D0874559

Gosford's
Daughter

Gosford's Daughter

MARY DAHEIM

Seattle, WA

Camel Press
PO Box 70515
Seattle, WA 98127

For more information go to: www.camelpress.com
www.marydaheimauthor.com

Cover design by Sabrina Sun

Gosford's Daughter
Copyright © 1988, 2015 by Mary Daheim
Originally printed by Avon Press under the title *Passion's Triumph*

ISBN: 978-1-60381-963-3 (Trade Paper)
ISBN: 978-1-60381-964-0 (eBook)
LOC Control Number: 2014957746

Produced in the United States of America

Dear Reader:

WHY DOES ANY AUTHOR WRITE a sequel to a story that appears to have already been told?

The characters, that's why. At least in my case. Over the course of what was originally 850 manuscript pages and I don't know how many years to create them, I became so immersed in Dallas's and Iain's Frasers that I couldn't get them out of my mind. *Love's Pirate* (reissued last year as *The Royal Mile*) was my first published book. In fact, it was the first book I'd tried to get published. Frankly, I was curious to see what happened to them—and to their family—in later years.

Quite a lot, it seemed. The Frasers lived in perilous times, especially for the Catholic minority. When we left them at the end of the first book, they'd sought sanctuary at Gosford's End, in the far north of the Scottish Highlands. To be candid, I wanted to find out how Dallas and Iain had fared during those turbulent years of James VI's minority. All things considered, they'd done rather well, mainly by keeping a low profile.

But that couldn't last forever. Not with the turbulent Scots and their history of clan feuds. As with all my historical books, I stayed closed to fact. Oh, yes, some of the real figures would get involved with my fictitious characters. If they didn't, there wouldn't be a story to tell. And I assure you there is. I hope you enjoy going along for the ride in the Frasers' later adventures.

—Mary Daheim, 2014

Author's Note

S INCE MARY, QUEEN OF SCOTS, clung to her French heritage and used the French spelling of Stuart, I've followed suit. In the case of others connected with her house, I've used the more familiar Scottish spelling of Stewart.

—Mary Daheim, 1988

Part One
1585-86

Chapter 1

THE PEBBLES AT THE BOTTOM of the burn glinted copper in the afternoon sun; the silver flash of the salmon broke water. Sorcha snapped her fingers in annoyance. She knew she should have come prepared to fish. The salmon going upriver from Beauly Firth were of a good size and wholesome color.

Tucking her faded serge skirt beneath her, Sorcha knelt at the burn's edge, savoring the dark earth's peaty smell, letting her heavy black hair swing free a scant inch above the rippling water. Two more salmon darted by, swimming effortlessly against the current. The pair must weigh at least a stone, she calculated, enough to provide supper for her parents, two brothers, and her sister.

Not that Iain Fraser's family would go hungry without the fish. Lord Fraser of Beauly had made a comfortable fortune from his seafaring enterprises, both legal and otherwise. Though it was whispered that Lady Fraser had done her best to spend his profits, they lived an affluent life in a fine home near Inverness. Too affluent, Iain Fraser often reminded his offspring; it was well for all of them, including Sorcha and her sister, Rosmairi, to learn survival should it ever be necessary.

The lessons were lost on Rosmairi, however, whose gentle nature precluded fishing or hunting. As second son, Rob felt compelled to keep up with his adventuresome older brother, Magnus. Yet Rob's heart never seemed quite in league with his arm when he sent the arrow soaring into a fine stag's neck or was asked to deliver the dagger's death blow to a wounded boar.

But Sorcha had taken to the hunt like a hound to the scent of fresh meat. " 'Sons of the hounds,' " her mother, Dallas, had often quoted, " 'come and get flesh.' " It was her MacKintosh clan motto, and Dallas Cameron Fraser often recalled it to her elder daughter. But Lady Fraser's tongue also had a sharp edge that was as legendary in the Highlands as the voluptuous attraction she retained into middle age and as acclaimed as the book learning she'd passed down to her children. Sorcha loved and admired her mother, but at seventeen, it was embarrassing to say so. Indeed, only that afternoon, Lady Fraser had lectured her daughter on her unkempt appearance. Still smarting from her mother's rebuke, Sorcha thought of reprisals.

By chance, another silver flash cut through the water, giving Sorcha inspiration. Her green eyes glinted as she stood up quickly, reaching under her serge skirts to rip off her tattered petticoat. The fish was only a few feet away, moving smoothly over the copper-colored pebbles. Timing her movements perfectly, she leapt into the rippling burn, plunged her arms into the cold water up to her elbows, and ensnared the salmon in the folds of white cloth.

Sorcha staggered in the water, her feet slipping on the pebbles; the fish fought for its life inside the lace-edged trap. It was of handsome size, and fought fiercely, tail thudding against Sorcha's thighs, head trying to force its way back under water. Sorcha dug her heels into the peat between the pebbles and gritted her teeth.

The fish's obstinacy matched her own. Its lurching movements became more frantic, and Sorcha almost lost her balance. "God's teeth!" she swore under her breath, but at last she managed to wrap the salmon securely in her petticoat. Its movements slowed at once. Sorcha caught her breath, regained her balance, and carefully made her way out of the burn and onto the rock-strewn verge.

Weary from her exertions, she collapsed on the damp ground, hands still clutching at the heaving fish. Through the flame-colored leaves of the plane trees, she could make out the chimney pots of Gosford's End some three hundred yards away. She wondered if she could haul the fish that far, but the ominously slow pace of its breathing told her it was too late to put it back in the burn. She had no cudgel, but a jagged rock lay within reach. Sorcha grasped the stone and, summoning all her waning strength, dashed it against the bulge in her petticoat. The salmon quivered and went slack. Sorcha let out a heavy sigh and pushed the thick black hair from her face. The sun was beginning to set behind Gosford's End, out over the great green glens to the west, and the air had suddenly grown chill. Sorcha got to her feet, bent to pick up the fish, and, with caution, carried it toward her family home.

Dallas Fraser was seated in her favorite armchair, a French import with ivory brocaded cushions. At her feet were three of their servants' children, two boys and a girl, all about ten years old, receiving instructions in grammar. All four stared at Sorcha as she entered the room with her muslin-wrapped burden held out like a sacrificial offering.

"Pray excuse my interruption, Lady Mother," Sorcha said with unwonted deference, "but I've brought fish for supper." Without preamble, she marched to her mother's chair and unrolled the muslin, dumping the bloody salmon at Lady Fraser's pearl-gray hem.

"Good God Almighty!" shrieked Dallas, leaping to her feet as the three children yelped in astonishment. "Get that wretched thing out of here! Sorcha, are you daft?"

Sorcha gave her mother the most innocent of limpid-eyed gazes. "I merely wanted to make up for my contentiousness this afternoon."

The honey-voiced assertion scarcely deceived Dallas. Her full mouth, so like her elder daughter's, set in a grim line as she eyed the slimy salmon and the murky puddle of water. The three children had begun to snicker behind their hands, further inciting Dallas's wrath. "Oh, hush. Hasn't any of you seen a dead fish before? Here," she said to the children, "remove this piscatory pest and take it home to your families. They can share it for supper."

Sorcha stood aside as the three children wrestled with the slippery salmon. At last, the two boys managed to carry it between them, and doing their best to salute Lady Fraser with brief, clumsy bows, left the sitting room, with the little girl trailing behind.

After the door had closed with an irritating creak, Dallas turned to her daughter. "I suppose you think I've lost my sense of humor?" But Sorcha noted that her mother's anger was waning. Though she was at least an inch taller than Lady Fraser, her mother seemed to tower over her, an intimidating silver-clad figure not unlike an ancient image of Saint Margaret of Scotland in the chapel at Beaufort Castle. Yet there was nothing saintly about Dallas Cameron Fraser. If ever a woman seemed rooted firmly in the rocky soil of Scotland, it was she. And like the native heath, Dallas seemed to thrive on adversity.

For a brief moment, Sorcha saw Dallas not as just her mother, but as a woman. Reflecting on her parents' past, Sorcha considered how Lady Fraser had grown up as a tutor's daughter, and had been left impoverished upon her father's death. She had been determined to provide a living for herself, her two sisters, and a pair of young nephews. Dallas had made a strange bargain with a man named Iain Fraser, whose dual role as courtier and pirate had been matched only by the mystery that had shrouded his birthright. Dallas had parlayed her knowledge of Fraser's piracy into a profitable if seemingly loveless marriage. But what had begun in brazen blackmail had ended in mutual passion. And Fraser had finally learned that he was the son of King James V of Scotland, the first of that profligate king's bastard sons, and thus a rival to the ambitions of James Stewart, Earl of Moray, and acknowledged illegitimate half brother to Mary, Queen of Scots.

After Mary Stuart had been deposed by James of Moray, Iain and Dallas and their two sons had moved north to Inverness to escape the vicious intrigues of the court. They had also fled from persecution of the Catholic minority. While Iain was not a religious man and Dallas was more worldly than devout, both held fast to the old faith that had been uprooted by James of Moray and other staunch Protestants. For the past eighteen years, Lord and Lady Fraser had lived in relative peace at Inverness, bringing their two daughters into the world, creating a gracious home overlooking the River Ness, and only occasionally venturing south to Dallas's beloved Edinburgh. Fraser had given up piracy for commercial trade. Or so he insisted, though Sorcha knew from her mother's ironic glances that perhaps not every cargo had been secured by honest means.

Still, such allusions only added to Iain Fraser's mystique in the eyes of his eldest daughter. And lawful or not, the lengthy trips at sea had bequeathed the burden of raising their family to Dallas. While quick tempered and sharp tongued, she was essentially not a disciplinarian. It had been left up to Fraser to restore some semblance of order to his unruly brood between voyages. But to be fair, Sorcha also knew that it had not been easy for her mother to carry a disproportionate share of the children's upbringing.

Even as she stood before her mother, the tension evaporated between them. Dallas, in fact, had gone to a side table to pour herself a glass of wine. Sorcha flopped down onto one of the pillows vacated by the children.

"I suppose you were vexed by my lecture about your appearance," Dallas said, settling not in her armchair but on one of the pillows next to Sorcha.

Sorcha sighed. "Who do you think is going to see me, some poacher who's more grime laden than I?"

Dallas wagged a finger in her daughter's face. "It's not a matter of grime, but of attending to your toilette. You're no longer a bairn, Sorcha, but a woman." She gazed down at her goblet, and a faint smile touched her lips. "I used to be rather careless about such niceties myself. Before I met your father."

"You were?" Sorcha's round-eyed look was now genuine. "Weren't you always modish?"

"Modish!" Dallas all but spat out the ruby claret. "I've told you a thousand times, we were poor! I had two dresses before I married your father. Two!" She made the number sound vulgar. Dallas put the wine goblet down on the Moroccan carpet and rested her hand on Sorcha's arm. "Now consider, you're quite bonnie, with those big green eyes and your olive skin and that wavy black hair. Closer to beauty than I ever was, and never mind comparing yourself to Rosmairi's red-gold locks and petal-pink complexion, you're just as different from her as Magnus and Rob are from each other."

That was true enough: like Sorcha, Magnus had inherited the dark coloring of his parents, but both Rob and Rosmairi had taken after their royal grandfather. Still, at fifteen, it was Rosmairi who drew the admiring stares of the local lads, whether they be Fraser kinsmen or sheep herders returned from their shielings. But Rosmairi turned to stone if one of them spoke—even George Gordon, the braw young Earl of Huntly, who caused her to heave great sighs of yearning. Sorcha was puzzled as to why her sister grew so tongue-tied. "What's the mystery, Ros?" she'd asked a dozen times. "Laddies like George want to talk of hunting and fishing and throwing the caber—and of themselves. Especially themselves."

But Rosmairi would only turn more pink than usual and shake her red-gold head. Hopeless, Sorcha would think, and knew instinctively that her mother agreed.

Somehow, Sorcha had managed to lose the thread of Dallas's discourse. Only the last few words caught her attention: "... Then, after Magnus's marriage to Jean Simpson, your father and I have agreed to concentrate on yours."

Sorcha's jaw dropped. "God's teeth! What of Johnny Grant? I thought the matter was decided."

Dallas waved her hands, the dying light catching a huge diamond set in silver. "Don't curse so, Sorcha. Johnny isn't suitable. Indeed," she added, getting up and going to a small, ornate silver casket where she kept her correspondence, "Johnny has written us the most appalling letter." Dallas unfurled the parchment and straightened it with a bat of her hand. "Heed this, Sorcha. 'Being that my grandsire is in poor health and that upon his departure from this vale of woe, I shall take on the burdensome duties as Laird of Freuchie, it will be incumbent upon me to choose a right-minded bride. This decision comes not lightly to me, but is made after much soul-searching.' "

Dallas raised flashing eyes from the letter. "You see—the witless wretch refuses a Catholic wife. Snaggle-toothed viper!" She flung the letter aside.

Sorcha sat very still, trying to absorb this shattering news. All her life, there had been a number of comforting certainties; it would snow in winter, the flowers would bloom in spring, the salmon would spawn in the Ness—and she would marry Johnny Grant. It was an ideal match, rooted in old if uneasy alliances with Dallas's MacKintosh clan. The Grants' native ground lay to the east and west of Fraser country, making marriage more feasible than war. Sorcha's dowry included a large parcel of land around Stratherrick's wild yet arable ground.

As for Johnny Grant, he was a personable, honest, intelligent youth, who—despite her mother's scathing remark—suffered from no worse a physical impairment than slightly crooked front teeth. Indeed, Sorcha found his fresh blond appearance rather attractive, especially since he had grown old enough to sport a jaunty beard. He was the same age as Sorcha, but had been left fatherless three years earlier, forcing him to grow up before his time. Unfortunately, the result was stodginess rather than maturity. While he visited Gosford's End no more than twice a year, he and Sorcha always found it remarkably easy to resume their camaraderie. Marriage to Johnny Grant seemed natural, comfortable, even inevitable. Until now.

"Is this Johnny's idea?" Sorcha demanded as anger began to overcome shock.

Dallas sat down on the cushions. "I don't know. The present Laird of Freuchie—as well as Johnny's father—always favored the match." She paused, casting a speculative glance at her daughter. "Mayhap seeing himself about to inherit the Freuchie lands and title, he is inclined to demonstrate his independence."

The green eyes glittered. "Or has found some other bride he thinks more comely?" Sorcha's words were tinged with bitterness.

"More Protestant," Dallas sniffed in response. "Your father and I would wager that young Johnny is casting his lot with the ruling majority."

Over the years, the Protestants in Scotland had become more firmly entrenched. Queen Mary's son, James VI, had been but a babe when his uncle had put him on the throne in his mother's place. James of Moray had carefully groomed little King Jamie to love the Presbyters and loathe the Church of Rome. Only now, Sorcha reflected, as Jamie grew from boy to man, was he beginning to demonstrate that while he might be an unwavering Protestant, he was learning to use one faction against the other. Yet the Catholics were clearly a minority, having lost ground even in their former Highland stronghold. It was no wonder that Johnny Grant was eager to show his allegiance to the reformed religion. But for Sorcha, it was no comfort.

She leaned toward her mother, chin jutting. "Will Father avenge this insult?"

Dallas actually retreated a few inches on the cushions. "Insult? Oh—well, nay, you know how he feels about unnecessary bloodshed. Besides," she added hastily, seeing the fire in Sorcha's eyes turn to ice, "there was never a formal betrothal. It was all … just understood."

"Understood poorly, it seems," Sorcha seethed. "Betrothal or not, am I to be unavenged as well as humiliated?"

Reasserting her maternal authority, Dallas squared her slim shoulders, managing to salvage some dignity despite her squatting position on the cushions. "Here, now—you are not the only one who has been insulted. We have all suffered, as a family. But would you send your father and Magnus and Rob off to be butchered in the name of honor? Don't be as brainless as Johnny!"

Sorcha shifted her body, one hand pulling at the long, black strands of hair. "If it's religion that has changed his mind, I won't feel injured. But," she said with a wave of her finger, "if it's some other chit who's lured him away, I'll see to it that he pays for his perfidy! Nor will I be content with a lesser laird!"

Fleetingly, Dallas considered reminding her daughter that vengeance belonged to the Lord, that a seventeen-year-old laddie wasn't old enough to know his own name, let alone his mind, and that, in reality, there was probably very little Sorcha could do to make Johnny Grant lament his decision. But two things held Dallas back: one was the Highlander's code of honor, which brooked no personal wrong; the other was Sorcha herself, wounded, determined, and incapable of permitting anyone to get away with what she considered an injustice. As if to prove the point, Dallas glanced at the floor, where Sorcha had dumped the slimy salmon. Even when her own mother seemed to have behaved unfairly, Sorcha would not, could not let the matter rest.

"The fact remains," Dallas began in a calm voice, "that we must now begin anew to find you a husband. Praise the Holy Mother, Rosmairi is still too young. As for Rob, he fancies himself in priestly vestments. Though God himself would risk the wrath of the Presbyters if He flaunted his Catholicism. Mayhap Rob will outgrow the notion, but until he does, your sire and I will bide as far as marriage plans are concerned." She paused to adjust the short, stiff ruff that fanned out from the bodice of her gown. "While that drooling nonentity of a king squats on Scotland's throne, neither your father nor I are anxious to have you join the court. But we have thought about your going to Edinburgh to live with your Aunt Tarrill and Uncle Donald."

Sorcha only half heard her mother's words. She stared at her tattered serge hem and dwelled on vituperative speeches to spew at Johnny Grant. All these years, Sorcha had counted herself fortunate for not having to suffer the indignities of being bartered away in marriage like a sow going to market. Now, it seemed, she was just another piece of goods, to be shunted about from this eligible young lad to that well-off widower.

"Edinburgh?" she said at last, scowling at her mother. "I would rather not."

Dallas shrugged, picked up her goblet, and took a deep drink. "You needn't decide immediately. Though if you are to go, it would be wise to leave before the weather turns foul."

Absently, Dallas tucked a strand of brown hair back under its silver net. Only the keenest pair of eyes could find any traces of gray, and her skin was remarkably unlined. Yet age had touched her about the eyes and jawline. It had also added character and strength. She made as if to get up, but stopped, resting on one knee. "There is no one else here you care about, I gather?"

The question was just a trace too sharp to be devoid of suspicion. But Sorcha met her mother's gaze head-on. "No. Certainly not." She suppressed a sigh of relief as she saw her mother give the briefest of nods.

IT HAD NOT BEEN A real lie. Sorcha knew her mother was asking if there was anyone else she wished to marry. And there wasn't. Niall Fraser had been a groom until just six months ago, when his master had put him in charge of the stables. He was some distant kin, of course, but of lowly birth and scarcely a suitable mate for the daughter of Lord and Lady Fraser of Beauly.

Nor was Sorcha assured of any deep, reciprocal affection on his part. He appeared to enjoy her company when they went riding or hunting or fishing or walking over the moors. He would take her hand when they were away from prying eyes, and there had been that magical if confusing moment just a week ago by the burn when he'd tentatively kissed her. Rawboned, tall, auburn haired but swarthy of skin, Niall had reached his twentieth birthday that summer. Like all the Fraser servants he could read and write—Dallas insisted upon that—and he was an expert horseman, a fine hunter, and an uncannily lucky fisherman. Besides his ignoble birth, Niall's only serious flaw was that he seldom laughed. It wasn't that he was so somber, but he rarely found humor in the commonplace situations that often sent Sorcha into peals of laughter.

It was to Niall that Sorcha fled the following morning. A heavy mist crouched low over Gosford's End, all but hiding the stables until she had nearly reached the door.

Niall was tending a fractious bay mare that seemed to be suffering from bloat. The feed, he explained, after dismissing two stable boys so that he and Sorcha might speak privately.

"It's new, from this year's harvest. She has trouble digesting it," He frowned deep furrows creasing the swarthy forehead. "But why only this one? I must make her a special brew."

"My parents want me to live in Edinburgh," Sorcha announced, more concerned about her own problems than those of the bay mare. "I think I'd hate it." Involuntarily, she glanced around the stable; such a disparaging opinion of Edinburgh would be heresy to Lady Fraser.

"I've never been there," said Niall, patting the horse's neck before turning to Sorcha. " 'Tis said to be fine, bigger than Inverness."

"I don't care if it's big as Spain," Sorcha declared, hands on hips. "I'd rather stay here where I can ride and hunt and fish." With you, she wanted to add, but lacked the nerve.

"You've been there. Are you so certain you'd hate it?" The blue eyes were probing, but then they usually were. Niall liked to ask questions, though at times he didn't seem to care much about the answers.

"It's full of people, many of them poor and ragged. It's noisy, and there are too many Protestants who make you spend hours in church singing tedious hymns. Some of the houses are so high you can't see the sun. I'd feel all closed up."

"Then don't go." Niall gave her the scantest of smiles. "His Lordship won't force you."

Sorcha mentally noted that Niall was probably right. But Lady Fraser was another matter. If her mother had made up her mind that Sorcha would go to Edinburgh, then it was only a matter of time.

"I'm not going to marry Johnny Grant." She gave Niall a sidelong glance. "He won't marry a Catholic."

Niall tested the hinges of the bay mare's stall. "Ah. Many won't. They hate popish ways."

"I think Johnny hates me." Sorcha pouted, but Niall wasn't watching her. "In all those years he visited, he never kissed me."

"Mayhap he lacked the nerve." Niall closed the gate to the stall and turned to face Sorcha. "I hear we're overrun with rabbits again. Would you be thinking of thinning them out with me?"

"Oh, aye, I'd like that." She smiled up at him, the bright, wide smile that made her features so vivid.

"This afternoon, then." Again, that hint of a smile before he opened the black gelding's stall. It was Lord Fraser's horse. Corsair, a descendant of Barvas, the horse he'd loved best until the animal's death some five years earlier.

Sorcha watched as Niall began to check the hooves of the gelding. He rarely talked while he worked, and she knew she must go back to the house to join Rosmairi for their weekly art lesson given by an expatriate Flemish painter. Reluctantly, she made her way from the stable, somehow feeling more downcast than when she'd entered. Niall had expressed no disappointment over the possibility of her departure, nor did he seem interested in her shattered marriage plans or Johnny Grant's lack of ardor. Depressed, Sorcha walked into the music room that served as a makeshift studio.

Rosmairi was already at her easel, paint brush poised. Jan de Bogardus, a thick-necked, fair-haired man of middle years, pulled at his whiskers and pursed his lips. "You are tardy, *signorina*."

Sorcha bridled at his Italian affectation. De Bogardus had studied in Italy and France. It was their father rather than their mother who had insisted upon the lessons. Lord Fraser had a great fondness for Italian culture, developed over the years during his visits to Genoa, Venice, and other Italian seaports. Since no one of that nationality could be found to teach painting in northern

Scotland, a Fleming who had at least studied in Italy was acceptable.

"Here, here," Master de Bogardus commanded, waving a landscape sketch at Sorcha. "You are to work on sky today, blues and grays and whites. Contrast, yet harmony, eh?"

The corners of Sorcha's wide mouth turned down as she viewed the primitive first strokes she'd put on canvas the previous week. Contrast and harmony, my backside, Sorcha thought; it looks like stripes to me. With a heavy sigh, she reached for her smock, then changed her mind. Turning abruptly on Master de Bogardus, she lifted her chin in defiance. "I'm sorry, the muse is not upon me. May I leave?"

Rosmairi's palette rocked in her graceful hands Their teacher stared at his temperamental pupil. " 'The muse'? Since when were you making the acquaintance of such muse?"

"Since today." Sorcha glared at de Bogardus and ignored her sister's shocked gaze. But the Fleming's expression held as much rejection as annoyance. Sorcha shifted from one foot to the other and tried to smile. "Truly, I'm not feeling well. My head aches, and I couldn't possibly concentrate."

The lie seemed to salvage Master de Bogardus's artistic integrity and Rosmairi's sisterly embarrassment. "As you wish," said the Fleming. He turned to Rosmairi, beaming through his fair whiskers. "I am paid the same for one as for two. Go rest your head. And think of contrast. Harmony, too, eh?"

"Oh, yes, I shall." Sorcha had to hold tight rein to keep from racing out of the music room. She paused long enough to glance at Rosmairi's canvas. "Dear Ros, your azure is wrenchingly beautiful!"

Even Rosmairi's credulity was compromised by such blatant insincerity. But the gray eyes looked the other way as Sorcha slipped past her toward the door.

Once outside, Sorcha could no longer control her impatience to return to the stable. She flew past the Italian fountain, the fading glory of the rose garden, and the deserted dovecote. She cursed herself every foot of the way for having played the simple maid with Niall. It was not like her, at least not like the woman she wanted to become.

At the stable door, she paused to catch her breath, then kicked it open so hard that it hurt her ankle. Gritting her teeth against the unexpected pain, she marched inside.

Niall was sitting on a mound of hay, eating a steaming beef pie made by his mother, Catriona, the doyenne of culinary arts at Gosford's End.

Back among the feed bins, two young boys tussled in mock belligerence. Sorcha called out, ordering them from the stable. Startled, they turned dirt-smudged faces in her direction, then reluctantly shuffled outside.

Niall was regarding her quizzically, a piece of flaky pie crust in his hand. "Your painting master didna come?"

"Aye, he came." Sorcha paused, tossing her thick wavy mane in a gesture of self-affirmation. "But I left. I'd no mind to dabble in contrast today."

The creases reappeared on Niall's swarthy brow. He knew little of painting and cared even less. Chewing slowly on the buttered crust, he watched Sorcha sit down next to him in the hay. "Have you eaten?" He proffered the half-consumed pie.

"No." Sorcha started to refuse Niall's offering, but the tender chunk of beef that bobbed atop the creamy golden gravy changed her mind. She devoured it quickly before speaking again. "I gathered you were indifferent as to whether I marry Johnny Grant or whether I leave Gosford's End. Could it be true that you go about kissing young lassies and not caring if you ever kiss them again?"

Only a faint flicker in the blue eyes betrayed Niall's surprise at her boldness. He swallowed half a carrot, picked up the remainder of crust, and swirled it in the gravy dregs. "I care." He set aside the small crockery baking dish and inspected his huge hands. "Yet I know it does me no good." His gaze bore deeply into her challenging emerald eyes. "You are of the Hall, I am of the stable. It can never be more than a kiss. If not Johnny Grant, you'll wed some other fine laird."

Sorcha's fingernail flicked at the tip of her nose, an unconscious sign of dismissal to the arguments of others. "Indeed. But I'm not talking of wedlock or even handfasting." She stopped, averting her eyes, wondering what, in fact, she *was* talking about. "That is, not every lad and lass who care for each other end up married. And I have a right to know if you care for me, or only found kissing … convenient."

Niall drew back at her choice of words. Then he laughed, the first time Sorcha had ever heard him do so, and it was more grunt than guffaw. He sobered at once, however, seemingly embarrassed at such an uncharacteristic display. "I care; I've cared since you were but a bairn. So fearless you were, yet small and like a waif. And now …." He stopped and put a finger to his lips, as if to stifle any foolish, possibly regrettable, words. "Aye," he said in a rambling sort of voice, "I care."

"Well." Sorcha's shoulders slumped in relief. She crossed her arms over her breast and let her feet dangle just above the stable floor. "I'm glad," she asserted, nodding her head and noticing that a seam had come unstitched in her green linen skirt. "I was certain you didn't mind if I left forever."

"Then you're not going?" Niall was bending closer, and she could feel his warm breath on her cheek.

"Nay, not if I can help it. How could I bear to be mewed up in a city, with Aunt Tarrill clucking over me, or reciting psalms with Uncle Donald?"

"That would be wrong. For you." His words seemed to come with difficulty. He touched her cheek and kissed the bridge of her nose. Sorcha lifted her face and closed her eyes, the long, heavy lashes dipping against her olive skin. "You are like a gypsy, not a waif," he murmured, burying his lips against her neck. She put her arms around him, feeling the hard muscles under the rough woolen shirt his mother had woven for him. Then his mouth claimed hers, hesitantly at first, but fired into urgency by her eager response. Sorcha felt herself being pressed backward into the hay, Niall's weight a crashing but welcome burden. At last he stopped kissing her as they both gasped for breath.

Sorcha knew she was smiling even as her lungs took in the hay-scented air. She knew, too, that Niall might consider her less than virtuous if she didn't break off their exciting embrace. It was one thing to discover that desire existed for both of them; it would be quite another matter to let passion overcome prudence.

Inexperienced as she was, Sorcha could not know that Niall had already gone beyond that incalculable barrier. Just as she was about to tell him they had better part until it was time to hunt rabbits, Niall put both hands over her breasts, molding them experimentally through the linen fabric of her bodice. He looked awestruck and his words were hushed.

"I have longed to touch you thus since you grew to ripeness. You fill my hands; I pray God you will not fill my heart, for 'twould break."

Sorcha regarded Niall with a bewildered mixture of excitement, pity, and fear. "Dear Niall, we must stop."

The swarthy face turned apologetic. He shifted his weight so that only one leg lay along her thigh. Tiny beads of perspiration glistened at the edge of his crisp auburn hair. "We will stop. I swear it. But first, let me see your duckies. Please, Sorcha, lady-lass."

It was the name he had called her ever since they were children, an acknowledgment of her status but also of their friendship. She started to shake her head, but saw the hopeless plea in his eyes, and though he had taken his hands away, she could swear she still felt his touch on her flesh. With trembling fingers she undid the half dozen mother-of-pearl buttons; there had originally been eight, but Sorcha had lost two of them long ago.

As the linen bodice parted, Niall slid the fabric over her shoulders, then more hurriedly pulled at the thin camisole. He gasped in wonder as his eyes feasted on the smooth, firm, pink-tipped globes. "You are too bonnie," he said so low she almost couldn't make out the words. Cautiously, he put the palm of his hand on each breast in turn, pressing very slowly, as if he were afraid the rigid nipples would pierce his skin.

Sorcha heard a moan and realized it had come from somewhere deep inside her being. Surely that didn't seem right; was just the touch of a man on naked flesh sufficient to arouse such an animal like response? But she must put an end to it; she couldn't love Niall, and she didn't want him to love her. Or did she? Dimly, she could make out the somber, rugged face, etched with yearning, softened by his need for her. She cared, too; if she did not, Niall's feelings would not have mattered. He moved down to seek out her nipples with his tongue, stroking them in rapid, darting, upward movements, as if he could make them burst from bud to blossom by sheer force of desire. She touched the auburn hair with one hand, the other gripping the hardened muscles of his shoulder.

Later, Sorcha could not believe she had never heard that familiar voice call out the first three times. It was only the sudden, frightening tenseness she felt in every fiber of Niall's body that made her realize they were not alone. Gallantly, he tried to shield her half-naked body with his own. But in vain: Iain Fraser stood in the doorway of the stable, riding crop in one hand, Corsair's bridle in the other.

"You have exactly one minute to prepare to meet your Maker if you don't take your hands off my daughter," Iain Fraser said in low, chilling tones. "And if you ever look her way again, you'll roam the Highlands a blind man."

As if already in pain, Niall rose slowly and covered his face with his big hands. Sorcha clutched her camisole and bodice around her breasts, desperately trying to fasten the buttons. Fraser still stood in the doorway, the lean features grim, the hazel eyes never leaving Niall for an instant.

"My Lord," Niall began, now spreading out his hands as if in supplication, "forgive me, but the lady-lass is so fair ...."

Fraser made a slashing motion with the riding crop. "Enough. You'll never mention this incident. Never." He swung the crop once more, this time within an inch of Niall's face. "Understand?"

Niall nodded slowly, then turned away from both Fraser and Sorcha. Her legs seemed to wobble as she walked the ten paces to join her father. Tears hovered in her eyes, and she noticed vaguely that she'd done up the buttons all wrong, so that one side of her collar poked up unevenly against her chin.

Fraser didn't speak until they were inside the blue-gray stone walls of the manor house. Time had not slowed his long stride nor diminished his panther-like grace, though his black hair was streaked with gray and the hawklike features had sharpened. Indeed, to Sorcha, her father had never looked as severe as he did in this moment of her stark terror.

Wordlessly, she followed him up the winding staircase with its hand-carved bunches of grapes and entwined ivy. They went directly to the family dining room, which adjoined her parents' sleeping quarters. Dallas was already at the table, but the others had not yet arrived.

"Sweet Jesu, Iain," exclaimed Dallas, looking from her stormy-eyed husband to the tears that now rolled freely down her daughter's face, "what's amiss?"

Fraser started to speak, suddenly realized he was still carrying Corsair's bridle and the riding crop, and tossed them onto a footstool. "I have discovered why Sorcha prefers Inverness to Edinburgh," he said with forced calm. "Master Niall seems to have captured her fancy."

"Niall!" Dallas turned visibly pale and seemed to shrink into the chair. But she took a deep breath, pressed her hands against the table's beveled edge, and stared at Sorcha. "Has the knave seduced you?"

"Oh, no!" Sorcha's denial was a virtual wail of indignation. "I'd only kissed him once until today!"

Her parents both seemed to relax. Fraser went to a side cupboard and poured himself a generous tumbler of whiskey. He sat down at the head of the table and motioned for Sorcha to sit, too. "Then you are not infatuated with the braw laddie?" His tone had lightened into the indolent cadence Sorcha knew so well.

Her initial reaction was negative. Yet Sorcha had learned that she could respond to a man's touch. Even with the heat of Fraser's anger still upon her, surely what she felt for Niall must be more than impersonal animal lust.

But to say so out loud would bring down the wrath of both parents. Suddenly it didn't matter. Johnny Grant had jilted her. Only Niall mattered— and he was worth fighting for. "I care for him, yes. And he cares for me." She sat up straight, brushing the tears away with her hand, looking first at her father, then at her mother. They both wore expressions of stony reproach.

Dallas was the first to explode into words. "Fie, Iain, tell her! We can't permit this. And she must know why!"

"Christ." Fraser set the whiskey tumbler down on the table and shook his head. "Christ," he repeated, this time more softly, the heavy dark brows coming close together. "All right," he said, settling one booted leg across the other and facing his distraught, mystified daughter. "You must put Niall from your mind. What may be worse is that you must never tell him why. Some things are better left that way." He paused to take a swallow of whiskey, while Dallas pleated her napkin in her lap. Sorcha heard herself sniffle but vowed to stop crying, no matter what her father said. Was there madness in Niall's family? Had he been handfasted to someone else? Was he not the normal, virile young man he appeared to be, but given to unnatural affections such as King James was said to pursue? She held her breath as her father resumed speaking:

"The only way you can ever love Niall is as a brother. You see, Sorcha, Niall is my son."

Chapter 2

ONLY AFTER THE ENFORCED SEPARATION did Sorcha realize how much time she had spent in Niall's company over the years and how precious those hours had been. Indeed, it had almost seemed as if they had been brother and sister all along; the intimacy they had shared had been little less than that between herself and her acknowledged brothers, Magnus and Rob.

Yet a much different feeling for Niall had emerged during their ardent encounter in the stable. Sorcha had sensed the power of love—and of being loved. And then the raw, fledgling emotion she had experienced with such delight had been snuffed out.

There were moments when Sorcha considered that her disappointment over Niall hurt more than the humiliation dealt her by Johnny Grant. But pride intervened; being discarded by Johnny still rankled.

After her father's anger had cooled, Sorcha had sought him out in his study. It was early evening, with the sun setting over the gaunt hills to the west, casting a burnished crimson glow through the mullioned windows.

"I am surprised, sir, that Johnny Grant's dishonor of our family hasn't provoked you to wrath," Sorcha began. "Are we so wedged between Grants and Gordons that our own clan lacks importance or power?"

Iain Fraser looked up from his inventory of the annual harvest. He surveyed his daughter with cool hazel eyes. "I'd hold no man to a bond he'd chafe at keeping. Would you prefer that I haul Johnny here in chains and force him to wed with you?"

Sorcha noted that while her father's face was serious, there was a touch of humor in his question. While she didn't wish him to turn his anger on her, she half hoped he might be incited to take revenge on Johnny Grant. "He's done me a great injury," she complained, surprised to discover that her voice was unsteady.

Fraser leaned across the paper-strewn desk. "To your feelings or your pride?"

Sorcha rubbed at her nose with her fist. "My p-pride," she mumbled.

"Did you truly care for him?" Fraser reclined in his chair, long legs outstretched under the desk.

As if in answer, in her mind's eye Sorcha saw Niall, not Johnny. "We got on well enough," she replied, sniffling against her fist. "Or so I thought."

Fraser nodded, his lean mouth turned up at the corners. "Lassie," he said, now smiling affectionately, "don't fash yourself over hapless Johnny Grant. Neither your mother nor I would wish for you to marry a man you didn't love."

Sorcha frowned, unable to meet her father's wry gaze, though she sensed the rightness of what he said. Yet she was confused, not because of Johnny Grant, who had stirred no more than amiable companionship, but on Niall's account, and the mutual ardor between them.

Noting the confusion etched on her face, Fraser came around the desk to put a firm hand on her shoulder. "Let me clarify a point," he said in the indolent way so familiar to Sorcha. "Passion wears false faces. Be very careful, lassie. Always."

For the briefest instant, Sorcha let her head rest against her father's chest. She wasn't sure that she might not pine for Niall, nor was she convinced that Johnny Grant didn't deserve retribution. But the one thing she knew for certain was that while parents were often dense, they were almost always a comfort.

Sorcha did not talk to her father about Niall—or Johnny—again, but she had spent part of an afternoon with her mother discussing her half brother's background. Niall had been conceived during a period of estrangement in the early years of her parents' marriage. While Dallas lived at court, Iain had spent some time at his former home nearby at Beauly, where Sorcha's late aunt had maintained the household.

"As you know, 'tis not unusual for a gentleman to dally with a serving girl," Dallas had explained in an even voice. "Your father was no different than most, and he'd just returned from a long sea voyage." She'd paused and looked out through the window toward the darkened cluster of buildings that was Inverness. Her mother's face was in shadow, and Sorcha thought that memory was holding back her tongue. But Dallas continued speaking as she picked up a small porcelain jar and began smoothing a honey-colored cream on her neck and bosom: "Catriona was a pretty wench, and your father fell prey to temptation. He didn't know about Niall's birth until we moved here from Edinburgh the year before you were born."

Sorcha remained silent for a few moments. It was disconcerting to hear her mother discuss her father's infidelity, impossible to see Iain Fraser as anything but her father and the husband of her mother.

"He told you, then?" Sorcha finally asked.

"I guessed. When Niall was very young, he greatly resembled your father. In any event, your sire wanted to see that the lad was brought up properly. When I inquired as to Niall's parentage, he told me the truth." Dallas replaced the lacquered lid of the jar and smiled fondly at Sorcha. "It's so ironic that you should have been attracted to him. And he to you."

It was not Niall, but Catriona whom Sorcha considered later as she walked her favorite mare, Thisbe, across the ripe, heath-covered moor toward the River Ness. A stout, fair-haired woman with cheeks that seemed perpetually warmed by the manor house ovens, Catriona supervised her domain with a kind but firm hand. She had three younger children, all apparently fathered by the man who had been her husband until his death the previous spring. Cummings, his name had been, distant kin to the Frasers' majordomo of many years. And so the other three children were called, but Niall had retained the Fraser surname. Strange that Sorcha had never thought to ask why. But then half the inhabitants around Inverness were named Fraser.

Thisbe had stopped to munch at a tussock of grass that sprang up between clumps of claret-colored heather. At least, Sorcha consoled herself as Thisbe began meandering down the gentle slope to the river, there had been no more said about Edinburgh. A drop of rain on her cheek made her look up at the sky; dark clouds had moved down from the north without warning.

Guiding Thisbe among the pine trees, Sorcha paused to gaze at the wooded isles that stood like primeval ships in the broad, brown Ness. It was a view she had loved since childhood, with the rippling waters, the heavy scent of pine, the backdrop of blue hills marching like a giant staircase to the distant mountaintops, where the snow never quite disappeared, even under the hottest summer sun.

A sudden movement nearby made Thisbe tense. Sorcha turned in the saddle to see a six-point stag standing aloof in motionless splendor. She knew the stag well. Two years earlier, her father and Magnus had determined to see which of them would bag the magnificent animal. But he had evaded them both, in a taunting, cunning match of human and animal wit. In deference to his victory, the Fraser menfolk had vowed never to kill the stag they had come to call the Master of Ness. Strangely enough, the animal had seemed to sense their concession and had boldly appeared before them at least a half dozen times the previous autumn. Sorcha lifted her head to touch her cap in salute as Thisbe's ears twitched in apparent awe.

"Stay still," Sorcha whispered, patting her mare's neck. "He'll go. It's his way of telling us he's guarding the Ness."

The stag turned slightly, antlers tipped back like a primitive diadem. Sorcha was still smiling with admiration when the arrow soared through the pine trees and found its mark.

It seemed as if at least a full minute passed before the stag's long legs buckled and he crashed onto the peaty ground. Horrified, Sorcha screamed and Thisbe reared up. Instinct alone saved her from being thrown as she clung to the mare's neck and uttered a sharp command.

Sorcha leapt from the saddle, running to the stag, which was already in the last stage of its death throes. It was useless to remove the arrow; it had gone straight to the heart. Sorcha was too angry to cry, too outraged to be surprised by the tall, imposing figure that emerged from the pine trees carrying a huge bow in one hand and a dirk in the other.

"You killed him!" she cried. "You killed the Master of Ness!"

The man looked more bemused than concerned. "Strange, it looks like a stag to me." He bent down to make sure the animal was dead, then sheathed his dirk. "Was he your pet?" The dark eyes were the color of the river itself, unrevealing and every bit as deep, set in a long face that struck Sorcha as wolflike.

His skin was dark, too, and the wavy hair was brown as a bog. The short-cropped beard and mustache made him seem older than he probably was. Not yet thirty, Sorcha gauged, and realized she was staring.

"Aye, he was, in his way. A family pet." She gripped one of the antlers and glared defiantly at the man. "Why did you do that? There are so many other deer nearby."

The man stood up and sighed. He was very tall and broad shouldered under the long black cape that covered him from neck to ankle. The beard, the cape, the guarded features, momentarily deflected Sorcha's attention from the slain stag. There was something clandestine about the man, as if his all-enveloping attire shielded him from much more than the weather. But his words were frank enough, if tinged with irony: "I didn't know I had to request an introduction to a stag before I shot him. Most do not have names. Or families."

"Well, this one did. We all were particularly fond of him." Sorcha brushed at her damp cheeks, lest he mistake raindrops for tears. She suddenly felt very young and vaguely foolish. "Do you have a name?"

The smile he gave her was surprisingly candid. "I do. It's Napier. Gavin Napier. And you?"

"I'm Sorcha Fraser of Gosford's End." She paused, waiting for the usual acknowledgment of her family's prestige. But Napier said nothing; he just continued to gaze at her from those deep, dark brown eyes. She shifted her weight from one foot to the other, wondering if Gavin Napier lived close by. But most of their clan came from much farther south, near Loch Lomond.

Before any coherent words could take form, Napier whistled. Within seconds, a handsome gray stallion trotted through the trees to stand by his master. "At least my horse is obedient," Napier said with a trace of impatience. "Now where are the others?"

"You are with a hunting party?" Sorcha inquired as the rain began to pelt down in stinging drops.

"Of sorts." He turned away, and she noticed that his profile was strongly etched, from the high forehead to the long nose, which had apparently been broken more than once, to the wide mouth with its slightly elongated lower lip. It was not a handsome face, Sorcha decided; it was too rough-hewn, too uneven. And definitely wolflike. But for some reason, she could not take her eyes from him.

"Damn." He uttered the word with resignation. "They must have gone farther upriver, to the loch." He unsheathed his dirk again and looked at Sorcha. "I don't suppose you'd care to watch me gut your friend?"

"Oh!" Sorcha clapped her hands to her cheeks. "No! No, not this one!" The mere idea shocked her. Yet she wanted Gavin Napier to know that she had not only watched but gutted many a stag in her time. It seemed vitally important that he should not mistake her for a fatuous, squeamish child.

"Then turn the other way or head on home." He had knelt down once more and was rolling the stag over onto its back. Napier moved with practiced assurance, reminding Sorcha of the poachers her father often winked at when he caught them on Fraser property. Napier obviously was no local poacher, but there was the aura of the hunter about him.

The rain was beginning to pierce the thick fabric of her woolen skirt. Sorcha was suddenly tempted to take Thisbe and flee to the manor house. But sheer willpower and a determination to prove herself forced a different decision.

"Oh, God's teeth, if you need help, I'll assist you. The poor creature can't be any more dead than he is already."

Napier glanced over his shoulder, a glimmer of surprise in his dark eyes. "Well. There's a good lass. You hold the forelegs and I'll do the cutting."

Steeling herself to watch Napier's every movement, Sorcha pried the legs as far apart as she could. The dirk plunged, and a torrent of blood spurted out over the animal's tawny belly. Sorcha choked and was afraid she was going to be ill. To distract herself, she tried to think of Niall and how she'd responded to his kisses and the touch of his hands on her breasts. Somehow, those images were almost as jarring as the carnage taking place just under her nose.

Napier worked swiftly. Not more than five minutes had elapsed before the heart, organs, and entrails lay on the peaty, rain-soaked ground. The downpour was washing the blood away, allowing it to merge back into the earth, as nature claimed nature.

Napier stood up and caught Sorcha off guard with a wide, appealing grin. "Well done, lass. I have a rope; I'll tie him to my horse."

She was about to ask where he was taking the stag when three riders appeared downriver. As Napier called out to them, Sorcha could see that they were all dressed alike. As they drew closer, she realized why: They were monks, wearing their white robes under riding capes, with hoods covering their tonsures to protect them from the rain. She recognized one of them, an elderly brother named Joseph from Beauly Priory.

"The Lord be with you," Brother Joseph said in greeting. Sorcha curtsied and replied in kind. "Ah, we'll feast well this night," he exclaimed, his faded blue eyes fixed on the stag.

"Aye," said Napier, unwinding the rope from his horse's saddle. "Though I feared Mistress Fraser here might do me a mischief when she discovered I'd slain her pet."

"Pet?" Brother Joseph's mouth was droll. "Ah, I believe I've heard of that one. The Master of Ness, is it not?"

Sorcha nodded. "It is. Was. But I would not begrudge it to you and the other holy monks. Consider it a reparation for sin."

"Sin?" Brother Joseph's scanty white eyebrows lifted. "You would have had to break most of the commandments to need such a handsome penance, my child. But we thank you all the same." He turned in the saddle with some difficulty. "Do you know Brothers Michale and Dugald?"

She did not and went through an introduction to the two younger monks while Napier secured the stag and mounted his gray stallion. The rain was already letting up, driven southward by a brisk wind that moaned through the pine trees and ruffled the river's steady passage.

From his place in the saddle, Gavin Napier seemed to tower over Sorcha and dwarf even the stiffened corpse of the great stag. She caught herself staring again and started to turn away. But Napier had a parting word: "If ever you find a man you care for as much as you did this handsome stag, he will be a fortunate lad."

His voice was light, but Sorcha detected an undercurrent of irony. Had the monks not been with them, she would have given Napier a sharp retort. Instead, she found herself uncharacteristically silent.

The brief, awkward moment was broken by Brother Joseph. "It is well to love animals, my child. But it is more pleasing to God to love people. I trust you will take Father Napier's words to heart."

Sorcha's jaw dropped. Now she could not possibly keep from staring at Gavin Napier. Sure enough, sitting astride his horse with the long black cloak blowing in the wind, she could see that he wore the garb of a priest. He was looking just beyond her, toward the drooping bracken near the water's edge. Despite his lack of expression, was he inwardly laughing at her? Sorcha wasn't sure, nor did she remember if she bade them farewell. The only image that lingered was Gavin Napier, guiding his gray stallion back into the pine forest with the Master of Ness dragging behind over the rich, rain-soaked ground.

Chapter 3

WHEN SORCHA ARRIVED OUTSIDE HER parents' chamber, Iain and Dallas Fraser were arguing. From beyond the carved door with its detail of wild roses and wood violets, she could hear her father expounding at length, but his precise words weren't audible though the heavy oak. Then suddenly Dallas's voice pierced the door.

"Even after nigh on twenty years, you've never gotten that bubble-brained half sister of yours off your conscience. Queen or not, she never wanted your counsel!"

"That's unfair. For many years, she did." Her father's voice reverberated clearly now, in rejoinder to his irate wife. "It was only when she fell under Bothwell's spell that she lost all sense of proportion. And her heart."

"Not to mention her crown," Dallas snapped.

Sorcha leaned against the door, relieved to discover that it was of Queen Mary, and not herself and Niall, that they spoke. Poor Mary Stuart, that pathetic creature who had been stripped of her royal powers by her bastard half brother, James of Moray, and kept captive in England for seventeen years. Moray was dead now, but Mary's son, Jamie, had reached his majority and ruled alone. Separated from his mother before he really knew her, King Jamie was devoid of filial emotion and had never lifted a finger to set his mother free. If Iain Fraser felt that his half sister's obsession with the Earl of Bothwell had eroded her ability to govern, he also felt that Jamie had proved himself a callous, ungrateful son, who had condemned his mother to a life of suffering.

Dallas had no quarrel with her husband's assessment of Jamie, but she'd never been able to forgive Mary Stuart for proclaiming Iain Fraser an outlaw. To Dallas, ingratitude ran in the royal family.

"Mary talks of ruling by association," Dallas countered, her own voice now less strident, forcing Sorcha to press her ear against the door. "Jamie will never permit it. Nor will that heathen, Elizabeth. And Jamie only does what his cousin Elizabeth tells him, because he's hell-bent to be king of England when the barren crone dies."

"It's only natural that Jamie dances to Elizabeth's tune," Sorcha heard her father say in a reasonable tone. "Would you prefer that the Queen of England name an heir who would have no regard for our own poor country? At least we can trust that Jamie won't invade his native land."

"He doesn't need to," Dallas snapped back. "We can draw enough blood on our own."

Unfortunately, Sorcha thought, her mother was right. In Jamie's youthful innocence, he had inherited the seething conflicts of an unruly nation. The vicious feuds spawned by the concept of clan and kin had been altered somewhat by the Reformation, but not necessarily for the better. While in many cases, traditional clan loyalties persisted, in others, members of the same house found themselves in opposition over religion. Those who remained Catholic generally favored Queen Mary's return to the throne; most of new Kirk's presbyters not only opposed Mary Stuart but had conspired for her downfall. An infant king had been more malleable than a grown woman. Little Jamie could be governed by his mentors, reared in the Protestant faith, and taught who to hate and who to favor.

But as Jamie grew older, those men who had been solidly united against Mary fell out with each other in their quest for influence over the young monarch. A Scot might rarely relinquish the tartan of his clan, but he'd change his badge of loyalty almost by whim. There was no simple way to define opponents. A Protestant house such as the proud Hamiltons might secretly support Queen Mary out of a personal sense of loyalty; a Catholic clan such as the Gordons might offer allegiance to the young king for the sake of ambition. To exacerbate the turmoil, the country itself was divided into three distinct regions, each with its own cachet of convictions: the Highlands, with a rigid code of honor and a fierce sense of independence; the tumultuous Border lands, where the English enemy was never more than a moonlight ride away; and the Lowlands, where sovereign and subjects convened to direct the country's government and commerce. Over the centuries, the Scots had fought each other more relentlessly from within than they had engaged any enemy from without. To Sorcha, it seemed a tragic waste for a land that was neither rich nor powerful.

It also seemed that in this instance both her mother and her father were right. But if Lord Fraser had an immediate reply, Sorcha didn't hear it. Rob had suddenly materialized in the corridor, causing Sorcha to jump. He looked at his sister in surprise and grinned. Sorcha put a finger to her lips and jerked her head in the direction of the door.

"Is it about us that they bellow?" Rob whispered, edging close to Sorcha.

"Nay, 'tis Queen Mary." Sister and brother stood facing each other, each with an ear to the door.

Apparently, they'd missed something. Dallas's voice was raised again, shouting that nothing could be proved by letting Rob join the Queen. Sorcha stared at her brother, who looked faintly sheepish. Obviously, he had been keeping a secret from her.

"It serves two purposes," Fraser declared in a louder voice. "He will be exposed to priestly ways and will show the Queen that we have not completely forsaken her."

"That *you* have not," Dallas retorted. "Have you no regard for your son's safety?"

"He's in no danger as long as he avoids those damnable intrigues."

Sorcha and Rob started as Cummings materialized in the corridor. For almost thirty years, Cummings had served as the Fraser steward. In that time, he had grown portly, and what little hair remained ringed his head like lambswool, yet his unmistakable authority stayed intact. Sorcha and Rob both flushed under his reproachful gaze.

"We were trying to see if our parents were … taking a nap," Sorcha said lamely before grabbing Rob to slink away without a backward glance.

They sought sanctuary in the library with Magnus, who was working on charts for his father's next voyage. Upon prodding, Rob admitted that for some weeks now he had been pressuring his parents to let him join Abbot John Fraser at Compiègne in France. A Recollect friar and writer, the abbot was descended from another branch of the Frasers at Philorth.

"Our Lady Mother thought it feasible," Rob told his sister and brother as they lounged by the cozy fireside.

"Didn't Father agree?" Sorcha asked, tucking her feet under her teal skirts.

Rob nodded, a lock of red hair dipping down onto his smooth forehead. "He's always had some prejudice about living in France. I think it's because he almost had to exile himself there before the Queen lost her throne."

"That's no reason to prevent you from going there," Sorcha said, lifting the lid of a crystal comfit dish and making a face when she discovered it was empty.

"Have you ever noticed that parents don't need reasons when they want their own way?" Magnus asked in a dry tone very like his father's. He had inherited Fraser's coloring and height, but was heavier of build and possessed his mother's brown eyes.

"Then what does Father want?" Sorcha asked. "I gathered it had something to do with serving Queen Mary in her English captivity."

"So it does." Rob pushed at the stray lock of hair that always seemed to have a life of its own. "Where I go isn't as important as what I do. The point is, I want to live in the company of the clergy in order to learn if I have a vocation. But I don't want to go somewhere close by, such as Beauly Priory. I feel I must put distance between myself and the life I've always known with my family. That way, I can better hear God's voice."

Sorcha averted her eyes, staring into the struggling orange flames on the library hearth. Somehow, it always embarrassed her to hear Rob speak in such pious tones. While she had grown up in a world where the Catholic clergy was sometimes prohibited from practicing the sacraments, and in the best of times, was watched closely by the authorities, the priests and monks she had known seemed to possess a spiritual aura that removed them from the realm of ordinary people. To imagine any of them having once been rollicking, mischievous, disobedient boys such as Rob, was unthinkable. He had even seduced a maid or two, though he insisted that temptations of the flesh could be avoided if he became a priest. Once he took religious instruction and made his holy vows, he'd be transformed into one of those exalted, holy beings and cease to be Rob. Perhaps it wasn't embarrassment that distressed Sorcha, but a sense of loss: He would no longer be her brother; he would stop being a man.

The flames suddenly spurted into life and crackled sharply. Sorcha jumped in her chair, not so much from the sound as from the image she'd suddenly seen in the fire: Father Gavin Napier, tall, broad shouldered, arrestingly masculine—and assuredly worldly. Obviously, all priests were not the same.

"And how does our sire think you'll hear God's voice in the company of a captive Queen and her mawkish minions?" Magnus inquired with a slight sneer. "It seems that petty plotting surrounds our former Queen like weeds overrunning a flower bed. Or do you fancy yourself her youthful savior?"

Sorcha wrenched her attention back to her brothers. Rob explained that their father knew one of Her Grace's chaplains and that the Queen had grown obsessively devout during her long years of captivity. Not only would Rob be able to observe the clergy at close hand in an isolated setting not unlike a religious community, but at the same time he would fulfill Iain Fraser's own wish to demonstrate family support for the half sister he'd once abandoned. As for serving Mary Stuart, Rob rather unconvincingly averred that his interest was strictly impersonal.

Magnus plunged his quill into the inkwell, heard the tip break off, and frowned. "Oh, by the Mass, Rob, half the lads in Scotland and England dream of rescuing the poor Queen. As for our sire, he has been guilt laden for years because he didn't bear arms to support her at Carberry Hill. The older he grows, the more he regrets it. As if he or his small band of Frasers could have saved the Queen and Bothwell from defeat."

"Mother says he'd have ended up as dead as Bothwell did eventually," Sorcha put in, rejoining the discussion to stifle the persistent image of Gavin Napier that seemed to bedevil her in the shadowy library.

Rob nodded. "Father felt Queen Mary was no longer capable of ruling Scotland. That was really what mattered most to him."

"What matters most to me is supper," Sorcha declared, getting up and stretching. "How long does it take our parents to decide your future, Rob?"

Rob looked up at his sister out of twinkling hazel eyes. "Making the decision was probably done with some time ago. It's the making up between them that takes much longer."

No DECISION ABOUT ROB'S FUTURE was announced immediately. Yet Sorcha knew he would somehow prevail. Frowning as she made her way down the central stairway, she paused in midstep, her hand on the balustrade as she saw Iain Fraser and Magnus come through the doorway with several other men. One was George Gordon, the ambitious young Earl of Huntly; another was Father Gavin Napier.

Sorcha started to turn around, but her father called out, "We have visitors, lassie. Go tell your lady mother that George Gordon is here with his followers and a clutch of holy men."

Sorcha glanced over her shoulder when she reached the landing. She could have sworn that Gavin Napier, attired in his long black robes, was watching her with his hunter's eyes. Quickening her step, she caught sight of Rosmairi peering around a corner at the top of the stairs. "Is it George?" she asked eagerly, her cheeks pink as peonies.

Sorcha grasped the gilded knob at the head of the balustrade. "Aye. And others."

Rosmairi's fine, fair brows drew together at the vexed note in her sister's voice. "Is aught wrong?"

"Is aught right?" snapped Sorcha, and was immediately repentant when she saw the hurt on Rosmairi's face. "I'm out of sorts, that's all. Go bedeck yourself for George and his party. I must tell Mother they're here."

Dallas was not pleased that Gordon and his men were in the house. "Rosmairi's swooning admiration to the contrary, George isn't half the man his sire was," she asserted, urging her maid, Flora, to work more swiftly at pressing a gown of lavender silk. "Not that his father was much of a man, either, which makes young George about one-quarter baked around the edges and all dough in the middle."

"Yet my father welcomes him," Sorcha put in as her mother stood still long enough to let Flora slip the gown over her head.

"Your father always was weak in the head where the Gordons were concerned. Mark my words, not one of them has ever been trustworthy though they vow they're as Catholic as the Pope. Ambition, not religion, rules their house." Dallas made a face in the tall mirror that stood on dragon's feet in a corner of the bedchamber. "This dress looks worn. Oh, fie, it's good enough for a Gordon." She whirled on Sorcha, a strand of gleaming pearls in one hand. "Muslin! Go change, child, you look like a ragamuffin!"

"But you yourself aren't wearing your finest …." Sorcha began to protest but caught the warning light in her mother's eyes.

"One needn't dress up like that overblown hussy, Queen Elizabeth! She doesn't put on her clothes; she gets encrusted! Vile creature, all jewels and wigs and paint so thick if she itches, she can't dig deep enough to scratch!" Dallas wound the pearls around her head, clipping a matching earring on each ear, and stuck a pearl-edged comb into her dark hair. Flora stood stoically by, her twenty years of service having inured her to Lady Fraser's flamboyant tongue. "Mind you," Dallas went on, wagging a finger at Sorcha, "it's because of that wretched old harridan that your sire allies himself with the likes of young Gordon, who is no friend to Elizabeth and her minion, Jamie the Jejune. Now hurry, Sorcha, put on a presentable dress and comb your hair."

Sorcha quickened her step until she was out of her mother's sight. In truth, Sorcha found George Gordon a jovial, handsome sort, a bit too taken with his wealth and title, but at least capable of speaking about hunting and fishing and sports. If he was ambitious, as her mother insisted, he came from a powerful family, the most influential—and feared—clan in the Highlands. They were, she reflected with a touch of spite, often pitted against the Grants. For that reason alone, Sorcha would change into a more comely gown.

IN THE MAIN DINING HALL, Cummings had the servants rushing about in a flurry of activity. A huge fire crackled on the wide hearth at one end of the room. The wall sconces had been lighted, for it was a gloomy October day. The long table was already set for at least two dozen people. Sorcha scanned the room: Her father, Gordon, Magnus, and Rob were clustered near the fireplace, drinking malmsey. Closer to the table stood several monks and men wearing the Gordon plaid. Directly under the great arched window with its perpendicular panes, Dallas and Rosmairi conversed with Father Napier. Dallas and the priest were laughing as Rosmairi demurely eyed her folded hands. Sorcha looked the other way and went to join the monks and Gordon clansmen.

Inevitably, the conversation was of politics. It always seemed as if the

Gordons—and Frasers and Stewarts and Sinclairs and Grays—talked nothing but politics. At least George could speak of catching trout and playing golf. Sorcha put a hand to her mouth to stifle an indiscreet yawn as one of the Gordons eyed her with a mixture of admiration and amusement.

"Are ye not caught up with how King Jamie mistreats his royal mother, or whether he'll remain Protestant?" he asked with a twinkle in his slate-gray eyes.

"The King will do as he's told," Sorcha replied in a bored tone. Her gaze wandered to Father Napier, who had managed to convulse Dallas. "He'll agree with any proposal that will make him sovereign of both Scotland and England after Elizabeth is dead."

"Ah," remarked one of the other Gordons, a slight, elfin man of uncertain years, "you consider our monarch a puppet of ambition, Mistress Fraser?"

Sorcha shrugged. "I seldom consider the King at all, sir." She had intended the reply to sound polite. But the stiff ruff of her gown pricked her chin, making her nose wrinkle in apparent disdain. The elfin man mistook her expression and suddenly grew somber.

"Even a Highlander should profess courtesy for his—or her—sovereign," the man asserted as the others leaned closer in to the little circle. "We may not always agree, but we must show respect."

Sorcha drew back, put off by so many keen stares. "Such peculiar words from a Gordon! By the Cross, is this the same clan that rose against Queen Mary twenty years ago and had to be hacked down like so many saplings in a stiff breeze?"

The elfinlike man whistled in shock; the Gordon with the slate-gray eyes froze in place; the monks exchanged glances of shock and annoyance. The ancient rite of hospitality was as ingrained in the Highlander as the love of the land itself; rude behavior toward a guest could be grounds for violence. Sorcha shifted from one foot to the other, feeling hemmed in by the circle of Gordons. She had overstepped her bounds, yet these men had baited her, and even the two monks in their midst appeared malevolent.

"At whose knee have you studied history, mistress?" queried the elfin man between curling lips. "Your Lady Mother's?"

Sorcha tossed her head, the black hair flying about her shoulders. "Aye. And my father's, since he was at Corrichie Moor when the battle took place between clan and Queen. He loved the Gordons, but he prized loyalty more highly."

There was a pause on the part of her listeners. Before any of them spoke again, Iain Fraser's affable, yet incisive voice cut into the group: "So I was and damned near died for my trueheartedness. The late Earl of Moray cared less for his half sister's victory than he did to send me to an early grave."

The tale of Iain Fraser's attack by an assassin after the battle of Corrichie Moor was a legend in the Highlands. Though he had fought for the Queen, her villainous half brother James had been determined to rid himself of any competitors for his role as Mary Stuart's favorite counselor.

George Gordon had ambled over to Fraser's side. "That was a confusing occasion, My Lord." He grinned. "God knows my sire never held it against you for fighting with the Queen. He often spoke of that sad day."

Fraser put a light hand on George's wide shoulder. "Indeed, I urged him to flee, lest your entire family be destroyed. Had he not agreed, I doubt that you would have ever been born." He gave George a kindly pat. "Show my eldest daughter how gallant a Gordon can be, George. I must attend to Father Napier."

George's perpetual, faintly lopsided grin remained fixed in place as the others melted away in Iain Fraser's wake. "Don't tell me my kinsmen were being unpleasant?" inquired George in a voice that always seemed just a bit too soft for his burly frame.

Sorcha's green eyes followed her father as he joined Father Napier. Though the priest stood almost the full length of the hall from Sorcha, she could have sworn his gaze locked with hers for just an instant. "Unpleasant?" Hastily, she turned to George, vexedly reminding herself it was he, not Napier, upon whom she should be concentrating. "Oh, nay, merely tedious. Are the salmon running at Strathbogie?"

The bland blue eyes sparked with interest. "They were, a fortnight ago. I took six within an hour just after first light. 'Twas wondrous sport."

Sorcha brightened visibly. "How large?"

George spread his hands a good twenty inches. "Mayhap more, at least two of them." He sighed and shook his head. "The next day, they started to turn color."

"A pity." Deliberately, she moved closer to George and put her hand through his arm. "I don't think we're ever going to eat," she grumbled, noting with vague chagrin that her hem had become unraveled just where it met the ivory underskirt. "I could devour at least one of those salmon you caught all by myself about now."

Somewhat to Sorcha's surprise, George placed his hand over hers where it lay in the crook of his arm. "Shall we walk, then?"

"Walk?" She wrinkled her nose up at him, catching a glimpse of Father Napier over her shoulder. He was moving toward her, with Rob at his heels. "Yes," she replied. "It's overbright in here. And too warm."

A moment later, they were in the entrance hall of the manor house, the sounds of the guests muffled behind them. Sorcha gazed at the whitewashed walls, the graceful stairway, the Fraser coat of arms cast in silver and etched with gold leaf above the door. Now that she had escaped, she was uncertain what to do with her companion. "Would you like to see Father's antlers?" she inquired.

George's silky blond eyebrows lifted curiously. "Antlers? Nay, I thought perhaps we could speak of more … intimate matters."

Caught off guard, Sorcha took a deep breath and regained her composure. Whatever did the braw laddie have on his not-so-agile mind? "Well, George?" Her smile offered encouragement. "Feel free to speak your piece."

He shifted his burly frame. " 'Tis Rosmairi." He swallowed once, but seemed relieved to have spoken her name. "She's so bonnie, yet timid as a doe when I try to speak with her alone. I was wondering if … you might … remind her what a good fellow I truly am."

So, thought Sorcha with a surprising sense of irritation, it was Rosmairi who had captured his fancy. She should have known it would be. "You mean to sue for Rosmairi's hand?" Sorcha asked, trying to keep the chagrin from her voice.

"Hand?" A puzzled expression crossed George's florid face. "I hadn't thought so far into the future. Rather, I felt we should each learn more of the other first."

Pushing aside the tinge of unreasonable jealousy his words had evoked, Sorcha considered. "Rosmairi's only fifteen. And while she may not find your attentions unwelcome, my parents may feel differently." With a beguiling smile, she patted George's arm. "A year or more, then seek Ros out. The wait will do neither of you any harm and may prove beneficial."

George's thick lower lip protruded stubbornly. "I'd no mind to wait that long!"

His obvious impatience nettled Sorcha. She didn't give a fig about George Gordon as a potential match for herself, but having just been jilted by another, it seemed unfair that Rosmairi should acquire a suitor before she did. However, that was scarcely an explanation that would carry much weight with the determined young clan chieftain. Sorcha was trying to extricate herself as gracefully as possible when the sound of heavy knocking and barking dogs erupted outside the carved main entrance. Ordinarily, servants would have rushed to admit visitors, but this evening all the Fraser retainers were attending the guests in the dining hall.

Briskly, Sorcha went to unlatch the door. She took no precautions, since few strangers came to Gosford's End. A moment later, Sorcha wished she had used the rusted iron peephole. Johnny Grant stood on the threshold, while three of the Fraser dogs yipped at his feet.

"I presume upon your hospitality," he said in his quick, choppy manner of speech. The autumn breeze ruffled his pale hair, and his gray eyes were somber. Though only seventeen, he had the air of a much older, more rigid man. "My kinsmen will wait outside."

Sorcha yanked the door all the way open. Down the drive, near the well, she could barely make out the forms of two men and three horses. Shooing the dogs back outdoors, she stepped aside to let Johnny enter. He stopped abruptly when he recognized George Gordon.

"I'll not speak in front of any Gordon," declared Johnny, bearded chin thrust out. "What I say must be directed only to Frasers. Only Frasers," he repeated doggedly.

For George, any aspersion cast on his family name drew instant ire. "By the saints, brash Johnny Grant, guard your tongue lest I hack it out!" George's hand had gone to his dirk.

"I come in peace," Johnny asserted truculently. "But I'll speak only to Mistress Sorcha and her kin. Spare us an ounce of courtesy, sir!"

"Spare us all," Sorcha murmured to George. "If there's mischief to be made, I'll be the maker."

George eyed Sorcha with vague surprise, then squared his shoulders, glared at Johnny, and stamped into the banquet hall. When Sorcha turned back to her unwelcome guest, she noted that he was flushing under his beard. "Well? What brings you here to visit a maid you've treated so shabbily?"

"Sorcha …." Johnny sighed and crossed his arms over his chest. "It seemed the manly thing to tell you face-to-face that despite my fondest wishes, I am unable to marry you. Quite unable."

"It is me or my religion you find unpalatable?" Sorcha demanded, feeling the stiff ruff agitate her skin.

Johnny's faint smile revealed his slightly crooked teeth. "I have always found you most bonnie. Alas, I cannot take a Papist to wife. For me, 'twould be a grave sin." The smile faded. "A very grave sin."

Sorcha flicked the end of her nose with her finger in that unconscious gesture of dismissal, then stared at Johnny Grant's youthful, compact form and pleasant bearded face. In days gone by, he had been good company, a good sport, and sometimes a good friend. But Niall's hard-muscled body, and even the hunter's eyes of Father Napier, stirred something more exciting in Sorcha than did Johnny Grant's camaraderie.

"I'd not invite you to sin on my account," Sorcha said rather stiltedly. Suddenly she laughed and put out a hand. "Don't fash yourself, Johnny. The match was made for us before we cut our second teeth. I'll not hold a grudge."

Tentatively, he took her hand. "I'm relieved. Most relieved. I thought you might be angry."

She wrung his hand, then withdrew her own. "I was. Infuriated, actually. But since you've taken the trouble to explain, that changes my feelings. Though why religion and politics must muddle up people's lives, I can't understand. You, however, believe otherwise, and I should respect that. At least I'm not being thrown over for some simpering, dimpled ninny."

"Oh, no! Lilias isn't like that!" Johnny stopped, flushed even more deeply, and clapped a hand over his mouth.

"Lilias?" Sorcha's eyes narrowed. "Traitor! Reiver! Knave!" She flew at him, nails going for his eyes.

Retreating, Johnny grappled with Sorcha, vainly trying to utter words that would soothe her. "It's nothing … I merely meant … Lilias is but fourteen."

Sorcha had him backed up against the wall. He averted his face, gripping one of her wrists but feeling the blows she rained against his temple. Johnny was again attempting verbal appeasement when he felt Sorcha being pulled away from him and heard her shriek in protest.

"Enough!" commanded Father Napier, one arm slung around Sorcha's waist. He had lifted her off the floor and her feet swung free above the flagstones. "You seem to be having problems getting along with your guests this evening, mistress."

"Let me go!" cried Sorcha, now directing her blows at Napier's arm. "This churl has shamed me most dreadfully! Swill-sucking pig!" she spat at Johnny. "I'll marry a man twice as noble, thrice as rich, or see you rot in hell first!"

Apprehensively, Johnny straightened his dark brown doublet. "I had wished to see your sire …. Ah!" He gasped in relief as Iain Fraser came into the entrance hall.

"Christ," muttered Fraser, "what's amiss now?" He glanced angrily from the combative Sorcha and Father Napier to the rumpled Johnny Grant. Napier set Sorcha on her feet but kept his arm tight around her waist. She quieted down in her father's presence but still strained to escape from the priest's firm hold.

"I came to apologize," Johnny explained swiftly. "I meant no dishonor to your daughter or your family. No dishonor at all. Despite what Sorcha may think, I am not betrothed to any other lass. Though in consideration of all these years I've spent paying her court and thus depriving myself of opportunities to find a more suitable bride, I must ask for your daughter's dowry of Stratherrick as recompense. Stratherrick," he repeated and licked his lips nervously.

"Why not ask for my ears as well, you greedy little swine?" screamed Sorcha, who was promptly muzzled by Father Napier's hand.

Iain Fraser had stiffened, though his face remained impassive. With a lazy jab of his thumb, he indicated the banquet hall. "The first course is about to be served. I don't wish to detain my guests any longer. You are dismissed and will never be welcome again at Gosford's End." He turned his back, brushing past Sorcha and Father Napier on his way to the banquet hall.

"Never," Johnny breathed, his gray eyes fixed on the double doors that had just closed behind Iain Fraser. Taking a deep breath, he managed to glower at Sorcha and the priest. "Now it is my honor that has been impugned." Johnny put one hand over his heart, the other on the latch of the front door. "My honor," he repeated in an ominous voice, and was gone into the brisk October night.

Slowly, Father Napier released Sorcha. Her temper had burned itself out, rendering her limp. "I'm sorry, Father," she began, "I must explain why I behaved so badly ...."

Napier shook his dark head. "No. It was all quite clear." He started back to the banquet hall, but Sorcha called after him.

"It's a matter of shame," she persisted, "and injustice."

Napier looked at her over his shoulder, the hunter's eyes deep and shadowy. "I doubt that you know what shame really is. Or injustice. And certainly not pain."

Sorcha paused, watching him stalk away. For one brief moment, she had seen not the look of the hunter in Gavin Napier's eyes, but of the hunted.

THE CHEERFUL VOICES AND BURSTS of laughter inside the banquet hall made Sorcha feel as if the past half hour had never occurred. Iain Fraser was herding his guests to the long trestle table as Dallas eyed her daughter questioningly.

"My Lord Huntly," she called over the throng, "pray sit by our Rosmairi and your humble hostess." With a flash of amethysts at one wrist, she motioned to Sorcha. "Your place is with Magnus and Father Napier." Dallas seemed to gaze at her eldest daughter a bit longer than was necessary, then smiled graciously in Napier's direction. "It is our wish that you give the blessing, Father."

Gavin Napier nodded once, then began intoning a familiar prayer in Latin. As he raised his hands over the table, Sorcha's eyes strayed to the strong, long, brown fingers that appeared too rough to belong to a cleric. Certainly they'd had the strength to subdue her fury only a few minutes earlier. Many priests and monks, however, were forced to earn their own living in these perilous times. The meanest, most common labor was often the only sure source of sustenance.

During the first courses of leek soup and boiled curlew and mussels in broth, Magnus monopolized Father Napier. That was as well with Sorcha, who needed time to recover from Johnny Grant's monstrous behavior. Yet as she watched Rosmairi engage in diffident conversation with George Gordon, her concern reverted to her sister. It was obvious that poor, naive, trusting Ros was smitten with the complacent young laird.

Sorcha sighed softly. If George proved persistent in his courtship, she would have to keep close watch over Rosmairi, lest the moonstruck lass lose more than her wits. Moreover, Sorcha was puzzled by George's choice. Tradition and religion bound Fraser and Gordon clans, yet despite his youth, George had already been involved in several major court intrigues. Slow of wit in social situations and seemingly phlegmatic, the Gordon chieftain was amazingly shrewd when it came to politics. Why would he ally himself with a house that was already part of his Highland power base? Iain Fraser's personal integrity and sizable wealth made him a man of importance, yet he had deliberately absented himself from the royal circle for almost twenty years.

So, Sorcha asked herself again, why Rosmairi? She seemed like a useless pawn in the scheme of George's aspirations. Noting her mother cast a disdainful glance in the young earl's direction, Sorcha recalled Lady Fraser's damning words about George's lack of character and abundance of ambition. In spite of the cramped quarters and the heat from the huge fireplace, Sorcha shivered.

Her musings were interrupted as the servants brought on the venison stewed in ale. As she began to eat, her attention was caught by Gavin Napier's account of his background. As near as she could make out, he had been raised at Inversnaid on the eastern shore of Loch Lomond. Unlike many of the Napiers, his family had not embraced the reformed religion. Their obstinate adherence to the Catholic faith had cost them considerable property, and while Gavin was still a lad, they had exiled themselves to France. Apparently, it was there that Napier had entered the priesthood.

A typical tale, Sorcha reflected, as she chewed on her venison and sipped the French wine from her father's ample cellar. Her plate was almost empty when Magnus's attention was diverted by a freckle-faced Gordon to his right. Father Napier turned back to Sorcha.

"Forgive me," he began. "Your brother's keen inquiries have made me neglect your company."

Somehow, his tone seemed too familiar to Sorcha, who frowned into her wine cup and fervently wished Father Napier would sound—and act—more like a priest. "Are you on your way home?" she queried at last.

"There is no home to go to. My parents died in France several years ago. The kinsmen I have in Scotland would disown me for becoming a priest." Despite the serious nature of his words, Napier was still smiling, his teeth a white gash in the dark beard. "I've come to offer support to Scotland's Catholic families."

"Oh." Sorcha riveted her gaze on her empty plate. "Are you one of those priests who would convert King Jamie?"

Napier shrugged. "I'm not as optimistic as some, especially the Jesuits. Tell me, is a knave such as Johnny Grant worth your obvious distress?"

Coming from Father Napier, a virtual stranger, the question seemed most inappropriate. Sorcha stiffened, shoving back strands of black hair that had escaped over one shoulder. "He humiliated me. Some day he'll be sorry for it."

Napier dabbed a crust of bread in the remains of his gravy. "Leave vengeance to the Lord, lass. You'll find many a man who will give up all for what Johnny threw away tonight."

Magnus was trying to peer around the priest's broad shoulder. Sorcha refused to look at her brother, nor would she return Napier's dark gaze. "The Lord has aplenty to do without fashing Himself over Johnny Grant. I'd prefer sparing Him the bother of divine retribution."

Father Napier turned somber, staring without focus at a silver tureen near his plate. "Retribution of any kind is only another word for pain. Spare not God but mankind with your petty pouting, Mistress Fraser."

"You upbraid me," she retorted, leaning forward and hoping the thick strands of hair would shield her flushed cheeks. "You are a strange, unfeeling sort of priest. Out there, in the entrance hall, you were too rough with me. See here," she said, lowering her voice and pushing back the ruffed edge of her sleeve, "you bruised my wrist."

Napier hesitated, then touched the red mark with his forefinger. "Not I, mistress. I had you by the waist." The shadows lifted from his face as he raised his hand to within a half inch of her lips. "And here, to silence your rampaging tongue."

Sorcha refused to meet his eyes. She could swear she still felt his fingers burning against the flesh of her wrist. Yet it was Johnny who had grabbed her there, not Gavin Napier. "Priests ought not to be so harsh with young maidens," she muttered, wondering why, with all the ease and glibness she usually displayed toward male companions, this strange clergyman should make her feel awkward and dull witted.

"Young maidens should neither attack visitors, nor lecture priests on behavior." Napier spoke not without humor, yet Sorcha sensed a hint of reproach.

At last, Magnus intervened. "My sister has many opinions, Father. Like our Lady Mother, she is inclined to give them voice." To lighten his remark, Magnus winked at Sorcha but received only a stony stare in response.

Napier's peat-brown eyes regarded Sorcha keenly. "I commend you on your wit. As for your fortitude," he went on, easing himself back from the table, "I would test it by inquiring as to how you enjoyed your fine supper."

"Mightily," replied Sorcha, folding her arms across her breast. "I find eating most satisfactory."

"Ah." Napier nodded solemnly while Magnus fingered his chin and looked on with amusement. "And," the priest continued, inclining his head toward Sorcha's plate, "did you find the Master of Ness satisfactory eating as well?"

Sorcha's green eyes widened with horror. She glanced from Napier to her empty plate and back again. Abruptly, she slapped a hand over her mouth, struggled with the voluminous skirts that were caught under the table, and awkwardly hurtled out of her chair to flee the dining hall.

Sorcha was sick three times after she reached the herb garden by the kitchen entrance. Steadying herself against the walls of Gosford's End, she wiped away tears of distress and anger with her fingertips. She hated Father Gavin Napier, hated his lack of priestly manners, hated his relentless taunting, hated his bold, unholy gaze, and most of all, she hated his cruel amusement over serving the Master of Ness for supper. He was not just a hunter, but a destroyer.

Sorcha turned her face to the brisk autumn wind, as she wrenched the prickly ruff from her gown and crumpled it in her hands. She would not, could not, go back into the dining hall. Naturally, her parents would be angry with her for leaving so hastily. But they would understand when she told them about the Master of Ness. At least her father would. She hoped.

It was chilly in the garden, but Sorcha needed the fresh, damp air to revive herself. Without conscious thought, she found her footsteps leading toward the stables.

Niall was just coming out, a pair of riding gloves in one hand. He froze in place when he saw Sorcha.

"Don't go," she called to him in a hoarse voice. "Please. I've been ill."

He moved forward slightly but again stopped. In the moonlight she could see his face working, as if he were trying to find the right words, but knew there was nothing he could say because he had been compelled to speak not at all.

"They made me eat the Master of Ness," Sorcha cried out to him, shaking the crumpled ruff in one hand. "It made me sick! Please, Niall, give me a drink of water!"

Niall shifted from one foot to the other, obviously torn by the commands of his master and the need of his beloved. He fervently wished he had succumbed to his impulse and run away from Gosford's End when Iain Fraser had ordered him to avoid his daughter's company henceforth.

Before Niall could respond in any manner, Sorcha heard her father's voice cut into the night: "Sorcha! Come here!"

She stood motionless for several moments, staring at Niall's outline against the stable door. He seemed as transfixed as she, the two of them fixed in time and place, with the shadow of Iain Fraser somewhere deep in the garden. At last, she raised the hand that held the ruff, dashed it to the ground, and turned toward her father.

Chapter 4

THE SUMMONS TO JOIN HER mother at daybreak boded ill; Dallas rarely attempted to cope with the world until at least nine o'clock. Upon those rare occasions when she rose early, her mood was invariably stormy and irascible. Apprehensively, Sorcha made her way to her mother's chamber. There were circles under her green eyes, and the olive skin was pale. Although her father had not upbraided her the previous evening after her brief explanation about the Master of Ness, she knew he had merely put his wrath in check while his guests awaited him in the dining hall.

Indeed, Sorcha was faintly surprised that it was her mother and not her father who commanded her presence so early on this gloomy autumn morning. During the night the wind had blown storm clouds in from the sea, though the rains had not yet started to pelt the Highland countryside.

Dallas was lying on her divan, fretting at the folds of a deep blue peignoir trimmed in miniver. She appeared somewhat sallow, and her own hair was almost unruly as her daughter's. Indicating that Sorcha should sit on a footstool next to her, Dallas put aside a tray of food that apparently had proved unappetizing.

"Your father has gone to Inverness," she said in a displeased tone. "Some fool of a Dutchman stole one of his ships."

For one fleeting moment, Sorcha was grateful for the Dutchman's greed. At least her father wasn't able to vent his anger, and experience told Sorcha that the longer the wait, the lesser the punishment.

Dallas, however, was biting her lip and frowning. "Your father and I stayed up late last night discussing certain matters. You were one of them."

"Me?" The green eyes flickered.

"Aye. We wish you to go to Edinburgh for a time, to live with your aunts and Uncle Donald."

Sorcha's hand flew to her breast. "So soon! Must I?"

Dallas slowly but firmly nodded her head. "I have just learned that your Aunt Glennie has sold her house and moved in with Aunt Tarrill and Uncle Donald, yet they still have ample room in their fine Canongate residence."

"I shall hate it," Sorcha blurted, putting her hands out to her mother in a pleading gesture. "I shall suffocate."

Dallas sighed wearily. "You shall not. Oh, daughter," she exclaimed, "I will never understand how you prize these Highlands so greatly! They're desolate, wild, lonely places where the wind soughs through the hills and tears out your heart! There is no comfort here, only an empty echo from the Ness to Norway!"

Startled by her mother's intensity and passion, Sorcha shook her head in jerky, rapid movements. "No, no, 'tis not like that—'tis balm in the wind, succor in the hills. The very ground soothes my soul. I know not city ways, nor do I care to learn. Please, my Lady Mother, let me bide here at Gosford's End."

Dallas seemed to have depleted herself with the tirade against the Highlands. She lay back against the brocaded cushions, her hair atangle, her eyes overbright. "Nay, dear Sorcha, that cannot be. Your father says you must go." She cleared her throat before looking straight into Sorcha's eyes. "Your sire is hard, but just. You know why you must keep away from Niall. But Niall does not know, nor will he be told. Since you persist in seeing him—or trying to, as you did last night—one of you must leave for a time. Your father believes it would not be fair to ask Niall, in his innocence, to go. Therefore, it must be you."

"Fair!" Sorcha spat out the word. "It's not fair at all!" Her infatuation with Niall suddenly seemed remote, unreal. "Or am I in disgrace over faithless Johnny Grant?"

A faint smile played at Dallas's wide mouth. "You forget, Niall is your father's son." She lowered her eyes, the slim fingers tracing a sketchy path on the arm of the divan. Dallas chose her next words with care. "As for young Grant, to discuss him further is a waste of breath. He has ceased to exist in the world your father and I inhabit."

Sorcha kneaded her muslin skirt as Dallas looked directly at her daughter. "I've a mind to send Rosmairi, too, but dislike straining my kin's hospitality. I'm afraid Ros has come down with a fatal fascination for George Gordon of Huntly." Dallas made a face, looking very much as if she'd swallowed sour milk. "George, in turn, must covet your father's commercial trade. Or, perish the thought, his properties."

Sorcha's green eyes flickered. "Oh?" Was the explanation so simple? For once, Sorcha doubted her mother's perspicacity.

Dallas mistook Sorcha's reticence for not wanting to criticize her sister's lamentable taste in men. "Fie, how Ros rattled on last night! 'So braw, so gallant, so kind, so courtly!' And Ros always such a shy one with the laddies! George is twenty-three to her fifteen and has the wit of wool! I pray to Saint Anne he's not leading her a merry chase."

"So do I," murmured Sorcha, wishing her mother would show as much concern over Johnny Grant's rude treatment. But her own immediate future was Edinburgh, and Sorcha forced herself to face it. "It has been some time since I've seen my aunts and Uncle Donald."

"They're good, kindly people," Dallas said, her face softening at the thought of her kinfolk. "Uncle Donald has done right well in the banking business, all things considered."

Indeed, Donald McVurrich's humble beginnings had shown no sign of his future prosperity and financial acumen. He had been raised on a farm at Dunbar but had found himself unsuited to the agrarian life. For a time, under Dallas's tutelage, Donald McVurrich had served in the Queen's guards. But eventually his natural talent for figures had surfaced, leading to a place in the royal almoner's household. A few years after his marriage to Tarrill, Donald had gone into the banking business, where he had prospered almost without notice. Reticent, stolid, cautious Donald McVurrich somehow had managed to outwit—and outlast—his more flamboyant brethren in the major financial centers of Europe. He and Tarrill had five children, four boys and a girl. As for Glennie, the older of Dallas's sisters, she was now a widow twice over, her two sons grown to manhood, with families of their own.

"Uncle Donald is oversomber," Sorcha protested. "He is Presbyterian to the toes."

"A common failing," Dallas murmured, "but Tarrill keeps the faith in which she was raised. At least as much of it as she can, given the odious restrictions enforced by the Protestants. You'll not find it a gloomy household. No place where Tarrill dwells could be that."

Yet Sorcha's memories of their visits to the house in the Canongate were of children lacking in frivolity, of hymns sung before supper, and of an absence of laughter whenever Uncle Donald was present. Except for Aunt Tarrill's more relaxed, good-humored approach to life, Sorcha could think of little that appealed to her within the McVurrich residence. For the first time, she reflected upon her mother's confinement to the Highlands. Though Dallas was scarcely reluctant to complain, her words of criticism were so commonplace that no one—at least not Sorcha—took them very seriously. But, Sorcha realized, her mother must have gone through difficult times, wrenched away from her beloved city and her only relatives. It was a measure of her devotion to Iain Fraser that she had ventured north at all; it was proof of her love that she had stayed for almost twenty years.

Dallas now avoided her daughter's gaze. "The roads should be passable for at least another month. It's best that you leave for Edinburgh soon. Rob will be traveling with you."

"He will?" Sorcha tried to evince interest. "That's … reassuring," she said tonelessly, and for a long time, neither mother nor daughter spoke at all.

ONLY UPON RARE OCCASION DID Sorcha have difficulty sleeping. That night, however, she found herself tossing and turning, no longer so sure of herself in the quiet hours of darkness as by the light of day. Sometime before midnight, she got out of bed to stand by her window and gaze at the moonlit landscape.

Across the valley, the shutters of Inverness were closed for the night. Nearby, the stables lay in shadow, as the persistent autumn wind stirred the leaves in the plane trees. Yet there was a strange movement close by the Italian fountain—a form that she began to discern as horse and rider, edging toward the manor house. Within a few more yards the rider dismounted and tethered the horse to a sapling by the fish pond.

It was a man, seemingly young, tall and broad of shoulder. Sorcha recognized something familiar about him as he moved toward one of the rear entrances. Sure enough, a door opened and the man slipped inside. Sorcha pulled away from the casement, absently untangling her hair with her fingers. Someone from the Fraser farmhouses, perhaps, enjoying a nocturnal liaison with a serving wench. While such activity wasn't condoned, it was doubtful that either Lord or Lady Fraser would interrupt a sound sleep to exert disciplinary action.

Slowly, Sorcha made her way back to bed. To her immense relief, she fell asleep almost immediately. The following day, she didn't even remember the stranger's visit, nor was it alluded to by anyone in the household.

But that night, as she lay abed reading a volume of newly published French sonnets, there was a tentative rap on her door. Irritated, she flung back the covers and crossed the room on bare feet. Rosmairi stood on the threshold, her pink cheeks aglow.

"You must come," she whispered urgently. "George and I are to be married this very night!"

Sorcha gaped at her sister. It was impossible. Had she fallen asleep and was dreaming? Shaking herself, Sorcha grabbed Rosmairi by the arm and hauled her inside the room. "Are you daft, Ros? How can you be married tonight? Have the banns been announced? Do our parents know?"

Still basking in romantic euphoria, Rosmairi shook her head. " 'Tis a secret. George fears interference from high places should anyone find out our intentions."

Noting that her sister was dressed in a mauve riding habit with her red-gold hair plaited under a high-crowned hat, Sorcha gazed down at her own night shift and bare feet. "I must dress," she muttered and started for her wardrobe before abruptly turning to face Rosmairi once more. "Nay, Ros, 'tis madness! Our parents will skewer George and pack you off to a convent! Think on it. Gordon chieftain or not, George owes you an honorable wedding day with clan and kin in attendance."

Rosmairi lifted her chin and, with the crowned hat adding height, looked considerably older than her fifteen years. "I hadn't thought you'd fail me in anything so important to my happiness. Are you rankled because I'm to wed first?"

However unwittingly, Rosmairi had struck dangerously close to a truth Sorcha was loath to admit. Feeling her face grow as warm as her feet were cold, Sorcha flipped her tangled tresses over her shoulders. "Nonsense. I'm not mad to marry. I just think you're behaving recklessly."

Unwontedly cool and self-possessed, Rosmairi shrugged. "Then give me your blessing, if not your company. I'm off to Beauly Priory to take my vows."

Sorcha advanced on her sister to proffer the requisite sisterly benediction. But as she leaned forward to kiss Rosmairi's smooth pink cheek, memories came flooding back. Baby Ros with her fluff of golden hair, little Ros taking her first steps to Sorcha in the rose garden, Ros with a skinned knee, Ros being teased unmercifully by Magnus, Ros crying in Sorcha's arms after Rob had broken her favorite doll ….

"Fie," whispered Sorcha, sounding very like their mother, "of course I'll come."

Not more than five minutes later, both girls were tiptoeing out the side entrance of the manor house. Only a few wisps of cloud marred the sky as they slipped through the darkness toward the stable. In silence, they led their horses outside, and as a dog howled at the crescent moon, they were on the road to Beauly.

Passing the low hedgerows and the drooping cornstalks, they crossed the Ness single file over a narrow stone bridge. Just ahead, near a gnarled, leafless tree, they could make out the silhouettes of a dozen men and their mounts.

"George!" breathed Rosmairi, and beamed with eager delight.

Sorcha suppressed a disapproving sigh and urged Thisbe around a deep pothole in the rough dirt road. She could see George, taller and broader than the rest, waving a welcome. Maybe, Sorcha thought with a sense of shock, the braw laddie really loves her. Why, she wondered vexedly, had that idea never occurred to her until now?

The sudden spurt of movement directly in front of them startled both Thisbe and Rosmairi's horse. The animals shied, while the two young women clung to their necks for dear life. It took some time for Sorcha to soothe Thisbe and then to realize what had happened: As she calmed the frightened animal with her hands and leaned across the saddle, she saw that a man and a horse blocked the road between the narrow bridge and the gnarled tree. The interloper wore a flowing black cloak and held a pistol in each hand. Peering more closely into the darkness, Sorcha recognized Gavin Napier.

"Back! Back, you Gordons, or your lives are forfeit!" Brandishing the pistols, he purposefully spurred his horse to rear up and let out an ear-splitting whinny.

"That priest!" gasped Rosmairi, still trying to calm her little mare. "George!" she cried, her voice atremble. "What's amiss?"

Her answer was two loud pistol shots. Rosmairi screamed, and Sorcha swore. George and his men pulled back closer to the tree, though Sorcha realized that Napier had shot harmlessly into the air.

Keeping his weapons trained on the Gordons, Napier turned quickly to look over his shoulder. "Go back! Head for home! Now!"

Either his urgency or her instinct told Sorcha not to disobey. Wheeling Thisbe about, she spoke sharply to Rosmairi: "Do as he says! Go, Ros. Ride!"

Whatever reluctance Rosmairi possessed was overcome by her horse, which took its head, stumbled slightly, and cantered back over the narrow bridge just behind Sorcha and Thisbe. Two more shots broke the silence of the night; then Napier was also riding with them, racing across the rolling fields, kicking up clods of mud.

To Sorcha's surprise, the Gordons didn't attempt to follow. Within a quarter of an hour, they were back at Gosford's End, silently leading their weary mounts into the paddock. It was only after they had watered and bedded down the horses that anyone spoke. As might be expected, it was Rosmairi, her high-crowned hat askew, her face pale with disappointment, but her gray eyes sparking with indignant wrath.

"You *will* explain, Father," she averred with a voice that shook, yet had somehow lost its youthful timbre.

Napier tilted his dark head to one side and regarded Rosmairi with a rueful expression. "The Earl of Huntly's intentions were not what they seemed. George sought to dishonor you, mistress."

"Liar!" Rosmairi flew at him, but Sorcha grabbed her sister by one arm and yanked her back. "Leave me be!" she screamed, trying to wrench herself free from Sorcha's determined grasp.

"Be quiet," Sorcha rasped in a low voice. "Do you want to rouse all of Gosford's End?"

Rosmairi's gray eyes widened; then, like a card house, she virtually collapsed against her sister. "I hate you," she snuffled, wiping her face with the back of one gloved hand, "you and that priest!"

"Father Napier must have his reasons," Sorcha insisted, and put a comforting arm around Rosmairi. In truth, Sorcha was as muddled as Rosmairi. Seeking support, she glanced at Napier. "Are you trying to tell us that George Gordon wished to ravish Ros rather than to marry her?"

Napier was hanging his saddle and bridle in a vacant place on the stable wall. "Aye," he replied shortly. "Fornication was his only aim."

For some reason, his utterance unnerved Sorcha. She'd heard other priests talk against sins of the flesh, warn of wanton desires, rail against illicit passion. None of them had ever really moved her, let alone caused any upset. Yet she found Gavin Napier's simple statement disturbing.

"We must tell my parents," she declared, forcing her mind from animal lust and priestly condemnation.

"No!" cried Rosmairi, pulling free of Sorcha's arm. "Spare me that!"

The heartfelt plea tugged at Sorcha, but it was Napier who responded. "I'm afraid that's not possible." To Sorcha's surprise, he suddenly looked tired, even haggard. "Lord Fraser must hear of this, though I am as loath to tell him as you are, mistress."

Rosmairi went rigid as a carved image. "You shame me, Father! What kind of priest are you?" Putting frantic hands to her pale face, she stared in desperation at Napier, then turned and fled the stable. Sorcha made as if to follow, but Napier put a hand on her arm.

"Stay, mistress. She'll merely go to her chamber and sob noiselessly into the night. 'Twill do her no harm and mayhap some good." He started to withdraw his hand, but bent down to study Sorcha more closely. "And you?" he asked, with unexpected anxiety. "Your sister's tribulations must distress you mightily."

Their gazes had locked, and Sorcha found herself strangely tongue-tied. Behind them in the stalls, the horses were settling down for a foreshortened night. "Well, of course," she managed at last, noting absently that the little lantern she had lighted upon their arrival cast a feeble amber glow among the piles of straw and bales of hay. A black cat with a white vest prowled hopefully, searching for a midnight mouse. "Poor Ros," Sorcha murmured, self-consciously aware of Napier's hand still on her arm. "Our Lady Mother said George wasn't to be trusted. Why didn't we listen?"

Napier's mouth twisted bitterly. "I wish I had been given such a warning. My mission seems doomed. George Gordon's iniquities mock my efforts to bring unity among the Catholic clans of Scotland." Slowly, he let go of Sorcha's arm. "Gordon's callow, ambitious. He has no conscience."

"He has no heart, either," Sorcha asserted, once more feeling pity for Rosmairi. She gave her arm a little shake, as if she could still feel Napier's hold on her, then noted that his brown eyes had grown shadowy. A trick of the lantern light, she thought, but cast another glance in his direction and was struck by the haunted expression on his lean, wolflike face. "George has betrayed us all," she said gloomily, and put a hand to her weary head.

Napier's mouth twisted sardonically. He took a step forward, so that Sorcha's riding skirts and his long cloak brushed against each other. For one tense moment, she thought he was going to touch her again. Instead, he gathered the folds of his cloak more closely around him and flung them over one broad shoulder. "Perhaps," he finally replied, the irony still visible on his face, "but I betrayed him as well."

Then Napier swerved on his heel and left the stable, the flickering lantern light making his shadow ominously large.

IN THE FALL, EVER SINCE Sorcha could remember, the Fraser offspring spent one Sabbath gathering up the leaves from the front of Gosford's End and piling them high for a bonfire after dark. When they were younger, the four children had tussled and tumbled and toppled among the piles, eventually requiring several servants to restore order. These past years, they had gone through the ritual with less ebullience and more efficiency.

This time, it was different. As the north wind kept the rain clouds at bay, Sorcha, Ros, Magnus, and Rob whooped and shrieked as they worked, occasionally pummeling one another or throwing huge handfuls of crisp leaves onto an unaware sibling. It was as if the years had rolled back, and knowing that this could be their last autumn together, all four Frasers were desperately clinging to childhood.

"Stop it, Magnus!" Rosmairi called out as her elder brother brandished a rake. "You'll give Rob a tonsure before he ever leaves home!"

"Maybe I'll pound sense into him so he won't leave," Magnus replied, making a mock thrust at Rob's head. "I tell you, Rob, there's land enough here to make us both a living." Rob threw a stick for the aged collie, Buchanan, to fetch. The dog looked up, reconsidered, and went back to sleep on a tussock of grass. "You plant the seeds of food, Magnus; I'll plant the seeds of faith. Though, soon you'll plant other seeds with Jeannie Simpson."

"I rather like Jeannie," Rosmairi remarked in a deceptively bland voice. "She has lovely manners. Or does she never interrupt because she has nothing to say?"

Sorcha cast a sidelong glance at her sister. Of all the Frasers, Rosmairi had always possessed the greatest sense of charity, even more so than Rob. But her thwarted elopement had sharpened her tongue and blunted her usual happy, gentle nature. To Ross's dismay, Gavin Napier had carried the humiliating tale to her parents. Lord and Lady Fraser had been outraged by George Gordon's shameless behavior, though Rosmairi refused to concede that her lover had connived at her seduction. Doggedly, she clung to the belief that George really loved her and that Gavin Napier, for some cruel, unfathomable reason, had prevented the wedding. Sorcha didn't agree with her sister, and said so, but when Rosmairi had asked archly why she'd put credence in a stranger priest rather than their longtime ally, Sorcha had no answer, except that the young earl was ruthlessly ambitious and used to getting his own way. And that somehow, inexplicably, Sorcha trusted Gavin Napier.

While this explanation made no dent in Rosmairi's staunch defense of George, at least the sisters had not broken with each other over the matter. Still, there was an uncustomary distance between Rosmairi and the rest of her family these days. Nor, thought Sorcha, were remarks such as the one Rosmairi had just made about Jeannie Simpson helping to narrow the gap.

Indeed, Magnus was giving Rosmairi a baleful look, but it was Rob who replied: "Like most wives, Jeannie will discover her tongue once she's wed. I'll wager your ears will wilt within a year, brother."

Rob ducked as Magnus reached out to cuff him. "Jeannie is as bonnie as bluebells and docile as Buchanan," Magnus bellowed, and tripped over a root. He righted himself before falling down, but Sorcha moved swiftly, dumping a basket of leaves over his head.

"If any man compared *me* to a collie, I'd saw off his ears," she asserted, dancing out of reach.

Snatching leaves from his hair, Magnus grimaced, while Rob grew thoughtful. "We are more thorough than we used to be," he remarked, indicating the tidy grounds.

"We had less to talk about," Rosmairi put in, setting aside her rake. "We had fewer ... troubles," she added on a wistful note.

Sorcha set her face against the brisk wind as she gazed from Rob's slim, fair presence to the pink-and-red-gold visage of Rosmairi to Magnus's tall, dark, sturdy form. She would miss the others, but at least Rob would be with her on the journey south.

As the wind grew even stronger, Sorcha shielded her face with her Fraser plaid. "Damn," she said in a muffled voice. "Mayhap we'd better torch these leaves before they're scattered halfway to Inverness. Moreover, it's going to rain."

She felt her sister and brothers stare at her for just a moment. They knew she was right, but the annual burning would mean an end to their day together, perhaps to their lives together. Sorcha smiled back feebly. A few seconds later, Magnus had lighted some twigs. The leaves caught and before long the flames shot heavenward, an orange-and-yellow signal to herald oncoming winter. Biting her lip, Sorcha watched the fire burn, aware that her youth had drifted away like the leaves themselves. Yet the tree still stood, tall and sturdy against the twilight.

So did another figure, some distance away by the side of the house. Sorcha caught the movement and felt tears sting her eyes. It was Niall, alone in the shadows, watching the Fraser heirs pass through the rites of autumn.

Part Two
1586-87

Chapter 5

THE FIRST TWO DAYS THEY headed southward were uneventful, with kind, mild weather favoring the little party as it wound its way along the Findhorn. Sorcha knew this wild, remote country well; she had hunted here at least twice each year with her family. It was also MacKintosh and Clan Chattan ground, the ancestral home of her mother's maternal kinsmen.

There were ten people in the group: Rob and his manservant, Torquil MacKemmie, a stout, flippant youth with an eminently practical nature; Arthur MacSymond, related to Iain Fraser by marriage and renowned throughout the Highlands for his instincts as a guide; Father Napier, and two monks, Brother Ninian and Brother Myles; Sorcha was accompanied by her maid, Ailis Frizell, an intelligent, doleful girl with extremely poor eyesight.

Dallas's self-control had crumbled at the time of departure, as she clung to both Sorcha and Rob outside the gates of Gosford's End. Rosmairi wept, too, and even Magnus's eyes were brimming. Only Iain Fraser retained a mask of nonchalance, though his farewell embraces were overlong and overtight. As the group trotted their mounts away from the Fraser home, Rob wiped a manful tear while Sorcha used a sleeve to dry her damp cheeks.

I will be back, she vowed silently, not daring to turn around for a final look at her beloved home. But the brave words could not stave off the gloom she felt the first day of the journey. However, the next morning Sorcha awoke in somewhat lighter spirits. As there was no turning back, she might as well try to consider the trip as an adventure. Rob and Torquil were already laughing a great deal with Father Napier. Since Sorcha preferred keeping her distance from the disturbing priest, she would try to find some source of mutual amusement with Ailis Frizell. Judging from the sour look on Ailis's face,

Sorcha decided she'd set an all but impossible task for herself.

But by the third day, the sight of the Grampian Mountains lifted even Ailis's spirits. It was a clear, crisp autumn morning, with the rugged peaks of Ben-y-Gloe, Beinn Dearg and Ben Macdhui rising proudly above the moorlands. When the travelers espied the Cairn Gorms, they could see the first heavy snows nestling in the cleft between the peaks. Crows called out from nearby trees as nimble horned sheep sought safety from the intruders next to low stone walls.

"Do you remember," Rob called out to Sorcha, reining in his mount so she could catch up with him, "how we came through here one summer and feasted on raspberries?"

Sorcha did. It had been on the last of the three trips she had made to Edinburgh with her parents. Magnus and Rob had chased some shaggy cows while Dallas and the girls filled their riding skirts with berries. It had been a raucous, happy trip despite Magnus's wandering off in Perth, and Rosmairi's suffering from a stomach upset near Kinross.

Now, more than five years later, they would spend the night in the shadow of Ben Lawers, at a rude inn on the edge of Loch Tay. It was there that Father Napier and the monks exchanged their clerical attire for secular garb.

"We're out of the Highlands," Father Napier said to the group at supper in the small common room of the inn. "It's not prudent to flaunt our faith."

Sorcha felt a pang of sadness at the thought of leaving her native country behind. Another two or three days would bring them to Edinburgh. But even as Sorcha tried to picture the route in her mind, Father Napier informed the party that they would make a short side trip to Doune.

"Doune?" queried Rob, with his customary habit of accompanying a question with the wrinkling of his rather foreshortened nose. "Is that not the dwelling of the Earl of Moray?"

Napier nodded, summoning a lame-gaited serving wench with brilliant flame-colored hair. He indicated the trenchers, requesting more roasted lamb. "If you find it strange that I would deliberately visit the home of a Protestant lord, rest easy, young sir." Napier sat back as the redheaded wench served him. "Moray is a very different man than was his late and unlamented father-in-law. He is fair-minded, cheerful, and quite the braw gallant."

Sorcha regarded Napier's remark with interest. For all the enmity which had existed between her father and the previous Earl of Moray, Iain Fraser had never criticized the title's present bearer. In fact, Fraser had spoken well of young Moray's courage and integrity.

"Will you tell him who—and what—you are?" asked Sorcha, refusing more lamb but pulling another chunk of barley bread from the loaf that sat on a thick board in the middle of the table.

"Nay, though he'd bear me no grudge for it. One thing to keep in mind," he admonished his listeners, "is that while Mary Stuart lives, no one with any foresight will openly persecute a Catholic priest unless they have ample grounds."

"But we *are* persecuted," Sorcha countered, her mouth full of barley bread. "Even now, you go about in disguise."

Napier smiled dryly, his peat-brown eyes on Sorcha's face. "Most Protestants aren't like Moray. After all, it's still possible that Queen Mary could be reinstated as cosovereign with her son. Or that James could be swayed by influential Catholics to embrace the Church of Rome."

Rob put his chin in his hands as a sanguine glow touched his face. "Think of it, a Scotland brought back to the true faith! How I should want to be part of that holy crusade!"

"Och," exclaimed Torquil, with his customary irreverence, "will we see ye hovering over King Jamie with a rosary?" Rob flushed but managed a feeble laugh. "I've no such grand ambitions, Torquil, my brash laddie. But don't think a day goes by that I don't fail to pray for His Grace's conversion."

Feeling vaguely guilty because there were days when she didn't remember to pray at all, Sorcha brushed the crumbs from her suede jacket and excused herself. "Ailis," she murmured, leaning over the other girl's shoulder, "will you walk with me for a while? It's too early to retire, and our room smells of peat and dust."

With a marked lack of enthusiasm, Ailis agreed. Like her mistress, she had not been anxious to leave Gosford's End. Dallas, however, had persisted, telling Sorcha she would be better served by the stolid Ailis than some feather-witted wench who'd get herself seduced upon setting foot in the High Street. As for Ailis, Dallas asserted it was part of the serving girl's education, a once-in-a-lifetime opportunity.

Outside the little inn, Sorcha and Ailis walked along the edge of Loch Tay as the pale autumn light faded beyond the Grampians to the west. "The land has changed a great deal since we left home," Sorcha said, wondering what the rest of her family was eating for supper that evening at Gosford's End. "See how civilized it becomes as we move south."

"I won't object," Ailis replied, squinting into the dark loch. A sharp breeze tugged at their riding skirts and made little tuftlike waves on the water. "The road today was so steep, and rough as well."

"It was tricky footing for the horses," Sorcha conceded, "but Arthur MacSymond is an excellent guide."

Even as Sorcha spoke, Ailis stumbled over a rock and uttered a shrill little cry. She had turned an ankle, and while Sorcha didn't think it was a serious injury, it seemed wise for Ailis to go back to the inn. "I'll go with you," Sorcha declared, but Ailis insisted she could manage by herself. Not really ready to return just yet, Sorcha agreed.

From somewhere close by, she heard a throstle pip noisily in the chilly night air. The breeze had died as suddenly as it had come up, and the loch was quiet. Unacquainted with the terrain, she was careful not to lose sight of the little inn's sole lighted window. After about a half hour, she turned back, making her leisurely way toward the beckoning amber glow and the smell of the peat fire.

She had gone about halfway when she saw a tall figure walking with long, sure strides in her direction. Though he now wore conventional garb, she knew immediately that it was Father Napier. Annoyance crept over Sorcha. Did he think she was lost? If so, why hadn't he sent Rob to fetch her? Sorcha slowed her step deliberately, perversely wanting to make him walk as far as possible.

"This isn't the garden at Gosford's End, you know," he called out when he got within thirty feet of her. "Wild beasts still prowl at night in these parts. Are you armed?"

Sorcha ignored the irony in Gavin Napier's voice. "There are more such animals where I come from." She couldn't control the goading glare she gave him as he stopped just a few feet away from her. "I've grown to distrust not beasts with four legs but those with two."

Napier seemed to ponder her remark as he stroked his short, thick beard. He wore a leather jacket over a light-colored shirt, his boots rose well up on his thighs, and the wide belt around his waist held a silver-handled dirk. The layman's attire seemed to suit him much better than his priestly garments.

"You don't trust me." The statement wasn't as casual as Napier had intended; his voice was flat, his eyes wary.

"I don't know you." Sorcha frowned at the muddy ground under foot. "You ... confound me."

A crow cawed shrilly from the pine grove that hid the little inn from view. Napier's gaze followed the sound, then came to rest on Sorcha. "Mayhap. But I haven't meant to."

Sorcha blinked. His words seemed lame. She stopped abruptly, turning to confront him. "Well, you managed all the same!" She batted at the tip of her nose, chin thrust out pugnaciously. "Priests must act like priests! Oh, aye, I know some are as wicked and debauched as the Protestants say, but I sense that you have honor." Seeing Napier's unfathomable expression, Sorcha let out a deep raspy sigh. "What have I said? I sound like such a fool!"

Napier moved a few paces away, staring into the lapping waters of the loch. "Why did you agree to go to Edinburgh?" The question came from over his shoulder.

Sorcha gazed quizzically at his broad back. "My agreement wasn't necessary. Though," she went on, fretting at her temple, "I suppose I hope I shall find a husband there. My prospects could hardly be less dim than at home."

Napier didn't reply at once, but seemed to be brooding. "By the Cross," he murmured at last, and turned to face her, an imposing figure etched against the loch's black-and-silver waters. "Marriage is dangerous. If any woman—or man—ever thought what marriage would bring, the wedding bells would peal no more."

Involuntarily, Sorcha shrank back into herself. Father Napier's cynicism seemed excessive, even for a celibate. He had started walking down the path again when Sorcha, scurrying to catch up, uttered her response: "Life brings good and bad things, whether a person marries or not. At least husband and wife can face the hard times together." With an air of defiance, she stared up at Napier, who kept striding purposefully toward the inn. "I know that. I've often heard my Lady Mother say so when misfortune struck while my sire was away at sea. 'If only your father were here,' " Sorcha quoted, " 'I could bear all this so much better.' "

Napier emitted a vague snort. "But she managed all the same. And having met your formidable Lady Mother, I suspect she did it with great competence. Still, her sentiment is well-intentioned." He paused as something rustled in the tall grasses just ahead of them. A deer, Sorcha thought, coming to the loch for an evening drink. "If she speaks the truth, your parents may have been singularly blessed," he went on, resuming his determined pace.

"I don't think you like women much," she asserted. "Is that why you became a priest?"

His answer was swift and wordless. In three long strides, he took her in his arms, capturing her mouth with his. Stunned, Sorcha's reflex action was to batter his broad back with her hands, but the gesture of resistance was feeble at best. The kiss deepened, stifling her breath, pressing her body against his. She was bent backward, yet held tightly in his grasp as his tongue delved between her lips, her teeth. The brutelike intensity should have enraged her sensibilities. Instead, it enflamed them, urging Sorcha to open her mouth wide to him, to surrender to the hands that moved purposefully from her waist to her hips and back to the soft, yielding flesh just beneath her breasts.

She had felt like this with Niall, and yet it was not the same—then, she had been in control, of him, of herself, of the situation. Now, in Gavin Napier's steel grasp, Sorcha was not merely helpless but had no will to fend him off, no shame to demand that he desist.

As she felt his fingers move to the swelling curve of her breast, he suddenly released her mouth, holding her away from him in the crook of his arm. The dark eyes seemed to sear her face. "Does that answer your question?" Napier's voice was a low, ominous growl.

Sorcha was shaking. She still felt that tantalizing hand just under her breast and tried to read what was going on behind the dark eyes and the fierce voice. Contempt, no doubt, for himself, for her. "Sweet Mother of God," Sorcha whispered through lips that barely seemed to move, "did I entice you?"

For one fleeting moment, the hunter's eyes grew not only soft but almost merry. Then Napier slowly withdrew his arms from Sorcha, the fingers just brushing the tip of her breast, as if by accident. He put a hand to his forehead and rubbed vigorously. "Christ," he murmured, "what have I done?"

For once, Sorcha squelched her natural desire to speak boldly, honestly. Gavin Napier had kissed her and held her and touched her—and she wished he hadn't stopped. But she dared not say so aloud; she was compelled to lie, at least to suppress the truth, and to hide her feelings. Sorcha shifted her stance and shrugged. "A regrettable lapse, I suppose," she said and was amazed at the leaden sound of her voice.

"Aye." Napier nodded once, started to lift his hand in some sort of salute, and then abruptly turned on his heel to head up the rocky path toward the inn.

A faint glow of light could be seen from behind the rude inn's window. Off to one side of the thatched structure, Sorcha heard their horses stir in the dilapidated stable. Fleetingly, she considered going to pat Thisbe's neck to feel a reassuring reminder of home.

Napier never looked back, but he left the door ajar for her. By the time Sorcha entered the inn, she could see his booted feet ascending the ladder to the loft where his straw pallet lay between Rob's and Arthur MacSymond's.

Sorcha ignored the curious stare of the burly innkeeper as she made her way up the short, winding staircase to her attic room. Ailis was sitting by a candle, looking through the tiny window. There was no glass or horn, only a piece of canvas to keep out the autumn chill. Sorcha silently blessed Ailis's poor eyesight; otherwise she might have observed the indiscreet moment by the loch.

"How's your ankle, Ailis?" Sorcha inquired in a kindly voice.

"Sore, but I'll manage." Ailis gave Sorcha a tight-lipped smile. "Did your walk refresh you?"

Sorcha turned away as she started to undress. "Oh, aye," she answered as casually as possible, and realized her mouth felt bruised. "I think I saw a deer by the loch."

"Are they like the ones in the Highlands?" asked Ailis, crawling under a patched blanket and stifling a yawn.

"They're smaller," replied Sorcha evasively.

"Oh," Ailis said, and closed her eyes. Sorcha held back a sigh of relief; she had no wish to carry on a lengthy conversation. Blowing out the candle, Sorcha wrapped herself in her own blanket, which felt scratchy against her skin. The place seemed free of vermin, she decided, trying to find a comfortable position on the straw pallet. They had yet to sleep in a bed with a real mattress. At least the McVurrich household would provide the amenities of life.

Outside, an owl hooted. Ailis was already snoring softly. The little low-ceilinged room still reeked of peat, though Sorcha knew the fire had been put out before she returned to the inn.

"God's teeth," she whispered, turning over and wrestling with the rough blanket. She had hoped to put Father Napier's reckless embrace from her mind. Had he thought she was taunting him about not liking women? Was he really a lascivious priest after all? Or was Gavin Napier insane? The deep sigh Sorcha uttered seemed to fill the cramped little room. She lay on her back, staring up at the low, patched ceiling. Suddenly she felt quite young, rather foolish, and very lonely. True, Rob was with her on the journey, but soon they would be parted. Only a few weeks ago, Sorcha had been dwelling comfortably within the bosom of her family and the familiar surroundings of Gosford's End. She had an excellent prospect of marriage and the future seemed secure. Now she had been jilted, wrenched from her sanctuary, and sent upon a journey to a city that oppressed her. Worst of all, she had found pleasure in the arms of an errant priest.

"Hopeless," she whispered into the darkness. Sorcha knew it was as hopeless to love Gavin Napier as it was to love Niall Fraser. In that moment, she made a vow—to marry a rich, titled husband. She would love him, of course, since he would be clever and handsome as well. Love must be commanded to come or go. Hadn't Johnny Grant turned fondness to disdain? Weren't her feelings for Niall already obscure? In a few days Sorcha would forget Gavin Napier. And somewhere, perhaps just weeks away, Sorcha's true love was waiting.

Chapter 6

FOR THE HOME OF ONE of Scotland's most important noblemen, Doune Castle was impressive only in its forbidding appearance. After two hundred years, it was still unfinished. The bulky towers were ragged; the two wings jutting out above the River Teith appeared stunted. Sorcha found the place a gloomy fortress on a barren hill, with only the arched entrance worthy of an earl.

But the man who dwelled within was far from gloomy or stunted. James Stewart, second Earl of Moray, was a tall, handsome man with dark red hair and a brilliant smile. His wife, Elizabeth, was scarcely older than Sorcha. The Countess of Moray appeared shy, her gentian blue eyes downcast, her soft voice barely audible. She was pretty, Sorcha decided, in a quiet sort of way, with the hint of dimples and perfect small white teeth. Elizabeth Stewart was yet another relative, being the elder daughter of Iain Fraser's late half brother and arch enemy, James, the first Earl of Moray.

"Does that make us half cousins?" Sorcha asked of Rob as they walked along the gallery toward the dining room. The castle, Sorcha had noted with relief, was far more inviting inside than outside, being decorated with bright tapestries and handsome furnishings and plush Persian carpets.

"I suppose," Rob replied. "But then it seems as if half of Scotland is kin to us in some way."

"Just think," Sorcha said, lowering her voice, "Elizabeth of Moray's father tried to kill our own sire! Do you think she knows?"

Rob shook his head. "I hope not. Her father seemed to want to kill a lot of people. It's only fitting that he should have fallen to an assassin's bullet."

"I remember when we heard he'd died. I was but three years old, yet I recall how our Lady Mother gloated for days." Sorcha could still picture Dallas, standing in front of the great fireplace at Gosford's End, calling on God and the Virgin and all the saints to witness how justice had finally been done. Iain Fraser, however, had not joined in his wife's jubilation. Despite all the grief that Moray had brought him, the man was still his brother.

The stark walls of the dining halls were partially hidden by huge vases filled with evergreens and autumn leaves. The chairs were covered in rich crimson damask, a runner of embossed Spanish leather traversed the gleaming oak table, and a silver chandelier shimmered with the light of five hundred candles.

Sorcha was suitably impressed. They were not the only guests at Doune, however. Francis Hepburn Stewart, the wily Earl of Bothwell, was observing the newcomers over his glass of port. His one-time enemy, the doughty Sir William Stewart of Monkton, was also present. William Stewart had lost two fingers in the quarrel between his brother, the Earl of Arran, and the Earl of Mar three years earlier. Both Stewarts, now at peace, sat flanked by two mastiffs in front of the vast stone fireplace.

"Jesu," whispered Sorcha to Rob after the introductions had been made, "I hope we're not kin to all these people. How can we tell?"

"Ask our host. He's a most congenial man." Rob grinned at Sorcha, then shook his head at the drab maroon gown she was wearing. "Didn't our Lady Mother insist you bring along something more ... festive?"

Sorcha grimaced at her brother. "Since when have you taken to caring what I wear? And, yes, Mother packed my saffron dress, but I'm not sure where it is. She said Aunt Tarrill would see that I got a proper wardrobe in Edinburgh." Sorcha tossed the long, loose black hair and glared at the other guests who were lounging about in various states of unregimented camaraderie. "I didn't expect to stay at an earl's home en route to Edinburgh."

In layman's attire, Father Napier was almost as casually dressed as Sorcha. Whiskey cup in hand, he had approached her and Rob to join their conversation. "The Earl of Moray is well known for his congenial hospitality. His wife was raised more rigidly, but tries to adapt to relaxed ways."

"Relaxed?" mused Sorcha, watching the demure Countess of Moray nod diffidently at the Earl of Bothwell. "She seems a timorous creature to me."

"She has a certain sense of dignity," Father Napier noted with approval.

Sorcha's green eyes snapped; she hadn't spoken to Napier since the previous night outside the inn. "Not to mention an earldom stashed in her dowry." Sorcha said bitingly. "Moray had to choose between her and a younger sister, isn't that so?" While Sorcha was confident of her ability to maintain a conversation in the great hall of a nobleman's castle, she was also relieved to be in such a large company. It was best that she and Gavin Napier didn't find themselves alone together for the duration of the journey.

Napier shrugged, one big hand cradling his whiskey cup. "I assume His Lordship was taken by her modesty and grace. But ask him yourself," he went on, gesturing toward their host who was approaching, a warm smile on his handsome face.

"We should have music or tumblers for entertainment," Moray declared, clapping Rob on the shoulder. "I had no notion our humble home would be welcoming so many visitors at once."

"Including turbulent Bothwell, I see." Gavin Napier gestured toward the curly-haired earl, who had captured Elizabeth of Moray's rapt attention. "He, too, is kin to the Frasers."

Moray nodded, his open gaze taking in Sorcha and Rob as well as Gavin Napier. "His father was yet another illegitimate son of King James, his mother, the sister of Queen Mary's third husband. A stormy petrel, but possessed of a certain charm."

Sorcha eyed Bothwell with curiosity. Somehow she'd expected the offspring of jaunty Johnny Stewart and the coltish Jean Hepburn to be an imposing figure. He was redheaded, barely of average height, and with an unimpressive physique. Yet his nervous energy exuded a peculiar magnetism.

"Bothwell and King Jamie have an erratic relationship," Moray remarked lightly. He turned to Sorcha and Rob, his hands spread in an expansive gesture. "So we are all kin to you, yet we've never met 'til now." The clear blue eyes rested a trifle too long on Sorcha. "I regret our acquaintanceship has taken so long."

Sorcha was only vaguely discomfited by Moray's gaze. What disconcerted her more was that for the first time in her life, she wished she were dressed in a more becoming style. Noting Elizabeth of Moray's pale blue brocaded gown, Sorcha suddenly found her outmoded, shabby maroon dress inadequate.

Father Napier filled the unexpected void in the conversation with ease. "The Fraser heirs have spent most of their lives in the Highlands. Visitors to that part of the world are rare, I'm told."

"A pity it is, too," Sorcha put in, trying not to think of feminine finery, "as it's beautiful, untamed country."

Moray's eyes crinkled at the corners. "As are the natives?"

Rob stiffened, prepared for a pert response from his sister. But Sorcha merely laughed. "Oh, aye, My Lord, some of us are downright primitive! Though," she went on in a more wistful tone as Elizabeth of Moray moved toward them with the candlelight giving a silvery sheen to her gown, "we are adaptable to more civilized ways."

Father Napier made a wry face, which only Sorcha saw. Rob opened his mouth to speak, but the words never took life. From the entrance hall, shouts and scuffling could be heard. Moray excused himself abruptly, Elizabeth froze in place, and a hush fell over the guests.

A figure stood in the arched doorway, sword in hand. Sorcha gaped at the man whose tall, athletic body cast a long shadow across the floor from the torches held aloft behind him. He wore chain mail but no helmet. His hair was the color of burnished copper, his face calling to mind a Grecian temple statue. For all the aggression in his stance, there was an elegance that made his sudden appearance as much of a pose as it was a threat.

Yet Sorcha realized that the others were uneasy, even frightened. Elizabeth of Moray had tiptoed to Rob's side, where she chewed on her fingernails. Sir William Stewart's face was contorted, his eyes narrow with menace. Bothwell looked interested, as if weighing sides to assess his own position. Moray stood just a few feet from the interloper, attempting to defuse the situation by his easy manner.

"Patrick! Since when have you had to hack your way into my home? Put down your sword, man, and join us for supper." Moray gestured with an open hand toward the table. "Tell your men to come in. We'll roast more capons."

The other man lowered his sword lightly. "I seek not food, but a villain," he declared, his compelling hazel eyes raking the company. "There," he called out, pointing with his empty hand toward Stewart. "He knows who I seek! Where is your vile brother, the treacherous Earl of Arran?"

Sir William stepped forward with a bristling air of anger. "Where you imprisoned him, at Kinneil!" His voice was gruff. "You weave wicked plots, Patrick, Master of Gray. And all to make yourself the King's favorite in place of my gravely wronged brother!"

Gray brandished his sword. "Liar! Arran escaped from Kinneil while I was in Perthshire. Either he is here—or has fled to King Jamie."

Sir William thrust out his barrel chest. "Paugh, if he were here, he'd face you like a man! I know nothing of this escape, but I thank God for it."

Moray had stepped casually between Stewart and the Master of Gray. "If I were hiding Arran, I wouldn't conceal it, Patrick. On the other hand, I wouldn't allow you to carry him away. Let's end this farce and be at peace before my digestion becomes unruly."

Gray regarded Moray with those hypnotic hazel eyes. "I'm not a man given to violence, yet I know that while Arran is free, my life is in danger. If he's not here, he must be headed for the court. So then shall I be." Gray sheathed his sword, and the perfect features broke into a dazzling smile. "My reputation for manners has been sullied by this untoward incident. I apologize for my boorishness and thank you for your offer to sup. Yet being an untrusting sort, I must ensure my safe withdrawal." He threw Stewart a venomous smile. "I'll take the serving wench here," Gray announced, putting a hand on Sorcha's arm. "She'll be returned after I've reached the King."

Gavin Napier moved forward in two long strides. He and Gray were of a height, but the priest was more solidly built. "She is no serving wench; she's Mistress Fraser of Beauly. Go with your minions; no one will chase after you and your petty plots."

Gray still held Sorcha's arm as his eyes seemed to dissect her. "If this ill-kept chit is Lord Fraser's daughter, I'm the King of France! I don't know you, sir, but if she's your bedmate, you'll have to sleep alone this night."

Moray made as if to speak, but Sorcha saw Gray's men behind him, quietly filing into the dining hall. She had no idea how many retainers Moray housed at Doune Castle, but at least fifty armed Gray followers now flanked the arched entrance.

"I'm not afraid," Sorcha declared. It wasn't precisely true; she had not yet had time for fear to take root. "If we can trust in the Master of Gray's honor, I should soon be back."

Moray appeared uncertain, Rob's face had turned alarmingly pale, and Stewart was clearly dubious. Gavin Napier brought the side of his hand down sharply on Gray's wrist. Elizabeth screamed as Sorcha felt Gray release her arm. Napier's fist struck out at Gray but it never connected. Bothwell leaped forward to slam the butt of his pistol against the priest's head. Napier crashed to the floor.

Gray grabbed Sorcha around the waist, pressing her tightly against him. Bothwell stood with his pistol aimed at the others, while at least a dozen Gray supporters also cocked their weapons. "I've cast my lot with you before, Patrick." The Border earl laughed gratingly. "We'll call on King Jamie together."

Gray's sardonic expression revealed pleasure at the other man's decision. But it was to Moray that the Master spoke. "My Lord, I want no bloodshed! Let us take the wench and depart."

With a sigh of resignation, Moray moved back a few paces. Stewart seethed next to Elizabeth, who was crying softly. Reluctantly, Sorcha allowed herself to be half carried out of the dining hall, through the entrance way, and into the damp October air. The image that lingered was of Rob, bending over the sprawled, inert form of Gavin Napier.

Chapter 7

IT WAS ONLY AFTER THEY had traveled about five miles that Sorcha stopped worrying about Napier and began to consider her own predicament. Riding next to Gray and wrapped in a cloak one of the men had given her, Sorcha tried to recall what she knew about the strange, elegant sixth Baron Gray, a schemer, like Bothwell, given to convoluted, cunning plots to ensure his influence with King James. That, naturally, would put him at odds with Arran, who had been Jamie's closest confidant. But Arran was also a conniver who had managed to acquire his title and properties from a demented Hamilton scion. As far as she could remember, her parents favored neither Gray nor Arran, considering them both self-seeking, ambitious, unprincipled scoundrels. Dallas despised Bothwell and his Douglas wife, who, she insisted, dabbled in black arts.

Yet Moray had welcomed them all. Perhaps Moray's open, gracious nature would have welcomed the devil himself. Sorcha glimpsed Gray's perfect profile and shivered. There *was* something Lucifer-like about him. All she could do was pray that the Master would keep his word and return her unharmed as soon as they reached court.

"Where are we going?" she called to her captor as they galloped along a road lined by short, sturdy, stone fences. Obviously, they knew the route well, for there was no moon to guide them.

It was the first time she had spoken since leaving Doune. Gray didn't hear her, so she spoke again, this time more loudly. "Stirling Castle," he answered, eyeing her with mild interest. "Will you be awed?"

"Doubtless." Sorcha spoke without inflection. Hopefully, someone at court would know her and put an early end to the masquerade. Sorcha was angry with herself; if she had dressed appropriately, she might still be at Doune, basking in Moray's charm and feasting on roast capon. And Gavin Napier wouldn't have fallen victim to Bothwell's vicious blow. Glancing up ahead at the Border earl's narrow back, she marveled at his wiry strength and loathed his wicked meddling.

Her thoughts were interrupted by Gray's smooth, yet incisive voice. "You handle your horse well. Were you brought up in the stables?"

Sorcha kept her eyes on what she could see of the road. A mental picture of Niall flashed through her mind. "Aye, much of the time. I helped the grooms." There was no point in arguing, at least not while riding swiftly through the night to meet the King of Scotland. Sorcha had seen her royal cousin, Jamie, just once, at Holyrood, when he was no more than ten years old. A sniveling, gawky lad, she recalled, who looked more like a pot-boy than a monarch. He was only a year or two older than Sorcha, but had been King since babyhood, when his mother was forced to abdicate. Until recently, he had been the pawn of various mentors and opposing factions, relying almost completely on whoever was his current favorite. Sorcha wondered if the Master of Gray was determined to perpetuate that arrangement.

"Have you been at Doune long?" For all that Gray regarded her as a servant, his tone was cordial. Perhaps, when he wasn't wreaking havoc, his manners were as elegant as his appearance.

"About three hours," Sorcha replied with a touch of asperity. "I came with the others from the Highlands."

"Ah, I should have guessed from your voice." Gray slowed his horse to a canter and the others followed suit. Sorcha scanned the horizon, barely able to make out a jutting hill on which a huge building seemed to be perched like an eagle ready for flight. Gray noted the direction of her gaze. "Stirling."

Sorcha had passed it on at least one previous journey south, but always in the daylight. "Is the King in residence there now?"

"He is," remarked Bothwell, who had drawn up beside them, "if that villain Arran hasn't kidnapped him."

The possibility wasn't an idle thought. Jamie had been abducted at least once before. Indeed, Sorcha knew there was some connection between that incident and the enmity between Gray and Arran. But the complexities of Scottish politics being what they were, she wasn't quite certain who stood in opposition to whom, let alone why. Growing up at such a distance from court, it seemed to Sorcha that her countrymen played at politics as other men might play at games. They needed no great principles or moral causes to provide a confrontation; they seemed to quarrel, intrigue, and even murder for the sheer excitement.

Under the protection of the cliff on which the castle rested, a small village lay in darkness, save for a handful of rushlights burning behind cottage windows. The men's voices hushed as the horses slowed to a trot. The Master guided his mount in front of the others, beginning the climb up the Carse of Stirling to the castle entrance. Sorcha glanced down, somewhat unsettled by the long, sheer face of the basalt rock that rose like a truncated mountain above the town.

Moments later, they were halted by the guards. Sorcha wondered if Gray would resort to arms as he had done at Doune. But after only a minute's discussion, the guards stepped aside to let the Master and his men pass. As they dismounted, Sorcha turned to Gray. "May I ride back now?"

Gray, absorbed with whatever plan he was concocting, didn't answer directly. When he finally looked at Sorcha, he seemed momentarily puzzled. "What? Oh, aye. Nay," he contradicted himself, "you might get lost, and I can't spare men to accompany you. Wait until morning. I'd not have it said I didn't keep my word where a lass was concerned."

Sorcha's eyes snapped in annoyance. From what she'd heard, the Master of Gray wasn't one to worry about keeping his word. Perhaps the Earl of Moray evoked honor even from rogues. "What am I to do, then? Sleep under the King's bed?"

Bothwell had sidled up next to her. "You may sleep in mine," he said, his wily gaze resting on her bosom.

Sorcha emitted a snort and refused to look at him. But now that Sorcha had served her purpose, Gray had no further interest in her, nor in Bothwell's lewd suggestion. "Go to the kitchens. They'll see to you."

Not having yet had supper, Gray's idea suited Sorcha just fine. Relieved that her brief captivity was over, she simply walked away, wondering where the kitchens were located. Behind her, she could hear Gray giving orders to his men. It occurred to Sorcha that it might be amusing to watch the confrontation with the King, particularly if Arran had indeed sought royal protection. But her stomach was growling, and she had no real desire to become involved in politics, even on the periphery.

Stirling Castle was large, however, and while Sorcha had passed at least four guards and two servants, she hadn't troubled to ask for directions. Now, close to a quarter of an hour had gone by and she was growing ravenous. At last she caught up with a lad of short stature and a stealthy if shambling step. If he were up to no good, Sorcha reasoned, he'd only be too glad to send her along to the kitchens to be rid of her.

The lad jumped when she called to him and turned around, his homely face wearing a suspicious look. His clothes were well cut, but he seemed faintly imbecilic, with his gaping mouth and wary eyes. As Sorcha drew closer, she noted a spark of keen intelligence that surprised her.

"I've just arrived," she began, hoping to sound amiable. "Where are the kitchens?"

The lad blinked. "Kitchens? Why do you seek the kitchens?"

Sorcha wondered if she'd been mistaken about the intelligent spark. "I'm hungry. I'm afraid I was kidnapped before supper." Annoyed, she hoped her unconventional approach would swiftly elicit the information she wanted.

"Do you jest?" He spat as he spoke, and the eyes, which were very deep set, glowered at Sorcha.

"I do not. I seldom jest about being kidnapped. Or being famished. If you'd prefer bringing me food, I'll rest content. But one way or the other, I must eat."

"Who kidnapped you? Was it the Master of Gray?" The lad's face leaned closer. He had big hands and feet for his size, Sorcha noted, and one foot turned outward.

"Jesu, yes, yes, it was. News races swiftly at Stirling, I see. I wish victuals did the same."

"Who are you? Why were you kidnapped by Gray?"

Sorcha felt like boxing the impertinent lad's ears. "If you'd like to hear the tale, bribe me. Like a Gaberlunzie man. If you feed them, they'll tell you a story. So will I. Please." Sorcha sounded desperate.

"Mistress, do you know who I am?" The lad drew himself up to his full height, which wasn't much greater than Sorcha's.

A dim recollection of a homely, furtive boy at Holy rood stirred Sorcha's memory. "Oh, sweet Jesu!" she gasped, at least remembering to bob a curtsy as her stomach growled like an active volcano. "Your Grace?"

King James of Scotland looked severe, his face taking on the wizened appearance of a waspish old man. "That is correct. I, mistress, am your sovereign lord."

Sorcha clapped her cheeks with the palms of her hands. "And I, sir, am an idiot. Why, may I ask, are you skulking about your castle? Oh, by the saints, I'm not supposed to put such questions to you. Forgive me!"

Jamie's features softened. "They're all looking for me. Gray. Arran. Hamilton. Bothwell. No doubt half the nobles of Scotland are rambling about Stirling like cats searching for a mouse. I'm tired of people telling me what to do. I'm nineteen years old, with a God-given right to rule. I wish they'd all go away and leave me alone."

"If you'd had two parents instead of a councilful, maybe it wouldn't be so bothersome." Sorcha bit her tongue, chiding herself for her complete lack of courtly manners. But Jamie seemed unperturbed by her words. Indeed, he was nodding.

"They forget I'm grown up. I should have a wife, not a teacher." Jamie struck a fist into his palm. "Someone small and blond, with dimples and blue eyes." He cast a sidelong, diffident glance at Sorcha. She noticed that he seemed to spit a great deal when he spoke. "Would she have to be a Swede?"

"No, not necessarily. We could discuss it … over a bit of food, perhaps?"

"Oh! I forgot, you're starving. I must remember, I'm to watch over my subjects with more concern." Jamie warily looked around the empty hallway. "I know, we'll find Simeon. He's my manservant. He'll bring us something to eat, and we can talk, and perhaps I can figure out what to do with odious Arran and worrisome Gray."

"How very clever of Your Grace," Sorcha murmured, bobbing another curtsy, just in case it was expected. "Have you any rare beef with hot juices?"

Jamie was leading the way toward a winding staircase. "Alas, no. We seem inundated with mutton lately. I must issue a command to the cooks. I'm not fond of mutton, are you?"

Sorcha shook her head. "Not terribly. But I'd eat an old saddle about now."

The King giggled, a high, giddy sound that made Sorcha jump. She steadied herself against the stone wall as Jamie pushed open a door. It led into a small chamber where a young man with very fair hair reposed on a bed reading a book. He looked up and smiled when he saw the King, but suddenly stared when Sorcha entered.

"I found a hungry lassie wandering about the castle," said Jamie, going to the small fireplace to warm his hands. "She's starving to death. Could you bring her something? I'll have wine, of course, Simeon."

Simeon put down his book, first carefully marking the page where he'd left off. He bowed courteously to Jamie, nodded at Sorcha, and left through the room's other door, but not before the King called out to him: "If anyone asks, don't tell them where I am."

Jamie sighed when the door closed, then sat down on a battered sea chest that stood at the front of the bed. The room apparently belonged to Simeon; Sorcha assumed the King's own chambers were close by.

"Do sit," Jamie said rather vaguely, gesturing to the only chair in the room. Sorcha lowered herself onto the leather-covered seat and felt the legs creak beneath her. Now that they were alone, the King seemed at a loss for words. Strangely, Sorcha did, too, though she reminded herself that Jamie was, after all, a young man. If she didn't know how to converse with a king, she'd proceed on the assumption that he couldn't be so different from other lads of his age.

"Do you hunt here?" she asked, resting her chin on one hand.

"Not as much as at Falkland." He looked ill at ease and seemed even smaller than when he was standing up. "Who are you?"

Sorcha couldn't help but smile. "I'm Sorcha Fraser, daughter to Lord Iain Fraser of Beauly. We're kin, Your Grace, in some tenuous manner."

Jamie turned thoughtful. "Fraser. *That* Fraser. Another of my grandfather's bastards. I can't always keep them straight. Your sire didn't approve of my mother marrying Bothwell, did he?" Sorcha knew that Jamie had been carefully schooled not to approve of the Queen's hasty, ill-fated marriage, either. "Nay, the union cost her my father's allegiance, I'm afraid." Sorcha did not remind Jamie that her father had also disapproved of Mary Stuart's marriage to Lord Damley, the King's own sire. "It may be impertinent to mention it, sir, but the Master of Gray doesn't know who I am. Or, at least, doesn't believe it."

"Oh." The King frowned, his lower lip sticking out. Absently, he wiped at the saliva on his chin. "You said he kidnapped you. Why, if he didn't know who you were?"

"As a hostage, to keep anyone at Doune from following him. Arran's brother was there. And Bothwell, who rode with us." Sorcha turned to the door as Simeon entered, bearing a tray with covered dishes, two goblets, and a bottle of red wine. She all but fell upon the boiled mutton until she realized she should probably wait for the King's permission to begin eating. Jamie, however, was telling Simeon to retire. When the servant had left again, the King crossed his spindly legs and gave no indication that he was concerned with etiquette.

"Arran has been good to me, in his way," he mused, staring into the fire, which burned fitfully. "Yet the people hate him. The Master of Gray is cunning, but beautiful. Don't you think so?" His wistful gaze fixed on Sorcha.

"Mmmmm." Sorcha hurriedly swallowed a mouthful of mutton and carrots. "Impressive, to be sure. Though I would have preferred meeting him under other circumstances."

Jamie nodded, then once more turned diffident. "And me, Mistress Fraser? Would you have known who I was if you'd seen me sitting on my throne surrounded by fawning courtiers?"

Sorcha smiled at the irony. "Well, certainly. I hardly expected to find my sovereign lord prowling about the hallways. But then, the Master mistook me for a stable wench. It seems to be a day of mistaken identity."

The King brightened. "How true! We have more than our lineage in common, mistress." The smile he gave Sorcha was quite winning. "I don't talk much to lassies; it's not permitted. What do you like to hear?"

Sorcha paused between bites of potato. "I'm not typical, perhaps, Your Grace. Most lassies want to be told how bonnie they are and how sweetly they speak and that they move like a flower swaying in the breeze. I prefer to speak of other things. For example, I'm told you're very learned …."

Putting one hand to his narrow chest, Jamie did his best to puff himself up. "I have had a superb education, that's true. My elders often forget how shrewd and clever I truly am. I can," he added slyly, "sometimes be as devious as the next one."

"I suppose you've had to be," Sorcha conceded. Strange, she thought, until now, her image of Jamie had been almost totally unpleasant. Yet he was a rather appealing, if pitiful, laddie, with his exaggerated sense of grandeur and his naive frankness. Sorcha liked him and knew instinctively that the feeling was mutual. Inspiration struck between mouthfuls of mutton.

"Sir!" she exclaimed, one hand held out as if in supplication. "Would you know of any eligible young noblemen who'd wed with a Highland Fraser?"

Jamie's small eyes grew quite wide. "You?" He licked the moisture from his lips. "Oh—well—there's usually some distant Stewart kin seeking a bride." A sudden glint of suspicion flickered across his homely face. "Do you think you need a husband after being abducted by the Master?"

Sorcha flushed. "Nay, Your Grace! It's merely that I'm of an age to wed, which is part of the reason I am going to Edinburgh. And," she went on, after taking a deep breath, "I've been jilted by Johnny Grant."

"Grant." Jamie spoke the name without much interest. "His appearance doesn't move me." The King dismissed Johnny Grant with a wave of his hand. "Surely there is someone more suitable." He gave Sorcha a superior, yet conspiratorial wink. "We shall mull the matter over in our leisure," Jamie declared with a majestic intonation.

"Excellent," murmured Sorcha, hoping she sounded sincere, but wondering precisely how much real power Jamie had in such affairs. She was about to give further voice to her gratitude when the door burst open; Sorcha spilled gravy on her bodice and swore aloud. Jamie swiveled in his place, then leapt to his feet. Simeon all but fell into the room, followed by a dozen other men, including the Master of Gray, who dropped on his knees before the King.

"Your Grace," he exclaimed, his head thrown back, the firelight catching the copper glints in his hair, "am I to be slandered by the Earl of Arran after my selfless attempt to preserve his life? He is guilty of ingratitude as well as treason!" Another man, shorter and more squarely built than Gray, but seemingly possessed of equal audacity, also came forward to fall before King Jamie. "When did I ever do anything except to serve Your Grace? I desire no great rewards, though I've assuredly not earned the calumny spread by my enemies." Sorcha, discreetly trying to wash down her supper with a swig of wine, decided that the second man must be the Earl of Arran. His assertion of not wanting any reward struck her as strange, since he'd already wrested his title from another noble who still lived; though a Stewart, Arran had been made head of the House of Hamilton.

Jamie, appearing so young and insignificant beside the other two men, gazed fretfully at them both. "Your incessant quarrels distress us," he declared with more force than Sorcha had expected. "If you would truly please me, pray desist."

Arran all but growled his response: "I've tried to make peace with this two-faced scoundrel, but each time, he betrays me. My life is in danger as long as the Master of Gray lives!"

The Master got to his feet. For the first time, he saw Sorcha, sitting behind Simeon, a tray in her lap, a wine goblet in her hand. "By Christ's beard, what have we here, a serving wench dining with a king?"

To Jamie's credit, he never flinched. "Mistress Fraser is my guest. And my cousin. I find it soothing to have at least one relative to whom I can speak without fearing the consequences."

Gray threw Sorcha a furious look, but quickly composed his features. She had a fierce desire to stick her tongue out at him but controlled herself. Once this unpleasant scene was over, she would somehow have to express her gratitude properly to King Jamie.

Arran had also stood up. "My Lord," he intoned, ignoring Sorcha altogether, "I can no longer tolerate the presence of this man in Scotland." He gestured harshly at Gray but kept his eyes on the King. "He has deceived every man and woman he has ever dealt with, including the wife he abandoned. The Master has conspired against your mother, against Elizabeth of England, against the Protestants and then the Catholics. If he betrays me today, will he do less with you tomorrow?"

Sorcha didn't hear the King's reply. Sir William Stewart and at least six other men hurtled into the room, filling it with hailing bodies. Gray went down under the assault, but Bothwell was in the doorway shouting, "No more! The banished lords have returned!"

The room froze in a bizarre tableau. Gray lay under Stewart and two henchmen. Arran loomed over them, his hand on his dirk. The King had a finger pressed alongside his nose, as if contemplating a move in a chess game. The others remained in varied states of animation, apparently depending upon whose badge they wore.

Arran broke the spell with a snap of his blunt fingers. "Christ Almighty, we are done for!" With a heavy sigh, he bowed to King Jamie. "I ask your leave to retire."

Stewart and the others stood up, while Gray stretched his long legs and gazed up at Arran with malicious satisfaction. Jamie waved a hand at the room in general. "You may all go. Swiftly, I command you."

They obeyed, Gray and his men departing through the door to the winding staircase, Arran and his followers leaving from the other exit. Simeon trooped after them, though he gestured to the King to indicate he'd remain outside.

"Jesu," gasped Sorcha, setting down the tray and brushing crumbs from her skirt, "were they going to murder Gray?"

Jamie flopped onto the bed. "It would seem so, just as my mother's secretary, Rizzio, was done to death before her very eyes." He put a hand over his forehead. "I was in her womb then, you know."

Sorcha nodded vigorously. "My own mother was there, too. My brother Rob was born that night at Holyrood."

"Oh?" Jamie peered at Sorcha with renewed interest. "We do have much in common, Coz. Do you think I ought to ran away from here?"

Sorcha wrinkled her brow. "Isn't it more likely they'd run away first?"

"Arran will. The lords who have returned are his enemies. But I'm not so certain I want to see them, either. They're yet another passel of nobles who think me too young to rule." Jamie sat up straight, considering his plan. "Yes, I'll go to Edinburgh. Will you come with me?" There was an oddly plaintive note in his voice.

Getting to her feet, Sorcha paced the room. The past few hours had been the most disconcerting of her entire life. First, she'd been kidnapped, then she'd ridden some ten miles to Stirling Castle at breakneck speed, she'd mistaken the King of Scotland for a page, and witnessed a near murder. The idea of tearing off again into the night struck her as impossible.

"It must be well on to midnight," she began, wondering how to phrase her lack of enthusiasm for taking part in Jamie's escape plans. "Perhaps you ought to sleep on your idea."

But the King shook his head vehemently. "Nay, I go now or not at all." Hesitantly, he put a large, clumsy hand on Sorcha's arm. "Come. We'll take Simeon with us."

It was, after all, a royal command. Sorcha forced a smile and agreed. Ten minutes later, the three of them were walking with careful tread down a flight of stairs that led to the postern gate. Enveloped in the cloak she'd borrowed from one of Gray's men, Sorcha hugged it closely around her as they stepped outside. There, high on the hill at the castle's edge, the wind shrilled through the battlements, making Sorcha's teeth chatter. Simeon went to the postern gate, testing the latch.

"My Lord," he whispered in alarm, "it's been locked!"

"It's never locked," Jamie retorted sharply. "It must be stuck."

Simeon's head wagged in denial. "It's locked. Your Grace, I swear it."

Helplessly, the King looked in every direction. "The water gate, then," he said at last, but a voice from behind him cut against the wind.

"The water gate is also locked," said the Master of Gray. "Though it was not a few minutes earlier when ruthless Arran scurried through it."

Jamie whirled on Gray, his cape flapping like the tail feathers of an angry rooster. "How dare you! Arran escapes, but you prevent your King from doing the same! I shall have you both proclaimed traitors!"

Gray smiled down on his king. "Nay, My Lord, I only sealed off the castle to protect you. The banished lords are but a mile away. You could easily fall into their hands. We must discuss what course of action to take with them. If I may humbly suggest it, let us all go to our beds and rise early to chart our course."

Jamie seemed to wither under Gray's persuasion. "Very well." He motioned to Simeon and Sorcha. "I'm tired, in any event." He uttered a small, strangled laugh. "I loved Arran once. Why couldn't he have been more kind?"

Gray put a proprietary hand on the King's shoulder. "He doesn't know kindness. He never understood you. He always put his own interests first." The Master turned to Simeon. "Take gentle good care of our sovereign lord. I'll see to Mistress Fraser."

The King made as if to protest, but thought better of it. Docilely, he let Simeon lead him away without another word. Sorcha, still holding her cloak fast around her body, looked directly at the Master but winced slightly at the compelling hazel eyes. "If you think I intend to sleep with the horses, you're sadly mistaken, My Lord," she announced boldly.

"I had no such thought." He didn't bother to offer his arm but strode to the castle door and pushed it open. Sorcha dutifully preceded him up the staircase. "This way," said Gray, nudging her arm. "What did you talk about with His Grace?" The voice was smooth, almost unctuous.

"Mutton." Sorcha clamped her teeth together.

Gray emitted an exaggerated sigh. "I can't trust you. You spend an hour or more with the King, then try to help him escape during a most delicate political crisis, and insist you only talked of mutton."

"We began with beef," Sorcha said with impatience. "I want to leave this place."

"I told you we cannot." Gray sounded as if he were talking to a recalcitrant child. "You may leave tomorrow, after the King and I decide how to deal with the banished lords."

Sorcha swooped around, hair and cloak flying behind her. "You! Why should it be you any more than Arran or whoever else wants to control that poor laddie? He's the King; leave him be!"

"Christ's Beard," Gray exclaimed in mock wonder, pausing by a torch which still flickered fitfully. "The urchin wants to tell the Master of Gray how to conduct himself! Do they not teach you manners in the Highlands! They surely don't teach you grooming."

"You, sir, may put your manners up your arse," Sorcha raged, fists on hips. "If my father were here, he'd skewer you for speaking so to me!"

Gray leisurely moved to within a half foot of Sorcha. Deliberately, he reached out to pull the cloak from her shoulders. "Your dress is not only hideous, it's dirty." He put a finger on the gravy stain that rested against the cleft of her bosom. Sorcha pulled back, infuriated by his audacity.

"Don't touch me!" Sorcha's eyes darted from one end of the hall to the other. She lunged for the torch but Gray's long arm snatched at her wrist.

"Stay, urchin. I'm not going to deflower you, merely detain you." He gave her arm a little jerk, and Sorcha swore under her breath. Resignedly, she let him lead her past a pair of narrow windows where the wind blew through the cracks in the embrasures. They rounded a corner, all but crashing into Gavin Napier.

Napier's hand went to his dirk. Momentarily taken aback, Gray recovered his aplomb at once. He struck an indolent pose, half leaning against the wall, regarding Napier and Sorcha with an insolent smile. "Don't be a fool, man. If you kill me within these walls, you'll be just as dead within the hour."

Napier's shoulders relaxed slightly, but his fingers were still wrapped around the dirk's hilt. "Here or elsewhere, it matters not to me." His other hand lashed out, catching Gray sharply just below the left ear. The Master reeled and slumped against the wall but saved himself from falling to the floor.

"Whoreson!" breathed Gray, venomous eyes not quite in focus.

Napier grabbed Sorcha by the wrist. "Come, before I decide to kill this whelp of hell after all."

Sorcha shuddered and instinctively moved closer to the priest. Gray was pulling himself to his feet as Sorcha and Napier hurried down the corridor. "He's evil," she whispered, picking up her skirts in order to keep apace with Napier's long stride. "Bothwell, too. Poor Jamie!"

Napier's grip on her wrist grew tighter. "Did he harm you?"

"Oh, no—he was pleasant enough. For a villain." She craned her neck to look up at Napier. "But you—he won't forget, priest or not."

They had reached the east side of the castle, by the entrance to the great Parliament Hall. "Rob's outside," said Napier, ignoring her words. "He bribed the guards."

Anxiously, Sorcha peered back down the dimly lighted corridor. Despite all the tumult of the past hour or more, the castle was deceptively quiet. Sorcha saw no one. Not even the Master.

Napier had released her wrist, but Sorcha made no move toward the stout oak door. "I said you are in danger. I'd wager Gray is a vengeful sort."

"He doesn't know who I am." Napier tested the iron bolt; it slid back easily. "Quickly, before Rob grows apprehensive."

Sorcha still didn't move. She wanted to thank Gavin Napier for rescuing her, yet she was afraid to encourage any familiarity. With another man, she'd offer a kiss on the cheek, a hug, at least her hand. But she dared not touch this volatile priest for fear of leading him—and herself—into temptation. Abruptly, Sorcha turned away. "I'm grateful to you, Father. You were brave to come here." To her surprise, the words were a mumble.

Napier, however, acknowledged her appreciation with a shrug as he shoved the heavy door open. "Your care was entrusted to me by your parents. I'd have been derelict in my duty if I'd acted otherwise."

He spoke offhandedly, but as Sorcha passed over the threshold into the brisk night air, she felt Napier's hand press against her back as if to provide direction. Yet even as she saw Rob's form outlined against the castle battlements, Sorcha's flesh tingled from Napier's touch, and she cursed herself for nurturing what seemed to be a shameless, impossible desire.

Chapter 8

"**H**OW FORTUNATE!" CRIED AUNT TARRILL, leading Sorcha and Rob into the McVurrich parlor. "It's Donald's birthday! We're having a party!"

Sorcha and Rob exchanged bemused glances. The idea of dour Uncle Donald enjoying a celebration, even in his honor, seemed incongruous. However, the five McVurrich children, Aunt Glennie, and an elderly couple were indeed gathered around the fire, eating saffron cakes and drinking brandy wine.

"You must change," Aunt Tarrill said after the introductions had been made to the old people, who were Donald's parents from Dunbar. Tarrill inclined her head, looking thoughtful. She was a tall, statuesque woman, her dark hair streaked with gray, her aquiline profile softened by time. "You'll take the room over the Canongate, Rob. And, you, Sorcha, the one above the garden." She stopped speaking as Aunt Glennie sidled up to her niece and nephew, blue eyes bright, faded blond curls bobbing. "Well, Glennie," said Tarrill, "what do you think of Dallas's bairns?"

"A handsome pair, I must confess." Glennie smiled, blinking rapidly as she always did when agitated or excited. "Yet very different, with Rob's red-gold hair and Sorcha's dark locks. But then, the three of us were unalike. In many ways," she added wistfully.

Within minutes, Sorcha was upstairs with Ailis, sorting through their luggage. Having noted that the household was in mourning, no doubt for Glennie's late husband, Sorcha hoped she would not have to purchase an entire wardrobe of black. Such somber garb could hamper attracting rich, handsome suitors. For now, a crimson gown made over from one of her mother's dresses would have to do. Sorcha had been disinterested during the fitting sessions at

Gosford's End, but now she appraised herself critically in the bedroom's three-quarter mirror. The color suited her, but the dated style did little to set off her figure, except for the bodice, which revealed the curve of her bosom and just a hint of the cleft between her breasts. Another gown in the same shade, with the new V-neckline and a wide ruff fanning out behind the head would be more fetching. A narrow-waisted dress with a small farthingale would add height, too. As for her hair, she supposed she'd have to buy some caps, or at least veils and nets to keep it in place. It was hopeless to attempt taming the long, unruly strands at the moment. Sorcha stepped into the only new item she'd brought, a pair of black calfskin shoes with dainty heels.

Rob had already changed and joined the others by the time Sorcha returned downstairs. Henry, the eldest of the McVurrich offspring, was playing the pipes while the others sang a hymn. Sorcha slipped quietly into the group, between the youngest boy, Thomas, and Aunt Glennie. The hymn seemed to last a very long time. Sorcha noted that Glennie didn't join in, though Tarrill did. Rob, of course, was silent but wore a pleasant smile, as if to prove that he was enjoying the music.

The last notes died away in a minor key. Donald McVurrich rose from his place next to the hearth, a psalter in his hand. He was a tall, rawboned man in his forties; his blond hair had darkened over the years, and his beard reached his breastbone. Though he opened the book of psalms and gazed down at the page, the words he spoke were his own. "Sorcha Fraser, this is a godly house. Gentlewomen do not expose their bosoms, nor do they wear brazen colors. Particularly while mourning a loved one." Only upon conclusion of his reprimand, did Donald look directly at Sorcha. The eyes held no warmth, and Sorcha felt herself blushing.

"I'm sure she hasn't had time to go through her wardrobe, good husband," said Aunt Tarrill mildly. "Indeed," she went on, turning to Sorcha with a fond smile, "I remember your mother wearing that dress when she was in Edinburgh the last time. Or at least one very like it."

"I should expect Dallas would," Donald commented dryly. He ignored his wife's vexed look. "Let us recite the psalms." It seemed to Sorcha that Uncle Donald intended to recite all of them. An hour later, he was still droning on, though by then, the rest of the family responded only fitfully. Sorcha and Rob exchanged impatient glances. They were both hungry, not having eaten since breakfast in Dunfermline. To Sorcha, it seemed like much longer, though she had been relieved when Gavin Napier and the others had parted from them near the Netherbow Port, where Edinburgh's High Street met the Canongate. Both Sorcha and Rob remembered how to reach the McVurrich house in Panmure Close. Father Napier had left Rob with assurances that in a few days' time they would meet to discuss their plans. Sorcha considered it might be best if she didn't see the priest again.

At last, Uncle Donald closed the psalter. Yet another hymn followed, before the family relaxed, pressing Rob and Sorcha with questions about their journey. As if by some secret, mutual pact, neither Fraser related the incident with the Master of Gray or Sorcha's adventures at Stirling Castle. Nor were they specific about why Rob had come to Edinburgh. Candor would invite criticism—or worse—from Uncle Donald.

After a fine supper of salmon baked in a flaky crust and pheasant served with a thick, rich gravy, Sorcha felt very sleepy. When Uncle Donald began to read from the Old Testament, she had to struggle to stay awake. Sorcha had not heard so much of the Holy Bible in a year at Gosford's End as she had in the four hours since arriving at the McVurrich house.

"I'll perish," she moaned to Rob when they finally were permitted to escape upstairs. "You'll be able to leave ere long, but I must stay! How will I bear this stultifying Presbyterian gloom?"

Rob was looking out Sorcha's window into the darkened garden below. "I suspect it's because this is Uncle Donald's birthday. Apparently he celebrates with prayer and hymns."

Sorcha hurled herself onto the bed, kicking off the new shoes, which pinched most painfully. "If you go off to become a priest, I'll take the veil! Then Uncle Donald will be forced to throw me out of the house, and I'll be saved from dying of boredom!"

Rob chuckled as he turned away from the window, while Ailis moved discreetly about the room, putting the last of their belongings away. "In truth, Sorcha, when I'm a priest, I'll spend many hours each day in prayer."

"That's different—you'll be a priest, not a banker." Sorcha fixed Rob with obstinate green eyes. "I still hope you're wrong about having a vocation."

Rob inclined his head. "I may be. Time will tell."

Sorcha didn't answer. Time would tell a lot of things, she reminded herself, wondering how long it would be until she would meet acceptable suitors. It had already occurred to her that Uncle Donald would not allow Catholic gentlemen to call on her and that perhaps even lively Protestants would be discouraged. Sorcha's vaunted hopes for a fine marriage seemed remote.

SORCHA FELT AS IF SHE were some sort of prey, being stalked by the most dogged of hunters. The argument with Gavin Napier had raged for ten minutes. Napier was relentless, repeating his request to Sorcha over and over. She, however, had countered with at least a dozen good reasons why she should not approach the King to seek permission for Rob and Napier to attend Mary Stuart. But Napier had the perfect opportunity for Rob. Queen

Mary's strict new Puritan gaoler, Sir Amyas Paulet, had dismissed the Queen's chaplains and was threatening further reduction of her suite. However, Napier learned that she retained a man to read with her in French. Some thought he was actually a priest. Whatever his true calling, the household's move to dank Tutbury had eroded the man's health. With so many years in France, Napier could easily fill the position. As for Rob, he would go to England in the guise of Napier's manservant.

Outside the paneled library, sleet dashed against the two tall, narrow leaded glass windows that flanked the fireplace. Sorcha stood next to a bookcase, hands on her hips. "For the last time, I cannot! I keep telling you, we talked for a while, that was all. His Grace may have forgotten who I am."

Napier leaned against the solid dark wood of Donald McVurrich's desk. At least Uncle Donald was out of the house; with any luck he'd never hear of Father Napier's visit. "The King is unaccustomed to lassies, but I doubt he'd let you slip from his mind." If the words were meant as a compliment, Sorcha was determined not to notice.

She shook her head vehemently, the black hair sailing around her shoulders. "No, no! You must know someone at court with genuine influence."

The brown eyes continued to stalk her as she moved restlessly around the room. "I've been gone almost fifteen years. My family never spent much time at court. You must approach the King."

Sorcha let her hands fall limply to her sides. She stood quite still, giving Napier a little shake of her head. "Please. You persist, yet I cannot acquiesce. Please stop. It's pointless."

Napier brushed his beard with one long forefinger. "Your gentle brother's life may depend on it," he remarked without inflection.

"God's teeth!" exploded Sorcha. "And the future of Scotland as well, I suppose!"

He nodded, the wolfish face solemn. "Oh, aye, that, too. Through at least four generations."

Sorcha rubbed her left eye fiercely and blinked. "You play by no rules," she accused him. "You don't behave like a priest. I don't understand you; I don't know how to deal with you. Father, and that's the truth." Sorcha sighed loudly and rubbed her other eye.

Moving with his usual purposeful step, Napier crossed the room to put a hand on Sorcha's arm. "There is truth to what I say about your brother. I didn't intend to alarm you, but if it's the only way to make you see reason, then I'll be blunt. Without the King's permission, Rob could be arrested and executed as a Papist spy, either at the command of Queen Elizabeth or Jamie himself."

Sorcha felt the weight of his hand on her arm and wanted to shake free. But more than that, she wanted to prove to Gavin Napier that his touch didn't tempt her. "It just seems unlikely that His Grace would see me."

Sorcha felt Napier's hand tighten on her arm. She stiffened but refused to flinch. "This is Rob's future." Napier was very somber, his wolfish face looking down at Sorcha. "Would you ruin his hopes?"

"Oh …." Sorcha thrust out her chin at Father Napier. "I'll think on it, at least." It galled her to capitulate.

The sleet rattled the windowpanes and splattered onto the empty grate. Slowly, Napier let go of Sorcha's arm and stepped back a pace. "Thank you." The words were low and deep.

The awkward silence that followed seemed to bring the storm inside the paneled library walls. Sorcha felt the thrumming of the rain echo in her ears as she locked gazes with Gavin Napier. At last, he spoke again. "Do you hate me for what happened by Loch Tay?"

Sorcha blinked, then passed a hand over her mouth, as if she could still feel Napier's kisses. "Hate?" The word sounded thin, reedlike. She gave a little shake of her head. "Nay. I—well, it's occurred to me that …." She bogged down, unable to say aloud that the fault was hers as well, for goading him. Most of all, she couldn't possibly admit that she had savored those kisses, forbidden or not. She saw Napier watching her intently, the hunter's gaze probing, yet touched with sadness. Sorcha winced inwardly and considered her next words with care. "It's human to do foolish things. Don't fash yourself over it." She lifted her shoulders, signaling indifference.

Napier's brow furrowed. "You consider the episode trivial?"

To her horror, Sorcha felt tears well up in her eyes. She opened her mouth, then closed it again, and turned away. "Don't," she whispered shakily. "Please—speak of other things."

Napier took a single step toward her, but halted, a tall, rigid figure staring beyond Sorcha with unseeing eyes. "Damn," Napier breathed, and slammed a fist into his open palm. He turned sharply on his heel and strode out of the library.

For a full five minutes, Sorcha remained where she was, the tears unshed, but cursing herself over and over for being weak, for lacking pride, and, for once in her life, being utterly incapable of speaking with candor.

A week passed, and the King did not return to Edinburgh. Rob was the only person in whom Sorcha could confide, but he had no advice. "I hear the court will move to Linlithgow at the end of November," he told his sister, trying to be helpful.

"God's teeth, Rob," exclaimed Sorcha, "does Father Napier expect me to go there?"

Rob looked up from the fishing rod he'd been repairing. Along with three of his male cousins, he'd just returned from the Nor' Loch at the edge of the city. Their expedition had been cut short when a heavy, wet snowfall blew in from over the Firth of Forth. As Rob started to reply, Doles, the only McVurrich daughter, slipped into the parlor. Her hair was as dark as Sorcha's, but pulled straight back and kept tidily in place with a wide bandeau. She had recently turned ten years old, but was tall for her age, having inherited both her parents' height. She was not a pretty child, with her long face and straight nose, but the regularity of her features indicated she might someday become a striking woman. Doles folded her hands and fixed her somber gaze on Sorcha.

"Are you going away, Cousin? I shall miss you."

Sorcha smiled blandly, and Rob sucked in his breath. "I may visit the court, yes." She glanced at Rob. "My brother wishes to travel, to broaden his education."

"Ah." Doles's eyes sparked with comprehension. "My father isn't much for traveling, though I think my mother might enjoy it. Where would you go, Cousin?" She gazed with interest at Rob.

"Oh," Rob replied, lowering his voice confidentially. "Any number of places. The Indies, perhaps, or Araby. Where would you like to go, sweet Coz?"

Doles was thoughtful, the smooth brow puckering. "Mull. I should like to go to the Hebrides and see Mull."

"What an excellent idea!" exclaimed Sorcha, trying to remember precisely where the isles lay off the Scottish coast. Her father had sailed there often, but for Sorcha, their location remained somewhat vague.

"There are fascinating rock formations there, I'm told," Doles went on, her dark eyes sparkling. "They have wild goats and sea otters and red deer and buzzards and peregrine and … oh, so many wondrous creatures! Do you know," she said, dropping her voice and looking over her shoulder to make sure they could not be overheard, "I've never been to Glasgow?"

"Neither have we," Sorcha admitted, though it hardly seemed like a deprivation. "When I return to the Highlands, you must visit. We have some fine beasts and birds there, too." Sorcha smiled wide, though she felt a pang; now that the snows had started, it would be several months before she could contemplate going home.

"There are waterfalls on Mull," Doles informed them, now looking quite animated. "They are very high and cascade down to the sea."

Sorcha found her attention wavering as her young cousin burbled on about the magic of Mull. Somehow, the recital only intensified Sorcha's yearning to be in the Highlands once more. Though it had only been slightly more than a month since she had left Gosford's End, Sorcha seemed to have been away forever.

"I AM UNACCUSTOMED TO ADVISING young ladies on proper behavior in these situations," said Donald McVurrich, inclining his head toward the large group of people who chattered and laughed in the Earl of Moray's banquet hall not far from Holyrood Palace. "Doles is too young to attend such functions, but I would urge modesty and circumspect speech above all."

Since Sorcha was attired in black from head to foot and had restrained her hair under a heavy net, she felt Uncle Donald's advice unnecessary. Except for her speech. She did have a habit of letting her tongue go unchecked.

"Doles is very well read," Sorcha noted, hoping to divert the conversation away from a possible lecture on moral turpitude. "She has studied geography and topography extensively for one so young."

Somewhat to Sorcha's surprise, Uncle Donald responded with a show of pride. "She has read more at her age than I have ever done. Except for matters pertaining to finances. A canny lassie is our Doles."

Aunt Tarrill emerged from the throng of guests, two mugs of mulled wine in her hands. Her eyes were bright, and her skin had a youthful glow, as if her unaccustomed attendance at an elegant soiree had taken at least a dozen years from her age. "Here, good husband, drink deeply to savor the forthcoming spirit of Christmas."

Uncle Donald raised one blond, bushy eyebrow. "Will we once more argue about the frivolity of Christmas?"

"Certainly," replied Tarrill cheerfully. "We'll argue for hours. And then I shall decorate the house, rehearse the children in their carols, and fill the wassail bowl, as always." She reached up to touch her husband's bearded cheek. "I swear, Donald McVurrich, it wouldn't be Christmas if we didn't debate the season!"

Uncle Donald gave his wife a vaguely sheepish look, then patted her arm rather clumsily. "I fear I'm becoming embroiled in a conspiracy. Our host approaches, no doubt to urge me to join in the dancing."

"No doubt," Tarrill replied, offering her hand to the Earl of Moray. "My Lord, you are the model of a gracious nobleman! I have already plundered your sideboard until my stays have sprung!"

Moray smiled in that engaging way Sorcha remembered so well from Doune Castle. He saluted Uncle Donald, then bowed to Sorcha, his hand still firmly clasping Aunt Tarrill's. "I am delighted to see you're … free to enjoy our hospitality once more, Mistress Fraser. I fear we did not have time to fete you sufficiently when you visited Doune."

Sorcha was grateful for Moray's discretion. She deemed it a measure of his consideration for others that he would take care not to bring up what might be an awkward subject.

"Our party was anxious to reach Edinburgh," Sorcha replied, hoping she sounded sincere. In the background, several musicians were tuning their instruments, the random notes making a counterpoint to the laughter of the guests. The overcrowded hall smelled of perfume, perspiration, wine, spices, and roasting meat.

The Countess of Moray had joined them, her slender figure encased in a vermillion brocade gown with underskirts and sleeves of flowing pink moire. Sorcha's smile had grown taut; inwardly, she cursed Walter Ramsey for dying and forcing his survivors into mourning.

"We scarcely had an opportunity to speak at Doune," the Countess said shyly, as her pale lashes seemed to dip in deference. "Being cousins, we ought to be friends."

The overture took Sorcha by surprise. "Our sires weren't," she blurted and felt her olive skin flush.

Moray, however, chuckled. "All the more reason for our generation to sue for peace." He took both Sorcha and his wife by the hand. "Come, let's move out to the gallery for a few moments. It's too warm in here."

The Countess gave her husband a sweet smile but demurred. "We mustn't both leave our guests, My Lord. You walk with our cousin and refresh yourselves. I'll see if the musicians are ready to play."

Noting that Uncle Donald and Aunt Tarrill were too engrossed in their conversation with the Earl and Countess of Mar to notice her departure, Sorcha dutifully followed Moray from the crowded room. Once in the gallery, Sorcha took a deep breath. "Did you actually invite all those people, or did some of them wander in from the Canongate?"

Moray chuckled again. "To be frank, we had assumed that about half of our guests would still be at Linlithgow, waiting for the new Privy Council to be formed."

"Apparently, they'd rather wait here." Sorcha patterned her step after Moray's as they ambled down the gallery. It was narrow but not long, embellished with some fine portraits of very ugly people. Sorcha hoped none of them were her ancestors. She was about to ask when Moray spoke.

"I felt most distressed at my inability to keep you from being taken by the Master of Gray as his hostage. He had my small household garrison outnumbered, yet my inadequacy doesn't excuse me. I wish there were some way I could make amends."

The earl's handsome, candid face looked so chagrined that Sorcha was compelled to dismiss the incident out of hand. "It was quite harmless. I met the King, in fact, which was rather amusing."

"Well!" Moray seemed pleased. "Poor Jamie, so put upon by his elders! I try to offer him cheer and good fellowship, but others accuse me of ulterior motives." Moray shook his head sadly. "That's not fair, really, since my only ambition is to provide a comfortable existence for my family. Despite the grandiose title, my wife's dowry was meager."

It hadn't occurred to Sorcha that as the daughter of an assassinated regent, Elizabeth Stewart would have found her patrimony dissipated by the time she reached a marriageable age. "But you don't seem poor," Sorcha remarked, as they reached the end of the gallery and turned back the other way. "Why, this party alone must cost a great deal."

Moray looked rueful. "So it does. But I think of it as an investment. I've invited several important personages who may be able to improve my financial state."

Sorcha craned her neck to look up at Moray. "Such as Uncle Donald?" Seeing Moray nod, she laughed. "I wondered. He seemed like an odd choice of guest for you."

The Earl shrugged and took Sorcha's arm. "Oh, perhaps. But Donald McVurrich isn't quite as somber as he appears. As with many people who've come from humble origins, he is preoccupied with dignity and status." Moray's clear blue eyes rested on Sorcha. Beyond the gallery doors, the musicians had struck up a lively tune, drowning out the merry chatter of the guests. "Alas, some men of exalted birth overemphasize their state." Moray's mouth turned down at the corners. "George Gordon comes to mind." He shook his head with regret. "And, like others, he considers me a rival for the King's affection. Especially so, since the Moray title was once a Gordon prerogative before Queen Mary arbitrarily bestowed it on my late father-in-law. Yet," he went on, halting to stand by a pedestal upon which rested a marble bust of a jutting-jawed Roman senator, "I bear him no grudge. His enmity frankly puzzles me."

"So much antagonism exists among our people," Sorcha commented in a tone that sounded too breezy for its subject. "Surely George poses no danger to you—nor the other way round, I assume."

A smile eased the concern on Moray's face. He reached out to take Sorcha's hand, the warm, candid blue eyes crinkling at the edges. "I hope not. Yet ...." He shrugged. "Enough of my woes. Tell me, who is this fellow Napier? Surely he doesn't come from the Highlands."

Sorcha assumed a bland expression. "He's lived abroad for years. He arrived at Gosford's End only recently." The evasion wasn't quite a lie, Sorcha told herself, and wished Moray would let go of her hand.

Moray considered the explanation for a moment, then nodded. "And has come to court to seek his fortune?"

"Ah ... not precisely." Stalling, Sorcha smiled back at Moray. "He and Rob plan to travel." She hesitated again, wondering if she should name their destination. Moray had the ear of the King; perhaps he could serve as her emissary. Yet she hardly knew the man. With ambivalent feelings, she looked away from her host to the hem of her black mourning gown.

"A shame," Moray remarked, giving her hand a squeeze. "Napier struck me as the sort of ally I would like to have at court. He's intelligent, forthright, and brave. I should have been the one to chase after Gray and Bothwell, not Napier." The blue eyes had turned rueful, apologetic.

"He promised our parents he'd give us protection," Sorcha replied casually. She inclined her head toward the gallery doors. "Such gay music! Don't you feel like dancing?" Indeed, Sorcha had heard that Moray was a superb dancer, yet another asset which had earned him the soubriquet "the Bonnie Earl."

But Moray assumed a self-deprecating air. "Let us merely say that I'm less clumsy than some." He uttered a little laugh and moved another step closer to Sorcha.

The sudden, intimate silence was awkward. Sorcha gave her hand a slight tug, but Moray didn't seem to notice. The blue eyes were unblinking, fixed on her face as if they'd been searching for something that had long been lost and finally was found.

"Those drumsticks filled with Flemish cheese," Sorcha said, overenthused, "have they all been devoured?"

It took a moment for Moray to focus on Sorcha's query. She was about to repeat it when he laughed again, this time more heartily, if self-consciously. "Nay, unless your Lady Aunt stuffed the rest in her bodice." He kept her hand in his, but swung back toward the banquet hall. "I forget what hearty appetites Highlanders possess," he added lightly. "Have you tasted the candied fig tarts yet?"

The tension that had begun to creep over Sorcha like a chill began to drain away. Yet, except for holding her hand, and the lingering warmth of his gaze, Moray had done nothing to disturb her. Nor would he, Sorcha reassured herself—the Earl of Moray's vaunted reputation had been earned not just by athletic ability and a gift for the social graces, but by his unblemished gallantry with women.

EDINBURGH LAY UNDER A THICK blanket of snow that first week of December. From the pinnacle of Castle Hill to the gates of Holyrood Palace, residents slowed their pace and muffled their voices against the swirling snow that blew down from the north.

At Linlithgow, the King had brought his new Privy Council together. Many of the previously banished lords were restored to favor. Arran was said to be in hiding on the western coast. And plying the strings, as if the realm's most important personages were mere puppets, was the Master of Gray.

To Sorcha, these political events had but one significance: she could not reach the King to ask permission for Rob and Father Napier to join Queen Mary in England. By mid-December Rob was growing as impatient as his mentor. Immediately following a scripture lesson delivered by Uncle Donald,

Rob and Sorcha fled the McVurrich house to the snow-banked streets of the city. The snow had stopped falling just before supper, but the few barren spots on the cobblestones had already iced over. Keeping close to the lanterns that hung along the Canongate, brother and sister walked carefully in the direction of the High Street.

"As soon as the weather improves, I'll ride with you to Linlithgow," Rob said as they approached the Nether Bow Port that marked the end of the Canongate and the beginning of the High Street.

"If I'm to beg a favor of the King," Sorcha replied peevishly, putting a gloved hand over her nose as they passed the Fish Market, "I'd rather wait until he returns to Edinburgh. You could hardly make the journey to England now, with snow barring the roads."

"We're heading south, not north," Rob retorted, equally pettish. "Once this thaws a bit, we should get through."

"God's teeth, Rob, I don't see why you're so eager to exchange one prison for another. I can't imagine anything more gloomy than sitting around all day in a dank English manor house, listening to the Queen of Scots bemoan her fate and recite French sonnets." Sorcha ploughed purposefully through the virgin snow, leaving deep footprints. Her black skirts were already wet but her booted feet remained dry.

"I'm not joining the Queen to be entertained," countered Rob, glancing at two footmen who strained under the weight of a heavily curtained litter. "Not only am I committed to serving her, but I can also be taught by Father Napier."

"He can teach you here." Sorcha gave her brother a baleful glance. "Though perhaps if you see the Queen in all her human frailties, the experience will dampen your ardor. Then you can look upon lesser lassies without a prejudiced eye, and fall in love."

Rob shook his head, as if confounded by Sorcha's simplistic view. "You see things only in earthly terms, dear sister. Can you not raise your eyes heavenward upon occasion?"

"I can hardly raise one foot after the other in this damnable snow," Sorcha retorted crossly, momentarily slowed by the drifts that had accumulated next to the massive bulk of Saint Giles. "I can't help it if I'm an earthbound creature who—"

Sorcha's words were cut short by the sound of loud voices outside one of the entrances to Saint Giles. Several men appeared to be arguing, and her initial reaction was that they were drunken brawlers. But in the still night air, she could hear one of them cry out over the others, "I'll commit my soul to Christ before I let my body utter your vile confession of faith! Let the Devil take you all!"

The man was cuffed smartly by a stout figure whose back was to Rob and

Sorcha. At least two of the others wielded clubs. Sorcha counted the men, discerning that there were four assailants, yet only a single victim. "Where's the night watch?" she whispered to Rob, as they edged close to the side of the church.

"I don't know. I haven't seen anyone since we passed the Nether Bow." He had already felt for his dirk, but remembered he hadn't bothered to put it on. "Damn," he breathed, "I wish I knew more people in this pestiferous place."

The stout man's words were too low to distinguish, but the reply was clear. "No, by the sweet Virgin, I will not! Do what you must!"

To Sorcha's horror, the men closed in on their victim, wielding fists and clubs. Frantically, she turned to Rob, gripping his arm tight. "We must stop them! I don't care who they are, they'll kill that poor soul!"

She was not encouraged by Rob's look of complete helplessness. "They may kill us, too. We dare not, Sorcha. The man may be a criminal."

"God's teeth," Sorcha cried, letting Rob go and trudging purposefully through the snow. "Stop!" she called out, within twenty feet of the men. "Stop, for the love of God!"

The men paused, startled at the sound of a woman's voice. The victim was on his back, legs writhing wildly, emitting strangled groans from his throat. Sorcha was now only a few steps away. The stout man eyed her with contempt. "Make for your bed, wench! We want no meddling here!"

Rob had followed Sorcha, and now stood at her side. "Mind your manners, churl, or I'll call the watch."

A roar of laughter greeted Rob's threat. "Och, ye do just that," said a second man as the guffaws died away. "I *am* the watch!"

To prove his statement, the man moved to stand under a lantern that hung from the wall of the church. His chest was emblazoned with the city's arms, and his headgear boasted Edinburgh's crest.

Sorcha looked from the men, who still had their prey pinned on the ground, to her bewildered brother. In the next instant, the men fell once more upon the hapless victim as a soul-wrenching scream escaped from his lips before he lapsed into ominous silence.

The stout man stood up, turning back to Sorcha and Rob to dust off his hands as if he'd just completed a particularly irksome chore. "That's how you deal with obstinate Papists, my lad and lassie. If they won't recant on earth, let them do so before the Devil."

The others had also got to their feet, retrieving caps and clubs and other gear they had lost in the melee. Sorcha moved closer to Rob as the stout man saluted them with a mocking bow. "Let this be a lesson," he said, waving a hand carelessly toward the inert figure behind him. "And a bonnie night to ye both." The men were laughing and clapping each other on the back as they turned in the direction of Fish Market Wynd.

Rob moved swiftly to the man who lay on the ground, but Sorcha held back. She could already make out the spreading patch of red that blemished the snow. "Is he … alive?" Somehow, it was very important to form the words in a hopeful voice.

"No." Rob slowly stood up, fixing Sorcha with a stricken face as white as the snow itself. "Holy Mother of God, he was a priest!"

Chapter 9

THE CHRISTMAS SEASON PASSED PRECISELY as Aunt Tarrill had predicted. Despite Uncle Donald's reluctance to join in the festivities, he had been unable to maintain his opposition for more than a day. When Tarrill encircled his head with a garland of cedar, stuck a sprig of holly behind one ear, and tweaked his beard, he capitulated. To Sorcha's surprise, he seemed to enjoy himself, particularly on Christmas Day, when the wassail bowl turned magically bottomless.

By Twelfth Night, Rob was again urging Sorcha to request an audience with the King. He had not mentioned it since the priest's murder, making Sorcha speculate that Rob had been frightened out of his vocation. She would scarcely have blamed him. And though she told herself over and over that there was no way they could have prevented the priest's death, even if they'd acted sooner, she still felt guilty.

But Rob revealed that the incident had only strengthened his desire to join the clergy. "I hesitated; I'm at fault," he lamented to Sorcha late one night in her room. "You urged me on, but prudence made me stay. Now I must offer up my life for his."

Sorcha shook her head. "That makes little sense to me. But," she went on, trying to blot out a wine stain she'd gotten on her black gown, "it's hopeless, Rob, with the Master of Gray overseeing everything the King does. We must wait until his influence wanes." Sorcha examined the dress with a critical eye, noting to her chagrin that the stain still showed. "Unless we find someone else to intercede," she added and tossed the garment onto the bed. "I considered Moray earlier, but decided it would be impertinent. Yet now that Uncle Donald has made him a loan, I don't feel so cheeky."

Rob wrinkled his nose at Sorcha as Ailis slipped into the room, candle in hand. She was attired in her nightclothes and looked startled to find Rob in his sister's room so late. Sorcha contemplated Ailis briefly, then gestured for her to stay.

"Your apparel is sufficiently modest for mixed company," Sorcha asserted, with a dry smile. Indeed, Ailis was muffled to her chin, with yards of heavy flannel shrouding her body. The maid looked primly from Sorcha to Rob, then moved quietly to close the shutters.

"Uncle Donald was generous with the Bonnie Earl, I hear. But why," queried Rob, "would Moray want to offer succor to the Queen when his future is in the hands of her enemies—including her ungrateful son?"

"He's friends with devious Bothwell, who, for all his other faults, is also devoted to his royal aunt." Sorcha had spoken more to herself than to Rob, as if she were trying to support her argument.

Rob got up from the armchair in which he'd been lounging. "Well, Moray could hardly procrastinate any longer than you have," he said dryly. Seeing the spark in Sorcha's eyes, he held up his hands as if to ward off potential blows. "Nay, nay, I tease. Go to Moray. But for the love of Saint Joseph, mind what you say. Especially about Father Napier."

Sorcha gave Rob an enigmatic look. "Don't fret, my brother. I already know what I'm going to say. Especially about Father Napier."

WARMER WINDS HAD BLOWN IN from the sea to melt most of the snow. The Canongate was full of puddles and slush as Sorcha made the brief trek to the Earl of Moray's handsome town house. Ailis had offered to accompany her, but as the maid was engaged in a chess game with Doles, Sorcha was reluctant to disrupt the match. She was still smiling inwardly at the sight of the two intent, somber faces poised over the chessboard when she pulled on the heavy brass ring which adorned Moray's front door.

A pockmarked servant with hair the color of corn silk admitted her. He indicated the drawing room, where Sorcha found Moray, Bothwell, and a sulky youth she didn't recognize practicing putts on the Persian carpet.

"Cousin!" greeted Moray warmly, setting down his golf club and coming to take her hand. "Welcome. Bothwell and Caithness are helping me keep up with my game during this cold weather."

Bothwell gave Sorcha a sniggering smile; Caithness made a vague, clumsy bow. He was half a foot taller than Bothwell, but fair haired and lanky. All three men were in their shirtsleeves, and tankards of ale sat on a tiny tiered table near the fireplace.

"So you really are Iain Fraser's bairn," Bothwell remarked after the formal introductions had been made. "Did you ever convince Patrick Gray?"

"Did I ever need to?" Sorcha snapped and promptly flushed. "Forgive me, but that wild ride from Doune still rankles." Caithness was looking puzzled. He was not much older than she and, if memory served her, had a most unsavory reputation for mayhem. Moray appeared to take all manner of men under his good-natured wing.

"Braw Caithness here is half brother to Bothwell," Moray explained, quite unruffled by his guests' disparate emotions. "Here, mistress, join us," he urged, picking up one of the tankards. "Or would you prefer wine?"

Sorcha shook her head. "Nothing, thank you. I must keep my visit short." She gave Bothwell and Caithness a questioning glance. "It concerns a family matter."

"Ah." Moray nodded at the other men. "Be good fellows and see if you can find that club with the new shaft. It may solve my pesky problem of veering to the left."

Bothwell smirked. "Don't veer too far with the lass. I'm told she's kin to me." He gave Sorcha an oblique look and all but shoved Caithness out of the room.

Moray laughed ruefully as he offered Sorcha a chair. "Neither Bothwell nor Caithness has had much formal upbringing. Both their sires died young, you know, and their mother let them run roughshod. Caithness is still a lad, but Bothwell can be an amusing rogue."

"Oh?" murmured Sorcha, having second thoughts about the wine as Moray sat down opposite her. "Bothwell is a friend of Gray's as well as yours? It's all very confusing."

"So it is," Moray allowed, rolling a golf ball out of the way with his foot. "Now—what troubles you?" he inquired with kindly concern. "Are you and Rob suffering from a plethora of Presbyterianism?"

Sorcha laughed. "Oh, no—well, from time to time." She paused, growing more serious. "In a sense, the problem does pertain to religion—and politics. It's Rob, you see." She saw Moray's straight brows lift and hurried on. "My brother has a silly notion about serving Queen Mary in her English captivity. He's quite a dreamer, and has long fancied himself her champion. I would hope—indeed, I beg—that you would ask His Grace to let Rob join the Queen's household."

Moray had grown quite solemn while listening to Sorcha's request. "It's very difficult," he said slowly, fingering his chin. "King Jamie has little influence over his mother's imprisonment. Queen Elizabeth makes those decisions."

Sorcha sniffed with disdain. "It seems to me a king ought to have some say when it concerns his own mother. I can't imagine Jamie is so helpless. Or devoid of spirit."

Taking a deep swig from his tankard, Moray acknowledged Sorcha's allegation with a nod. "Our King plays a canny game, knuckling under to the English queen at one moment, flirting with the Catholic powers the next. But he knows that if he's to succeed Elizabeth, he must ultimately play by her rules. Just last month, he signed a bond with England to solidify relations between the two countries."

Sorcha stood up abruptly. "By the Virgin, I'd no idea how weak-willed we Scots really are until I came to Edinburgh! You would think Elizabeth was Queen of both England and Scotland. Perhaps it's well I've never thought of myself as a Stewart but as a Fraser. Highlanders have more pride than to let a foreign hussy lead them around on a leash."

Moray set his tankard down and also got to his feet. He put a gentle hand on Sorcha's arm and gave her his self-deprecating look. "You make me ashamed of my heritage. As perhaps I should be. See here," he said, tapping her nose with his finger, "I'd like to make amends for what happened at Doune. I'll go to Jamie, if you insist. But you must come with me."

It was Sorcha's turn to prove she had the courage of her convictions. She shifted from one foot to the other, as Moray's hand moved down to cup her chin. "Very well. But you—we—must also ask permission for Gavin Napier to join Rob. My father has refused to let my brother go to England alone."

Moray's hand fell to his side. "Napier? Very well. You mentioned they would travel together. So be it, mistress."

Sorcha felt flushed with triumph, though the idea of going to Linlithgow was not appealing. Still, it was a small price to pay for Moray's cooperation. She offered him what she hoped was a fetchingly grateful smile, but he waved her thanks aside.

"Never mind; we're even now. I've been all but moping since the Master carried you off from Doune." Moray picked up his golf club and proffered it to Sorcha. "Do you play?"

"A little." Sorcha felt the club with experimental fingers. "My father and my brother, Magnus, are quite good. They have a makeshift links near our house, though the sheep get in the way."

"We'll play when the weather is better," Moray said. "Winter is a trying time for me. I grow bored indoors."

"So do I." Sorcha set the club down and gathered her cloak around her. "The city pens me in. I miss the Highlands."

Moray eyed Sorcha thoughtfully. "I see that. You possess remarkable energies. A child of nature, perhaps?" He saw Sorcha's blank expression and frowned. "Nay, you are no longer a child," Moray asserted and uttered his self-deprecating laugh. "I'm reminded more of Diana, or Artemis. I've seen a most wonderful sculpture of Artemis with a magnificent stag. It's a perfect rendering of the Goddess of the Hunt."

The words nettled Sorcha. No bronze or marble figures came to mind, but rather herself, angry and rain soaked, mourning the Master of Ness. And looming over them both in her mind's eye was Gavin Napier. She had tried not to think of him in the past few days, and now she resented Moray for unwittingly bringing him to mind.

Nor could Moray be blamed for misreading her reaction. "It seems you find me too forward, mistress," he declared, wearing a shamefaced expression. "I intended no dishonor."

"What?" Sorcha snatched her cloak even closer to her body. "Oh, no, I suppose not." In her attempt to exorcise Gavin Napier's image, she had forgotten what Moray had said to evoke it. She looked sheepishly at her host. "I was thinking of my … my pet. He was a stag, in the Highlands, and was killed this past autumn by a … hunter." Sorcha forced herself to smile. "I miss him too," she added rather lamely, and didn't know if she spoke of the great stag—or of Gavin Napier.

IT HAD JUST STARTED TO drizzle when she got outside, a fretful rain mixed with a few flakes of snow. The clouds hung close in over the city, casting a gray gloom on the Canongate and the Girth Cross. Nevertheless, Sorcha was relieved to be gone from the Earl of Moray's company. As charming and kind as he was, his presence had a peculiar effect on her. Perhaps Moray was a born womanizer, skilled in the arts of enchanting ladies, capable of flattery designed to provoke flirtatious banter. It was an art practiced by many, and often quite harmless. Certainly Moray's name had never been tainted by scandal. But, Sorcha thought as she waited for a coach and four horses to labor by, she didn't wish to offer him any encouragement.

Looking across the street through the drizzle, Sorcha sucked in her breath. Gavin Napier was directly opposite her, wrapped in a long black cloak, bareheaded and staring straight toward her. He didn't move, but waited for Sorcha to join him.

"You come from Moray's." It was a statement of fact, not a question.

Sorcha rearranged her hood to keep the rain off her face. "Aye, for Rob's sake and yours." She misliked his stern tone and willed him to smile at her as easily as Moray did. "Moray will intercede. Aren't you pleased?"

Napier started walking quite fast, forcing Sorcha to fall into step beside him. "I ought to be," he replied, his voice very deep. Napier gave Sorcha a sidelong glance. "What wiles did you use to convince him?"

Sorcha started to balk but shrugged instead. " 'Twas simple enough—I offered him my body. It rarely fails when dealing with men."

They were passing the Canongate Tolbooth, where a half dozen beggars huddled by a brazier next to the edifice's gray walls. Napier all but stepped on one of the men as he whirled around to confront Sorcha. "Christ! You did no such thing!"

It never occurred to Sorcha that Napier would take her seriously. The blazing brown eyes told her otherwise, however. She backed off a pace, one heel splashing into a puddle. "And if I did? Wouldn't it please you if it meant gaining your objective?" Her chin shot up, the hood falling from her hair.

In the folds of his black cloak, Sorcha could see Napier's hand tighten into a fist. His face was grim. "Don't talk drivel," he growled, lowering his voice as the beggars looked on with interest. "Whatever you did was for Rob, not for me." He glanced over his shoulder, started to tell his ragged audience to mind their manners, but instead, dug inside his cloak and tossed out a few coins. The beggars scrambled among themselves amid a mingling of vile curses aimed at each other and grateful cries directed at their benefactor. Napier, however, had grabbed Sorcha by the arm and was steering her along the Canongate.

"Let go; I can walk," Sorcha rasped, using her free hand to struggle with her hood. "God's teeth, did you truly think I'd give myself to Moray—or any other man?" She darted Napier an angry look. "What must you think of me!"

"What I think of most women," Napier snapped back as a scruffy mongrel scampered close to his feet and shook himself, water flying from his fur. The animal yapped noisily, but Napier paid no heed. "Why should you be different?"

The mongrel had raced away after a rooster that had strayed from a nearby close. Napier's response had further nettled Sorcha. "It sounds as if you've heard too many lewd women in confession."

Napier's profile was stony, though his grip remained firm on Sorcha's arm. They passed the Canongate Kirk, where an angry woman scolded two young boys who had been taunting a tearful little girl. "You comment on matters of which you know little," Napier finally said in a harsh note of reproach. "At the very least, your notion of humor is perverted."

"At least I have a notion of humor," Sorcha retorted, and yanked her arm free. "Whatever became of fat, jolly priests with rosy cheeks and rotund bellies?"

"They went the way of Chaucer," Napier replied, but his voice had lost its edge. He glanced to his right, toward a deserted close that was sheltered from the rain by an archway. Abruptly, he pushed Sorcha over the cobbles until they both stood under the protected entrance. Beyond, a fallow garden lay at the front of a house with closed shutters and dormant chimneys. "Tell me," he implored, more solemn than stern, "do you find me disagreeable?"

Sorcha gave the query the consideration it deserved. "I find you strange," she answered after a moment's reflection. Pausing, she searched the long, wolflike face. "There are tiny lines of laughter around your eyes—I think you were happy once. But there's sadness, too, and somehow, I sense a contradiction, as if …." Fretting her upper lip with her finger, she made a frustrated face. "I don't know. I think perhaps you find faith and charity easy to come by. But not hope." She shook her head slowly as she saw Napier retreat behind the familiar mask. "As for being disagreeable, you *do* tend to disagree." She shrugged. "But I don't mind arguing. Just don't be unreasonable as well."

The glimmer of a smile tugged at the corners of Napier's mouth. "For such a young lass, you speak freely to your betters, mistress."

Sorcha flicked at the end of her nose in dismissal. "Pah! I'm a Highlander—there are no 'betters.' Or," she went on, feeling a vague sense of remorse, "if there are, it must be proved."

Napier considered her statement. His dark brown hair was soaked, and it curled slightly over his ears and forehead. Just a few yards away, in the street, the heavy wheel of a hay cart fell off and rolled down the Canongate toward the entrance to the close. It careened into the archway just as Napier pulled Sorcha flat against the wall.

"Jesu," Sorcha breathed, as the wheel bounced off the stonework a scant foot away and crashed onto the cobbles. "How fortunate there were no small children playing nearby."

The driver of the cart was huffing and cursing in his pursuit of the wheel. He was followed by a lad younger than Sorcha, whose coloring and build resembled the driver's. The two of them righted the wheel and began rolling it back toward the cart.

Sorcha moved as if to step from Napier's protective embrace, but he didn't seem ready to yield her up. His reluctance was considerably less astonishing than his words. "Did he suggest a price?" The inquiry was hoarse, almost diffident.

"What?" Sorcha craned to look up at Napier's face, her hood slipping off her head again. It occurred to her that what was most bothersome about Napier wasn't his intransigent, solemn nature but his unpredictability. "Did who do what?"

The dark eyes were focused on the unruly tangles of her damp hair. "Moray. Did he suggest such a payment as you mentioned?" Again, Napier's words didn't come easily.

"Moray?" Sorcha was incredulous. "Naturally not! His reputation is spotless! Really, Gavin, you have the most—" She jerked up her head to stare at him, as startled as she thought he would be by her use of his Christian name. "Forgive me, Father … I meant no disrespect." Sorcha was flushing, her hot cheek suddenly pressed against his chest.

But Napier said nothing, nor did he seem shocked by her lapse of etiquette. One big hand moved to pull away the mass of hair from where it lay caught in the fallen hood. "Still," he said, ignoring her apology, "doubtless Moray has the usual masculine weakness for virgins. No man is to be trusted, under certain circumstances."

Recalling Napier's impassioned kisses all too vividly, Sorcha was about to respond that she understood his words well enough. But she could feel his heart beat against her ear, and she smelled the virile warmth of his body next to hers. It was not the moment for rancor.

Nor was this the man for romantic dreams, Sorcha reminded herself sharply. Better to moon over the married Moray than the forbidden Father Napier. She made a tentative effort to pull away, and to her surprise, the priest released her at once. "I still feel responsible for your safety—spiritual as well as otherwise," he declared in a tone Sorcha found unconvincing. Apparently, her reaction showed; Napier scowled and kicked at a piece of masonry dislodged by the runaway cart wheel. "You have every right to despise me, you know."

They had taken up a brisk pace, moving back through the Canongate toward Panmure Close. "And you, me," Sorcha replied in a dismal voice. She didn't bother to put her hood back. They were only a few steps from the McVurrich residence, and Sorcha suddenly felt as if she deserved to catch cold.

They concluded their brief journey in silence. At the wrought iron gate that separated Uncle Donald's fine house from the Canongate, Sorcha stole a glance at Napier from under the wedge of unruly hair that all but covered one eye. "I'll hate it when you—and Rob—go away." She swallowed hard, but still couldn't quite look directly at Napier. "Yet it will be a good thing, I think."

The hunter's gaze was compelling. "Will it?" He bit off the words and made as if to reach out for her. From somewhere on the second story of the house a shutter slammed, making both Sorcha and Napier jump. "I must go," she breathed. "Uncle Donald mustn't see you." Whirling, she pulled open the iron gate and raced along the flagstone path to the McVurrich front door and Presbyterian sanctuary.

Chapter 10

THE MUDDY ROADS SLOWED THEIR pace as Sorcha, Rob, Ailis, and Moray rode to Linlithgow the third week of January. The weather had turned unusually mild, melting all but the most sheltered patches of snow along the route. They arrived at the castle shortly before noon. The King was closeted with his council, but Moray assured Sorcha and Rob that he would grant an audience later in the day.

"The Master will try to thwart me as he always does, but Jamie will be gracious," Moray said as they shared their noon meal in the earl's quarters. "I like to think he finds my undemanding company pleasurable."

Moray's prediction proved accurate. King James sent for his cousin just after four o'clock. Two hours later, however, Moray had not returned.

"I considered Moray a most persuasive man," Rob fretted, pacing the chamber as the shadows crept across the rushes.

Sorcha looked up from a book of Italian sonnets she'd been scanning. "I suspect he must prove entertaining as well. They may be playing cards or draughts."

"While my fate hangs in the balance," Rob retorted with unusual impatience. He snatched his cape off a peg and threw it over his shoulders. "I need some air. Do you wish to join me?"

Sorcha gave him a caustic look. "Not when you're so cross. I'll go see if Ailis is still napping."

Rob nodded tersely, then left the chamber. Sorcha returned the book to its place on the shelf, paused to gaze out the window into the dusk, and wandered to a sideboard, where a silver bowl filled with dried fruit sat next to a miniature of Elizabeth, Countess of Moray. Examining the little portrait closely, Sorcha noted that the artist had given his subject more animation in his brush strokes than she possessed in real life. Absently picking up a date and popping it into her mouth, she chewed thoughtfully, the miniature still in her hand. She turned abruptly as Moray entered the room, an anxious expression on his face.

"His Grace wishes to see you," he said, then noticed the little portrait. "Ah," he said, his voice softening, "you're admiring my Countess?"

"It's a reasonable likeness," Sorcha replied noncommittally, setting the miniature down and hastily swallowing the date. "Why does the King want to see me?"

Moray laughed, though without his usual ease. "I believe he wishes to have feminine wiles worked on him, Cousin. Thus far, he's proved obstinate."

Sorcha sighed. "I'm not very guileful. Candor and camaraderie are my strong suits." And little good they've done me, she thought, turning to a small oval mirror to survey her image. The black riding habit, borrowed from Aunt Tarrill, was too long and too large, though the cut of the bodice set off her bosom and the small ruff around the neck provided a satisfactory frame for her face. She had bundled her hair into a heavy jet-studded net, which had looked well enough under the high-crowned riding hat, but without it, now seemed incomplete. Experimentally, she piled the hair on top of her head, but realized she had no pins to hold it in place.

Sorcha threw her hands up in the air. "Oh, damn all, I shall go as I am. I was once taken for a serving wench, so why should I fash myself now?"

But Sorcha stiffened as she looked in the little mirror and saw Moray close behind her. "You look like a Gypsy queen, with that black hair and those green eyes. Your skin is sun kissed even in winter, and your smile would melt the deepest snows."

From any other man, Sorcha would have found such fulsome words insincere. But from Moray, they had the ring of authenticity. She stood as if rooted to the floor as Moray slipped his arms around her waist and brought his lips against her ear. "My Lord!" she gasped, feeling the pressure of his muscular body next to hers, "this is most unseemly! I must go to the King!"

He lingered for just a moment, fingers gently stroking the slender waist. "Forgive me," he murmured. "You tempt me like no other woman."

Her breath too rapid, Sorcha turned swiftly as he released her and stepped back several paces. She saw the abject look on his face and felt a pang of remorse. Yet, she told herself sternly, he had no right to make such advances. Nor did she dare believe his words.

"A lamentable lapse," she said crisply, trying to smile, yet knowing it was a puny effort at best. "Where is His Grace?"

Moray gave concise directions, his manner tense, the blue eyes no longer merry. Sorcha found the King's chambers without difficulty and was admitted at once.

King James of Scotland sat cross-legged on the floor of his audience chamber, a fur-trimmed robe draped ungracefully about his gangly body, a scowl on his face. He was alone, and several sheets of paper lay scattered in front of him.

"Coz," he said by way of greeting, looking up briefly. "Why do I have to read all these documents when Gray will tell me what to do?"

Sorcha had made a deep curtsey but remained standing uncertainly as James flicked a sheet of paper with his fingernail. At last he gazed at her fully, shaking his head. "Silly, this business of being a king. Oh, pray sit, Coz, if you can find a place that isn't covered with the governance of Scotland."

"I thought you might be composing," Sorcha remarked, settling down on the floor and arranging her skirts as carefully as possible without disturbing the documents. "I understand you write rather well."

"Extremely well. Brilliantly at times, if you must know." Jamie grinned unabashedly at Sorcha, spitting slightly as he spoke. "Why haven't you been to visit me until now?" He lowered his long chin almost to his chest and attempted looking formidable. "Or are you here only because you want something?"

Sorcha flushed but didn't falter. "In truth, you're right. If I weren't seeking a favor for my brother, I would have waited until I got an invitation. Since one wasn't forthcoming, it seemed prudent to use Rob's request as an excuse to see you."

Jamie brightened. "Is that so? God's eyes, I should have sent for you sooner. But the Master of Gray and Lord Hamilton and the rest of the lords who had been in exile have all but monopolized my time." Jamie sighed, tugging at one fur-trimmed sleeve. "In faith, I sometimes think my nobles forget that I have a God-given right as their sovereign to chart my own course for Scotland."

"How very thoughtless of them," Sorcha commented, picking up a sheet of paper and scanning the page. "What is this? A letter?"

Jamie leaned over her shoulder, the fur on his robe brushing Sorcha's cheek. "Mmmm? Oh, yet another plea to Elizabeth, asking her to name me as her successor. As if there were anyone else! But the old hag keeps putting me off, just as she's done with the suitors who have tried to woo and win her. She'll never marry, but she *will* die. And when she does, I shall be King of England as well as of Scotland. Mark my words." Jamie rocked back on his heels, smiling in anticipated triumph.

Sorcha tossed the letter aside and stretched her legs. She still wore her riding boots, not having remembered to pack a pair of shoes. Indeed, Sorcha had hoped they would not spend the night at Linlithgow, but it was now dark, and obviously they couldn't return to Edinburgh until the next day.

"How strange it will be when the two countries are governed by one monarch," Sorcha mused, wondering how she could work Jamie's complaints about his nobles and Elizabeth to her advantage. "Though your mother maintained she was the rightful heir to both thrones, since Catholics considered Elizabeth a bastard."

"Catholics are wrong. Or so I'm told." Jamie scratched his long chin thoughtfully. "Are you a Catholic, Coz?"

Sorcha shifted uncomfortably. "Well, yes, most of the Frasers are, Your Grace."

Jamie shook his head sadly. "That's a pity. I'll have to ask you to renounce your religion. I'm head of the Kirk, you know."

Clearly, the conversation was going in the wrong direction. Sorcha leaned on one elbow, surveying her sovereign with dubious green eyes. "Being raised in a Catholic home far to the north, I know nothing about your church, sir. If I were to renounce my own faith, I would have no idea of what I was renouncing it *for*."

"Ah!" With surprising alacrity, Jamie jumped to his feet. "Then I shall instruct you!" He clapped his hands together as several sheets of paper fluttered at his feet. "It will be an excellent way to keep you in my company."

The idea wasn't totally unappealing to Sorcha; at least it would free her from the tedium of the McVurrich household. But if Jamie's bored, fretful attitude was any indication, she might be exchanging one sanctimonious lodging for another. Unless, of course, there were suitable young men on hand. From what Sorcha had seen so far of the nobles who swarmed about the King, that seemed unlikely.

"Your suggestion is most gracious," she said at last, deciding she had also better stand up. Somewhat to her surprise, Jamie didn't offer his hand, but let her struggle rather clumsily to her feet. In her riding boots, she was almost as tall as he was. "If I'm well versed in the tenets of the Protestant faith, perhaps I can dissuade Rob from his madness."

"Rob?" Jamie looked blank.

"My brother. Didn't Moray mention him?" Sorcha's patience was wearing thin. It was also growing close to the supper hour, and she was hungry.

"Oh! Of course, he wishes to attend my mother at Chartley. Why?" James seemed genuinely puzzled, rubbing a fur-trimmed wrist against his chin.

"Perhaps to make up for my father's desertion of her when she eloped with Bothwell." Sorcha tried to sound wistful. "Such a tragic mistake on her part, if I may speak bluntly. My sire had always felt close to her, even though he didn't realize they were half brother and half sister for many years. It was almost a personal betrayal for him. It's sad to think how we Scots can violate the affections of even our closest kin."

Jamie's high forehead creased with sorrow. "Aye, you put it well. My mother betrayed my father, too. And so, in a sense, me. Yet some would insist I've abandoned her, that I'm an unnatural son." He stretched his hands out to Sorcha. "Can you blame me?"

Sorcha tilted her head and smiled gently. "You were but a bairn when she lost her throne. And now … well, you hardly know her, mother or not. Yet it must be a source of great sadness to her, alone and unwell in a foreign prison."

Sorcha wondered if she had gone too far. But Jamie sighed, a long, drawn-out breath that seemed to echo in the audience chamber. Except for two tapers on the fireplace mantel, the room was shrouded in shadows. A spaniel with a game leg hobbled out from under the dais at the end of the chamber, apparently awakened from its nap. The dog sniffed at Jamie's foot, then limped to Sorcha and barked once.

"Enough, Morton," Jamie commanded. The spaniel sat down on some of the papers still lying on the floor. The King of Scotland paid no heed. "I am not as cold and calculating as my critics would like others to believe," he said petulantly. "If you think your brother might bring some cheer to my mother, perhaps he should go."

"Rob's a cheerful sort," Sorcha replied, reminding herself to speak cautiously, lest her apparent victory be snatched away by Jamie's legendary shifts of mood. "And he *is* kin, of an age with yourself. Our mothers were with child at the same time," she reminded him. "My Aunt Tarrill brought him to see your mother the very morning after he was born at Holyrood. You were still in the womb."

Jamie's eyes, which had grown wide, narrowed in concentration. "It's providential, is it not?" he asked at last. "In a sense, it's like sending part of myself to my mother. Yes, yes, Coz, your brother must go." He nodded again, this time with great vehemence. "And if Elizabeth quibbles, I'll brook no interference. I shan't allow her to meddle in family matters."

Since Queen Elizabeth had been meddling with the Stewarts ever since ascending the English throne, Jamie's words struck Sorcha as almost comic. She dared not laugh, however, and tried instead to appear overwhelmed by his generosity. "Your Majesty's gracious gesture honors my brother—and me. Rob will bless you a thousand times. As will his tutor, Master Napier."

A hint of suspicion flitted across James's long face. "Tutor? What sort of tutor?"

"French, of course. A most insufferable pedant, but according to Rob, a gifted teacher." Sorcha winced inwardly at the conjured-up image of Gavin Napier as a crotchety, gnarled scholar wallowing in French verbs and tenses.

King James lifted one narrow shoulder. "So be it. To Chartley they shall go."

Sorcha was about to reiterate her thanks when the chamber door opened to reveal the Master of Gray. He paused on the threshold, stared openly at Sorcha with those hypnotic eyes, and bowed low.

"Your Grace," he said to Jamie, barely concealing the anger he felt at Sorcha's presence, "I marvel at the company you keep! The lords of your realm await you at supper."

"A pox on the lords of the realm!" Jamie threw Gray an indignant glare, but not before he'd glanced at Sorcha as if for approbation. "Tell them I'm detained on family matters."

Gray gazed from the King to Sorcha and back again. The spaniel, which had dozed off again on the state papers, looked up and growled. Ignoring Sorcha, Gray made a distasteful face at the animal, then smiled pleasantly at Jamie. "We await your pleasure, sire." The graceful figure bowed again and withdrew.

As the door shut, Jamie giggled with glee. "He's jealous! The Master is jealous of you, Coz! Oh, such a delightful circumstance!" He grasped Sorcha by the arm, his eyes suddenly pleading. "When will you come to court? Soon, please do!"

"I must see my brother off to England first," she replied, aware that she was increasingly loath to join the court, no matter how tiresome life in Panmure Close had grown. "A month or so, perhaps?"

The lower lip dipped into a pout as Jamie's hands dropped to his sides. "I'd hoped you would stay on at Linlithgow." He brightened. "I shall find you a rich husband. An Erskine, perhaps, or a Farquharson?"

Sorcha paused, momentarily distracted. "Oh? A handsome one?" She saw Jamie turn vague and regretfully shook her head. "I appreciate your concern and know you will ... ah, continue your search. But, for now, I dare not stay at court, sire. I must help Rob make adequate preparations for his journey. He hasn't had the advantages of being self-sufficient as you have."

"I've not had the advantages of brothers and sisters to see to my well-being. Nor parents, either." Jamie leaned down to scoop up the spaniel. "I envy Rob." He scratched the dog's ears and held it close as if it were a small child. "You won't tarry, will you, Coz? I shall seek out the most gallant mate for you, I promise!"

Sorcha felt her heart melt in her breast. Jamie looked so pathetic, attired in his royal robes, clutching the spaniel, both master and dog sad eyed and craving affection. Raised in a loving, boisterous family, Sorcha had a hard time imagining how isolated and lonely Jamie's youth must have been.

"A month, no more," she vowed. Impulsively, she leaned forward to brush

Jamie's cheek with a kiss. "I shall relay the news of your kindness to Rob at once. Take care, Your Grace." She patted the spaniel. "And, you, Morton." With a quick curtsey, Sorcha moved across the audience chamber. As she opened the door, she heard a little moan and wasn't certain whether it came from the spaniel—or the King.

Chapter 11

R OB WAS SO ELATED OVER King James's benevolence that for the first time in his life, he drank himself into a stupor. Half annoyed and half amused, Sorcha and Ailis put him to bed in the chamber hastily provided by Moray. A short time later, Ailis was about to retire and Sorcha was getting undressed when the earl knocked at their door. Signaling that Rob was already asleep, Sorcha stepped out into the hall. "Jamie approves," she said in a low voice. "I thank you for your assistance. So would Rob, if he were sober enough to speak."

Moray smiled indulgently. "I sensed Jamie would be more easily persuaded by you than by me. Every time I mentioned the subject, he diverted the conversation."

"I can understand that," Sorcha said dryly, recalling her own initial attempts. "Incidentally, if he should ever ask, Gavin Napier is an aged French tutor, withered as a prune."

Moray made a wry face. "Hardly an apt description of the stalwart Napier." He gave a little laugh, then sobered, and met Sorcha's gaze head-on. "I must remain at court for a time. I offer my apologies for not being able to escort you and the others back to Edinburgh."

To her surprise, Sorcha felt a pang of disappointment. "We'll manage," she said in reassurance. "It's a short journey, and the weather is holding."

"Aye." Moray paused, looking strangely uncertain. Briefly, the blue eyes flickered away, then returned to dwell on Sorcha's upturned face. "If I were a sane man, I'd say I made a fool of myself today. Sane or not, am I forgiven?"

Sorcha tried to avert her gaze but could not. The distress on Moray's finely molded features held her like a physical force. "We'll pretend it was a game.

And I shall forfeit my right to cry foul." She spoke lightly, but felt an inner heaviness.

"A game?" Moray's mouth twisted slightly. "Ah, I would that it were so!" He retreated a pace, one hand fretting at a sapphire ring set in silver. "To think I am hailed as a master at games! Yet you are the prize I'll not win."

Distress ebbed through Sorcha like a rising tide. "Sir, don't fash yourself! You confuse me. But I find you most … kind."

From the end of the hall, two pages raced exuberantly after each other. Sorcha and Moray stepped aside as the youths slowed their pace, but cast saucy glances in the direction of their betters. When they had disappeared in the opposite direction, Moray took Sorcha's hand and pressed it to his lips.

"There should be no confusion," he said clearly. "I love you." Seeing the disbelief on Sorcha's face, he squeezed her hand and shook his head. "Nay, don't protest. I've stated my feelings. I have no right to do so, but it would be less than honest of me if I did not." He smiled softly, though his eyes were in shadow. "Damn me, revile me, curse me. But never doubt me, Sorcha Fraser."

Sorcha felt as if she were suspended in space. James Stewart of Moray, the Bonnie Earl, the most personable, admired man in Scotland had declared his love for her, an unworldly, unkempt Highland lass more at home in the wild northern glens than the elegant banquet halls of Edinburgh. As the epitome of Scottish manhood, Moray was the ideal mate for Sorcha. Yet he belonged to another.

But she had already seen the loneliness of her King and kinsman that evening; now another Stewart stood before her, yearning and disturbed. Whatever common strain ran in their blood, it seemed to call out to her own. Even as he pulled her into his arms, she was unable to lash out her rejection.

"Jesu God," he whispered, holding her so that her head was tipped back against his arm, "could you ever love me?"

Sorcha felt numb. "I don't know what love is." The black hair had tumbled from its net, reaching halfway to the floor. Her breath came rapidly through parted lips; the green eyes were wide and questioning. If Moray could rouse her senses, then perhaps she could break the spell Gavin Napier had cast upon her.

She sensed his hesitation before he lifted her high in his arms. Sorcha felt herself being carried down the corridor, and watched over Moray's shoulder as he somehow managed to unlatch the door to his chamber. Only a rushlight burned low next to the bed. It was there that Moray set Sorcha down, kneeling beside her on the floor.

"If it were possible, I would go to Jamie now and ask his permission for us to marry within the hour. Alas," he said sadly, "I cannot. I can offer you only myself, my life, my heart, my very soul." He bent down, his cheek brushing hers. "Will you accept my poor gift?"

Sorcha felt the faint new growth of beard against her face and his breath on her ear. "I can't," she all but wailed, struggling to rise from the bed.

"Is there someone else?" Moray gently but firmly pinioned her with one arm.

Sorcha wagged her head from side to side, strands of hair flying about the counterpane. "No."

Moray's brow furrowed. "Napier?"

Sorcha all but bolted in his grasp. "Napier!" She felt her already flushed cheeks turn to fire. "No! There's no one!"

Moray smiled uncertainly. His free hand slipped over one breast, cupping it gently. "You're irresistible. That's your charm, an infectious, earthy sort of magnetism."

Sorcha felt his hand tighten almost imperceptibly around the firm globe of her breast. "Please let me go now," she implored, aware that her mouth had gone dry. "You must give me time."

He pulled away just enough to scrutinize her face. "I can give you time. But the world may not." He leaned down again, to kiss her ear, her temple, the hollow under her eye. The hand at her breast moved to the fastenings of her riding costume, parting the fabric to reveal the creamy silk chemise that strained over her bosom.

The rushlight flickered, catching the russet glints of Moray's hair. Sorcha knew she had to end this madness. But Moray moved with such quiet deliberation, his mouth trailing down the curve of her throat to the valley between her breasts. Still on his knees, he straightened up to slide one arm under Sorcha's body, raising her so that he could strip away both riding jacket and creamy silk. Sorcha waited for his touch to fire her senses, to drive out the image of Gavin Napier. But she felt nothing. "No," she cried as the silk slipped below her waist and the jacket dropped from her arms. "No, no, this must not be!" The beseeching words seemed lost on Moray, who smiled at Sorcha with great pleasure and placed his fingers on the hollow of her belly. With that same sweet determination, he pulled the riding skirt down still further, carefully removing the undergarments at the same time, down over her hips, pausing in wonder at the bold, black triangle of curling hair, teasing her thighs with his fingers, then removing the garments over the black leather riding boots, and dropping them at the edge of the bed.

Sorcha struggled to sit up against the pillows, her brain reeling. She made up her mind: She had to dissuade Moray from folly. It was insane to think that sacrificing herself to any man, however eager or noble, would erase her feelings for Napier. Hot tears stung at her eyes, causing Moray to regard her with alarm. "Sweeting, are you so frightened? Or unwilling?"

"Both." Sorcha gulped and then screamed in horror. Beyond Moray, standing in the doorway, was the Master of Gray. Now bare chested and barefooted, the earl leaped to his feet. Gray was laughing almost hysterically, the handsome head thrown back, fists on hips. But even as Moray reached for his doublet with the courtier's sword, Gray's laughter ceased, and he went for his dirk.

"Stay, Moray, I'll not play the interloper to your ignoble seduction. Next time I'd urge you to latch your door." Gray gingerly tossed the dirk from one hand to the other, a sardonic smile on his lips. He kicked the door shut, and walked leisurely to within a few feet of the bed. "Mistress Fraser, you are ubiquitous. You are also troublesome." Appraisingly, he let his eyes wander from the top of her head to the tip of her boots. "Perhaps worth the trouble to some, but not to me." He heard Moray's sharp intake of breath and whirled menacingly, the dirk only inches from the Earl's bare chest. "I'm in no mood for mirth, contrary to what you may think. Our King has grown fractious." Gray glared at Sorcha. "Who fuels the fires of his independence, I wonder?" He motioned with the dirk. "Come, I shall return you to your owner."

Moray ignored the dirk pointed at his chest and made a slashing gesture with one hand. "She goes nowhere. End your devilish intrusion and leave. At once."

But Gray only chuckled, a sarcastic, insulting sound. "I will take the urchin with me." He saw the refusal settle on Moray's face and pressed the edge of the dirk against the earl's throat. "So you doubt I'd kill you? One James Stewart is sufficient in this kingdom. I'd not hesitate a moment to rid Scotland of the one who doesn't wear the crown."

It seemed to Sorcha that madness gleamed in the Master's eyes. Cowering on the bed, she grabbed the counterpane to cover her nakedness. Sorcha was trembling, from fright and humiliation. To her horror, Moray stepped aside. "Take Mistress Fraser, if you must. But if you harm her, your life is forfeit."

Gray sneered at Moray. "I'm not afraid of your threats. For all of your camaraderie with the King, he loves me best." The mesmerizing hazel eyes bored into Sorcha. "Come, urchin, I'll escort you … home."

Moray lunged with his entire body, catching Gray momentarily off guard; he fell against the armoire but held onto his dirk. Yet Moray had gained that precious second to retrieve his own weapon. He brandished the sword at Gray, forcing the other man's back up against the armoire.

"Get out!" Moray cried, as Gray's handsome face contorted with wrath. "Now, or you die!"

Gray's dirk crashed against Moray's sword. Earl and Master parried and thrust for what seemed to Sorcha like an eternity. Moray had more reach with his weapon, but Gray's advantage was maneuverability. He ducked under Moray's outflung arm, going for his opponent's bare chest. Moray dove to one side, as Gray, off balance, staggered and almost fell. Spinning around, Moray cracked Gray's wrist with his sword and the dirk clattered to the floor.

The Master's glare was murderous. But before Moray could pick up the dirk, the other man bellowed in a voice that made Sorcha's ears reverberate: "Caithness! Aid me!"

The Earl of Caithness hurtled into the room, scarcely pausing to size up the situation. He held a hackbut in one hand, a rapier in the other. Moray whirled on him, but Caithness slashed at his upper arm and brandished the gun in Sorcha's direction. "I've killed men before. I'm not squeamish about killing women." The sullen face was enflamed, as if by some primeval blood lust.

Moray put a hand on his bloodied arm. "Caithness, you traitor! I thought we were friends!"

"Friends are for fools. Gray is my patron." Caithness prodded the earl with the hackbut. "Drop your sword. Or the baggage dies."

Reluctantly, Moray did, the sword falling at Gray's feet. He was about to speak when the Master, again holding his dirk, ordered Caithness to bind and gag the earl.

"Another prank on my part," Gray said with sardonic humor. "Nor can you explain it otherwise to the King without dishonoring Mistress Fraser."

"He's wounded!" Sorcha exclaimed, astonished that she could still speak. "Leave him be!"

"It's but a graze," Moray said, eyeing Sorcha with remorse as Caithness roughly shoved him onto a chair. Secured with his own belt, Moray stoically refused to flinch when Caithness stuffed Sorcha's undergarment into the earl's mouth.

"Ah," murmured Gray, "the Bonnie Earl is quite helpless to save his ladylove." He smirked at Caithness, then turned to Sorcha. "Up, urchin. Once more, we ride by night."

"My clothes," Sorcha protested. "Hand them to me!" She still held the counterpane under her chin, pointing frantically at the riding habit by the bed.

Gray gazed at the garments with apparent interest, picked them up, started toward Sorcha, then strode to the narrow window, opened it, and threw the little bundle out into the night. Sorcha gasped, trembling even more violently. "Swine! If Moray doesn't kill you, I will!"

Gray grasped her arm and yanked the counterpane away. "It's mild out this evening. Come, it grows close to midnight."

"I will not!" Sorcha held her hands across her bosom as she knelt on the bed. She flinched as Caithness devoured her with his eyes and Moray writhed impotently in the chair.

"You will," drawled Gray, who appeared immune to Sorcha's naked body, "or the Bonnie Earl will no longer be so bonnie. Caithness is clever with the rapier."

Sorcha didn't doubt Gray's words. Both were fiends, spawns of the Devil, and there was no choice but to obey. Shakily, she got off the bed, letting the long black hair fall over her shoulders to hide her nakedness. But Gray picked up a cloak the earl had draped over a high-backed chair. He handed it to Sorcha with an elegant flip of the wrist.

"I wouldn't wish you to die of a chill. You may prove useful yet." He grasped her shoulder, steering her toward the door. She cast one last glance at Moray, whose blue eyes followed hers in desperate, miserable farewell.

THE ROAD TO EDINBURGH HAD dried out the past few days, so that a coach could travel the route without much difficulty. Sorcha sat next to Caithness, with Gray opposite them. She could already imagine the shock with which she'd be greeted in Panmure Close. Uncle Donald would send her packing to Inverness, she was certain of that, yet the thought did not cheer her. Moreover, she'd lost Aunt Tarrill's black riding habit.

Moray would no doubt free himself before long, but he'd have no idea where Sorcha had been taken. As for Rob and Ailis, neither would miss her until morning. She cursed herself over and over for dallying with Moray. Nor had it served any purpose—despite the Bonnie Earl's charm and good looks, she had not responded to his embrace.

They had gone about half the distance when Caithness leaned forward and whispered something to Gray. The Master looked dubious, but then shrugged. "You've earned some slight reward. Though we're a bit cramped for space."

Sorcha, who had sat in rigid silence while Gray taunted her during the first few miles, felt Caithness edge closer on the wooden coach seat. Wordlessly, he reached up to unfasten the brooch which held Moray's cape in place.

Batting at his hand, Sorcha swore. "God's teeth, leave me be!" But Caithness paid no heed either to her blows or her words. The brooch fell to the floor, rolling past Sorcha's feet.

"What think you?" Gray inquired lazily. "Pretty duckies, though a bit dark-skinned for my taste."

Caithness didn't reply. His hands engulfed Sorcha's breasts, squeezing them as if they were ripening melons in a Grass-market stall. Sorcha pulled away, but could only move a few inches before finding her back pressed against the corner of the coach. Caithness lowered his head to suckle her breasts noisily, his hands moving to her hips, forcing her down onto the seat. One booted leg was lodged against the far door, the other dangled awkwardly over the edge of the seat.

Sorcha pounded Caithness' head with her fists, then screamed in terror as Caithness shoved her onto the hard floor. Gray shifted his legs and chuckled. "She's fierce, that urchin." Raking her nails along Caithness' cheek, she heard him mutter an oath, yet knew she did little damage. The sullen face loomed above her, his breath coming rapidly. He was fumbling with his clothes and Sorcha cried out again as she saw him hold his stiff, red member in one hand and open her thighs with the other.

"Stay," Gray said casually. "You may yet need Iain Fraser's alliance if all goes ill with Huntly. We'll take no chances of making the wench bear fruit."

"Jesus," moaned Caithness. "You promised!"

The coach was slowing down. "I promised sport, not ravishment." Gray sounded half amused, half piqued as he moved the curtain aside and looked out the window. "Ah, we are at the city gates. Cover the wench up, and if the watch stops us, kiss her into silence."

The moment Caithness eased himself away from her, Sorcha clambered back onto the seat, cape in hand. Sure enough, the watch halted them, and Sorcha caught a glimpse of the Nether Bow Port before Caithness crushed her in his arms to close her mouth with a harsh, wet kiss. She heard Gray casually mention "His Majesty's business," and then the coach rumbled on over the cobblestones. Caithness released her and a few moments later, they came to a halt.

"Our destination is at hand." Gray stood up, careful not to bump his head on the low roof of the coach. The door opened. He stepped into the High Street, holding out a hand to Sorcha. "You recognize this place?" he asked in a low, cheerful voice.

Sorcha put one booted foot on the cobbles. They had gone beyond Panmure Close and the McVurrich house, toward the Lawnmarket. Despite the darkness, she could make out a handsome carving of the Twelve Apostles and the Trinity on the exterior of the house before her. It had been her parents' home years ago, located in Gosford's Close, and sold before Lord and Lady Fraser moved from Edinburgh. Sorcha knew that Gavin Napier was staying there now, a guest of the present owner. She looked again at the ornate facade and desperately wanted to flee.

It took several minutes before anyone responded to Gray's knock. At last, a serving man opened the door a crack, peering out inquisitively.

"We bring Master Napier a gift," Gray announced, as casually as if it were Christmas.

"He's asleep," the servant answered, sounding none too alert himself.

"We have something worth waking him for." Gray jabbed Caithness in the ribs. "Eh, Georgie? Succulent goods, in many ways."

Sorcha flinched. The serving man had disappeared, presumably to fetch Gavin Napier. A withering sense of dread filtered through every inch of her body as she stood silently on the front stoop with her tormentors.

Napier swung the door open wide. His dark hair was tousled. He wore breeks and a shirt so hastily put on that it was not tucked in, and his wolflike face was thunderous.

In one deft motion, Gray tore away the cloak and shoved Sorcha across the threshold. She sprawled at Napier's bare feet, as Gray's words rang in her ears. "Fresh meat from Moray's bed, sir! Your mistress has not slept this night!" And before Napier could step around Sorcha's prone body, Gray and Caithness were down the steps, into the waiting coach, and rollicking off up the High Street.

"Jesus God!" Napier called out. He stood with one fist raised, as if rooted to the entrance hall floor. At last Sorcha whimpered and tried to sit up. Napier leaned down, his face cast in white hot fury. "What is all this?" he demanded. "Are they daft?"

"Please," begged Sorcha, unable to get up. "Help me!"

"Christ." Napier's tone was a shade less sharp. He knelt beside her, propping Sorcha up against his leg. "What did they do to you?"

She leaned against him, surprised to discover she was no longer afraid. "Caithness tried to ravish me." Sorcha started to cry.

Napier let out a foul, garbled oath. He stared at the mass of black hair and the curve of her back. "Wait." Steadying her with one hand, he made certain she could kneel on her own, then hurried to retrieve the cape, which still lay on the stoop. Slamming the heavy front door, he spread the billowing garment over her before picking her up in his arms. Head drooping against him and eyes shut, Sorcha lay all but lifeless as Napier carried her up the stairs. Faint noises could be heard along the passageway, as the servants peered from their doorways to see what was happening.

The door to the bedroom was open. Napier set Sorcha on the bed, arranging the cape to cover her nakedness. Without a word, he poured two cups of brandy and handed one to Sorcha. She drank deeply, coughed, and drank again. Slowly, she felt the vitality return to her body, and with it, rational thought.

"I swear I'll kill them," she vowed, wiping the green eyes that snapped over the brandy cup.

"Caithness is a young fool, and Gray is a whelp from hell." Napier spoke in a tight voice as he lowered himself onto an aged divan. "Will you tell me what happened?" He winced visibly. Sorcha wondered if he was afraid of what she would say.

"I was at Linlithgow, to see the King. About you and Rob." Sorcha gulped some brandy before continuing. "Jamie was kind. He has given permission to you both." She paused, expecting some response from Napier.

It came, but lacked enthusiasm. "Good." His voice was low, encouraging, yet oddly detached. Sorcha felt as if she were in confession.

"I saw Moray later. He … he declared his love for me." She felt her cheeks flush and drained the brandy cup. "I was confused …." Sorcha stopped and gulped. She could hardly tell Napier the whole truth.

Napier waved a big hand at her. "Go on."

Sorcha lowered her eyes, staring into the empty cup. "The earl wanted to make love to me. I tried to prevent him, but …." Her voice trailed away; Napier was rigid on the divan.

"But *what*?" The question was almost bellowed.

"But Gray came. And then Caithness. They attacked Moray and tied him up before carrying me back to Edinburgh. In the coach, Caithness tried to force himself on my person in a most revolting manner."

Napier looked mystified, the sharp features faintly twisted in an attempt at comprehension. "You were or were not violated by any or all of these lords?"

"I was not," Sorcha retorted indignantly. "But Caithness was repulsive all the same."

Napier gave her a brooding, black look. "Yet you are still a maid?"

"I am." Sorcha lifted her chin and held out the brandy cup. "I want more. This has been the most terrible night of my life."

Napier took a deep breath, then picked up the brandy decanter and poured a generous measure into Sorcha's cup. Instead of moving back to the divan, he remained standing over Sorcha, one finger hooked around the decanter's neck.

"Do you love Moray?" The words were deep, a virtual growl, his peat-brown eyes hard and unblinking.

"No." Sorcha shook her head. "By the Mass, I do not." Napier banged the decanter down in exasperation. "You're a chicken-witted wench, Sorcha Fraser! You play games with a married lord and tempt…." Now it was Napier who found words difficult. "No wonder you arrive on my doorstep wearing naught but your boots! What's to become of you?"

Sorcha took another drink, set the cup on the nightstand, and wound the cape more tightly around her. "I shall go to sleep. I hope. I'm tired, I hurt, and I'd like to die of shame. Whatever happens to me next will have to wait until morning." Throwing; a fierce look at Napier, she curled up under the rumpled bedclothes and closed her eyes. She was asleep before Napier could remind her she had commandeered his bed.

* * *

THE NIGHTMARES WOKE HER SHORTLY after dawn: the distorted faces of greedy-eyed men, drooling with lust, groping Sorcha with coarse, hairy hands. She kept running from them, but never quite eluded their grasp. At last, she was falling into endless space, unable to scream, a mute, wingless bird doomed to infinity.

She sat up, shaking from head to foot and not certain where she was. The faint pale winter light made the room look as if it were shrouded in fog until her eyes adjusted and she became aware of her surroundings. Sorcha started in surprise as she saw the recumbent form of Gavin Napier asleep on the divan. He lay on his side, one arm carelessly raised above his head, the long legs extended beyond the divan's edge. His breathing was deep and regular; the rugged features were softened in repose. Indeed, there was a vulnerable, appealing quality about him, now that all the defenses of the waking hours had been stripped away.

The shaking abated; Sorcha got up, keeping the cloak around her, and went in search of a place to make her morning ablutions. A few minutes later, she emerged from the little closet to find Napier still sleeping. He had shifted onto his side and was smiling. For one fleeting instant, Sorcha saw what he had looked like ten years ago, when he had been more lad than man.

Sorcha was wandering about the room, inspecting the sparse furnishings and gazing out the window when Napier woke up. He stretched and yawned, momentarily looking as puzzled as she had upon awakening.

"Do you suppose this was my parents' bedroom?" she asked as Napier vigorously ran his hands through his wavy dark brown hair and stood up.

He shrugged and yawned again. "Possibly. It's the biggest of the bedchambers. Most of the others are closed off." Napier frowned at Sorcha. "We must find you some clothes. The wind's come up."

Sorcha almost missed the glint of humor in his brown eyes. "I must confess, I'm weary of bundling this great swatch of cloth around my person. Breeks and a shirt will do."

Napier nodded, tucking in his own white cambric shirt. "We'll find something. Are you hungry?"

"Famished. Last night I thought I could never look at food again."

"Time is the greatest healer," Napier replied dryly. He pulled a bell cord by the bed. "How do you feel?"

"Better. But I had such nightmares! And I still ache." She mustered a smile. "Whatever shall I say to Uncle Donald and Aunt Tarrill?"

Napier strolled to a dresser on which sat a small mirror with wavy glass. He gazed at his image and scowled. "Tell them only what they need to know." He turned to look at Sorcha. "Gray and Caithness tried to rape you. They failed. The greatest loss was your clothing. That's all."

"My aunt's clothing, that is." Sorcha reflected upon his words. "I didn't tell them about Gray before. I suppose I'll have to mention Doune."

"Probably. But they can't blame you." Napier had come to stand in front of Sorcha, gazing down at the black-shrouded figure with the thick strands of black hair, and the toes of her riding boots peeking out from under the cloak. At first glance, she looked like a wood-witch, with only her face showing. But as Napier's stare lengthened, he noted how forlorn, yet valiant she was—a battered, wounded creature prepared to leave her lair to face the dangers of the forest.

The servant who had first opened the door the night before answered Napier's summons. If he seemed surprised to find her in Napier's bedroom, he gave no sign. The man nodded several times as Napier requested fresh buns, slices of ham, baked apples, oatmeal with cream, and hot cider.

After the serving man departed, Napier began rummaging through the wardrobe. He finally pulled out a costume that included a light woolen tan shirt, brown breeks, and a rather handsome green vest. "Our host is rather short, it seems. Try these." He handed the garments to Sorcha and turned his back.

It was, of course, precisely what she would have expected from a priest and a gentleman. Yet somehow his gesture touched her. Perhaps it was the comparison with the satanic Gray and the brutal Caithness, or even the importunate ardor of Moray, but Sorcha felt ridiculously sentimental. Swiftly, she removed the cloak and put on the garments Napier had laid on the bed.

"I'm dressed," she announced, pleased that the outfit was not as ill suited to her figure as she had feared. "Where's our breakfast?"

Napier turned around, looking strangely tense. "Be patient. We are the only guests at this time." Scowling, he went to the window and pushed open the casement. "We need fresh air. These rooms are musty."

With growing curiosity, she watched him open the other window, then fold Moray's cloak and put it in the wardrobe. He struck flint to light the fire and used a little broom to sweep the ashes into the grate. He made up the bed and arranged the pillows on the aged divan.

"What do the servants do?" Sorcha finally asked with a nervous little laugh.

"Make breakfast, I hope." Even as Napier spoke, the serving man arrived with a huge tray of covered dishes. Moments later, Sorcha was seated next to Napier on the divan, scattering brown sugar on her oatmeal porridge. He seemed less tense but was uncommonly silent while they ate from the teakwood table the servant had set out for them.

"Excellent ham," Sorcha finally exclaimed. "And the buns are so light! Is there more butter?"

Napier handed her a glass-covered dish. He watched with amusement as she chewed lustily on a slice of baked apple. "In all, you are most remarkable. Another lass would have swooned and stayed abed all day."

Still chewing, Sorcha shrugged. "I'm upset, of course." She paused to pour cream on her porridge. "But there is much to be done. Not only must I face my aunt and uncle, but no doubt Rob and Ailis will come racing into town, certain that I've been killed. And Moray is doubtless distressed, too." She popped half a bun into her mouth, then dabbed at some melted butter which had escaped onto her chin. "Is there jam?"

"Honey." He proffered a tiny china pot. "All right," he said with a sigh of resignation, "I must ask the question. Why were you not disturbed that I saw you naked?"

Sorcha stopped in the act of spreading honey on her buttered bun and blinked at Napier. "Why, I have no idea!" She stared at Napier in amazement. "I never thought about it. So much else had happened."

Napier grasped the wrist that held the bun. "Is it because you think I'm not a man?" The words were low and harsh, the deep, brown eyes piercing.

"Oh, no!" Sorcha gasped. She looked away, biting her lower lip. And in that moment she knew the truth: it was not just desire that Gavin Napier aroused, but love. Priest though he was, she had given her heart to the hunter, the man whose grip grew painful on her arm, whose peat-brown eyes could be felt if not met. It made no difference that he had seen her naked body because she already belonged to him. But he must never know, lest he break his sacred vows and send them both to hell. She forced her lips to form meaningless words: "I was so upset. You were my savior from those hateful beasts. Whatever you might do, it would not be stained by evil." The smile she gave Napier was tremulous. He let go of her wrist and turned back to the breakfast table.

"That's so. I wouldn't harm you." His movements seemed heavy as he lifted the cider tankard and poured the murky, amber liquid into pewter tumblers. "Don't tarry if you wish to reach your relatives' house before Rob does."

Sorcha nodded, but her usual ravenous appetite had fled. Somewhere in her breast, where she had supposed her heart to be, Sorcha felt a stone weighing her down. It had been sufficiently cruel of fate to let her become infatuated with a lad who had turned out to be her half brother; it had been demeaning to have been jilted by a callow Highland laird; it was wretched luck to have been enticed by the charms of a married man; but surely no future could be more bleak than to fall hopelessly, desperately, in love with a priest who had committed his body and soul to God.

For the first time in her life, Sorcha cursed the Catholic Church and the devastating misfortune of having been born into its faith.

Chapter 12

IN FEBRUARY, WHEN THE HOARFROST silvered the city, King James commanded Sorcha's presence at Falkland. But Rob had not yet left for England, and both their aunts were suffering from grippe. Sorcha dispatched a tactfully worded letter to Jamie, expressing her regrets and looking forward to joining the court in March.

By that time, King James was headed north on a progress, stopping first at Wemyss. Sorcha delayed once more. His Grace was to be accompanied by Moray, Gray, and Caithness. She had no desire to spend time with any of them. The tedium of Panmure Close was preferable to the overtures of Moray and the brutalities of the Master and his minions.

Moray's innate gallantry had prompted a letter of abject apology, accompanied by an exquisite gold chain with a heart encircled by amethysts. He reiterated his love and spent several pages reviling himself for not being able to save Sorcha from Patrick Gray's cruel machinations. Sorcha, having no wish to encourage him, did not respond.

Ignoring her feelings for Gavin Napier was more difficult, though, but circumstances came to her aid. While Napier had managed to smooth over her return to the McVurrich household, she didn't see him alone after that night. Except on two occasions when Uncle Donald was away, Napier met Rob elsewhere to discuss the preparations for their journey. Aunt Tarrill and Aunt Glennie were finally told of Rob's plans and were both present when the hour of leave-taking was at hand. With great effort, Sorcha had maintained her composure right up until Rob gave her one last hug. Over his shoulder, she could see Napier, the hunter's eyes shadowy and solemn. Or was it sadness that touched him? she suddenly wondered—and promptly burst into tears.

As the two men rode up the High Street, Sorcha let her aunts assume that she cried solely for Rob.

To Sorcha's distress, the days that followed failed to dim her feelings or alleviate her loneliness. She spun out the hours by reading with Doles or playing cards with her aunts. There were long talks in the winter evenings with Ailis, of books and geography and history. Ailis's stolid presence was a comfort, and on rare occasions, she would exhibit a dry sense of humor that made Sorcha smile.

Yet no suitors approached Panmure Close. The McVurrich sons' friends came to call, but they were uniformly and unyieldingly Presbyterian. The mere idea of courting a Catholic lass would have scandalized them.

As the weather improved and the days grew longer, there was more opportunity to go outdoors. Walks along the Nor' Loch, horseback riding outside the city gates, and even an expedition to the sands of Leith helped pass the time.

On a windy April day with fitful sunshine, Dallas Fraser arrived with Rosmairi, Flora, seven trunks, five boxes, and a large sea chest. Iain Fraser and Magnus had sailed to Italy in mid-March. Dallas had decided to visit her relatives in Edinburgh and announced that she and her daughters would join the court as soon as the King returned to Edinburgh.

"He's gone north to patch up some wretched quarrel between Huntly and Caithness," Dallas said, as Flora and Rosmairi unpacked their baggage. "I believe Huntly's sister will wed with Caithness to cement the reconciliation of the two families."

Sorcha blanched at Caithness' name. "Caithness is a vicious beast," Sorcha declared, noting her mother's scrutiny. "I feel sorry for the Gordon lass."

"I don't," said Dallas. "She has the brains of a pigeon. And how do you know Caithness?"

Sorcha winced. "I met him here in Edinburgh. He makes a poor impression."

"I haven't seen him since he was a lad." Dallas flipped her unbound hair over her shoulders. "Yes, I do believe he murdered some people. His father's gaolers, as I recall." She shrugged and began to remove the mauve riding jacket, with its padded shoulders and black-braid trim. "How I wish I'd arrived before Rob left! Do you know, I was absolutely certain he'd never get permission?" She sighed and shook her head. "I'm uneasy. Mary Stuart has never brought our family anything but trouble."

Sorcha could hardly refute her mother's words. She glanced at Rosmairi, who was hanging up a dazzling ball gown of teal satin brocade shot with gold. Rosmairi looked taller, more composed, yet somehow detached. Sorcha wondered if she'd seen George Gordon since the attempted elopement. She was anxious to talk to her sister alone.

The opportunity came that night. Aunt Tarrill had rearranged her guests, putting Sorcha and Rosmairi together, while Ailis joined Flora in a smaller bedroom. Dallas took over the chamber vacated by Rob, though part of her wardrobe had to be stored elsewhere.

"It would appear that our Lady Mother intends to stay awhile," Sorcha remarked as she and Rosmairi prepared for bed.

"She does." Rosmairi brushed her red-gold hair vigorously. "Father will be away until August. I doubt that we'll go home before then."

"Damn." Sorcha snatched her nightshift and put it on over her head. "I'd begun to yearn for summer in the Highlands," she said, her voiced muffled by the shift.

"What? I can't hear you." Rosmairi stood up, impatiently thrusting the hairbrush aside.

Sorcha repeated her words, but didn't wait for a response. "Tell me, Ros, what makes you so cross?"

With brisk, efficient motions, Rosmairi wound her hair into a single plait. "What would you think?" She threw Sorcha a challenging look. "Did you really believe that I'd forget George Gordon so easily?"

Sorcha stared at her sister. "Well … I suppose I haven't thought about it much one way or the other." She saw Rosmairi's cheeks turn pink as cherry blossoms. "I mean, I thought about *you* a great deal. But I hoped you'd dismiss George from your mind, seeing that he was a feckless sort."

For one brief instant, it appeared that the overbright gray eyes would shed tears upon the flushed cheeks. But Rosmairi drew herself up straight and emitted a sharp little laugh. "What does it matter? What's done is done, but that doesn't mean I can't regret it." She moved with unwonted dignity toward the casement that looked out over the Canongate. "I've had time to think since you left home." She glanced down into the street, where a McVurrich servant was extinguishing the light that each burgher was required to keep burning until curfew. Church bells sounded, from nearby Holy Trinity, and farther off, from Saint Giles. Rosmairi turned back to gaze unblinkingly at Sorcha. "I lost George; Johnny Grant threw you over. But it's not the same. I love George." She lifted her chin, and suddenly Sorcha saw less of the lass and more of the woman.

Rosmairi was gliding to the prie-dieu, where she fell to her knees. "I must say my prayers. Good night, Sorcha."

Sorcha tugged the counterpane back and crawled into bed. Rosmairi was wrong, at least about one thing—Sorcha also knew of love. But she dared not admit it.

Rosmairi's nocturnal devotions went on and on. Drowsily thinking to herself that such piety would make Uncle Donald envious, Sorcha drifted off into an uneasy sleep.

HOLYROOD PALACE WASN'T ONE OF King Jamie's favorite residences. He preferred his country dwellings, particularly Falkland, where the hunting was superior. But a king must occasionally live in his capital, so Jamie returned with his court the last week of April.

Dallas had been surprised to learn that Sorcha already had an invitation to court, personally extended by the King. Sorcha, however, was vague about how she'd met Jamie and suggested that they should seek formal permission for her mother and sister to visit Holyrood. Dallas merely scoffed, asserting that Jamie was her nephew by marriage and that she needed no such ceremony.

As it turned out, Dallas was right. While Jamie welcomed Sorcha with considerable warmth, he seemed well pleased to see Dallas and to reacquaint himself with Rosmairi, who had been a very small child the last time they'd met. But it was Sorcha he sent for the next day, greeting her in his chambers just before noon.

"We're to have a tournament for May Day," he announced, piling up a stack of books and haphazardly shoving them onto a shelf. "It will be very dull, with Moray winning all the prizes. But at least it will make the Master of Gray envious. Though," he added, thoughtfully pulling on his long chin, "I dislike it when Patrick is angry. He becomes quite ungovernable."

Sorcha picked up Morton and set him on her lap. "Moray and Gray are both at court?"

"Oh, yes, and at each other's throats like two cocks in a pit." The King glanced out the window, which looked toward the adjacent rocky mount of Arthur's Seat. "Pray tell me, Coz," he asked with a tinge of diffidence, "is your sister like you?"

Still considering the dilemma of eventually confronting both Moray and Gray, Sorcha was caught off guard by the question. "Rosmairi? Well, not exactly. She's quieter. And more sweet natured. Usually," she amended, thinking of her sister's recent change in temperament.

"Ah." Jamie nodded, still in a ruminative mood. He looked at Sorcha with cautious eyes. "She is bonnie, is she not?"

"Aye, very bonnie." Sorcha spoke with a sister's loyalty, though bemused by Jamie's comments. "Your Grace, don't tell me Ros caught your fancy!" She gave the King a teasing smile.

Jamie stood very straight, his face quite solemn. The spaniel grew alert in Sorcha's lap, his ears pricked with apparent interest. "I'm of an age where dalliance is part of my royal prerogative," he declared, then seeing Sorcha's flabbergasted expression, hastened to add, "I mean no dishonor to your sister. Many highborn ladies, including your own Fraser grandmother, have been eager to let the Kings of Scotland bestow ... uh, favors upon them."

"Favors, my backside," Sorcha retorted, then softened as she noticed that Jamie was flushing. "Excuse my capricious tongue, Your Grace, but I can't speak for Rosmairi. And to be honest, I'm somewhat surprised."

Jamie's flush deepened. "You've heard ... tales?"

Having bearded the subject, Sorcha could do nothing but plunge ahead. She felt Morton quiver in her lap and patted him reassuringly. "You've scarcely kept your preference for males a secret, My Lord. Nor should you, if that is your predilection. You are, after all, the King."

Jamie let out a long breath in apparent relief. The narrow shoulders slumped as he flopped down in his chair of state, one leg flung over the carved oak arm. "Many despise me for such perversities. But I've never known the affection of women, save for my wet nurse. Frankly, I always thought *her* a trifle odd."

Morton had grown restive. Sorcha let the dog down from her lap and smoothed her black skirts. "If you seek female companionship, you'll find Rosmairi personable. However, I doubt she'd be willing to follow in her grandmother's footsteps," Sorcha added with a wry smile. "We need no more royal bastards to complicate our family situation."

Somewhat to Sorcha's surprise, Jamie's chest seemed to expand with pride at the suggestion he might father a child. "I shall respect her virtue, yet I find her comely. She doesn't paint her face, though her hair is too long. But then," he added musingly, "so is yours. I've been taught that cosmetics and flowing tresses are lures of the devil."

As if by reflex, Sorcha ran a hand through her own long black hair. "I'm not one for paints and such myself, but I should find bald women devilishly frightening."

Jamie burst into a giggle, the high, piercing sound that Sorcha was getting used to. Clearly, it bothered Morton not a whit, as he shambled into a corner of the audience chamber and relieved himself in a gilded box.

A discreet rap on the door cut short Jamie's laughter. Simeon appeared, announcing that the King had a visitor. Sorcha stiffened in her chair, almost certain that either the Master of Gray or the Earl of Moray was about to appear. But it was Lord John Hamilton, tall, broad shouldered and distinguished in a blue doublet that flirted with the royal purple.

Hamilton bowed courteously before the King. "The tournament is about to begin, Your Grace."

Jamie turned fretful. "Is it to last all afternoon?"

An indulgent smile touched Hamilton's mouth. "Not quite. We'll adjourn before five to a fountain of wine in the courtyard."

"Ah." Jamie nodded in satisfaction, then motioned at Sorcha. "Have you met Lord Hamilton? He is recently returned from exile." The King spoke with a certain smugness, as if he enjoyed putting one of his most important lords in a potentially embarrassing situation.

But Sorcha had stood up, proffering her hand to Hamilton. "I've not seen you in several years, sir. I'm Sorcha Fraser of Beauly."

Hamilton expressed his pleasure as he kissed Sorcha's fingertips, then gripped them firmly in his own. "Why, my dear child, I'd not have known you! It's been so long since I've ventured into the Highlands." He smiled broadly, surveying her from head to toe with his frank brown-eyed gaze. "Who do you look like? Your father's coloring, I'd say, but your mother's features predominate. It's an enchanting combination."

"Thank you." He let go of her hand, and Sorcha bobbed him a curtsy. "My mother and sister are also at court," she blurted.

"Are they indeed?" Hamilton's smile stayed in place. "I shall be delighted to call upon them, as will Margaret. My wife is very fond of your Lady Mother." He turned back to the King, who was clearly bored by the entire exchange. "Shall we go, Your Grace?"

Jamie went, with Hamilton following, and Sorcha was left standing alone in the middle of the audience chamber. She supposed she should also attend the tournament, but was even less enthused over the idea than King Jamie. The prospect of watching Moray devastate his opponents and bask in the acclaim of the courtiers was unsettling. Sorcha had been at court for only a day, and already she was restless and uncomfortable. The song of the sea and the scent of the pine called her home, though she knew she could not escape from herself.

SORCHA WAS RESCUED FROM THE May Day tournament by her mother, who had summoned the best dressmaker in Edinburgh to Holyrood. If Dallas had been surprised that her eldest daughter seemed to prefer a two-hour fitting session to an afternoon of athletic competition, she made no comment. At least not then. But after supper, which Dallas had elected to take in their rooms, she dispatched Rosmairi on an errand and sat Sorcha down for a serious talk.

"If you think I've been unaware of the change in you since my arrival in Edinburgh, you're mistaken," Dallas announced, plumping up the pillows behind her on a delicately carved French divan. "I've merely been waiting for you to come to me. But since you've kept silent, I think it's time to discover what troubles you." She gave her daughter a sardonic, but loving smile. "Mothers have a way of knowing."

Sorcha's initial reaction was to deny that she had any problems. Certainly in the first seventeen years of her life at Gosford's End nothing more serious than a quarrel with her sister and brothers, or rebellion against her parents' discipline had raffled the calm waters of her life. Until she'd been jilted. Then there was Niall, of course, and the Earl of Moray. Most of all, there was Gavin Napier. Sorcha's life had been turned upside down.

In an uncertain voice that gathered strength as she went along, Sorcha unwound the tale of her adventures since leaving the Highlands. To her daughter's astonishment, Dallas listened in virtual silence, only occasionally offering a word of encouragement or understanding. It was strange, Sorcha thought fleetingly, how her mother could rant and explode over life's minor irritations, but when it came to serious matters, Dallas was amazingly self-controlled.

She was, of course, visibly upset by Sorcha's somewhat abbreviated account of the carriage ride with Gray and Caithness. And when Sorcha finally admitted that she was in love with Father Napier, Dallas almost dropped her wine goblet.

"Sweet Jesu," she breathed, the brown eyes wide, "that priest! Dear child, you've been beset by an uncommonly cruel fate these past months. Only Moray sounds normal!"

"If being married is normal for the seducer of maids," Sorcha murmured, biting her lip.

Dallas snorted. "It often is. Oh, fie, Sorcha, what a dreadful thing to happen with loathsome Caithness! How sorry I feel for his Gordon bride. If we tell your father, he'll kill him. Perhaps we'd better keep it to ourselves."

"I've considered killing Caithness myself," Sorcha remarked dryly. "Indeed, I'm not anxious to see Gray again. Or Moray," she added on a lower note, plucking at the hem of her peignoir, which she'd put on after the fitting session. "I like Moray," Sorcha said, looking somewhat confused, "but I shouldn't wish to encourage him."

"Remarkably mature of you," Dallas stated in a firm voice, but her thoughts were already elsewhere. "By the Mass, I wish you and Ros could have more governance over your hearts!" Dallas was on her feet, marching up and down the bedchamber, her rust-colored gown snapping around her heels like the flames of a crackling bonfire. "Fie, why Ros tried to run off with that wretched rodent, Huntly, baffles me! I worry about her." Dallas stopped stomping and eyed Sorcha directly. "And you—I wonder." The brown eyes were speculative but compassionate.

Sorcha looked away and changed the subject. "I saw Lord Hamilton today," she remarked in a matter-of-fact tone. "Lady Hamilton is here, too, I gather."

"Oh?" Dallas picked up a slim silver vase, rearranging some errant jonquils. "It's been a long time since I've seen them. John was sent packing with the other Lords of the Congregation when Arran assumed influence and stole both lands and title from John's brother, James. Of course," she went on, placing the vase back down on a marble-topped table, "James has been quite mad for years. I trust John is using Gray's influence with the King to set matters aright."

"Lord Hamilton has always seemed like a kindly man," Sorcha said, wondering if such a breed truly existed. "I remember when he and Father took us fishing in Glen Urquhart."

A reminiscent smile touched Dallas's lips. "Ah, so do I. Ros developed a stomach complaint and Margaret Hamilton talked of nothing but the children she'd born by her first husband, the Earl of Cassilis. The woman has a penchant for bed-wetting anecdotes. Still, it will be pleasant to see her. And John." Dallas was at the dressing table, sorting through a jewelry case. For Sorcha, it was a comforting sight. She felt better for pouring out her problems to her mother. Yet Sorcha knew that even her resourceful mother could not resolve the problem of Father Napier. No one could do that; it was up to Sorcha to find an answer for herself.

ROSMAIRI HAD GONE HUNTING WITH the King. Her aversion to the kill had evoked resistance, which Jamie mistook for maidenly modesty. But Sorcha had argued that Jamie was in dire need of female companionship. If only to help him break the spell of such unnatural beings as the Master of Gray, Rosmairi must accept the royal invitation.

"She insists I should have gone instead," Sorcha told her mother as they strolled the gardens of Holyrood on a fine May morning. "In truth, I wasn't asked."

Dallas smiled at her elder daughter. "Nor was I, but they'll spend most of their time seeking game instead of killing it. No wonder the King, with his love of the hunt, prefers his residences outside the city."

Sorcha concurred, though she suspected that the royal party would go no farther than Hunter's Bog and Salisbury Craigs, which lay not far from Holyrood. Even now, she and Dallas were heading in the same direction, with Saint Margaret's Loch just ahead. The area was part of the royal park that Jamie's—and Sorcha's—grandfather, James V, had converted into a hunting area. Guarded at one end by the rocky mound of Arthur's Seat, and Saint Anthony's Chapel at the other, it had also provided Queen Mary with many hours of sport during her brief reign. For Dallas, their stroll was evocative, taking her back in time to the years she had spent serving Mary Stuart, a bittersweet time of political betrayal and the discovery of love for Iain Fraser.

"Sweet Jesu," Dallas mused, glancing back toward the gray stones of the palace, "such memories!" She drew a deep breath, as if savoring those far-off days in the air itself. Sorcha expected a wealth of oft-told stories to tumble from her mother's lips, but instead Dallas spoke of the present. "I've been meaning to tell you," she said in a brisk, yet unnatural tone, "that Niall sailed with your father and Magnus. Your sire hopes it is a way of … making amends."

Ignoring her mother's inquiring sidelong glance, Sorcha said nothing. She was glad for Niall, but somehow their brief romantic interlude seemed as long ago as her mother's reminiscences.

Yet the past suddenly merged into the present as Sorcha looked up to see Lord John Hamilton, who had strolled out along the edge of Saint Margaret's Loch with his young wife.

Both Hamiltons smiled broadly as they recognized Dallas. Lord John held out his arms in greeting, and Dallas embraced him warmly. She kissed Margaret on both cheeks, then brought Sorcha forward.

"How she has grown!" Margaret exclaimed. "My good husband told me he'd seen her here at Holyrood, no longer a wee bairn but a bonnie lass." Margaret Hamilton was in her thirties, a ruddy-complexioned redhead with a boyish figure and a radiant smile.

As her elders turned their talk to Hamilton's exile, Iain Fraser's commercial ventures, and whose kinfolk had married whom, Sorcha grew bored. Discreetly withdrawing, she wandered off to seek the shade of birches that grew close to Saint Anthony's Well. Sitting down on a grassy mound, with a view of the small chapel to her right, Sorcha picked off a buttercup and wished the heavy feeling inside her breast would go away. She managed to mask her longing well enough during the day, but at night, alone in the dark, she felt lost and empty. The worst time was upon awakening, when her wits were still dulled by sleep and it would take a few slow, agonizing moments to remember that Gavin Napier was gone, perhaps forever.

"Have you made a wish in the well?" The pleasant voice came from behind Sorcha, but there was no mistaking its owner. Slowly, she turned to see the Earl of Moray, attired in hunting garb and leading a sorrel gelding. When Sorcha didn't reply at once, Moray tethered the horse to a sapling and spoke with less than his usual assurance: "My mount went lame while we pursued a deer in the direction of Crow Hill. I decided to return to Holyrood this way."

Getting to her feet, Sorcha tossed the buttercup aside and shook out her skirts. "Your horse is a fine animal," she said without emotion. "How did it become lame?"

"I'm not certain. We were racing along between the bog and the hill, having flushed the deer from a nearby copse. Suddenly Stow faltered, so I turned back this way." Moray forced a smile. "Strange that I should find you here … alone."

"Not so strange, since I had an urge for solitude." She gave Moray a stony look, then swiftly strode to the horse, which was munching the long grasses. Sorcha bent down and gently lifted first one front hoof and then the other. "Ah," she exclaimed, "it's but a pebble. Have you got a knife?"

Moray did, and handed the weapon to Sorcha, who deftly excised the pebble while the horse stood patiently, as if aware that she meant to help, not harm. "There," said Sorcha, dropping the pebble at the foot of the sapling and patting the horse's neck. "Now you can gallop again, Stow." She barely glanced at Moray as she brushed past him. "And you may rejoin the hunt, My Lord."

Moray put out a hand to touch Sorcha's arm. "Please … Sorcha, please." His tone was urgent, almost desperate. "I must hear you say you don't despise me for what happened at Linlithgow."

"God's teeth." Sorcha stood motionless, Moray's hand still on her arm. Painfully aware of the sadness in his usually sparkling blue eyes, she turned to face him. "I don't despise you, sir. I respect and admire you immensely. But I don't love you. You have a wife. There can be nothing between us, unless we can be friends. The burden of restraint lies with you."

A faint breeze stirred the birch trees. Stow looked up from the grasses, stretching his graceful neck skyward. Moray's grip on Sorcha's arm tightened as his face grew darker. "Do you think I married for love? I had both of the late Regent Moray's fatherless daughters thrust upon me and was forced to choose one as my wife. I'm fond of Elizabeth; she's a sweet child, but I don't love her. Am I to be condemned to a lifetime of being loveless and alone?" Moray spoke with passion, no vestige left of the proud Stewart or noble earl, but only a young man facing rejection by the woman he loved.

Sorcha could scarcely remain unmoved, yet she hesitated to offer him comfort lest he mistake it for acceptance of his advances. "I don't know what to say," she confessed in a hollow voice, the green eyes troubled.

Moray sighed as he finally let go of her arm. "As you will. But I don't intend to give up so easily. For now, I'll rest content that you don't find me contemptible."

"Of course not." Sorcha spoke more briskly. "I find you most gallant. And—" Sorcha cast about for the appropriate word—"appealing." She winced inwardly as she saw Moray's gaze turn quizzical. "Imposing? Gracious?" Sorcha threw up her hands. "God's teeth, you'd be as fine a man as I know if you weren't in love with me! I feel like a twittering ninny!"

Moray couldn't repress his laughter. "Which is doubtless why I love you. There's no pretense, no guile." Reluctantly, he moved toward Stow, who was still cropping what was left of the grasses in the vicinity. "At least think on my words. You may find the world a more loveless, lonely place than you imagined."

Sorcha saw the bittersweet smile and raised a hand in farewell. Moments later, she was hurrying past the chapel, along Saint Margaret's Loch, and through the gardens of Holyrood with the wind in her hair and sadness in her eyes.

THE KING OF SCOTLAND WAS greatly agitated. He shambled about his chamber, rubbing his temples and spitting even more than usual when he spoke. Despite his youth, he looked old and wizened. "I am sick of them all!" he cried, pounding a fist against the stone wall of Holyrood. "Most of all, I am sick of my mother! Is there no end to her complaints?" He whirled on Sorcha and wagged a finger in her face. "I will not write to her again! Never, do you hear? She has plagued me since I was born!"

Sorcha tried to conceal her ironic expression. "Has she reacted badly to the bond of association you plan to sign with Queen Elizabeth?"

"Naturally." James looked highly indignant. "She feels that the bond will forever cut off her chances to rule with me. God Almighty, I'm a man, not a child! She hasn't reigned over this country for almost twenty years. Nor did she do it well while she was on the throne." He loped over to an _écritoire_, where sheaves of correspondence lay in an untidy heap. "What's more, she constantly whines about her household. Paulet, her latest gaoler, has eliminated several positions. I'm amazed your brother and his tutor weren't turned back. But now, one of her ladies is with child." James flipped up a long sheet of paper and peered at the elegant French handwriting. "Barbara Mowbray, married to a man named Curle." He studied the letter for a moment, then tossed it aside. "Barbara has a sister, Gillis, who is being allowed to replace her. However, Gillis is a timid creature and unwilling to travel to England without a lady of equal social status." Jamie made a distasteful face and shook his head. "Females! Sorcha, why can't they be more like you?"

"I have no idea," Sorcha replied with a little shrug. "I'm an ordinary person, just a simple Highland maid." She pointed to a silver bowl that boasted a design of entwined ivy. "Are those oranges in there?"

The King glanced at the bowl. "Aye, bounty from King Philip of Spain's emissary. Would you like one?"

"How kind of you to ask," said Sorcha, grasping an orange and peeling it with her fingernails. "And you?"

Jamie shook his head. "They give me a rash. Or do I get that from some sort of melon?" He frowned. "No matter, I'd prefer a rash to these plaguing women." The King turned suddenly shy and shifted from one foot to the other. "Will you go with Gillis?" he asked in an anxious voice.

Sorcha had just put two orange segments into her mouth. The green eyes widened and she all but swallowed the fruit whole. "To England? To serve

Queen Mary?" She made no attempt to conceal her astonishment. "God's teeth, I'd rather go to Africa!"

Jamie waved his big, awkward hands at her. "Nay, nay, Coz, it's not so terrible in England. My mother lives in a fine manor house, only recently built, and she's allowed to ride and hunt, and eats well. It wouldn't be for long, just until Barbara Mowbray has her bairn. Or Gillis becomes brave." He approached Sorcha, who was shaking her head even as she devoured more orange slices. "I thought it would be ideal, since your brother is there. And his venerable tutor."

Sorcha choked on the orange. Being mewed up at Chartley with Gavin Napier would be heart-wrenching. Yet such propinquity might dispel her love for him. If she could see him daily, carrying out his duties as a priest—offering up Mass, changing the bread and wine into the body and blood of Christ—perhaps she would be able to still her longing.

"I would like to see Rob," she said in an uncertain voice. "We haven't heard from him since he left for England."

"Correspondence is guarded most closely," James said, looking both hopeful and forlorn. "Truly, I wouldn't let you go if I didn't think you'd return soon. We haven't yet had an opportunity to discuss religion. Perhaps you could remain here this afternoon. The Master of Gray is coming, and the three of us could discourse. He knows a great deal about Catholics and Protestants, having been both."

"On several different occasions," murmured Sorcha through the remaining piece of orange. But the last person she wished to discuss religion—or anything else—with was Patrick Gray. At least in England she wouldn't have to face him or Moray. "Let me think about it," she finally said, giving Jamie's arm a pat. "In fact, I shall go to my rooms and make up my mind now."

"Ah, good lass!" Jamie rocked on his heels in relief. "I'd be so grateful. You have no idea how hard it is for me to keep refusing my mother's requests. No matter how sorely she tries my patience, I still endeavor to be a dutiful son. And depend upon it, when you return, a rich and handsome husband will be yours!"

Again, Sorcha had to mask her expression. She had no illusions about Jamie's efforts to find her a suitor. As for his avowal of filial devotion, Sorcha was unconvinced.

HER OPINION WAS ECHOED BY Dallas. Though she rarely defended Mary Stuart, Dallas listened to Sorcha speak of the King's request with a set face. "He seems to have conveniently laid the burden of his mother upon our family," Dallas noted with asperity. "Surely you will refuse?"

"Can I?" Sorcha asked, thinking it would be much easier if Dallas had agreed to the King's proposal outright.

Dallas resumed plucking her eyebrows in front of a handsome mirror embellished with chunky cherubs. "You wouldn't refuse outright. You'd think of six good reasons why it was impossible as well as detrimental to the King."

"At least," remarked Rosmairi, who had been sketching by the window that overlooked Arthur's Seat, "we'd find out if Rob is dead or alive."

"Of course he's alive," Dallas shot back, and pinched herself with the tweezers. "Fie, I almost drew blood!" She turned away from the mirror to face her daughters. "Rob couldn't be in any real danger, could he? Surely he and Napier have been cautious about their mission?" She saw Sorcha turn away at the mention of Napier's name. "Oh, by heaven, I didn't think ... Sorcha, do you truly *want* to go to England?"

Rosmairi threw Sorcha a sharp glance. Only the previous evening Sorcha had confided her feelings about Gavin Napier. "I think," said Sorcha with conviction, "there are many reasons why I should go. Mostly, I want to leave the court."

Dallas settled her little chin on her fist. "Yes, and so you should, all things considered. Though Chartley may present as many ... complications as life does for you here."

Slipping down from the window seat, Rosmairi confronted both Sorcha and Dallas. "You head for terrible temptation. Will you resist or succumb?" Rosmairi's gray eyes glittered with challenge.

Sorcha exchanged pained expressions with her mother. "Fie," Dallas breathed, getting up and going to a cupboard where she took out a bottle of wine and three goblets.

"As if there were none here?" Sorcha countered.

"How could you love that priest?" Rosmairi cried, waving a hand as if to fan herself. In truth, it was cool for late May, with heavy dark clouds hovering on the horizon and a damp feel to the spring air.

"So?" snapped Sorcha. "Aren't you pleased that my heart's desire is as unattainable as your own?" Sorcha stared boldly at her sister. "You might have better luck capturing Jamie Stewart than George Gordon."

Rosmairi tossed her long, red-gold braids. "I might. Jamie is fond of me. He calls me his 'Primrose.' "

"*Primula vulgaris*," Sorcha snorted. "The scientific name, as I recall."

"You're vexed because Jamie finds me good company," accused Rosmairi, now standing almost toe-to-toe with Sorcha. "You thought you had him all to yourself, the first lassie he'd ever noticed! And now you're chasing after a priest! At least I set my sights on eligible gentlemen!"

Sorcha's eyes narrowed. "Jamie would rather sleep with Patrick Gray than he would with you! In fact, he'd probably rather sleep with his spaniel, Morton!"

Juggling goblets and a wine bottle, Dallas tried to interject herself between the two quarreling girls. "Children! Hush! You're giving me a headache! Have some wine. And sweets. We've at least half a stone of marchpane on the sideboard."

"I hate marchpane," Rosmairi asserted. "Father is the only one in the family who likes it."

"It *is* a great favorite of his," Dallas allowed, all but forcing a goblet into each of her daughter's hands. "Now please calm down. Neither of you has any right to chastise the other, since you both seem exceedingly dim when it comes to falling in love."

Sorcha let her mother fill the wine goblet with a deep burgundy. "I fail to see where intellect plays any part in love. It seems to me it just happens."

Dallas poured wine for Rosmairi, and then for herself. "Alas, there's truth in what you say. But the trick to which we can put our brains is to blot out love when it's impossible."

"And how is that managed?" Rosmairi demanded, taking a sip from her goblet with an unusually reckless air.

Dallas looked blank. "It isn't easy. Perhaps," she said slowly, both hands wrapped around the stem of her goblet, "it's the art of forgetting. With love that cannot be, memory—or the lack of it—is the greatest ally." Her pleading brown eyes turned to Sorcha. "That's why I don't want you to go to Chartley. When you are with Gavin Napier, there will be no way you can forget. I've seen that man, Sorcha, and I know he will break your heart."

Chapter 13

IN THE END DALLAS GAVE in. She had no wish to force her daughter into remaining at court and facing either the Master or Moray. To further console herself, Dallas reasoned that Napier's priestly vows would protect Sorcha from any harm to her virtue. Dallas, however, remained uneasy, though she realized that Sorcha had to learn about life on her own.

King Jamie was elated with Sorcha's decision. A passport had been produced almost at once. So it was, that in the last week of June, Sorcha, Ailis, several retainers, and Gillis Mowbray left Edinburgh.

Gillis was small and dark, with a rabbitlike face that was pretty only when she smiled. Fortunately, she did so often, though usually in a tremulous, nervous manner. Sorcha tried to put Gillis at ease during the journey, but failed. For every note of optimism Sorcha struck, Gillis could conjure up two omens of doom. On the fifth and final day out, Sorcha attempted to enlist Ailis's aid to lighten the pall of pessimism that hung over the little party. But the dour Ailis was almost as gloomy as Gillis, and Sorcha mentally referred to them as the Un-Lissome Lasses.

Sorcha was sorely in need of humor by the first day of July as they rode into Staffordshire under sunny skies. Her relief at leaving the court behind had sustained her through the first two days. Yet, as she drew closer to Chartley, Sorcha became apprehensive. Rob, no doubt, would be delighted to see her. But Gavin Napier, whom she had thought never to meet again, was a different matter. Sorcha desperately tried to armor herself against her chaotic emotions.

They reached Chartley late in the afternoon, a hot and tired group, expressing pleasure at the great house that stood on a hill overlooking a fertile green plain. The surrounding countryside was lush with the promise of summer. For the first time since crossing the border, Sorcha paused to appreciate the gentle, orderly beauty of England. All her life, that country had been the Enemy, the source of so many Scottish woes. She had imagined it as formidably foreign, even dangerous. But after they left the turbulent Borders where men had quarreled and pillaged and murdered for centuries, the land had taken on a less menacing aura. Now, at the entrance to Chartley, Sorcha took in the prosperous, beautiful earth that had nurtured Scotland's ancient foe.

"Somehow I thought we'd be surrounded by dark woods and jagged hills," Sorcha said, leaning in the saddle toward Ailis. "Chartley doesn't look at all like a prison."

"Maybe not," replied Ailis, "but the number of guards indicates otherwise." She gestured toward several soldiers who stood stiffly at the gates. They wore Tudor-green, and for the first time, Sorcha saw the badge of Queen Elizabeth.

A long discussion ensued between one of the guards and Gillis Mowbray's serving man. The Scottish retainers could not be admitted to Chartley, even for rest and refreshment. Woefully, Gillis paid them off as they were directed to the nearest inn. In the morning, they would return to Scotland.

As the gates finally swung open, the three women were met by a somberly dressed man of middle years, with a trim mustache and beard setting off a tight, prim mouth. He bowed stiffly, the black feather on his bonnet dipping low. "I am Sir Amyas Paulet," he intoned in a surprisingly deep voice. "I am told you have come to wait upon the Scottish king's mother." His gaze was imprecise, as if not focusing on the young women would make them cease to exist.

"If," replied Sorcha, perspiring freely under her deep blue riding habit, "you speak of Queen Mary of Scotland, you're correct, sir."

Paulet's colorless eyes flicked over Sorcha with distaste. "We have no queen in residence here, only a vexatious Papist woman who plots against the English throne."

At one side, Gillis twittered anxiously, and on the other, Ailis's mouth formed into a tight line that almost matched Paulet's. Sorcha considered the grim reality of their situation—too much cheekiness might provoke Paulet to refuse them admission to Chartley. Fleetingly, she wondered where Rob and Father Napier were. If Paulet had been notified of her arrival, they probably knew, too.

"We are here to attend Mary Stuart," Sorcha said in what she hoped was an amiable voice. "I am Sorcha Fraser, daughter of Iain Fraser of Beauly. This is Gillis Mowbray, whose sister, Barbara, has been in service here. And," she added, motioning at the grim-faced Ailis, "this is my attendant, Ailis Frizell."

"An attendant for an attendant?" Paulet's face puckered with disapproval. "I was not told of a third person."

"An oversight," Sorcha commented blithely. "Ailis is extremely capable and can do the work of a half dozen other women." It was true enough, and Sorcha hoped her appeal to Paulet's reputed penchant for economy would sway him. Ailis, however, was glaring indignantly at Sorcha from under her thick brows. In the months that she had served Sorcha, Ailis had acted more as secretary and companion than as maid or servant.

"I don't endorse having any of you join the household, if I may speak bluntly." Paulet tried hard not to squint into the late afternoon sun, which made his face seem more pinched and priggish than ever. "But I have received orders, and in this instance, I'll relent." He gestured to the guards to let the women pass. "You will, of course, be searched."

Sorcha turned in the saddle so quickly that her riding hat almost fell off. "Surely you jest, sir! We aren't English citizens, but answer only to the Scottish crown!"

Paulet stood rigidly in place. "Please proceed inside."

For the moment, that seemed like a reasonable suggestion. Sorcha was relieved to be out of the warm sun. As servants led their horses away, she walked briskly into the entrance hall, noting the fine workmanship and handsome appointments. The young Earl of Essex's country home, she'd been told, and decided that he must have inherited great wealth.

"Is My Lord of Essex in residence?" Sorcha inquired with an air of dignity.

"He is in the Low Countries, in the service of Her Majesty the Queen." Paulet scarcely moved his head but motioned to a trio of drab matrons who seemed to have materialized from nowhere. Though one was tall and gaunt, another short and birdlike, and the third of middle height and stocky, there was a sameness about them that made Sorcha think of crows sitting in a row on a stile. "These gentlewomen will take you to your chambers," Paulet announced before making a stiff bow and withdrawing from the entrance hall.

With dogged step, the tall woman led them to a stairway that wound up to the next story. An airy, intimate gallery connected the two wings. The newcomers' rooms were at the far end of the west wing. Once inside, the three matrons stood by the door, with arms folded across their bosoms.

Sorcha took off her riding hat and unpinned her hair before she spoke to the women. "We'll have lamb, with some of those excellent fresh vegetables we saw growing nearby. Spring potatoes, with parsley, and bread. You generally drink beer, I'm told. We'll have some of that. And trifle for dessert." She turned her back as if to dismiss the matrons.

"Supper isn't served for another three hours," the stocky woman replied in a nasal, English accent. "Tonight, it's sparrow pie. Now we must conduct our search."

By the bed, Gillis's eyes darted from Sorcha to the three women. She seemed on the verge of tears. Sorcha surveyed their adversaries and wondered if it came to physical force, who would win the day. She and her companions had youth on their side, but Gillis might simply go to pieces. As for Ailis, she was as trim and fit as Sorcha. Still, Sorcha questioned Ailis's nerve.

That was a miscalculation. The stocky woman had advanced on Ailis, who held her ground and assumed a lethal expression. "If you touch me, I shall gouge out your eyes." With astonishing quickness, Ailis put up her hands, contorted into claws. The woman stood stock-still, staring in disbelief. But there was no mistaking the chilling threat in Ailis's words. She seemed rooted to the floor, like a primeval goddess sprung from a Highland bog.

"We are doing only what we're told," the tall matron said from her place by the door. "Sir Amyas's orders must be obeyed."

"I doubt that Sir Amyas wants a blind gentlewoman on his hands," Sorcha asserted, moving casually to stand by Ailis. "At Inverness, we call Ailis 'The Bat.' " Sorcha smiled sweetly. "That's because she has made so many people sightless. But they should not have vexed her."

Ailis hadn't moved. She still crouched, her grasping hands a scant six inches from the stocky matron's face. The tall, gaunt woman cleared her throat. "If any of us is harmed, you'll all hang."

"Perhaps." Sorcha flipped the long black hair over her shoulders. "But you won't be able to see it."

A low, guttural growl erupted from Ailis's throat. Gillis shrieked in terror, falling to her knees and cowering against the bed. Sorcha threw her a reproachful look. "Oh, Gillis, don't fash yourself! The Bat has never disfigured or maimed anyone unless they annoyed her! Except for Margery MacKim, and that was a misunderstanding. A pity, too, since she was such a fine needleworker."

Sorcha gave the three matrons an apologetic smile as Ailis snarled again. "I'm afraid she's gone beyond my control. Forgive me if I look away. It's quite a gruesome sight."

The stocky woman sucked in a deep, rasping breath. Gillis whimpered by the bed. The tall, gaunt matron exchanged terrified glances with her birdlike companion. Sorcha had turned her back, barely able to stand still, but determined to display an air of calm. The tension in the room was oppressive.

A firm knock on the door snapped the spell. Gillis's whimpering melted away, Ailis stood up straight, dropping her hands to her sides, and the three matrons all gasped in audible relief. The birdlike woman opened the door to admit Sir Amyas Paulet. He surveyed the entire group with cold, probing eyes. "Is the search completed?"

The hesitation on the matrons' part was barely noticeable before the tall, gaunt matron replied, "Yes, Sir Amyas, it took just a few moments once our visitors realized how vital security is here at Chartley."

"Excellent." He nodded in a detached manner at Sorcha. "Very sensible." His hand waved at the matrons. "Come. As always, there is much to be done." The trio followed him out of the room, with not one backward glance.

As soon as the door closed behind them, Sorcha rushed to Ailis and hugged her. "God bless you, Ailis! You're brilliant!" She felt the other girl stiffen slightly and then relax. Sorcha stepped back to scrutinize Ailis's bland, oval face. "Tell me—would you have actually gouged the old hag?"

Ailis looked thoughtful. "I shouldn't think so. I find violence most repellent." She tapped a finger against her cheek. "Still, I was put out."

Gillis had struggled to her feet. "Do you mean," she gasped incredulously, "that Ailis isn't ... The Bat?"

Sorcha laughed and gave Gillis's arm a little shake. "Oh, by the Mass, no! 'Twas all a ruse. And, as ruses go, quite a good one." She smiled broadly at Ailis, whose mouth twitched in droll response. In that moment, Sorcha knew that the prickly, somber Ailis was more than a Fraser protégée—she was also a friend.

ROB JOINED THEM AFTER SUPPER. He was thinner, and his boyish aura had dimmed. But his spirits were good, his humor intact, and his delight in seeing Sorcha was evident. Since Gillis was unaware of his real purpose in joining Queen Mary's household, Ailis tactfully led her out of their rooms after the first few minutes. Though Sorcha's most burning question was the whereabouts of Gavin Napier, she refrained from asking straightaway. Instead, she queried Rob about the Queen and his duties in attending her.

"She is in better health than I'd expected," Rob said, sitting cross-legged on a cushion opposite his sister. "Indeed, she has become quite merry in recent weeks. I spend some two hours a day reading French with her and helping with her correspondence, though Master Nau does most of that, as is his duty. Little freedom is allowed here, and no trappings of the Catholic faith are permitted." He paused to drink from a tankard of beer. "It's far worse than Scotland," he added, lowering his voice. "Someone in the household was rumored to have attended Mass a while ago, and Paulet had him hanged in full view of the Queen."

Sorcha shuddered. "God's teeth, how horrible! You mean the Queen can't receive the sacraments?"

Rob shook his head sadly. "Paulet is a Puritan, more vehemently opposed to Catholics than are other Protestants. I fear he takes great pleasure in tormenting Queen Mary over even the smallest matters. In all the years of her imprisonment, she has had no gaoler as severe as Sir Amyas."

While Sorcha was genuinely dismayed at the Queen's plight, she was still anxious to hear about Father Napier. And unwilling to ask outright. "What of you, Rob? Do you still wish to be a priest?"

Rob brushed at the stray lock of red hair. "Oh, aye, my desire to take Holy Orders has been strengthened since I've been here. The evil opposition fuels my resolve. There is persecution here in England ten times worse than in Scotland. The days of Edmund Campion—God rest his soul—have not fled."

Sorcha crossed herself rather absentmindedly. "Campion … ah, the Jesuit martyr. Poor man." She racked her brain to find a natural way of turning the conversation to Gavin Napier. "If … Napier can't give the Queen the sacraments, what does he do?" she asked, hoping her voice contained no more than ordinary curiosity.

Apparently it did not, for Rob merely shook his head. "There's little he *can* do, save pray with her and meditate. He reads with her, as I do, of course." He gave his sister a rueful look. "You'll find us dull company. I was astonished to learn you were coming with Gillis Mowbray."

"King Jamie was set on my attending his royal mother." Sorcha stood up and stretched, her muscles weary from long hours in the saddle. "When do I meet Her Grace?"

Rob fretted at his unruly lock of hair. "Tomorrow, perhaps. She was feeling unwell this afternoon. Though," he added, setting his tankard aside and also getting to his feet, "I've been told by Secretary Nau that her spirits are much lighter these days because she has been able to renew her correspondence abroad since coming to Chartley."

Sorcha turned skeptical. "And how is it that the strict Sir Amyas permits such freedom of the pen?"

Rob gave Sorcha a tight little smile. "Paulet doesn't know. It's a secret system devised by Nau and someone in the village. The brewer, I believe."

"It sounds most strange," Sorcha said with a deepening frown. "To whom does Her Majesty write?"

"I'm not sure." Rob adjusted his somber doublet. Everyone at Chartley seemed to be attired in severe, even drab, clothing, no doubt in deference to Sir Amyas Paulet. "I've not been asked to write anything but the most official sort of letters. Eventually I may, when I win her trust."

Sorcha began to pace, vexed at the sense of restlessness that was creeping over her. She had been at Chartley but a few hours. There was great pleasure at seeing Rob again, and shortly she would meet the tragic, charismatic woman who had once been Queen of Scotland, yet Sorcha was still discontent. She paused by the casement, pushing it wide open to feel a warm summer breeze touch her cheek.

A single rap on the door made Sorcha jump and Rob turn questioningly. Gavin Napier's muffled voice sounded on the other side of the heavy oak, deep but scarcely audible. Sorcha started for the door, hesitated, and watched Rob glance quizzically at her before he got up to admit their visitor.

Gavin Napier was dressed as somberly as the rest of the household, in black doublet, hose, and boots, relieved only by a thin silver chain draped across his chest. He could not have looked more austere had he been attired in clerical vestments. Greeting Sorcha with a curt bow, he rested his dark eyes somewhere beyond her face. "It seems that our sovereign lady has changed her mind and wishes to see you now. Will you come?"

"Of course." Sorcha glanced at Rob, as if for reassurance. He lifted one shoulder and smiled faintly. "Will you join us, Rob?"

Napier answered for him. "No. Too many would tire her this time of night. I will escort you only as far as her chamber door."

Sorcha couldn't suppress a look of annoyance, though whether it was for the Queen's nervous state or Napier's arrogant indifference she could not be sure. Hastily, she rummaged about in a partially unpacked trunk for her mirror and a hairnet. The mirror proved elusive, but at last she pulled out a wide green velvet bandeau that would serve to keep her unruly hair in place. Her appearance was hardly suitable for meeting the former Queen of Scotland, but then, this sudden invitation was not a formal state occasion.

Nor, Sorcha thought with bitterness, did it matter how elegant she looked as far as Gavin Napier was concerned. She dared not be comely; she must force herself to resist any show of encouragement. If she had been resolute in turning Moray away, she must be ten times as determined with Father Napier.

So ran her thoughts as Napier closed the door behind them and led her down the shadowy corridor. While Chartley's tall windows might fill the manor house with sunlight on a summer day, Sir Amyas's economies didn't permit the luxury of more than an occasional sconce at night. Sorcha imitated Napier's purposeful step as they passed two guards and a pot-boy on their journey to the Queen. Napier didn't utter a single word, nor did he so much as glance at Sorcha. At last, even as she could see two more guardsmen flanking a chamber door near the end of the long passage, Sorcha bit off the question she had vowed not to ask:

"Are you truly displeased that I came here?" She was startled by the harsh sound of her voice.

Napier paused almost imperceptibly before speaking. "Aye." The affirmation rambled out like an animal growl.

Of course there could be no other answer; Sorcha had known that before she asked. So why did she feel that heavy, dull thud in her breast; why had the color drained from her face? She was afraid to look up at the grim, set profile, well aware that it exhibited all the rigid self-control she had promised to show him.

"It was a royal command," she replied with a crispness she scarcely felt. Nor was the explanation entirely accurate; Jamie's self-righteous pleading had been more likely an apologia. But Napier needn't know that. Like her kingly cousin, Sorcha felt obligated to make excuses.

"As you will," Napier muttered, waving one hand toward the mildly curious guards. "Her Grace awaits." He turned on his heel, leaving Sorcha to face Mary Stuart alone.

Over the years, Sorcha had heard the Queen of Scots described in great extremes. She was frivolous; she was plagued by bad luck; she lacked political acumen; she was blindly willful; she was easily swayed; she paid no heed to sound advice. Depending upon individual bias, Mary Stuart ran the gamut from saint to whore. But virtually everyone who rendered an opinion agreed upon one thing: the former Queen of Scotland was a charismatically lovely creature whose charms were either heaven-sent or the work of the Devil. Tall, graceful, auburn-haired, skin like alabaster—even Mary's enemies had to acknowledge her beauty.

It was natural then that Sorcha should almost make the second mistake of her life in failing to recognize a royal Stuart. Yet there could be no doubt that the sad-eyed, sallow-skinned, middle-aged woman who sat up in the heavily curtained bed was Mary, Queen of Scots. A terrier lay on the counterpane, and a lady-in-waiting announced Sorcha in a mournful tone.

Sorcha took a deep breath before dropping to her knees. The hand that reached out to her was stiff with rheumatism, and the lips that formed a smile seemed so thin as to almost disappear inside her mouth. Yet the eyes were bright and lively; the voice held the famous lilting French inflection from the Queen's youthful years abroad.

"*Ah, ma petite*! Another Fraser joins us in our English cage." She gestured clumsily toward a high-backed chair as the terrier stirred on the bed and went back to sleep. "Pray sit. Tell us fresh news of your family."

Sorcha composed herself as decorously as possible in the chair. Swiftly, she calculated the Queen's age—middle forties, younger than Lady Fraser. Yet she looked at least ten years older, no doubt the result of too little exercise and too much sorrow. Sorcha was moved to pity.

"There is nothing much to tell," Sorcha said carefully. "My father is away on a voyage." She saw the Queen's lips twitch slightly. "My mother and my sister, Rosmairi, are at court. Though," she added hastily, "this is their first visit in many years."

"So your gentle brother tells me." A flickering smile touched the Queen's mouth. "Ah, *ma chère*, are there many in Scotland like your father?"

Sorcha could not keep the puzzlement from her green eyes. She saw the lady-in-waiting cast an urgent glance in her direction. "My father … you refer to his concern for your welfare, Your Grace?"

The faded lashes drooped against the waxy cheeks. "Ah, yes, our welfare. From this distance in time and place, we cannot be sure how many care about us."

"He cares very much," Sorcha replied stoutly. "He always has." She saw a trace of color creep into the other woman's face, and continued with more vigor. "I'm sure there are many who lament your fate. And who keep you constantly in their prayers."

It was probably true enough, Sorcha told herself, though her primary concern was to give this pitiful, tragic woman a word of cheer. Surely she must hear few of them, shut off from the rest of the world for so long. Fleetingly, she thought of Jamie Stewart and cursed him for treating his mother so shabbily.

"We wonder," Mary Stuart said in a low, musing voice. "We have so little else to do … except wonder. And pray." As if to prove the point, she slowly placed the tips of her crippled fingers together on her breast and closed her eyes.

Sorcha glanced at the lady-in-waiting, who made a small gesture with her hand signaling that the Queen was not yet finished. Patiently, Sorcha sat very still, though Mary Stuart's eyes remained shut and her breathing seemed labored.

"Better times are coming." The Queen spoke without appearing to move her lips. The eyes slowly opened again. "Your arrival is most propitious." She smiled at Sorcha, this time with greater warmth, and the years receded from her face. "Our fortunes have changed since Rob came. He brought hope and springtime. Now that you are with us, mayhap we'll look forward to the harvest." Mary groped for Sorcha's hand and gave it an awkward pat. "So often your sire brought me good luck. Now you and Rob, *eh bien*?"

"I hope so, Your Grace," Sorcha replied with a smile, though inwardly she questioned the Queen's optimism. The company of any sympathetic newcomers must buoy Mary Stuart's spirits, especially, Sorcha decided, when her gaolers were so odiously oppressive.

A sudden spasm of pain twisted the Queen's face. The lady-in-waiting rushed to the bedside, motioning for Sorcha to move away.

"It's nothing," gasped the Queen, stiff fingers waving the woman aside. She smiled with majestic apology. "Still, it grows late, and you've had a tiring journey." Without further resistance, she allowed the waiting woman to make her comfortable among the pillows. The terrier remained where he was, snoring softly. Sorcha bade the former Queen of Scotland a restful night and curtsied her way from the room.

MUCH TO HER CONSTERNATION, SHE did not see the Queen, Rob, or Gavin Napier during the next few days. Gillis Mowbray was summoned to attend Mary Stuart, but Sorcha was informed by the gaunt matron that there would be no crush of ladies in attendance on the royal prisoner. "You will bide until it is your turn," the matron had informed Sorcha with unconcealed malice. "Sir Amyas's understanding was that only one waiting woman would be sent to replace Mistress Curle."

Sorcha hadn't given the woman the satisfaction of a response. But once she and Ailis were unpacked and settled in their cramped quarters, time hung heavy on their hands. There were no playing cards available, though an aged chess set was unearthed by a surprisingly cooperative servant. Despite the fine weather, they were not allowed outside the manor house precincts. What few books they could find were mostly turgid Puritan tracts. By comparison, Sorcha's stay with Uncle Donald was beginning to seem like a bacchanal.

Finally, at the end of the first week, Rob came to see Sorcha. She was so glad to have him join her that at first she didn't notice the overbrightness of his eyes or the unaccustomed excitement in his manner. For Sorcha, there could be only one welcome explanation.

"God's teeth," she exclaimed as her brother accidentally upset a vase of lilies Ailis had picked outside the manor house, "if I didn't know better, I'd say you were in love!"

Rob flushed as he stooped to help Sorcha retrieve the long-stemmed flowers and restore them to the vase. "Nay, nay. Nothing of the sort." He looked up into his sister's probing eyes. "Why? Do I behave strangely?"

"A bit. You're standing in a puddle of water in your house slippers. Isn't that a trifle odd?"

Startled, Rob stared down at his feet. "The soles are quite thick." He gave his sister a sheepish smile. "Perhaps I seem strange because I've been mewed up so long," he went on without much conviction. "That's why I've come. Incredible as it may sound, tomorrow Sir Amyas is permitting the Queen to go riding. He and his minions wish everyone out of the manor house so that they may give it a thorough cleaning."

"Everyone?" Sorcha tilted her head at Rob. She wasn't satisfied with the explanation about his behavior but realized it would do no good to pry.

Rob nodded, as he searched the cupboards for a rag with which to wipe up the spilled water. "You and I, Ailis, Father Napier—everyone. It should be a fine day."

Sorcha agreed. She wondered, however, if Mary Stuart were capable of several hours in the saddle. But when she put the question to Rob, he laughed. "The mere idea of fresh air and exercise transforms Her Grace. She is already in a state of excitement, choosing which costume to wear and how the others should dress."

For the Queen's sake, Sorcha was pleased. Reflecting on the famous Stuart charm, Sorcha finished tidying up after Rob had departed. No wonder most of the Queen's gaolers had been accused of falling in love with her. Except for Sir Amyas Paulet.

It was Paulet who stood in the courtyard, his shadow long in the setting sun, his head inclined as he engaged in earnest conversation with two other men. Servants, thought Sorcha, leaving the window as someone rapped at the door. Ailis, perhaps, returned with the laundry she'd collected from the washer women down by the moat.

It wasn't Ailis, it was Gavin Napier. Surprised, Sorcha all but fell back a step or two when he strode into the room. "Are you alone?" he asked, glowering at the room in general and Sorcha in particular.

"Aye." Sorcha closed the door firmly behind her. "Rob just left."

Napier gave a brief nod, appeared to consider sitting down, but remained standing in front of Sorcha with a grim look on his face. "Did Rob tell you about the hunt?"

"Hunt?" Sorcha was annoyed to hear her voice sound unduly high-pitched. "A riding party tomorrow, he told me. Yes."

"All right, then." Napier put his hands on Sorcha's shoulders, forcing her to meet his dark eyes. "Now hear me out—you must convince Rob to run away while he has the chance. I don't know how, but you must do it." Napier took a deep breath as his grip tightened. "His life depends upon it."

Sorcha was staring at him openmouthed, as disconcerted by his touch as by his demand. "Why? What's happening?"

Napier shook his head. "I'm not sure. But I do know Rob is in mortal danger."

Sorcha thought back to Rob's giddy behavior. He had denied being in love, but it was clear he kept some sort of secret. A dangerous secret, it seemed, and Sorcha felt the perspiration break out on her palms and her back.

The dark-eyed hunter's gaze still held hers. So did the strong hands at her shoulders. Sorcha forced herself to concentrate on Rob, yet despite the urgency of Napier's tone, it was the physical contact that sent her mind into turmoil. "I can't think," she protested. "I don't know how I can convince him when I don't know what I'm talking about. Why don't you speak to him?"

Gavin Napier let go of her and stepped back a pace. "I have. He will not listen. But he might, to you."

For several moments, she stood in silence, gazing without sight at the bouquet of lilies Rob had toppled earlier in the evening. "I'll go see him," she finally said. "Where would he be this time of night?"

"With Her Grace." Napier moved about the room, going to the window, where the last rose-hued streaks of sunset rode low in the western sky. "It's unlikely you could get word to him this late. You know Sir Amyas's curfew is very strict."

The green eyes were curious. "How is it that you're abroad. Father Napier?"

For a moment, Napier didn't respond. Then he pointed to his boots which were covered with dust. "I've been further abroad than you might guess. Don't ask more questions, mistress. Tomorrow, just do what you must to get Rob away from here. Go with him, if need be."

And leave you! The question clamored unbidden at Sorcha's inner ear. For the first time, she realized that he might be in danger, too. Without thinking she put out her hands to shake Napier by his black-clad arms. "What about you? Will you come with us?"

Napier's heels locked into the floor. He stood like a graven image, though his stern expression had softened slightly. "Nay. There is no need. Believe me, Sorcha." The last three words were a low rumble. Resolutely, he pulled free, and was gone.

SIR AMYAS PAULET COULD NOT have chosen a better day for the buck hunt. It was high summer, those green and golden days when England sparkles under the friendly sun and winter is no more than nature's empty threat. The party rode toward the moors, where purple heather bloomed like a royal carpet, awaiting the Queen's pleasure.

Rob had been right—Mary Stuart was indeed transformed, her thickened figure jaunty and erect in a handsome, if outmoded, black riding habit set off with bold touches of white and red. She rode at the head of the group, in the company of Secretary Nau and Sir Amyas. Sorcha purposely lagged behind with Gillis Mowbray and Rob, wondering how and when she'd have an opportunity to speak privately with her brother.

"How welcome is the breeze, the sun, the wide horizons!" exclaimed the Queen as they trotted up a hillock toward Tixall. "Sir Amyas, how do you fare? You've been indisposed of late, I'm told."

Sorcha, straining to catch Mary Stuart's words, marveled at the Queen's gracious manner. "I should have hoped the old goat would perish from his lack of charity," Sorcha murmured to Rob.

But Rob gave a little shake of his head. "Scarcely a charitable wish on your own part," he chided gently.

"Paugh," retorted Sorcha, eyeing the broad back of Gavin Napier just ahead. She wished they were riding through less open country, or at least could drop further behind. Nor was Gillis's presence any asset. Sorcha had already suggested that she might prefer the company of Jane Kennedy, but Gillis had timidly demurred, asserting that she would rather keep to those she knew better.

As for Rob, he seemed blissfully unaware of his sister's concern. His mood was lighthearted, though Sorcha noticed that he lapsed into moments of deep thought. Or was it prayer? She was about to ask, when a company of horsemen appeared in the distance, galloping rapidly in their direction.

"Who might they be?" Sorcha inquired of Rob as their own party reined up.

Before Rob could reply, Father Napier turned in the saddle. "It's time," he announced, his dark, now fierce gaze on Sorcha.

Gillis's rabbitlike face paled at the ferocity of Napier's words. He motioned for Sorcha to move closer to him; she obeyed, as if by instinct.

Rob was clearly puzzled as he gazed from Napier to Sorcha and back again. The horsemen were now just a few feet away. Mary Stuart sat tall and majestic on her black gelding, the white egret plumes of her hunting hat drifting with the wind. Except for Secretary Nau, who seemed to be asking a great many questions of no one in particular, the little group had fallen ominously quiet.

With one eye still on the approaching horsemen, Sorcha leaned toward Rob. "We must flee," she whispered in as urgent a tone as she could muster. "Don't talk, don't argue, just ride!"

But the intransigent gaze that met hers dashed Sorcha's hopes for a clean, swift victory. "Don't fash yourself, Sorcha," Rob whispered back. "These men may be friends, not foes."

Rob's optimism was unfounded. The leader of the horsemen, an imposing figure wearing the badge of Elizabeth Tudor, dismounted and walked quickly toward Mary Stuart. Sir Amyas Paulet introduced him formally as Sir Thomas Gorges, Queen Elizabeth's emissary. Sorcha's hands froze on the reins, and Thisbe seemed to shudder beneath her as Gorges made his ringing, damning announcement.

"Madame, the Queen, my mistress, finds it very strange that you, contrary to the pact and engagement made between you, should have conspired against her and her state, a thing which she could not have believed had she not seen proofs of it with her own eyes and known it for certain."

For once Mary Stuart's royal aplomb deserted her. Turning to Nau and gesturing freely, she protested Gorges's words. "My royal cousin must be mistaken! Surely I am the victim of malicious gossip!" Mary stared at the implacable Paulet and the stalwart Gorges. "There must be a wicked plot afoot, dressed in lies and riddled with innuendo!"

"There is no mistake," Gorges declared in brusque, even tones. "You will come with us, and your servants will be taken away, since they are as involved as yourself in this vile scheme against our sovereign lady."

"Now!" hissed Sorcha, wheeling Thisbe around and rapidly spurring her to a gallop.

Rob sat as if paralyzed, then followed his sister, their mounts plunging through the heather, voices shouting out to them on the clear summer air. Sorcha's plum-colored riding hat blew off, her skirts whipped at her legs, and Thisbe broke into a sweat. Rob and his horse were right behind, but three riders were in close pursuit. Daring a backward glance, Sorcha saw that one of them was Gavin Napier.

Seconds later, Sorcha heard the scream of horses and the thudding of bodies. Curses rent the air, then Napier's cry resounded like summer thunder: "Don't stop! Ride on!"

Against her will, Sorcha obeyed. But again she looked over her shoulder, glimpsing a frenzy of activity among the purple heather. Two of the horses and all three men were down, though one of the riders appeared to be very still. Sorcha couldn't be certain, but she thought the third man and Napier were grappling on the ground.

Sorcha had no idea how long or how far they rode. At last they came to a copse and slowed their horses to a walk. "God's teeth," gasped Sorcha, as winded as Thisbe, "I can't guess what's happening. Or perhaps I can," she added, taking several deep gulping breaths and turning to Rob, whose face dripped with perspiration. "All I know is that you must head for Scotland."

"I can't!" Rob slapped angrily at the stray lock of red hair. "I can't desert Her Grace! Not now!"

Sorcha reined up Thisbe, wishing there were a stream or pond nearby. The sunlight filtered through the beech trees, dappling the mare's sweaty flanks. "Don't be a fool, Rob." Sorcha tried to keep the fear from her voice. "It's not just you I'm thinking of—it's all of our family. What will King Jamie do if he learns you've plotted to free his mother?"

Rob's mouth was set in a stubborn line. "He's a heretic usurper. Queen Mary is our true sovereign."

Sorcha shook her head. Secretly, she gauged that Jamie would do little more to his Fraser kin than wave his hands in dismay over Rob's defection. But bending the truth would sit far more lightly on Sorcha's conscience than a dead brother. "That weakling king of ours is under the Master of Gray's thumb. And Gray hates me." That much was true. She saw the first flicker of misgiving on Rob's flushed, perspiring face. "You know that. Nor do we have the old Gordon alliance to fall back on. Would you sacrifice our family for an aged and infirm relic like Mary Stuart? Our sire would not."

Rob, still panting, wiped his face with his sleeve. Sorcha's cruel words about the Queen rankled, yet he had to acknowledge his sister's perspicacity.

"Sweet Jesu." Rob spoke low, his hand covering his eyes. "How can I leave Her Grace?"

"Paugh, Rob, she has made her own fate, whatever it is to be." Yet even as she spoke, Sorcha felt a pang of compassion for the poor Queen, caught in a deadly trap. "We Frasers have always stood together in time of trouble, you know that. Will you let Mary Stuart once more play havoc with our clan?"

Rob gazed up through the trees, squinting against the morning sun. At last he looked again at Sorcha. "Will you come, too?"

Sorcha sat very still in the saddle. There was no question but that she should ride away with Rob. It might be the only chance she'd have to escape for some time, perhaps forever. A tingling of fear crept along her spine as Thisbe pawed at the ground and whinnied softly.

"No, Rob." Sorcha saw him start to contradict her, but she held up a gloved hand. "I must stay to defend you. And I can do it honestly, since I've no idea why you're in trouble." Recognizing that he was about to interrupt her, she waved the hand at him with vehemence. "There is Ailis, as well. I can't leave her to fend for herself. Nothing will happen to me—whatever has transpired cannot touch me. I haven't been at Chartley long enough. And I came with King Jamie's blessing."

Rob let his mount wander for a few yards to crop at the patches of short grass. The flush had faded from Rob's face, which now wore a resigned expression. He nodded over his shoulder. "And Father Napier? What about him?"

Sorcha straightened her shoulders. "Father Napier can take care of himself." She spoke the words with authority, yet the pang of fear twisted inside her rib cage. "Is he ... involved?"

"No." Rob looked away, gray eyes cast down toward the ground. "I still don't understand what's happened. It all seemed so ... certain."

"Most things in life are not." Sorcha gave her brother a wry smile. "I learned that much from Johnny Grant. Now ride away, Rob, or I'll take the crop to your horse myself."

Reluctantly, Rob guided his mount close to Thisbe. He leaned from the saddle to give Sorcha a tight, loving hug. "God help us." He chuckled. "I don't know whether I fear Queen Elizabeth's wrath more than I do our Lady Mother's if she learns about all this."

"I told you, I'm safer here than you're going to be there." Sorcha smiled as Rob adjusted his riding habit and patted his horse's neck. "Godspeed, Rob. You go with my prayers."

Her brother turned again in the saddle, blew her a kiss, tried to keep the distress from his eyes, and urged his horse into a trot. Sorcha watched him until he was swallowed up by the leafed-out trees, with only the echoing sound of hooves serving as counterpoint to the summer wind's stately song.

"Oh, Thisbe," murmured Sorcha, "I would to God we'd all stayed in the Highlands." With some annoyance, she brushed at a tear which had trickled onto her cheek.

The sun was at her right, halfway in its path to midday. Chartley must lie to the west. Sorcha had just guided Thisbe in what seemed to be the right direction, when Gavin Napier came plunging through the copse on foot.

"God's teeth!" exclaimed Sorcha, "you frightened me!" With trembling hands, she urged Thisbe to stand still and dismounted without waiting for Napier's assistance. "By the Virgin, I wish someone would tell me what's happening this fine summer morn!"

Napier brushed impatiently at a dead branch that clung to one sleeve. There was a bruise on his cheek, and his right knuckles were badly skinned. Yet despite his disheveled appearance, he appeared exhilarated. Sorcha had seen the expression on stable boys after a particularly exuberant fistfight. She had also seen it on the faces of her father and brothers, depending upon which one had emerged victorious from some sporting event.

"Rob is gone?" Napier was actually smiling through the dark beard. He saw Sorcha nod, and his wide shoulders relaxed. "Praise God." The smile faded. "And you? Why didn't you join him?"

Sorcha was tempted to tell Napier the truth. *Because I want to stay with you. Because I want to make sure nothing horrible happens to you. Because I love you, Gavin Napier, priest or not.* Instead, she merely brushed the long black hair away from her forehead and lifted one slim shoulder. "I couldn't leave Ailis. And Rob can travel faster without encumbrance. Where's your horse?"

Napier made a face. "He went lame. I shouldn't have rammed him into the other mounts. But I could think of no other way to prevent the guardsmen from following you and Rob. One of the men was knocked unconscious. I managed to help the other follow suit." Gingerly, Napier touched his skinned knuckles.

Sorcha winced at the bloody, broken skin. "Where is the Queen?"

Napier shook his head. "I'm not sure. God help her. I fear the worst will befall her now."

"Can you tell me why?" persisted Sorcha, letting Thisbe wander at will in the little clearing.

Napier paused, apparently reluctant to enlighten Sorcha. At last, he eased himself onto the ground, leaning against a sturdy tree trunk. "It was a wily trap, set and sprung by Queen Elizabeth's secretary, Master Walsingham." Napier sneered slightly at Walsingham's name. "It would seem there were two plots, but both involved messages sent by Queen Mary in the beer kegs that were delivered to Chartley's brewer. Alas, the brewer was employed by Walsingham. And the correspondence, which was in part exchanged with a fervent young Catholic noble named Anthony Babington, involved the assassination of Elizabeth and setting Mary in her place." Napier stopped speaking and shook his head ruefully. "Most dangerous. And foolish."

Sorcha fingered her lower lip in puzzlement. "Queen Mary consented to the murder of Elizabeth?"

Napier lifted his palms upwards. "So it would seem. But after all these years, she would pay any price for freedom. With a crown thrown into the bargain, mayhap she can't be judged too harshly. At least by us. After all, to Catholics, she is the rightful queen of England as well as of Scotland."

"And this Babington? Was he in league with Walsingham, too?" Sorcha had dropped to the ground beside Napier, heedless of a patch of damp earth near her hem.

"Nay, he was genuine in his wish to rescue Mary and dispatch Elizabeth to her eternal reward. A silly young man, caught up in chivalrous deeds and misguided theology."

"But Rob—how did he come to find out?" Sorcha was so engrossed in Napier's story that she failed to notice her skirts rested on the priest's booted leg.

"It took some time for him to win Her Grace's trust, but within the past few days he had been asked to help with her infamous letters. The plotting has been afoot for some months, and I suspect Queen Mary convinced Rob it was close to fruition. I daresay she thought this morning that the horsemen had come to save her, not arrest her." Napier's brow furrowed as he absently plucked at a tuft of grass. "Mayhap Rob thought so, too. It would appeal to his youthful ideals and religious zeal—as it did to Babington and like young gentlemen in London. By God, our bonnie lady has been the undoing of many a man, from one end of her life to the other!"

The full implication of what Napier had revealed began to creep over Sorcha like a huge, smothering hand. "Jesu! If Rob is caught, he may die for his folly! Will they follow him?"

Napier looked down at the folds of plum-colored fabric that covered his knee and part of his calf. He frowned, then turned to Sorcha. "I doubt that he'll be pursued. He came late into the conspiracy and, with luck, has gotten far enough away to elude the English."

Sorcha slumped against the tree, one hand raking through her hair. "How did you learn of this?" she asked, almost afraid of the answer.

Napier shifted his legs, shaking free from Sorcha's skirts. She felt rather than saw his gesture and was suddenly embarrassed. The priest, however, seemed to pay no heed. "It was all wrong, this flurry of letter writing, though I knew not what it concerned. Here was our Queen, with a gaoler more strict than any she had ever endured—and yet her spirits had soared, her optimism flowed more freely by the day. Finally, when Rob confided that he was helping with some very special correspondence, I knew there must be a new scheme afoot, even though he refused to tell me. He had been sworn to secrecy, of course. But for three days, I kept close watch, eventually discovering that letters were being smuggled out of Chartley in those damnable beer kegs. I managed to slip away the other evening to visit the brewer." Napier paused, fingering his bearded chin. "I misliked the man; I didn't trust him. Call it instinct, but I knew that Rob—and the Queen—were in mortal danger. I also knew his only chance of escape was during the hunt, and that I couldn't speak to him before then, nor could I convince him if I did. So," he added with a shrug, "I had to leave it up to you."

"Jesu," Sorcha murmured again, grateful for Napier's omniscience, thankful for her own powers of persuasion. She turned wide green eyes on Napier, one hand outstretched. "What can I say? I owe you my brother's life."

Napier gazed from her face to the slender hand that almost touched his chest. "You can say your prayers, for him, and for the Queen. Doubtless this means the end for Mary Stuart." He was frowning again, his voice gruff.

Sorcha's hand fell into her lap, limp as a wilted rose. "And what of us?" she demanded in a tone that was surprisingly angry. "Are we to suffer for a crime we didn't commit?"

Abruptly, Napier got to his feet. "You could have gone with Rob. Why didn't you?" He loomed over her, appearing almost as tall as the beech trees themselves. "You don't belong here, after all."

"Nor do you," Sorcha shot back. "You can't perform your priestly duties, and in any event, the Queen has been stripped of her household. Isn't your first duty still in Scotland, mending the rifts between the Catholic families?" None too gracefully, Sorcha also stood up. She almost tripped over an exposed root but Napier didn't offer a hand to steady her.

"Someone with a cool head should remain with the Queen's people." Napier sounded defensive as he once again touched the tender knuckles. "Who else, since Secretary Nau is implicated up to his eyes in this ghastly affair."

"Oh, rot!" Sorcha cried, throwing up her hands. "Those people have been together for years and years! See here," she said earnestly, waving a forefinger at Napier, "we could still ride away to safety. I worried about Ailis at first, but she's really quite self-sufficient. And unquestionably innocent of this matter. Why shouldn't we go, while there's still time?"

The guarded, hunter's look faded from the brown eyes. For one moment, Gavin Napier seemed very young and guileless. He moved swiftly to Sorcha, gathering her into his arms. She had no will to fight him, though she knew she should. His hand was in her hair, as his mouth came down hard and feverish on her own. One kiss, thought Sorcha dazedly, one kiss will not send us straight to hell. Mayhap it's all we'll ever have ....

She clutched at his back, feeling his tongue delve inside her mouth, sensing the surge of longing that fired through both their bodies. If this be sin, Sorcha told herself, then I'll welcome the flames of purgatory.

Napier drew back just enough to look into her upturned face. To Sorcha's astonishment, there was no arrogance, no stern authority; Gavin Napier's searching gaze revealed only an uncertain man. But there was something more, Sorcha realized, the shadow of bitterness, or a haunting memory. She had seen it there before and knew it was a warning. Sorcha paid no heed.

"Why did you stay?" Napier's voice was low, almost desperate.

Sorcha leaned her head back against his hand. Maidenly virtue required that she not tell him the truth; the vows he had taken demanded a lie. But Sorcha's innate honesty compelled her to candor. "I couldn't leave you," she said simply. "Having come this far, I couldn't go back."

The full meaning of Sorcha's words only struck her after she had uttered them. But it didn't matter; they were true, in every sense. Napier saw the thick black lashes dip against her cheeks, the white teeth bite her lower lip, the flurry of long, dark hair sprawl over his arm and her shoulders. "God almighty," he muttered fiercely, "I wish it were otherwise!"

The green eyes flew open. "I know, I should never have spoken! Or let you kiss me or come to Chartley or thought about you twice!" With great effort, she strained away, though he still had a hand at her waist. "It would seem that I am doomed to choose the wrong men in my life. Am I accursed?"

His fingers dug into the flesh between her ribs. "Nay!" He hurled out the word defiantly, pulling her close to him once more. "I am the one who is accursed," Napier asserted, gripping her chin and bringing it within a scant inch of his face. "Don't blame yourself, Sorcha. Nor ever let me blame you."

His words confused her, but it was scarcely a time for concentrated thought. She closed her eyes, anxiously awaiting his ardor.

A few yards away, near a moss-covered log, Thisbe reared and nickered sharply. Sorcha and Napier both froze, stared at the startled horse, and then listened intently to what sounded like approaching hoofbeats.

Sorcha gestured at Thisbe. "Shall we flee?"

Napier shook his head. "Your mount is weary. She'd have to carry us both, in any event." He bent to kiss her temple. "We're too late. But then we knew we would be."

As the horsemen came nearer, she pressed against Napier. "I love you," Sorcha whispered. "It may be a sin, but I love you."

Napier's reply was to hold her so tight she wondered hazily if her spine might snap. Then he released her abruptly, just as a half-dozen members of Sir Amyas's household came into view among the beech trees.

Their leader was a deceptively cherubic man who hissed slightly when he spoke. "You are both to return to Chartley, or suffer Her Majesty's grave displeasure. Where is the other one?" He gestured at the air with his riding crop.

Sorcha started to reply, but Napier stepped in front of her. "He had been ordered home. By King James of Scotland." Napier planted one booted foot in front of the other. "His sister remains, at His Grace's request."

The cherubic man fingered his round chin thoughtfully. The Scots were all a pack of devious, cunning liars. Sir Amyas Paulet and Sir Thomas Gorges had no wish to expend a great deal of effort on any of them, but two of the three proved easy prey. The household guards would not return empty-handed.

Napier was ordered to ride Thisbe back to Chartley, while Sorcha had to endure sharing a mount with a buck-toothed boy not much older than herself. Fortunately, he seemed far more embarrassed by their close contact than she was. There was some good-natured banter between the other men, but Sorcha paid little attention. Her mind was filled with different matters, though she managed to offer a prayer of thanksgiving for Rob's apparent safe deliverance. Now, she must concentrate on her own—but whether she wished most to be delivered from English hands or the spell of love cast however unwittingly by Gavin Napier, were questions she could not answer. As they cantered out of the copse and across the moors under the brilliant summer sun, Sorcha knew that both she and Napier might face great dangers in the days to come. But at least, she thought, with a bittersweet smile, they would face them together.

Chapter 14

MARY, QUEEN OF SCOTS, HAD been taken to Fotheringhay Castle, a dank, gloomy place whose very walls seemed to scoff at hope. For over two weeks after the fateful outing in the park at Tixall, Mary had been confined there at Sir Walter Aston's country house. It was during that fortnight that Gavin Napier secretly made his way out of Chartley and seemingly evaporated into the late summer air of Staffordshire.

After Mary's confrontation with Elizabeth's men, virtually all of the Scottish Queen's attendants had been returned to Chartley. Each had been interrogated relentlessly by Sir Amyas Paulet and his cohorts. Nau and Curle were deeply implicated and carted off to London. Sorcha's obvious innocence of the plot spared her more than the others, though Paulet persisted in his questions about Rob.

"Think you," Sorcha inquired archly, "that the man designated by King James himself to attend his mother would connive at a matter so transparently opposed to his master's best interests?" While her scornful manner annoyed Paulet, the rationality of her words eventually satisfied him. Sorcha was dismissed just in time to help Jane Kennedy and Gillis Mowbray deliver Barbara Curle's baby.

From that point on, the Scots entourage was permitted more freedom within Chartley. Sorcha's first excursion outside of her quarters was to seek out Gavin Napier, whom she had not seen since the day of the stag hunt. But to her cruel disappointment, she discovered that he had been gone from the manor house for almost a week. Sorcha passed through the early days of autumn in frustration and despair. The news that Mary Stuart had been removed to grim Fotheringhay moved her not half so deeply as Napier's disappearance.

"Where can he be?" she demanded of Ailis for what seemed to the serving girl like the hundredth time. Only that morning they had learned that Mary's steward, Master Melville, and a handful of others, were heading out for Fotheringhay. "Surely he would not have gone there before them?"

"We'd have heard if he had," replied Ailis with a squinting stare. "Why do you fash yourself so? If ever a man could take care of himself by himself, I'd set my money on that one."

Sorcha wasn't reassured in the least. "As a priest, he's in mortal danger wherever he goes in England. To make matters worse, he's known as a supporter of Queen Mary."

Ailis lifted her square shoulders. "He's not known as a priest in these parts. It seems wasteful to me to fret over a man you hardly know."

If there was a trace of curiosity in Ailis's voice, Sorcha decided to ignore it. Not that she couldn't trust the serving woman; Ailis was as discreet as she was loyal. But Sorcha couldn't admit the truth aloud—that she was madly, passionately, in love with a priest. She didn't worry about losing Ailis's friendship, but she did fear losing her respect.

"I'm going outside." Sorcha gathered up a light cloak and waited for some comment from Ailis. "I said I'm going outside," Sorcha repeated. "I mean, outside the confines of this damnable manor house."

Ailis looked up from a hairnet she was mending. "Can you?"

"I'm going to." Sorcha's mouth was set in a grim, determined line. Now that Sir Amyas had taken up residence with his royal prisoner at Fotheringhay, restrictions at Chartley had begun to slip away almost imperceptibly. "Don't worry, I'll come back." She glanced at Ailis, who was meticulously tying two strands of gold thread together and not looking worried in the least.

DESPITE HER BRAVADO, SORCHA WAS somewhat amazed to discover that she was at liberty to walk abroad as long as she never lost sight of the manor house and returned by noon. At first, she assumed she would be followed, but after ten minutes in the mild open air, she could detect no one in sight. It made sense, Sorcha decided—the defection of an unimportant lady-in-waiting was of no concern to the English. Indeed, Sir Amyas was still searching for ways to cut back on Queen Mary's retinue and expenses. The previous day he had ordered that her coachmen be dismissed.

It was a fine morning to be outdoors, with a light breeze and a full sun. The newly harvested earth was headily fragrant, the oak trees up ahead were splendid in their full-leafed grandeur, and the beeches beyond the low stone hedge had already turned from gold to flame. There was just enough of a chill when the wind picked up to make Sorcha wonder about the first frost.

She had deliberately avoided the village, as she didn't wish to speak to curious local gossip mongers. In consequence, she had no idea where she was heading, though it was south and east, as far as she could judge by the sun. No matter, she couldn't get lost as long as she kept to the rutted dirt track, which was blessedly unpeopled this bright October morning.

Yet as she rounded a curve, only a few yards ahead, Sorcha saw two figures sitting by an ancient, gnarled tree. Farmers, perhaps, or travelers. As she drew closer, she noticed another figure and several horses off to one side near a narrow stream. As she drew abreast of them, one of the men rose to his feet to join the man with the horses. Sorcha glanced without much interest at the seated figure, who wore a heavy cloak and hood. Idly, she wondered if he—or she—wasn't overwarm on such a fine day.

Sorcha stopped and stared. The bearded face and dark eyes that looked out at her from under the hood belonged to Gavin Napier. With a little cry, she rushed to him and sank to her knees.

"Thank God!" she gasped. "Where have you been?"

He gazed at her with curiosity—but nothing more. "I crave your pardon, mistress," came the deep, smooth voice which betrayed no accent at all, "are we acquainted?"

Sorcha saw the dark eyes twinkle with amusement. And realized there was no trace of the hunter, no haunted, vulnerable, searching gaze in this stranger's face. Nor, up close, was the resemblance to Gavin Napier quite so remarkable. This man was thinner, his features more refined, probably not nearly as tall or as broad when standing.

The other men were watching them but made no move to intervene. Sorcha knew she was flushing deeply, but was too flabbergasted by the coincidence to care. "I'm sorry, sir," she said in apology, "but I mistook you for someone else."

"A very fortunate someone, I'd wager." He gave her a wide, winning smile. "I hope you find him soon."

"So do I." Sorcha didn't try to hide her worry. "I don't suppose you've seen anyone in these parts who looks a lot like you?"

The man's grin widened even further; then it suddenly died away at the corners. "No." The reply seemed abrupt, considering his previous good humor. But the eyes were still kind, and he pushed back the hood to reveal hair as dark as Napier's but neither as thick nor as rich in texture. "Are you a Scot, by chance, mistress?"

Sorcha hesitated, then nodded. "I'm … I've been staying at Chartley." She could see no harm in telling this pleasant man the truth. "I just went for a walk. We haven't been able to get out much until recently."

"Ah." He made a rueful face. "I hear the fair Queen of Scots is at Fotheringhay now."

"That's so." Sorcha started to get to her feet. "I'd best be on my way. Do you head north, sir, or west?"

He uttered an odd little laugh. "We follow the wind, my friends and I." The man's head nodded toward the others, who were conversing easily as they tended the horses. "The one you mistook me for—has he been at Chartley, too?"

Surprised at the question, Sorcha sank back onto the ground. "Aye, but he left some weeks ago." She was wary now, wondering why this stranger should inquire about a man he couldn't know. Unless …. Sorcha leaned forward, the black hair falling over her shoulders to almost touch the grass. "Who are you?"

The stranger didn't blink. "I'm a Scot, like yourself. My name is Adam Napier."

THERE SEEMED TO BE A buzzing in Sorcha's ears, yet it was late in the season for bees. It also seemed strange that it should have got so dark so quickly, since it had been quite early when she'd left the manor house. Dazedly, Sorcha opened her eyes and tried to concentrate on her surroundings. Three men, an old tree, and sunshine. One of the men looked like Gavin Napier, but he wasn't. Except that he was a Napier. Sorcha rubbed her eyes and shook her head.

"You seemed to have had a dizzy spell," said the man who called himself Adam Napier. He was still seated opposite her, but the other two now knelt by Sorcha. "Are you all right?"

"I don't know," Sorcha answered truthfully. "I'm confused, I do know that. Are you Gavin Napier's brother?"

The man laughed lightly. "We are all brothers, are we not? No doubt you refer to a kinsman of mine, one I've not met. Still, if he's in the environs, I'd like to call on him. Did you say you knew where he's gone?"

"No," retorted Sorcha, feeling more like herself, but still light-headed. "I wish to God I did."

The man glanced at the others. "Could he be at Fotheringhay?" he inquired of Sorcha.

"He could be roasting Cecil over a spit at Windsor, for all I know." Sorcha knew she sounded vexed and didn't care. Her life was difficult enough without finding two Napiers tangled up in it.

"Mayhap we'll some day cross paths," the man said, signaling for the others to fetch the horses. "It might be amusing to see a face so like one's own. Especially one that inspires such concern from a bonnie lass." He gave her the wide, winning smile again and kissed her hand.

Startled, Sorcha awkwardly got to her feet. At least she wasn't dizzy anymore. "A fair journey to you all," she said, one hand waving in their general direction. "Wherever it may take you."

"Our thanks," said the man, still smiling. "Pray forgive me if I don't rise, mistress." He uttered a self-deprecating laugh of apology. "I'm lame, you see. I cannot walk."

Sorcha gazed from his covered legs to the other men who were carrying a litter to the edge of the road. "Oh!" she exclaimed with sympathy, "I'm sorry!"

"Don't be," the man said simply. "Better to lose one's legs than one's soul. No one yet has walked through heaven's gate." He bowed from the waist up as Sorcha gave him an uncertain curtsey. "Godspeed," he called after her, "and when you find your Gavin Napier, take good care of him!"

If only I could, Sorcha thought fervently, quickening her step back toward Chartley. After a few yards, she looked over her shoulder before rounding the curve in the road. The little party had started moving again, heading south. Toward Fotheringhay? she wondered—and felt as if she'd spent the last hour in a bizarre, disturbing dream.

ON THE LAST SABBATH IN October, Sorcha received several communications. First, there was a letter from Dallas, stating that Rob had returned safely in body, "though his brain be riddled by earwigs, or so it would seem," their mother wrote with some asperity. Obviously, Rob had told her about his small role in the Babington conspiracy. Dallas would have been outraged, not just because Rob had risked his life, but that he had done it in the cause of the unworthy Mary, Queen of Scots.

Dallas was somewhat less guarded in her wording about Rosmairi. "Her spirits have been revived by being so much in the King's company. Still, she seems unnaturally aged for her years."

The letter contained little else of importance—how the McVurrich brood and Aunt Glennie fared, a few bits of harmless court gossip, and plans for Dallas and Rosmairi to go home to Inverness soon to make ready for the wedding of Magnus and Jean Simpson. Wistfully, Sorcha envisioned the grand ceremony and unbridled celebration. She longed to be at Gosford's End for her brother's nuptials, but instead, she was closed up at Chartley, feeling as if she were in limbo.

There was no direct mention of Mary Stuart's tragedy nor of any reaction by her former subjects. Dallas had been very careful. Nor did she make any reference to Gavin Napier—unless it was a veiled one in her closing line: "God keep you in His tender care, my daughter, and may your journey prove to have done you no lasting harm nor given you unwanted sorrow."

The second piece of communication had come from Fotheringhay: The commissioners who had sat in judgment at Mary Stuart's trial had found her guilty of conspiring to assassinate Queen Elizabeth. It seemed to Sorcha that the verdict was a foregone conclusion. However, there was a rumor among the servants at Chartley that Elizabeth, never at a loss for coming up with surprises, would ask for clemency.

In the wake of that news came word that Sorcha and the remaining members of the Scottish contingent would be allowed to attend Queen Mary at Fotheringhay. Sorcha received this message with ambivalent feelings. If Gavin Napier were neither at Chartley nor at Fotheringhay, what difference did it make where she stayed? Except that upon reflection, she knew she owed the Queen of Scots her comfort and support.

The third and final missive was a brief, jerkily written note from Gillis Mowbray, who had been summoned to Fotheringhay a fortnight earlier. While she and Sorcha had hardly been close, an apprehensive Gillis had wept upon departure.

"The chit writes an appalling hand," Sorcha complained, knowing she sounded very like her mother. "I can scarcely make twixt or tween of this mess."

Ailis glanced over Sorcha's shoulder and snorted. "I can't see it at all. It looks to me like chickens' feet."

Sorcha shook her head. "She hopes we'll join her soon—I think. Truly, it reads as if she hopes we'll join her 'son.' But as she is unwed and childless, that seems unlikely." Sorcha made a droll face at Ailis over the rumpled parchment. "She says—perhaps—that the Queen spends much time with napping. Poor lady," Sorcha remarked, frowning at the note. "I suspect she is exhausted from her tribulations. Oh!" Tapping at the paper with her finger, Sorcha's eyes widened. "That's not 'napping'—it's 'Napier'! He must be at Fotheringhay, too!"

"Well." Ailis's tone was dry, her gaze speculative. "Do we pack and await our call?"

Sorcha felt her cheeks grow warm under Ailis's scrutiny. With unwonted care, she folded Gillis's note and shoved it under the other two letters. "Do you despise me, Ailis?" The green eyes invited candor.

Ailis's oval face held no expression, save for a certain thoughtful set of her small mouth. "No, certainly not. Nor is it my place to question your judgment."

The second statement seemed to detract from the first. Discomfited, Sorcha began to prowl the room. "I don't know how to explain. It's very distressing." Though the misery was apparent in her face, she stopped to regard Ailis levelly. "I didn't want this to happen."

"Mayhap it will pass." Ailis had folded her hands at her waist. In her somber gray gown and matching wide bandeau, she looked very like a novice nun. The mental comparison only made Sorcha more uncomfortable. But, though Ailis remained detached, she was not without compassion. "Someday you will find a fine young laird to wed. Once we are back in Scotland, of course."

"Of course." Sorcha couldn't help but smile, albeit weakly. She was touched by Ailis's concern. Any show of sympathy on the other girl's part was worth ten times that of a less taciturn, more extroverted sort of person. "Meanwhile, though," Sorcha said, unable to keep the eagerness from her voice, "you're right—we had best pack up our belongings."

But the trunks and boxes sat in lonely readiness for all of November and much of December. Summer now seemed long ago, as the trees around Chartley shed their leaves to stand starkly barren against the gray, gloomy skies. Heavy rains filled the moat and flooded the duck pond in the manor house gardens. From Fotheringhay, word came that Mary, Queen of Scots had stood trial. Her bearing had been regal, her composure unruffled, her arguments irrefutable. Not that either matter or manner could change the verdict. It was a question of when, not if, Mary Stuart would be executed.

For the few of her followers who remained at Chartley, the news came as a devastating, if expected, blow. Sorcha was disturbed at the thought of Queen Mary's impending death, but she soon grew depressed as well. With the end no doubt near, it was possible that she and the other Scots would not be summoned to Fotheringhay at all.

Christmas was all but ignored at Chartley. Only a skiff of snow in the morning changed the dreary pattern of the winter landscape. Sorcha had a sudden, almost uncontrollable urge to go home to Scotland.

But at last, on a chill, bleak late December day, word came that all who supported the former Queen of Scotland should make ready for Fotheringhay. Despite herself, Sorcha's spirits soared as she and Ailis headed out with the others on the journey from Chartley to Northamptonshire. Whatever tragic hours lay ahead were all but obscured by Sorcha's knowledge that within the dark, stern walls of Fotheringhay, Gavin Napier also waited.

HANDSOME, STATELY CHARTLEY MIGHT POSSESS its own unhappy memories, but Fotheringhay's menacing towers and the double moat that ran along three sides made it impossible for Sorcha to think the castle had ever been used as anything but a prison.

"Jesu," murmured Sorcha to Ailis as they walked their horses up to the massive gateway that served as an ominous counterpoint to the hulking keep looming over the courtyard, "to think I found Doune Castle ugly!" She shivered in the saddle as the pounding waters of the River Nene beat against the worn stones of Fotheringhay's unmoated side.

If the structure itself seemed inhospitable, the inhabitants of Fotheringhay were even less inclined to offer a gracious welcome. To Sorcha's surprise, she and the rest of the little party were met not by Sir Amyas Paulet, but Sir Drue Drury, who had been appointed by Queen Elizabeth to share the burden of Mary Stuart's captivity.

Drury was a balding, boxlike man with pale blue eyes and a small scar on his full upper lip. He scowled with disapproval when the Scots rode into the courtyard. "This is a most unseemly arrival, seeing as how you were told not to come to this place," intoned Drury, the pale eyes focusing somewhere near the ground rather than on any individual face. "We are at a time when less, not more, attendants are required herein."

Sorcha and Ailis exchanged perplexed glances with the others. "We were summoned here, sir," Sorcha said at last, realizing that no one else in their small party was about to speak up, "by express command of Sir Amyas Paulet. Who countermands his orders, may I ask?"

Drury made a quick shift of his feet, looking rather like a portly court dancer responding to a cue. "That was the original order," he replied, still avoiding Sorcha's gaze, "but a second message was sent the following day. It nullified the original." Drury lifted his chin, now appearing to stare off in the direction of the northwest castle turret.

"Well, we missed it, then," Sorcha said, as a snowflake drifted down to touch her nose. "We left immediately."

They had, indeed, with Sorcha so anxious to head for Fotheringhay and no one at Chartley outranking her authority among the Scottish contingent. Her hands and feet were already numb from the last raw miles over the bleak plains of Northamptonshire, and Sorcha's patience had begun to ebb. Ironically, she was reminded of her arrival at Chartley under a sweltering summer sun half a year ago—and of the equal lack of civility shown by Mary Stuart's English gaolers.

"Come now," urged Sorcha, wondering how—and why—a middle-aged subject of Elizabeth Tudor's would bend gracefully to the will of an unknown Scottish lass not yet twenty. "Will you let us freeze our haunches out here in the courtyard, or may we at least come in to warm ourselves?"

Drury's pale eyes darted in the direction of Sorcha's wool-covered "haunches." He flicked his tongue over the scarred lip and cleared his throat. "Ah, since there is clearly a misunderstanding, we can allow you to enter the castle. For a time, however. Only for a time." He held up one pudgy thumb.

Sighing, Sorcha dismounted and let a servant lead Thisbe away. "Your messenger must have missed us," she said, now on eye level with Sir Drue Drury. "Perhaps he passed by in the night."

Drury still did not meet her glance, seemingly diverted by the flurry of activity among Scots and serving people. "Perhaps, perhaps. Yet it would have been better for you all to have stayed at Chartley. Or," he added in ominous tones, "to have returned to Scotland."

He started to turn away, but Sorcha was at his heels, like a worrisome terrier. "Why? What's amiss?"

At first, Drury didn't respond, but kept walking briskly toward a side entrance between what appeared to be a chapel on the right and a great hall on the left. "Amiss?" Drury all but snorted. "Even now, the scaffold's abuilding for the prisoner." He jerked his head in the direction of the great hall. "All that is needed is our gracious sovereign's word to proceed with the execution. But does that word come? My, no!" Leaning against a heavy, ancient battered door, Drury tugged at the latch and looked fretful. "The warrant is drawn up, we're told. The prisoner is ready, she says. The ax is sharpened, it's said. And nothing happens—except that Sir Amyas gets sick!" Drury threw up his hands in helpless exasperation, the picture of a frustrated civil servant, charged with a duty he was powerless to perform.

Only Drury's words about the scaffold had really sunk into Sorcha's brain. She was barely conscious of Ailis, who had followed them to the side entrance and was looking much put out. The door suddenly opened from inside, revealing the tall, imposing form of Gavin Napier.

It was all Sorcha could do to keep from hurling herself into his arms. Napier, however, seemed as astonished to see Sorcha as she was relieved to see him.

"You came," he stated without inflection, and stiltedly stepped aside to let Sorcha, Drury, and Ailis pass through the doorway.

"You know them, I assume?" Drury inquired peevishly of Napier. "Then," he went on as the other man nodded, "take charge of them. I must go see if Sir Amyas improves. Such a time for ill health on his part!" Drury fussed off down the narrow corridor, the quick little steps again reminding Sorcha of a performer in a court masque.

Aware that she spoke too quickly, Sorcha explained why they had come to Fotheringhay despite orders to the contrary. Napier, leading them in the opposite direction from Drury, nodded once or twice, then headed up a twisting stone staircase to a drafty wing of the castle that looked out directly over the River Nene.

"Our quarters are cramped," he told Sorcha and Ailis, pausing midway in the corridor and fingering his bearded chin. His preoccupation with practical matters provided a more relaxed veneer. "Let me think—you could stay with Gillis Mowbray and Elizabeth Curle." Napier finally turned his hunter's gaze on Sorcha. "I suspect, alas, it will not be for long."

"Then it's true? The Queen will … be executed soon?" Sorcha's voice was wispy in her ears.

Napier nodded gravely. "All is prepared. Though," he added, gazing from one end of the empty corridor to the other, "there is a curious reluctance on Elizabeth's part to act. It makes me wonder, as I did when I followed Her Grace here." He shook his head, and gave a rueful little laugh. "Either way, our poor sovereign lady will die. Unless, as Patrick Gray has hinted to Elizabeth, Jamie intervenes."

"Gray!" Sorcha involuntarily stepped back a pace at the Master's name. "And how does that loathsome creature figure into all this?"

Napier brushed Sorcha's wool sleeve with his fingers. "He has written to the Queen of England, stating that King Jamie will not tolerate the execution of his mother. I think Gray blusters. Jamie will not sever the bond between himself and Elizabeth, not even to save his mother's life."

"I would to God it were Gray going to the block, instead of Mary Stuart!" Sorcha couldn't still her tongue and felt herself flush. "As for Jamie, I am embarrassed for his lack of heart."

Again, Napier touched Sorcha's arm. "So are we all." He glanced at Ailis, who still had her cold hands tucked up her sleeves. "Come, Gillis will see to you. I believe Elizabeth Curle is with the Queen."

As Napier opened the chamber door, Sorcha lifted searching eyes to his face. But the priest avoided her gaze, ushering them into the room with only a brief greeting for Gillis. The rabbit-like face twitched with excitement, but Sorcha was still eyeing the door as it closed behind Napier. So, she thought to herself, here I am at Fotheringhay, and so is he, but what good does it do us? In her frustration, she snapped at Gillis who was trying to lead her toward the fireplace.

"Hold on, let me take off my cloak*" said Sorcha crossly. She saw Gillis step backward in confusion and immediately became contrite. "I'm sorry, Gillis, I'm weary. And cold." She made a vague gesture of appeasement in Gillis's direction. "Nor does the news which met us bode well."

" 'Tis terrible!" moaned Gillis, pushing the settle closer to the fire. "Yet our sovereign lady is so brave and cheerful. She writes her last letters and disposes of what little is left to her and spends much time in prayer. Her chaplain, de Preau, was allowed to visit for a time. Queen Mary is a saint, mark my words," asserted Gillis. Her hands fluttered nervously, as if to excuse herself for speaking with such conviction. "Though who wouldn't pray, being so near to judgment?"

"Aye," agreed Sorcha absently, dropping down onto the settle to feel the warmth of the fire touch her face. As Gillis chattered on and Ailis responded in her terse, unemotional manner, Sorcha stared at the flames, wondering if fervent prayer at the close of one's life did indeed help pave the way to heaven. Burdened with her own sin of loving a man who had taken Holy Orders, Sorcha questioned her right to salvation. Perhaps she could neither bid love to come nor to go. But she had willfully, shamelessly, pursued Gavin Napier to Fotheringhay. Sorcha meant to tempt him—why else had she come? And how could Napier ever love her when she clearly dismissed the jeopardy to their souls? Yet Sorcha knew she could not stay away from him. She was drawn like a river to the sea, like a flower to the sun. And even the threat of hell couldn't seem to stop her.

Chapter 15

THE QUEEN OF SCOTLAND'S CHAMBERS were far more austere at Fotheringhay than they had been at Chartley. Gone was the royal dais, removed by Sir Amyas Paulet, and in its place hung a stark crucifix. The furnishings were old and shabby; the room itself seemed very damp. Nor did Mary Stuart's spirits appear as buoyant as Gillis had described them. Sorcha found the Queen doleful, devoid of energy, and considerably more crippled than she had been just three months earlier at Chartley.

"I have written twice to my cousin, Elizabeth," Mary said querulously to Sorcha and Elizabeth Curle on a dark January afternoon. "I have begged her to end my misery, not for my own sake, but for yours. You are both peaked, Jane Kennedy is unwell, my poor maid, Renée, cries all the time, Gillis trembles whenever someone comes to the door. Father de Preau has been sent away. Yet I hear nothing—Sir Amyas remains ill, unable to bring me news." She paused to wave away a bowl of beef broth proffered by Elizabeth Curle. "Now my household is being further reduced. Melville is removed; so is my butler—who will be next?" Mary moved fretfully in the bed, where she had spent the past two days.

"Still," interposed Elizabeth Curle, "you must eat. Shall I have chicken fetched? Or fresh salmon?"

Sorcha, who hadn't eaten since breakfast, felt her stomach stir with hunger. But Mary Stuart shook her head. "No, *ma chère*, I have no appetite. Nor could the English ever cook properly." She uttered a feeble laugh. "Mayhap that has been the hardest part of my captivity—being subjected to English food."

"Then we should request something French," Sorcha declared brightly, unable to pass up an opportunity to quiet her own hunger pangs. As the

Queen started to protest, Sorcha gently waved her hand. "Please, Your Grace, I insist on having the cooks create a delicacy to tempt you. Please?" She gave Mary Stuart a winsome smile.

The Queen relented, and half an hour later Sorcha had all but miraculously reappeared with broiled trout stuffed with nuts and raisins, slices of sugared apple in cream, and a plateful of honey tarts. "It may not rival Chenonceaux, but it smells most enticing," Sorcha asserted, placing the large tray before her mistress.

"La," exclaimed Mary Stuart, taking one look and falling back among the pillows, "it's very good of you, but I cannot." She shook her head in apology. "Forgive me, *ma petite*, food turns my stomach more than it tempts." Seeing Sorcha's face fall in apparent hurt, the Queen held out her hands. "Oh, dear Sorcha, I mean no ingratitude! Here," she said, pointing at the tray, "you and Elizabeth eat. I shall receive pleasure from watching you."

Sorcha, with visions of apples, trout, and tarts being thrown to the castle hounds, all but snatched the tray from the bed. However, Elizabeth Curle merely nibbled at the food, apparently sharing the Queen's loss of appetite. At first, Sorcha ate somewhat self-consciously, but so sweet and tender was the trout, so crisp and tangy were the apples, so light and flaky were the tarts, that within less than ten minutes, the entire meal was devoured. After all, thought Sorcha, using her napkin to stifle a hiccup, the Queen of Scotland's stomach disorders were well known. In such a time of great stress, it was no wonder the poor woman couldn't eat.

She could pray, however, and expressed a desire to say the rosary. Brushing crumbs from her bodice, Sorcha knelt with Elizabeth Curle by the bed to tell their beads in French. Since Mary was inclined to spend several minutes meditating on each of the Sorrowful Mysteries, nearly an hour passed before they kissed the small crucifixes and put their rosaries away.

It had started to snow by then, persistent small flakes that swiftly covered the ground outside Fotheringhay Castle. Mary Stuart declared that she would take a nap. Moments later, she had fallen into a fitful sleep, and Elizabeth Curle suggested that Sorcha might as well leave.

Somewhat sluggishly, Sorcha agreed. Her digestion was unsettled, no doubt the result of eating too fast. When she reached her quarters, Sorcha told Ailis she wanted to lie down and rest.

"Are you ill?" Ailis inquired with a hint of concern tugging at the corners of her small mouth.

"Nay. Mayhap I'm bored. Where's Gillis?"

Ailis pulled back the counterpane and the sheets. "Tending to the laundry." She stepped aside as Sorcha fell onto the bed, shivering slightly. "You appear flushed. Are you feverish?" Ailis's glance had sharpened as she peered at Sorcha.

"Flushed? Her Grace said I was peaked." Tentatively, Sorcha touched one cheek. "God's teeth, I am overwarm. And thirsty. Is there water or beer?"

"Certainly. Wine, too." Ailis waited for Sorcha to state a preference, but she merely nodded and closed her eyes.

By the time Ailis had poured her a cup of water, Sorcha appeared to be asleep. Yet Ailis noted that her breathing was irregular and her face was a blotchy crimson. Alarmed, Ailis hurried from the chamber to fetch Dr. Bourgoing, but she almost collided with Gavin Napier at the end of the corridor.

With her usual economy of words, Ailis explained Sorcha's condition. Napier told her where she might find Dr. Bourgoing, then headed for Sorcha's quarters, where he, too, was distressed at her feverish state and unnatural breathing.

"Sorcha!" Napier whispered her name hoarsely, then bent to shake her by the shoulders. She flopped about in his grasp like a floundering fish, but her eyelids fluttered open.

Napier grabbed the cup of water Ailis had left on the night table and forced it between Sorcha's lips. "Drink this," he commanded. With a flickering, glazed stare, Sorcha gulped down a swallow or two, then pushed the cup with one weak hand. But Napier batted her away, bringing the cup back to her mouth. "Drink, by God, or I'll pour it down your throat!"

The fury masked the fear in his voice, and Sorcha drank again. With his free hand, Napier searched under the bed for the chamberpot. "Take more, Sorcha," he ordered. "It's dog piss."

Sorcha's eyes flew open, her body convulsed, and she screamed just once before vomiting into the chamberpot that Napier had swiftly hauled up onto the bed. As she retched violently, he held her shoulders tight and relaxed his own ever so slightly.

At last, Sorcha went limp. Napier still held her, but pulled the long, tangled hair back from her face and waited to make sure she was through being sick.

"Was it truly dog piss?" Sorcha whispered hoarsely.

In spite of himself, Napier laughed. "No. I only told you that to make you retch. 'Twas water." Carefully, he laid her back among the pillows and was shocked to see how suddenly her flushed face had turned pale. "Sorcha, what did you eat today?"

Sorcha grimaced at the mention of food. "Trout. And apples and honey tarts. I was greedy." She attempted a smile, but it was a pathetic effort. "I'd had the meal prepared for Her Grace. She had no appetite so I ...." Sorcha paused as the door opened to admit Ailis and Dr. Bourgoing.

Napier rose from the bed to greet the Queen's physician. "Mistress Fraser vomited everything," he told Bourgoing as Ailis went to tidy up. "It was poison, I'll stake my life on it."

Bourgoing's thin face turned grim. "Henceforth no one must serve the Queen but her people." He waited until Ailis had removed the chamberpot, then sat down next to the bed. "Poor child, such an irony that you ate that food! Yet you are young and strong. No doubt Her Grace would have perished." Gravely, he crossed himself.

A trace of color was returning to Sorcha's cheeks. "I don't understand— why would anyone poison Queen Mary when she is to be executed?"

Napier had moved next to the physician but remained standing. "She is sure to be killed, yes. But all along I've feared a treacherous end for her, rather than a public, legal one. Elizabeth dallies and dithers over the warrant. Ever since Queen Mary grew ill a week or so ago, I suspected that she was being slowly poisoned. I also suspect that's why Sir Amyas is ill as well."

Sorcha tried to sit up but failed. Slumping back against the pillows, she gazed in bewilderment from Napier to Bourgoing. "Sir Amyas is being poisoned, too?"

Napier shook his head. "No, no. I mean that it may have been suggested to him that he do away with Queen Mary by other than legal means. His strict Puritan conscience would balk at that. So he took to his bed, claiming illness as an excuse to not carry out such an odious order."

"Then who?" asked Sorcha, realizing that her voice had grown stronger, though her body was still weak. "Drury?"

Napier shrugged. "Perhaps. But it could be anyone who feels compelled to murder a Catholic sovereign or please Elizabeth. The reward, after all, would no doubt be great."

Ailis, who had completed her domestic tasks, came round to the far side of the bed. "I beg leave to inquire. My Lords, why Mistress Fraser became so violently ill when the Queen has not." She turned her myopic stare on the priest and the physician. "Pray enlighten me, if you will."

Bourgoing sighed, bony fingers brushing at the scant gray hairs that grew long across his balding pate. "We can but assume Her Grace was being given poison in small doses that merely weakened her and made her lose all appetite. The less she ate, the longer she lived. The assassin must have decided that a large measure would result in immediate death." He lifted his narrow shoulders in an expressive gesture. "So, this time the poison was sufficient to prove fatal for one already ill. Praise our Holy Mother that it was consumed by someone in good health."

Sorcha gave Dr. Bourgoing a skeptical look. "You may speak thus from not having eaten it, sir. I am grateful to be alive, but not for suffering from a great deal more than acute indigestion."

Dr. Bourgoing had the grace to appear chagrined. However, he reassumed his professional aplomb by way of apology and made several suggestions as to Sorcha's recuperation. "Indeed, by tomorrow you should feel almost like yourself, my child. Sleep is your greatest ally."

Ailis saw the doctor to the door. Napier seated himself in the chair Bourgoing had vacated, and took Sorcha's hand. "We'll not speak of this to anyone," he said quietly. "It would be useless, even harmful, for Her Grace to find out."

Weakly, Sorcha tried to squeeze Napier's fingers. She was trembling, no doubt in reaction to the shock of her close brush with death. "It's horrible … I might have died … What if you hadn't known what to do?" She stared at Napier with huge, wide green eyes.

"Don't think about it." He spoke more gruffly than he'd intended and looked away to the corner of the room, where Ailis was busying herself with the instructions Dr. Bourgoing had given her. "It may be that you would have merely been very ill for a few days."

"But you came," Sorcha persisted. Feeling Napier start to take his hand away, she clung to it as if it were a piece of shipwreck on a storm-tossed sea. "You were *here*. You saved me." This time her smile was real, if tremulous.

Napier smiled back, though there was nothing wolflike in his face, and Sorcha was reminded of the other Napier. She wanted very much to ask the priest if he'd ever encountered the man who looked so much like him. But sleep tugged at her eyelids, and very soon Sorcha was dreaming of the Master of Ness, gliding majestic and free through the tree-shaded glens of the Highlands.

SORCHA AND THE QUEEN BOTH rallied over the course of the next few days. While no one had informed Mary Stuart about her lady-in-waiting's critical attack from poison, Sorcha caught her mistress regarding her inquisitively on at least two occasions. Perhaps Queen Mary had noticed the vigilance of her attendants over her food, or had heard a rumor of Sorcha's sudden, violent illness.

Ironically, Sir Amyas Paulet still lay abed, arms and legs swathed in bandages to cure either alleged gout or, as lane Kennedy put it, "other ill humors." And still no messenger rode posthaste from London with a warrant for the Queen's execution.

It hadn't snowed for almost a week, but graying patches lingered on the plains around Fotheringhay. On a clear but cold late January evening, Sorcha grew restive as she watched the Queen and Gillis Mowbray play piquet. Gillis,

Sorcha noted with some disdain, had no card sense, and was beaten easily by Mary Stuart. The Queen invited Sorcha to play. Unable to sit still, Sorcha suggested that Elizabeth Curle take her place. Asking to be excused, Sorcha exited the royal chambers to wander aimlessly through the drafty halls of Fotheringhay.

Despite Elizabeth Tudor's vacillation, eventually the time would come for Mary Stuart's final scene. It was a subject Sorcha had dwelled on at length in the days since her illness. Once the Queen was dead, her household would be quickly dispersed. Sorcha, Gillis, Ailis, and most of the others would return to Scotland, though some of the French attendants might go back across the Channel. In any event, Sorcha thought glumly as she passed a scrawny tabby cat that seemed to be in search of the castle kitchens, she was almost certain that Gavin Napier would go out of her life forever. It was an overwhelming thought, pressing down upon her with the weight of a powerful fist, unleashing her need for him at the same time that it stifled her soul.

Not that it did any good to be near him, she reminded herself for the hundredth time; yet at least she could derive some pleasure from his presence, his voice, his searching hunter's gaze. How he had reacted to her declaration of love she could not guess. They had not really been alone since that August morning when Queen Mary had been led away and Rob had fled to Scotland. Either by chance or by design, Gavin Napier did not seek her out. It was right, of course; it was honorable. For all Sorcha knew, Napier had been shocked and horrified by her ardent avowal.

She had seen him only once since her recovery, in the Queen's chambers while he read aloud from a tattered book of French sonnets. Sorcha had met his gaze just briefly, as he looked up at the end of a particularly affecting verse, and she could have sworn that the dark eyes bore right through her like twin torches.

A noise made her whirl around, but as she peered about the dimly lighted corridor, Sorcha saw only the tabby cat, which had apparently followed her. She bent to pet the animal but it flew off in the direction of an ancient but elaborately carved door. Unless she had lost her bearings, Sorcha had reached the inside entrance to the chapel. It was no longer used, she'd heard, but she tried the latch, on the slight chance that it might be unlocked.

To her surprise, it was. The door creaked open to reveal a high-ceilinged nave, a handful of rickety chairs, and a sanctuary that had been stripped of decoration. Sorcha jumped as the draft caught the door behind her and slammed it shut. From behind the latticed chancel, Sorcha sensed rather than heard movement. She was about to head for the door when Gavin Napier's voice called out.

"Is that you, Sorcha?"

"Oh! Aye." She slumped in relief and tried to adjust her eyes to the gloom. "Where are you?"

Napier stepped out onto the altar, then descended the three steps to the center aisle. "What are you doing here?" His voice sounded strangely suspicious.

Sorcha tried to move so that the faint moonlight that filtered through the clerestory windows might offer further illumination. "I was … exploring." She cleared her throat and attempted to walk nonchalantly up the side aisle. "I've never seen the chapel. It's been stripped by the reformers, hasn't it?"

"Years ago, I should guess." Napier's words echoed slightly in the empty nave.

Pausing in front of the altar, Sorcha shook her head. "I was about to genuflect. But of course there's no host or tabernacle."

"Nay." Napier stood with his boots firmly planted on the worn rounded stones of the chapel floor. "Why are you not with the Queen?"

Sorcha twisted her hands in a nervous gesture. Their lowered voices sounded loud in the echoing chapel. "I grew restless. Her Grace gave me permission to withdraw." Forcing her hands to her sides, Sorcha gave Napier a sidelong glance. "And you?"

"I?" There was defensiveness in the word. "I come here to pray sometimes. 'Tis still a chapel, after all."

"Oh, well, yes." Sorcha peered upward, as if envisioning the large crucifix that must have once hung over the altar. Yet she could see nothing, except the vague outline of Napier's tall figure on her left. She could feel him, sense him, as if they were already touching. Sorcha shuddered and abruptly turned back toward the side aisle.

"Wait!" Napier sounded an urgent note in his command.

Sorcha hesitated, took another step, and then stopped to lean against an aged confessional. "Why?" She turned questioning green eyes upon him, demanding not a reason, but asking everything of Gavin Napier.

His answer was to sweep her into his arms, covering her face with hungry kisses—her eyes, her forehead, her mouth, her cheeks. He held her with that same fierce intensity she remembered from the morning in the copse, as if he expected demons to try to drag her from him. His tongue delved into her ear, his lips caressed her throat, he buried his face in the masses of her black hair. Sorcha moaned in his arms, digging into his back with her fingers.

Slowly, inexorably, he was lowering her onto the hard, cold stones of the chapel floor. He cushioned her body with his arm, as he lay down beside her. Her eyes now accustomed to the gloom, Sorcha glimpsed the naked passion on the dark, ragged face and let out a little gasp, though whether it was of awe or pleasure, she neither knew nor cared.

Napier pulled at the fabric of her moire gown, heedless of buttons or the small ruffed collar. Somehow, Sorcha thought hazily, I should stop him. But I can't. Nor do I want to. This was not a braw laddie like Niall, nor a debonair lord like Moray; this was Gavin Napier, the man Sorcha loved and wanted above all else.

The flame of his desire slowed apace as he freed her breasts to hold them in his hands. "Oh, my love," he breathed as the hunter's gaze locked with her glittering green eyes, "you are so fair!" Napier lowered his head to the valley between her breasts, then brushed each nipple with his beard and grinned. "Are we mad, sweet Sorcha?"

"Yes!" She grasped his hair in one hand and flicked her tongue over her lips. "I thought you didn't want me!"

"Oh, God!" The words were a groan of denial. "Can you guess the struggle I've endured with myself?" His dark eyes held shadows of secret, scarring conflict. "How many times did I almost flee to France? No heretic ever stalked his prey as you did me!"

The accusation should have stung, even inspired fear, considering Napier's priestly status. But Sorcha shut out everything except her need for the man whose head rested on her bared breasts. "I couldn't stop myself," she admitted. "If it be wrong, then what's right is meaningless."

The shadows seemed to deepen in Napier's eyes. "For us, for now, there is neither right nor wrong." He took a deep breath, and Sorcha felt the weight of him more keenly and welcomed its burden. "There is only us," he averred, "and all else is a sham." Slowly at first, then with the animal intensity returning, Napier mouthed her breast, sending sharp shocks of yearning throughout Sorcha's entire body. She strained toward him, instinctively arching her womanhood against his chest, demanding that he assuage her all-consuming hunger.

He had lifted his lips from her breast to sweep up the skirts and petticoats, attempting to pile them under Sorcha for comfort's sake. But the hard stones could have been a swans-down couch; the only agony Sorcha knew was the incessant throb which cried out for Napier.

There was just a moment's hesitation before he slipped down her undergarment. She caught the shadowy, haunted look in his eyes and stifled a little cry. Did he perhaps not really want her after all? Was he thinking of the sin they were about to commit? Was he unwilling to take her here in the chapel, even though it had already been desecrated by the hands of heretics?

And even as his mouth touched the soft flesh of her belly, Sorcha knew the truth. Her heart, her soul, her whole spirit, soared with joy that was matched only by the ecstasy of feeling Napier's deft fingers probe into her very core. She writhed with pleasure, pressing her thighs together, trapping him within her, then letting go so that he might at last unite them in the ultimate gift of love.

The pain was sweet, swift, and piercing. Sorcha's scream floated up into the nave to mingle with the lost music of forgotten choirs. In that moment, the night seemed to open wide with a brilliant glow, bathing the chapel in light. Sorcha felt Napier flood her with his passion, and she went limp in his arms. He stayed within her for several moments; with the burnished sheen of an unnatural midnight turning their entwined bodies into molten gold.

IN OTHER PARTS OF FOTHERINGHAY and all over England, it was said that someone great was about to die. The brilliant, blazing comet was an ancient sign, and even those who had long ago given up popish ways crossed themselves and closed their eyes.

Chapter 16

SORCHA AND NAPIER HAD NOT spoken until after they left the chapel and were back in the Scottish household's part of the castle. Even then, Napier discouraged conversation. "I hear voices everywhere," he cautioned. "This heaven-sent radiance has awakened the lot of them."

"But Gavin …." Sorcha interjected, as two young scullery knaves ran past them, "there are many things we must talk about. Urgent matters that can't wait."

He put a finger over her mouth and shook his head. "They'll have to. I must go to the Queen. I suspect the comet will be taken as a sign, even by her." He saw Sorcha start to protest further, but pressed the finger against her lips. "No, not now. Tomorrow."

Sorcha couldn't keep from pouting, though she was still so dizzy from the joy of surrender that she couldn't be angry. Half expecting Napier to kiss her good-night, she waited with upturned face, but he merely patted her arm, grinned somewhat sheepishly, and strode away down the hall.

It was just seconds later that Sorcha realized she was practically ready to fall on her face with weariness and repletion. Somewhat shakily, she continued in the other direction to her rooms, hoping that Ailis wasn't awake. If anyone could sleep through a natural phenomenon, it would be the dour serving girl.

But not only was Ailis sitting up by the window watching the dazzling nocturnal display, so was Gillis Mowbray. Neither, however, seemed much interested in Sorcha's arrival. After exchanging a few words with the other women, Sorcha, shielding her torn dress with her hand, hurriedly got into bed.

The whole world could come apart and England might catch fire from one end to the other, but this night Sorcha didn't care. She had tasted love, and for the moment, there was nothing else in life but Gavin Napier.

Nor was she touched by guilt. Sorcha had found more than love in the chapel at Fotheringhay; she had also discovered truth. Whatever dire fate the comet that blazed across the winter sky might portend, Sorcha saw only the promise of hope.

As EVER, THE HOUSEHOLD WAS too taken up with its mistress's nerve-racking dilemmas to note anyone else's troubles. Sorcha told herself that was just as well; until she could unravel the skein of deception that Gavin Napier had wound, it would be much better if they kept the secret to themselves.

Still, Sorcha felt as if she would burst unless she talked to someone. Ailis, perhaps, with her guarded tongue and dissuasion to judge others. Not that Ailis would understand how gloriously happy Sorcha was or the cause for her unbridled joy. Nor would anyone comprehend why Sorcha wasn't in despair over losing her honor. Certainly she had been brought up to guard her virtue, but Sorcha's instincts told her that Gavin Napier was the man who held her life in his hands. As before, when he had seen her naked at his dwelling in Edinburgh, Sorcha knew no shame. Despite the impossible barriers between them, she had recognized that they belonged together. It was as if they already were one, from the beginning, for all time. The happiness Sorcha derived from the consummation of their union could not be tarnished by anything on heaven or earth. She needed very much to share these overwhelming feelings, to hear the reasons for her bliss being uttered aloud.

Sorcha, however, retained enough basic common sense to realize that the atmosphere at Fotheringhay was not conducive to the euphoric ramblings of a lass in love. Although Queen Mary had rallied from her digestive indisposition, the chill, damp February days made her rheumatic joints swell and pulse with pain. If that suffering weren't enough, the uncertainty of her fate still dangled over her like a boulder suspended on a fraying thread.

After two days had passed since the passionate encounter in the chapel, Sorcha's state of elation began to erode. She had learned that Napier had been closeted with the Queen for most of Monday, and the following day he had gone with Dr. Bourgoing to search for herbs that might alleviate the Queen's rheumatism. On Wednesday, wherever she went in the castle, she seemed to miss meeting him. Outside the Queen's rooms, Jane Kennedy told Sorcha that he had just left for his own quarters; there, Dr. Bourgoing informed her that Napier had gone to inquire after Sir Amyas Paulet's health; at the entrance to Paulet's suite, an English servant professed to have no idea where the Scotsman was. Her once-ecstatic emotional state was gradually being reduced to rubble. Impatient and anxious, Sorcha stomped back to her own chamber, where Ailis reported that she'd seen Napier in the courtyard only ten minutes earlier. He was, of course, gone when Sorcha descended to the main entrance.

Sorcha spent most of the next day with the Queen. "England does not agree with you, *ma petite*," Mary Stuart declared that afternoon as Sorcha brushed the Queen's thinning gray hair. There were still hints of the auburn tresses that had complemented Mary's youthful alabaster complexion, but for years she had tried to conceal some of the ravages of age by wearing wigs. "It was only a few days ago that you were quite ill," the Queen went on, turning with effort to look up over her shoulder at Sorcha. "I had thought you fully recovered, yet today you are peaked again."

"It's being cooped up so much," Sorcha replied, remembering to say as little as possible about her violent illness lest she reveal that there had been an attempt to poison her mistress. "At home, in the Highlands, I spent much time out of doors, even in winter."

"Ah, yes, the Highlands." A reminiscent expression crossed Mary Stuart's face. "Your sire taught me those strange dances. So many of the people in the North were loyal to me, yet I found it a desolate, alien place."

"My Lady Mother would agree with you," Sorcha said, pausing to pluck a few strands of hair from the tortoiseshell brush. "She has always preferred the city."

"Edinburgh, you mean?" For an instant, the Queen's face showed disdain. "Oh, but of course, your mother was born and raised there. For me, there could never be a city such as Paris or a court such as that of France, with the great chateaus along the Loire and the Cher. If only I could have been permitted to return there, to live out my last days in peace. At a convent, perhaps ..." The shadowy lids drooped over Mary's eyes, making her seem suddenly ancient and corpselike. "One of my four Maries," the Queen went on, looking up again as she made reference to the quartet of Scottish noblewomen who had served her devotedly from childhood, "retired to the convent of Saint Pierre at Rheims some years ago. How I longed to join her there!"

To Sorcha, it sounded much like exchanging one prison for another. Still, within the sanctified walls of the convent, there would be no Puritan gaolers or prying eyes to hound Mary Stuart's every word and step. From the perspective of the Queen's age and experience, a cloistered life might have great appeal. But for Sorcha, not yet twenty and wildly in love, the notion seemed as hopelessly bleak as the dreary winter day. The late afternoon was overcast, a cruel wind cut through the drafty walls of the castle, and if this first week of February brought any small signs of spring to Northamptonshire, they were well camouflaged by the stark, fiat, colorless landscape that surrounded Fotheringhay.

When Sorcha returned to her chamber, a half dozen rushlights flickered next to the window seat where Ailis was reading, her face almost touching the pages of the book. When Sorcha entered the room, Ailis peered at her over the leather-bound volume. "I hear from one of the laundresses that Father Napier is ill." Ailis's features remained carefully composed. "It would seem that Fotheringhay Castle is not a healthy place for those who dwell here."

Sorcha twisted at the silver chain that hung from her waist. "I should ask about his welfare," she said, though there was a question in both her voice and her eyes.

"He was solicitous when you were sick." Ailis spoke without inflection, squinting once more into the pages of her book.

Pausing just long enough to make it appear she wasn't bolting from the chamber, Sorcha went back out into the chilly, ill-lighted corridor. At least she now knew why Gavin Napier hadn't sought her out in the past day or so. The fears that had been slowly building up inside the secret places of her heart were brought out into the open and summarily dismissed. Gavin Napier had not been overwhelmed with remorse, he had not found Sorcha undesirable, he felt no shame for their frank, ardent declarations of mind and body. Sorcha all but flew down the corridor, stopping to take a deep breath before she rapped on Napier's door.

Again, it was Dr. Bourgoing who answered her importunate knock. "A debilitating illness," he explained, the kind eyes not quite meeting hers. "Ague, or some other weakness, I should say. He is abed, mistress, and sleeps most deeply."

Sorcha fixed an appraising gaze on the doctor's face. Bourgoing was not only kind but trustworthy and honest. Yet Sorcha sensed he was being evasive, if not actually lying to her. It would be disrespectful to accuse him of perfidy, however well-intended. Was it possible that Gavin Napier was far more seriously ill than the doctor had acknowledged? A tingle of alarm crawled up Sorcha's spine.

"Is he in danger?" The words were spoken rapidly, but in a hushed, breathless voice.

Bourgoing's high forehead furrowed. "No, no. But he is very weak." He smiled at Sorcha in reassurance. "Tomorrow I shall bring you fresh news, perhaps of a more sanguine nature."

To Sorcha, tomorrow seemed very far away. Frantically, she searched her mind for a pretext to see Napier immediately. At the end of the silver chain she wore around her waist was a ball encircled with pearls. Sorcha snatched at it, cupping the bauble in her palm. "See here, good Doctor, I have a shred of the Virgin's mantle, brought to me by my father from Jerusalem." Inwardly, Sorcha blanched at the blatant tie; she possessed no such relic, nor had her father ever ventured as far as the Holy Land. But Dr. Bourgoing wouldn't know that. Gazing up into the physician's kindly face, Sorcha opened her green eyes wide and tried to strike a pose that she hoped would be simultaneously pious and appealing. "If I could but hold the blessed fabric against Father Napier's forehead, I'm sure he would recover more quickly."

The furrows deepened on Dr. Bourgoing's forehead. He looked from Sorcha to the silver globe resting in her hand. She had always struck him as an unconventional sort of maid, not given to girlish simpering or the exertion of feminine wiles. A bit untamed, no doubt due to her Highland heritage, but an open, intelligent young woman whose sense of duty had brought her to serve at Queen Mary's pitiful parody of a royal court.

Bourgoing shrugged and smiled. " 'Twould do no harm." He raised a cautionary finger. "But only for a moment. You must not wake him."

Sorcha nodded. "Of course. The Blessed Mother hears short petitions as well as lengthy ones." She gave Dr. Bourgoing a demure smile.

To Sorcha's relief, the physician didn't follow her into the bedchamber. As she closed the door quietly behind her, Sorcha was forced to adjust her eyes to the gloom. Except for one stubby candle, the room lay in darkness. The pale winter sun had already set, but while a fire was laid in the grate, no one had yet kindled it into flame.

Treading softly, Sorcha made her way to the bed. The outlines of furniture, hangings, walls, and windows began to take shape. Sorcha was still several feet away from the big canopied bed when she realized that it was empty. For one panicked moment, Sorcha feared that Gavin Napier had died. As a small child, she had imagined that dying meant people simply disappeared, with all earthly evidence of their existence being assumed into heaven. The youthful concept struck her for only a split second, but it was sufficient to send a violent shudder throughout her entire body.

"Brainless ninny," Sorcha murmured aloud, hoping that the sound of her own voice would bolster her courage. With an unsteady step, she went to the bed; the counterpane was pulled back, but the sheets were cool to the touch. The suspicions that Dr. Bourgoing's lack of candor had stirred now began to run amok. If Napier had been critically ill, he certainly wouldn't have risen from bed and climbed out the window. Yet if the illness was feigned, why had Dr. Bourgoing allowed her to come into Napier's bedchamber? Suddenly more frightened for herself than for Napier, Sorcha whirled around to race toward the door and test the latch.

Even as she reached out, Sorcha felt a movement as brisk as a winter wind from somewhere behind her; her hand fell away from the door at the same moment strong arms went around her shoulders.

"Don't cry out," commanded Gavin Napier. "You'll upset Dr. Bourgoing."

Sorcha had stiffened at his touch, but relaxed sufficiently to feel her body lean against Napier's. She craned her neck to look up at him. "God's teeth, what manner of prank is this?"

Slowly, Napier released her, though one hand lingered at her breast. She turned to face him, pushing the heavy hair out of her eyes. "You're not ill! Indeed, you're dressed to ride!"

Napier glanced down as if surprised by her declaration. He seemed to be studying the long, black leather boots, the heavy serge cloak flung over one shoulder, the roughly stitched calfskin gloves. "I am," he admitted, his mouth turned down at the corners in his dark beard. "I didn't know you were here."

Sorcha looked up into the hunter's eyes, which were in deep shadow. It seemed to her that Gavin Napier was already very far away, as if they had never made passionate love in the deserted chapel. She felt quite cold and had to step back to lean against a straight-backed chair for support. "Where are you going?" The words were thin and hollow.

Napier took a breath that seemed to tax him, opened his mouth to speak, clamped it shut, and turned to the bureau, where he picked up a black bonnet trimmed with a single gray feather. "I'm going away." He hesitated, still not looking at Sorcha. "My task is finished here."

Sorcha's teeth had begun to chatter as a fearsome chill overtook her. "I don't know what you're talking about. Or maybe I do," she amended unsteadily, "but you must take me with you."

"No." The word fell between them like the last mournful note of a dirge.

"Yes!" Sorcha flew at him, hands clutching at his arm. "I love you! You love me! You said so!"

He started to pull away, then stopped and turned to gaze down into her desperate face. "Of course I love you. But I'm a priest. It's impossible, Sorcha." He shook his head slowly, firmly.

Her nails dug deeper into his arm. "A pox on your priesthood, Gavin Napier!" Defiance strengthened her voice. "You are no more a priest than I am!"

Napier's jaw dropped just a fraction as he stared down at Sorcha. "You're daft. Where do you get such fancies?" His effort at laughing away her accusations degenerated into a grunt.

Sorcha's determination had helped quiet her trembling limbs. "I've met another Napier, Adam by name. He's your brother." She paused, seeing his mouth tighten. "And he's crippled and could not come to Scotland or England until recently because of his health. So now that he's here, you must leave. Though why at this precise moment, when you and I have just found love, I'm baffled thrice over." She dropped her hand from his arm to gesture toward the door. "I must surmise that Dr. Bourgoing knows the truth as well. Has he not interrupted us because he thinks we're in bed together?"

"Christ!" Napier flung the black bonnet back on the bureau so hard that it slid off the edge onto the floor. He reached out to grasp Sorcha by the wrist, giving her a sharp shake. The brown eyes narrowed, but his dismay was still evident. "How long have you known?"

Though Sorcha was still distressed and anxious, she couldn't help but savor her triumph of deduction. "I only realized the truth the other night. In the chapel." She refused to flinch from his glance but knew that her cheeks were flushing. "No priest would have taken me there, no matter what religion that chapel serves." Glancing down to where he still held her wrist, she smiled faintly at the strong, brown fingers that circled her flesh. "I can't believe how blind I was! I should have guessed months ago, back at Chartley, when I met Adam Napier along the road. From a distance he looked exactly like you. And while he didn't admit to your acquaintanceship, he asked too many questions regarding your whereabouts. The world may be riddled with coincidence, but two Napiers hovering around the Queen of Scots tried my credulity." She wriggled her fingers, but he still held her wrist fast. "Don't you think," Sorcha demanded, "that you should tell me the rest of your strange tale?"

Napier's jaw was set, and his eyes had turned hard. But he finally let go of her wrist and sat down on the bed, shoving the rumpled counterpane aside. "Your conjecture is damnably accurate," he admitted, indicating with an absent wave of his hand that Sorcha should sit next to him. "Adam is my older brother. He was ordained in France a few years after our family exiled itself there." Napier stopped speaking for a moment as Sorcha seated herself on the bed, feet dangling a few inches above the rush-covered floor. "Adam's great ambition in life was to bring unity to the Catholic clans of Scotland, so that they might join forces against the presbyters. He had also pledged himself to serve Mary Stuart as long as she lived. But," he went on, a painful expression crossing his face, "about two years ago, Adam was captured by the Dutch. They tortured him. He was crippled. But at last they finally let him go."

Sorcha shuddered, recalling the cheerful countenance of Adam Napier, who must have suffered unspeakably. "God's teeth," she breathed, "how valiant he must be!"

Napier's curt nod acknowledged the truth of her statement. "He was sent back at last to Amiens. We were sure he would die, but eventually he rallied, though he had lost the use of his legs. Twice he set out for Scotland; twice he was forced to return before taking ship from France. His health was still very poor, and at last he asked me to take his place until he grew stronger."

The stumpy candle was almost out. Napier leaned toward the little nightstand, extracted another candle from a sandalwood box, and lighted it from the dying flame. "I was reluctant to act out such a deceit, but I feared that if I did not and Adam worsened, I would never forgive myself for refusing his request. Nor," he added, turning to Sorcha and dropping his voice almost to a whisper, "was I certain that I, too, did not have a priestly vocation. At the very least, I was—I am—as concerned about the fate of the Catholic Church in Scotland and England as is my brother. In time, I shall also find out if, like him, I am also destined to take Holy Orders."

The fearsome chill began to creep over Sorcha again. "But … but you couldn't be a priest! How could you, when you love me?" She had to force herself to keep from clutching at him.

"Oh, Sorcha …." Napier shook his head, then rubbed his temple. "You open up my very soul! You dig into the raw wounds of my heart! Can you not leave me be, for the love of Christ?"

With a distress that matched his own, Sorcha saw the haunted look surface in his eyes and the pallor that seemed to lurk beneath his dark skin. "Why say that? I'm offering you my heart, my life! You've already taken my body!"

Napier's head sunk into his hands. "I know that!" His response was strangled deep in his throat. "I wish to God I had not! Then I would never have known how …." He halted abruptly, his head jerking up, his mouth locked tight.

Tentatively, Sorcha put a hand on his shoulder. "We've had so little time to think this through. Stay, my love, at least for a few days. Please!" For a brief moment, she let her head rest against his arm, feeling the rough serge cloak touch her cheek. "Please," she repeated, more softly this time.

Sorcha felt rather than saw him shake his whole body in refusal. "I cannot. Mary Stuart is to die within the next few days. The executioner is already on the road to Fotheringhay. My brother waits but a quarter of an hour from here to take my place and give the Queen the comfort of a true priest."

For a moment, Sorcha was distracted from her own problems. "Ah— then that is why you were supposedly ill—so no one would wonder why you couldn't walk." She saw Napier give a single nod. "But the Queen! Sweet Virgin, somehow after all this time, I thought perhaps she would be spared!"

"Nay, not with those English hounds of hell on Elizabeth's heels." With a swift motion, Napier rose from the bed to open one of the narrow castle windows. "The moon is rising. I must be gone. I'd hoped to leave without Bourgoing knowing, so that he could be honestly surprised if anything should go awry."

Sorcha was also on her feet. "Gavin!" she cried and then stared at him openmouthed. "God's teeth! I scarcely know you!"

Napier started toward her but stopped, planting his boots firmly among the rushes. "You know enough. But it's best if you forget. Oh, Sorcha," he said on a long, plaintive sigh, "I'm sorry!"

His assertion was so inadequate that Sorcha barely took it in. It was impossible that he was leaving. She wanted no highborn lairds, no wealthy noblemen, no royal princelings. Sorcha had set her heart—and her mind—on this man who was picking his bonnet up from the floor and adjusting the clasp of his serge cloak.

Sorcha set her fists on her hips and dug her heels into the rushes. "You will not go," she averred, the green eyes flashing. "Or if you do, you will not go without me." Seeing his big hand raised to refute her, Sorcha raced on. "I swear it, I'll bring the guards down upon you, and you'll never be able to reach your brother. I cannot lose you," she asserted, ignoring the catch in her throat, "for if I do, my world is ended."

The haunted eyes seemed to clear. An uncertain smile cut across the dark beard as Napier slowly moved toward Sorcha. "I underestimated your obstinacy. Though I should tell you that if you truly love me, you'll let me go." He uttered a short, hollow laugh. "You will not listen though, I fear."

As a wave of relief lifted Sorcha's spirit, she offered Napier a radiant smile and eagerly watched him reach out his left hand to her. She never saw the right fist that came up to catch her on the jaw. In the place where she dwelled for an unaccounted time, there was only a lush green meadow and a silver stream where Sorcha ran barefoot among the lilies and joyfully proclaimed her love for Gavin Napier.

When Sorcha awoke, she was in Napier's bed, and he was gone.

PART THREE
1589

Chapter 17

THE HEAVY SCENT OF LILACS mingled with the acrid odor of a hundred candles in the small stone chapel of the Dominican convent at Le Petit Andely. Through narrow windows wrought in exquisite stained glass, the morning sun cast a warm glow over the community as its members chanted Terce in Latin. In a pew near the back of the chapel, Sorcha knelt with Rosmairi, whose profile was all but hidden by the postulant's white flared coif.

The rustle of linen habits and the soft slapping of sandals on the stone floor were the only sounds when the service ended. Sorcha watched the nuns file out in decorous silence, then moved into line with Rosmairi behind the others.

Outside the chapel's arched entrance, Sorcha took a deep breath of the fragrant spring air and sighed. Beyond the lovingly tended garden of vegetables, herbs, and flowers stood the guest house with its slanting roof. Sorcha had resided there for over a year in a small, sparsely furnished room that looked out on the River Seine and across to the village of Le Petit Andely. She had come to the convent to keep her sister company while Rosmairi grappled with the festering wound of her aborted romance with George Gordon. Yet if Rosmairi found balm at Sainte Vierge des Andelys, Sorcha had few illusions about the religious life providing a solution to her own problems. Gavin Napier was the only answer, and Sorcha refused to believe she could ever find happiness without him.

Still, she found a measure of tranquility within the convent walls. Sainte Vierge des Andelys had been built on a small wooded island in the middle of the languorous Seine, giving the holy refuge an air of peaceful isolation.

Rosmairi was bending down to scold Marcel, an ill-natured goose that constantly bedeviled the convent's other geese and chickens. At eighteen, Rosmairi's soft features had turned more angular. If she had been a pretty child, she was growing into a beautiful woman. But the red-gold hair was hidden under a coif, the gracefully rounded body was concealed by a white linen habit, and even her perfect complexion was less remarkable without color to enhance it.

"Ah, your sister, she is the only one to make Marcel behave," said a droll voice just behind Sorcha. Mother Honorine's bowed upper lip smiled in a curious way that revealed only her two large front teeth. She paused, regarding Sorcha with a frank, yet confidential gaze. "It would seem Rosmairi has put misfortune behind her."

Sorcha turned pensive eyes on Rosmairi, who had joined one of the other postulants to scoop handfuls of grain from a sturdy wooden tub. "I pray she has," replied Sorcha with more fervor than conviction. "She rarely speaks of the past."

The bowed lips relaxed into a less jocular, though pleasant, expression. "Praise the Lord you two are so close. It must be a comfort."

A sidelong glance revealed to Sorcha that Mother Honorine wore no pious demeanor, nor rolled her eyes heavenward in the assumption that the *Bon Dieu* was nodding approval of her comments. Not only was the Mother Superior a Frenchwoman, but a Guise by birth, and a blood relation to Mary, Queen of Scots. She was a practical person imbued with sufficient worldliness to discuss the basest of human frailties without flinching. She knew why Rosmairi had come to the convent of Sainte Vierge des Andelys. It was not the first time a young woman had fled there to mend a broken heart. But Sorcha's reason for joining her sister as a guest in the convent had never been questioned. Until now.

"We shall see in good time if Rosmairi's vocation is sincere or merely of convenience," Mother Honorine went on as they began to stroll along the stone path between the rows of cabbage and lettuce seedlings. "As for you, *ma chère*, is your visit here gaining you spiritual or temporal grace?"

The inquiry was so artful and unexpected that Sorcha was caught off guard. She hesitated, distractedly watching Rosmairi scatter grain among the geese. "My parents didn't wish for Ros to come to France alone. Even though our brother Rob is studying with a kinsman at Compiègne, he isn't close enough to visit much." Sorcha avoided Mother Honorine's gaze, instead watching Rosmairi walk sedately toward the henhouse.

"Very sensible, yes." Mother Honorine nodded sagely, slipping her tapering fingers inside the draperies of her white linen sleeves. "Unselfish, too, is it not so?" She had turned to Sorcha, tilting her high-coiffed head to one side. "That is, you are young and lovely. Most sisters, I fear, would not surrender the days of their youth for the sake of another. Instead, *les beaux hommes* would divert their time and attention, eh?"

Sorcha knew her face had turned grim, and she was annoyed by Mother Honorine's perspicacity. "We are Highlanders," she said woodenly. "We keep close together."

In her mind's eye she could still envision Dallas Fraser refusing to hear of Rosmairi's professed desire to enter a French convent. "One son heading for the priesthood, one daughter in love with a man who is a priest and yet not a priest—and now this, a budding nun! By the Virgin and all the saints, was ever a mother so bereft of sensible children!" Dallas had stormed and raged for the better part of two days, only to surrender when Iain Fraser had threatened to marry each of his unwed offspring to the first tinker or tart who asked for them.

"Let the bairns find their own way in the world, no matter how ill chosen it may seem to you," he had admonished his wild-eyed wife. "At least Magnus is well settled with Jean Simpson. Didn't we promise long ago not to manipulate our children into futures they found repugnant?"

So, at last, Sorcha and Rosmairi had followed Rob to the Continent, each sister nursing a broken heart. As the months passed, Rosmairi became more like her former self, though with a new aura of gentle dignity. Sorcha's peace of mind proved more elusive.

Rosmairi had disappeared inside the henhouse. Mother Honorine turned back to Sorcha, as a pair of sparrow hawks darted overhead, then soared toward the river. "Your sister has shown signs of preferring a more contemplative life, perhaps." The black veil that fell from a stiffly starched linen crown fluttered in the May breeze. "But you, *ma chère*, you might find yourself suited to the role of a lay tertiary. I am told you get on very well in the village. They call you *L'Écossaise Noire, n'est-ce pas?*"

Sorcha was unable to suppress a smile. It was true—her foreign accent, the dark hair, and olive skin, had earned her the nickname of the Black Scotswoman. On the three days a week she spent in Le Petit Andely tending the ill, helping the poor, cheering the elderly, teaching the young, Sorcha forgot her own aching heart and allowed the townspeople to accept her into their community.

Still, Mother Honorine's suggestion of becoming a Dominican lay tertiary seemed premature. "It's fulfilling," Sorcha admitted as the mother superior paused at the end of the vegetable garden, where two nuns were chattering a few feet away by the stone well. "Not so very long ago, I should have scoffed at the notion of living in a convent. Now I find it ... soothing."

Mother Honorine nodded deeply. "Just so. For your sister, too, though she is quite different from you." The slate-gray eyes were frank, as always. "Yet I must ask myself, is it that you young people from Scotland—and England—have had so little opportunity to practice your faith that you find greater freedom here within the convent than at home? Freedom of the spirit, that is—you comprehend?"

It was not a question Sorcha had ever considered. While she chafed from time to time at the monotony of daily prayers and services, she had rarely rebelled, even within herself. There was a certain satisfaction in self-discipline. Yet Sorcha could not honestly state that she felt her soul growing closer to God. Perhaps, instead, she had grown further away from the world, which was not necessarily the same thing.

The nuns at the well had erupted into gales of laughter. Mother Honorine glanced inquiringly over her shoulder; the women subsided immediately. The reverend mother was not strict, but she was demanding when it came to excess of any kind. If there was one rule that superseded all others at Sainte Vierge des Andelys, it was moderation—in food, in speaking, even in religious devotion. Several weeks earlier, at the beginning of Lent, one of the young novices had declared a fast for the entire forty days and had vowed to remain at prayer in her cell except for morning Mass. Before the sun set on Ash Wednesday, Mother Honorine had the young novice in the refectory, taking bread and water.

Guilelessly, the reverend mother turned back to Sorcha. "Perhaps it is too soon for you to know." She removed her hands from the graceful draperies and gazed at the ring that had joined her to Christ. "I had many doubts." She frowned, then exposed those large front teeth in yet another smile. "Though my family did not. 'A fourth daughter,' said my dear departed papa, 'is a dowerless daughter. Guise though she may be.' And so it was into the convent I went, yet at the time I would have preferred a strong young husband and babes in the cradle." She arched her shoulders and back in a characteristic shrug. "But later, I found there was much joy here, great satisfaction. Though," she emphasized, waving a long, tapering forefinger at Sorcha, "not such peace as you might think. Oh, *non, non!* A convent, at least one where its inhabitants work in the world, is no place for escape!"

Sorcha started to respond, but Sister Marie Françoise was approaching in her plodding, bowlegged manner. Not that Sorcha had ever seen the middle-aged nun's bare legs, but she could guess from the woman's stride that she had spent much of her early life on horseback in her native Brittany. "It's the bees," Sister Marie Françoise was explaining, direct as ever, "the young are dying in the hives."

"The late frost, perhaps." Mother Honorine nodded to Sorcha before allowing Sister Marie Françoise to lead her back down the path toward the granary, where the convent's half dozen hives were kept. For a few moments,

Sorcha waited, watching the henhouse. But either Rosmairi was still inside tending to her chores, or she had left through the back door. No matter; Sorcha preferred a few moments alone. Mother Honorine's inquiries had brought Sorcha's hidden thoughts out into the open.

Glimpsing her murky reflection in the well, Sorcha tried not to think of Gavin Napier. Over two years had passed since he'd left her at Fotheringhay, bereft of his love and bewildered by his rejection. If Sorcha couldn't quite forgive him, neither could she forget.

Upon Napier's departure, his brother had come to offer the comfort of the Church of Rome to the doomed Queen of Scots. Sorcha never learned whether Mary knew there had been a change of identity. Father Adam Napier had only a few, furtive moments alone with the Queen before her execution. Then he, too, was gone, riding out after midnight, across the Northamptonshire plains. Sorcha never even saw him.

She did, however, see the Queen one last time. During the night Mary Stuart was permitted to spend her final hours alone with her loyal subjects. She distributed her last few belongings, wrote down some personal requests, and attempted—in vain—to shore up her companions' crumbling courage. For Sorcha, who had not known the Queen as long or loved her as well as the others, the long, pathetic night still had been deeply disturbing. Several times she felt her eyes brim with tears, and at one point, near dawn, when Mary Stuart offered that familiar, engaging, charismatic smile, Sorcha buried her face in her hands and turned away. At last, as the Queen was led away to the executioner's block in the great hall, she embraced Sorcha with as much fervor as rheumatic joints and royal dignity would permit. It was a piercing, brittle moment. Mary Stuart, so often foolish, reckless, obstinate, and flighty in her youth, wore both her royal diadem and her martyr's crown with an unquestionable assurance. She had drawn away from Sorcha and placed her gnarled hand over her heart. "It is here, *ma petite*, that truth dwells. May God keep you in His tender care. *Adieu.*"

The attendants who had spent so many years in captivity were allowed to accompany their mistress into the great hall, but Sorcha and Gillis Mowbray were ordered to stay behind. To her shame, Sorcha was immensely relieved. She had spent the next few minutes in prayer for the Queen's swift and holy death, but Mary's final words kept intruding. Had she spoken of love or faith? Had she guessed Sorcha's feelings in some instinctive, omniscient way? Had those years of enforced patience and inactivity made Mary Stuart more observant of others? Or was she merely offering a meaningless paean of farewell?

Absently, Sorcha tossed another pebble into the well, scarcely noting its soft splash as the two nuns who had been drawing water earlier returned with their empty buckets. They greeted Sorcha, replaced the containers, and made their chattering way toward the convent's arched entrance. Overhead, heavy clouds began to roll in from the north. The promise of a warm, sunny spring day seemed about to be broken.

Sorcha stood up, adjusting her drab gray skirts but unable to break the train of memory. Less than a month after Mary's death, she and Ailis had returned to Scotland. The entire Fraser family, except for Magnus and his bride, Jean Simpson, were in Edinburgh, anxiously awaiting news from Fotheringhay. Rob was despondent over the Queen's execution, but he was almost as dismayed when he learned from Sorcha that Father Napier had not been a real priest. Lady Fraser openly stated that perhaps this revelation would cure Rob of his clerical notions. But while he was shaken by the deception, it failed to deter him from his chosen course.

Rob's decision had its effect on Sorcha as well. Since he was going to France to visit various religious houses, she insisted that he make every effort not only to seek out Gavin Napier—or Adam, for that matter—but to learn as much as possible about them and their background. Somewhat reluctantly, Rob agreed. When he came home to Gosford's End that autumn, he had made up his mind to become a Recollect friar—but he had unearthed very little concerning the Napiers. Adam was a secular priest who had studied at Amiens and Cambrai. He had been captured and maimed by the Dutch. After his release, he'd recovered sufficiently to leave France the previous summer. He was said to be holy, kind, devout, and fervent to the point of militancy, at least as far as persecution of the faith in Scotland and England were concerned. Yes, he had a younger brother, Gavin, who had also lived as an exile in the vicinity. Beauvais, perhaps, or Clermont. No one Rob talked to in the Île-de-France region seemed to really know Gavin Napier, except as Father Adam's brother.

"Forget him," Dallas had told her elder daughter that Christmastide. Fortified by a great deal of mulled wine, she dared broach what had been virtually an unspeakable subject as far as Sorcha was concerned. "He's a strange one, mayhap touched in the head. Don't fash yourself, child, it's time, and past time, you and Rosmairi both put those feckless knaves behind you."

Sorcha hadn't replied. That Gavin Napier was strange, at least when it came to love, was hardly a startling observation. But touched in the head he was not, nor was he a knave such as George Gordon. Napier loved Sorcha—and she loved him. It was the world that was all awry, and Sorcha was convinced she would one day gaze out from her casement and see Gavin Napier riding up to Gosford's End.

But that day never came. And as Rob prepared to begin his studies at Compiègne and Rosmairi sighed and cried over George's impending marriage to Henrietta Stewart, for the first time in her life Sorcha yearned to leave the Highlands. She no longer found comfort savoring ripe berries in the bramble brake by the low stone fence; she had no thrill at the tug of a fish on her line in the peaty burns; she no longer was soothed on a restless night by the caw of the night corbie from a nearby tree. And when she hunted alone, or with other members of her family, the only time her blood sang with excitement was when she thought she'd glimpsed the long, flashing legs of the Master of Ness—and then realized that he was gone, killed by the man she loved. Along with the great stag, Gavin Napier had turned her heart to clay.

There was no succor for her at Gosford's End. While her parents did their best to cheer Sorcha, when Rosmairi made up her mind to go to France, Sorcha went with her. Whether she fled from her homeland or ran to that place where Gavin Napier had dwelt, she could not be sure. Sometimes it seemed as if her heartbreak had little to do with her disenchantment with Gosford's End. It was as if having been forced to leave home in the first place, Sorcha's ties hadn't merely been loosened, they'd been completely severed. Not even Niall remained as a bridge between her youth and her coming of age as a woman. He had gone with Magnus and his bride to live at the edge of the Muir of Ord.

And Sorcha had gone to live in France, on an island in the middle of the River Seine. If she could not find peace at Sainte Vierge des Andelys, perhaps she could learn to forget.

ON A SOFT SUMMER NIGHT following a vigil Mass to herald the feast of Saint John the Baptist, Sorcha and Rosmairi strolled along the river's edge, taking advantage of the long June twilight.

"Mother Honorine asked today if I would profess my wishes to become a novice," Rosmairi said matter-of-factly as they carefully skirted the edge of the little bluff that dropped sharply to the river. "I replied that I needed more time. At Advent, perhaps." Rosmairi lifted her chin, smiling serenely, if a trifle smugly, at the darkening periwinkle sky. It was an expression that she often assumed and that annoyed Sorcha considerably.

"You risk the wrath of our Lady Mother." Sorcha's remark was intended to goad.

But Rosmairi ascended from serene to sublime. "Even our dear mother should hardly complain if I became a Bride of Christ. Each day I pray that she may be filled with the grace of understanding and acceptance."

A molehill caused Sorcha to falter just enough to stifle her response. The idea of Dallas Fraser being enveloped in an ethereal glow of submissive comprehension seemed to demonstrate Rosmairi's apparent inability to distinguish fantasy from fact. Rosmairi's brief flirtation with reality had been short-lived. While their mother was still opposed to Rob's vocation, at least

Iain Fraser had managed to coax his wife's acquiescence with allusions to bishops' miters and even cardinals' red hats. Unfortunately, such goals were beyond a nun's aspirations.

"The fact remains," Sorcha asserted, deciding upon a more conciliatory note, "would either of us truly want to spend the rest of our lives on foreign soil, whether nun or not?"

"Oh …." Rosmairi gazed at the first faint shimmer of stars gathering beyond the wooded hills above the village. "It might be for the best, since our old faith is being beaten out like so many late summer brush fires."

Sorcha looked askance at the uncharacteristic turn of phrase. Yet Rosmairi was right—the previous summer, when the Spanish had sent their mighty armada to invade England and avenge Mary Stuart's death, all English Catholics had been deemed enemies of the Crown. Even in Scotland, Papists were looked upon as traitors, no doubt conspiring with King Philip II to foment rebellion all over Britain.

When the armada was defeated, the English interpreted the victory as a sign that God Himself was a Protestant. Catholics might disagree, but this was not the time or place to voice such an opinion. Clearly, Elizabeth of England and her Protestant faith were riding the high tide of political favor and influence in Europe.

"Just think," Sorcha said, pausing to observe how the dying light touched the slim silver spire of the Gothic church in the village, "in our grandparents' time, or mayhap before that, there was no such thing as different religions. People didn't fight over which version of the Bible was right, or whether prayers should be said in Latin or Scots, or if a clergyman should marry or be celibate." As she uttered the last few words, Sorcha frowned and looked down at the patch of clover that cushioned her feet. Even after she had discovered that Gavin Napier was not a priest, he had still refused to marry her. Why? she asked herself for the thousandth time—and, as always, found no answer.

"It would seem that men must always fight over something," Rosmairi said, sounding less ethereal and perhaps aware of Sorcha's sudden distraction. "In France, Catholic and Huguenot quarrel. Yet it seems more confusing than at home. Who is which?"

Sorcha resumed walking, though she turned toward the river as a fish jumped and then disappeared under an ever-widening halo of water. "At home, I felt people were sincere—if misguided—in their beliefs. From what we're told in France, religion is more weapon than dogma."

Rosmairi again wore her sublime expression. "How inconsequential to spend one's life using religion instead of being used by it. I wonder—if I were to become very holy and extremely wise, would Henry III listen to me as the Dauphin heeded Joan of Arc?"

In the twilight, Rosmairi couldn't see the vexed glance that darted from Sorcha's green eyes. "He might," she replied with some asperity, "though you ought to consider brave Joan's rather crisp demise."

"Sorcha!" Rosmairi's hand flew to her mouth. "You blaspheme!"

"Rot." Sorcha turned as the Angelus bells sounded from both the convent and the village. She couldn't help but give Rosmairi an impish glance as they crossed the little wooden footbridge that spanned a tiny stream flowing from the duck pond down the bank into the Seine. "If you wish to advise an errant king, you should have stayed in Scotland with Jamie."

Rosmairi tossed her head, the white linen veil whipping against her cheeks. "Jaimie wanted my admiration, not my counsel." The smug, serene aura had fled, replaced by resentment and a touch of chagrin. "Oh, aye, he found me fetching and a sop to his uncertain ego, but it was you, Sorcha, whose wit he craved."

Pausing to face Rosmairi, Sorcha stood with her hands shoved deep into the huge pockets of her simple gray gown. Beyond the wooded hills, the darkened sky was sprinkled with stars. "What poor Jamie really wanted was to be assured that he could function in the company of females. He will soon take a bride, you know."

Rosmairi nodded, her expression faintly rueful. "A Dane, isn't that so?"

"An odd choice, it seems …." Sorcha stopped, as the frantic movement of a lantern across the river caught her eye. It was just upstream from the village, near the Chai Vieux, the abandoned quay once used for boats crossing the Seine to the convent before the river had cut a new channel.

"What is it?" Rosmairi had turned, her linen veil catching in the folds of her wimple. "A lantern, is it not? Is someone signaling to us?"

An unwarranted sense of caution made Sorcha put a finger to her lips. It seemed that their voices carried unusually well on this fair summer night. "It may be. That far from the village, no one on the island but us could see the light." She moved a few feet to the very edge of the bank, treading carefully lest the ground be undermined. "Wave back, Ros. Whoever it is might be able to see your white robes."

Rosmairi lifted her arm, the flowing sleeve moving in the darkness like the sail of a phantom ship. Abruptly, the lantern came to rest.

"Well." Sorcha's hands flexed several times inside her deep pockets. "Are we to send a boat over or wait and see what happens next?"

Freeing her veil and worrying her lower lip, Rosmairi peered across the indolent, inexorable current of the river. There were no sounds from the vicinity of the convent. While the rules of the Grand Silence were not enforced on the eve of a feast day, it appeared that the inhabitants of Sainte Vierge des Andelys had settled in for the night. Indeed, across the way in the village only a few dim lights could be seen behind casement windows that had not yet been shuttered.

But the lantern near the quay had begun to bob once more with renewed urgency. "By the Mass," murmured Sorcha, picking up her skirts and heading back along the bank to the path that led down to the river, "I'll row over to see if someone needs help."

"Wait, Sorcha," Rosmairi whispered, hurrying to catch her sister. "If help is needed, the villagers are closer than we are."

"Then whoever is waving that lantern doesn't want help from the village, but from us." Feeling her way for footholds in the darkness, Sorcha climbed down to the narrow shingle. Moments later, her feet touched the rough pebbles. To her right, she could see the little boat tied to a young oak.

"We should tell Mother Honorine," Rosmairi asserted, stumbling slightly as her sandals slipped on the rocks.

But Sorcha was already in the little boat, untying the knot that held it in place. "We can tell her when we find out what's going on. It doesn't seem wise to waste time."

Reluctantly, Rosmairi clambered into the boat, wrestling with her robes, which had already gotten wet in the sloshing water under the planked seats. Sorcha was pulling on the oars, propelling them upriver against the current. Her back was to the lantern; she had to depend upon Rosmairi to serve as navigator.

"The light has stopped moving again," Rosmairi noted, trying to find a dry place to put her feet. "I wish the moon would come up so we could see better."

"It will give little enough light when it does, being the old quarter." Sorcha set her jaw, feeling the tug on the oars pull at muscles grown stiff from disuse. "God's teeth, we should have let these cretins come to us, not the other way 'round!"

"We're almost there," Rosmairi said in consolation. "Ah, I can see figures— two men at least, perhaps with horses." A sudden, frightening thought struck her; she put a hand over her mouth. "Sweet Virgin, do you suppose they might be thieves?"

Sorcha grimaced, as much at Rosmairi's irrational fears as at the ache of her upper arms and shoulders. "Do they expect us to have loaded this beanpod of a boat with the wealth of Sainte Vierge des Andelys? Come, come, Ros, it's more likely they've been set upon by thieves themselves." She felt the boat bump against an underwater snag and let go on the oars. As she turned to look over her shoulder, a man waded out from shore. A moment later, he had grasped the prow of the little craft in his hands and was pulling it toward the bank.

"Ah, mademoiselles!" He greeted them effusively, his hand stretched out.

A spate of French apologies followed, begging forgiveness for every sin from lack of social grace to presumption upon their good natures. Sorcha listened with growing impatience, then put up a hand.

"We would both forgive and forget your importunate signaling in a moment if only you would explain why you are here," she informed the man in her passable French. "Have you met with danger, or do you seek someone from the convent?"

The Frenchman, who had long since doffed his plume-festooned bonnet, smiled even more broadly, the even white teeth a perfect foil for deep blue eyes and sun-streaked blond hair. "You are foreign," he said, more amused than surprised, then turned to Rosmairi. "And you, so enchanting in your postulant's garb, are you also not French?"

Rosmairi was flushing in a becoming manner. "I am a Scot." She gestured at Sorcha. "As is my sister." Pausing, Rosmairi heard the second man stir from somewhere near the lantern, which was beginning to dim ever so slightly. "We are puzzled, sir, as to what you want."

"The game goes on too long," said a Scottish voice that Sorcha recognized instantly. Father Adam Napier was seated on the ground against the bank, his crippled body drooping with fatigue.

"Jesu," breathed Sorcha, ignoring a startled cry from Rosmairi. "Father—are you all right?" She all but knocked over the Frenchman as she fled to the priest's side. "I'm Sorcha Fraser," she said, sinking down beside him. "Do you remember me from Chartley?"

The sympathetic brown eyes brimmed with warmth as Father Napier offered a weary smile. "If I did not, I wouldn't be here on a late summer's eve." The smile ebbed as his body strained to seek a more comfortable position on the sandy ground. "Praise the Baptist himself, it must be his blessed intercession that brought you from the convent."

The words skittered in and out of Sorcha's brain without impression. She was too mesmerized by the likeness of Gavin and Adam Napier, too shaken by the assault on her senses that his brother's presence evoked. "Father," she all but gasped, edging closer, "where is he?"

The priest's dark brows drew together. "Why, Compiègne, of course. You seem to sense the urgency. How can that be?"

Rosmairi and the Frenchman had drawn within a few feet of Sorcha's flowing hem, but she paid them no heed. "It's not sensed—it's something I know." She placed her hand on her heart. "Here, Father."

"Ah." He nodded, the fusty hood slipping from his dark hair, which seemed a bit thinner than when Sorcha had last seen him. "Then you will go to Compiègne at once?"

"Of course!" Sorcha pressed the hand hard against her breast, feeling the rapid beating within. "Did he ask for me?" She was breathless, her face aglow with excitement.

"He did, though I questioned his wisdom." Father Napier's smile had faded, replaced by pain and worry. "I tried to tell him it was useless, but he insists you can help him. It would seem," he added wryly, "that your brother has great faith in your persuasive powers."

Sorcha felt her jaw drop as her fingers clutched the drab fabric of her bodice. "My brother?" She fell away from the priest, her excitement withering like delicate blossoms under a scorching sun. "Jesu," she whispered, her hand now covering her face. "I thought … I didn't realize …." As if from far away, she heard Rosmairi kneel beside her. "My wits are addled," Sorcha declared with forced briskness. "Somehow, I misinterpreted what you were saying, Father. Please explain, what troubles Rob?"

Father Napier was fingering his beard; the puzzled expression he had briefly worn now cleared as enlightenment dawned. But before he offered to clarify his statement, he glanced at Rosmairi. "So you are the other sister, my child. You bear a marked resemblance to Rob, if not to Mistress Sorcha."

"That's true," Rosmairi replied without interest. For quite different reasons, she also seemed bewildered. "Forgive me, Father, at first I thought you were someone else." A swift, sidelong glance at Sorcha elicited no response. "You are … Father Adam Napier?"

"Aye. I became acquainted with your brother through a Recollect friar, the renowned John Fraser. And I met your sister once in England, by chance, near Chartley." He paused, gesturing at the Frenchman. "Please let me introduce my companion, Armand, the Sieur d'Ailly." The white teeth flashed as d'Ailly made a lavish bow. "He has," Father Napier continued with a grateful smile for the Frenchman, "been my legs as well as my courage for the past year or more. I fear the dampness of England succeeded in providing me with more suffering to offer up to the greater glory of God."

A fleeting sense of compassion touched Sorcha, but so deep was her disappointment and so great was her curiosity that she could no longer control her patience. "What of Rob, Father? Is he with your own brother, Gavin?"

"Gavin?" Father Napier's visage turned deceptively bland. "I don't believe Rob has seen Gavin since Chartley. Or wherever it was they knew one another." With determination, he forced himself into a more erect posture. "At this moment, Rob is in Compiègne, expending his efforts to deter a most devout but misguided young monk from carrying out a dangerous, reckless mission." Father Napier didn't seem to notice that Sorcha had paled at his dismissal of Gavin's whereabouts. "Rob tells me you have a way with you when it comes to dealing with wrongheaded young men—such as the King of Scotland. He begs you to join him at Compiègne and speak with Brother Jacques."

Momentarily, the priest's recital about Rob and an unbalanced monk put Gavin Napier out of Sorcha's mind. She stared at Father Napier, then turned to Rosmairi, who was looking equally puzzled. "Could you explain more specifically what this Brother Jacques intends to do? Is he bent on burning Huguenots at the stake, or marching on Rome to make demands of the Holy Father?"

But the priest merely gave a little shake of his head. "It's best for Rob to tell you the rest. The less you know until you reach Compiègne, the better." He placed his hand on hers. "Will you come, my child?"

"I ...." Sorcha closed her eyes and grimaced. "Holy Mother, how can I refuse? We Frasers keep together, after all."

"We do," Rosmairi asserted, standing up and shaking sand from her habit. "We can get horses in the village."

" 'We'?" Sorcha craned her neck to look up at her sister. "But Ros, you can't leave the convent!"

"I can if Rob needs me." The fine features sharpened. "I'm but a postulant. Mother Honorine won't interfere."

"She will have no opportunity," Father Napier said quietly. "You must leave now. With Saint Christopher's protection, you should reach Compiègne by nightfall tomorrow. I will remain here, with the good priests in the village church. I can then explain to Mother Honorine, and in any event, my presence would only slow your journey."

Before Sorcha could comment, Father Napier whistled softly. Nearby, horses stirred in the bracken. D'Ailly vaulted up the embankment, calling to the animals. Moments later, the little party was in the saddle, with Rosmairi riding pillion behind the Frenchman. They rode in silence toward the village, though as the tall, slim spire of the church drew closer, Sorcha held back with Father Napier.

"Please, I must ask—what became of your brother, Gavin, after Fotheringhay?" The words were whispered, but on the still summer night air, they seemed unnaturally loud.

Father Napier didn't turn to look at her. The bearded profile remained motionless, staring straight ahead. "It matters not to you where Gavin went," the priest answered at last. His voice was suddenly heavy, not just weary but old. "Wherever he may be, you cannot reach him."

Sorcha's hand tightened on the reins. She wanted facts, not enigmas. If Father Napier has not been a man of God, she would have sworn aloud and demanded the truth. But so implacable, so remote, was the priest that she bit her tongue until she felt the taste of blood. Nor did she speak again until it was time to bid Father Napier farewell at the iron gate of the village church.

Chapter 18

THEIR PACE ACROSS THE ÎLE-DE-FRANCE had been steady, if tiring. At dawn, they paused long enough at a farmhouse near Gisors to eat and rest the horses. The farmer was generous with fresh-baked bread from his own wheat field, while his wife magically produced eggs and cheese. After the meal, Rosmairi asked if she might buy some clothing; she felt it inappropriate to ride through the countryside in her postulant's garb. Though the farmer's wife was twice Rosmairi's size, after a great deal of rummaging under the staircase, she presented her guest with an outmoded pale green gown that almost fit.

" 'Tis old," the woman explained apologetically, her plump cheeks flushed from exertion, "but it's seen many a wedding, feast day, and baptism in its time."

At first, Rosmairi had protested, thinking perhaps that having kept the gown all these years, the farmer's wife might be saving it for a daughter or granddaughter. But the woman had insisted Rosmairi take it, remarking cheerfully that if the gown traveled to Compiègne, it would go farther in its lifetime than she would in hers. After an embarrassed moment in which Rosmairi realized she had no money with her, Armand d'Ailly slipped several gold coins into the woman's pudgy hand.

"For your hospitality as well, Madame," he said with a deep bow and that glittering smile. "Your kindness is exceeded only by your generosity. And such remarkable eyes! *Ma foi*, were ever sapphires so blue?"

The woman had flushed again, while her jowls jigged with mirthful pleasure. A few minutes later, the three travelers were back in the saddle, cantering across the rich farmland, through the rolling woods, and past the tiny villages built of gray stone. They reached Beauvais by midafternoon, pausing at the monastery for refreshment. It had turned very warm, with the air stirring fretfully through the leafed-out trees lining the dusty road to Compiègne. In the heat of the day, they stopped again to drink from the slow-moving waters of the Oise. Rosmairi slept for a while, but Sorcha remained awake, despite the fatigue that seemed to tug at her very bones.

A few feet away, d'Ailly sat on a tree stump, vigorously rubbing his shoulder muscles. For the first time, Sorcha observed him carefully. The young Frenchman had been a pleasant companion. His lustrous blond mustache added maturity, as did his exuberant self-confidence, yet Sorcha decided he was probably not much older than herself. His riding clothes were well cut, if more dapper than a Scot or even an Englishman would wear. He was just over average height and sufficiently muscular to convince Sorcha he could defend them against a roving bandit or a zealous Huguenot. He spoke with wit and eloquence, changing easily from French to English, occasionally uttering appropriate phrases in Latin. He also had let his eyes linger on Rosmairi—at least after she had discarded her postulant's habit.

The sun had shifted, so that it shone directly down on Sorcha. She stood up, moving into the shade almost at d'Ailly's elbow. "You are from these environs, Seigneur?" she asked, casually dropping down beside him.

He stopped rubbing his shoulder and rested his hands on his knees. "I come from not far away," he replied with a friendly smile. "Somewhat north, toward Amiens."

The place name caught Sorcha's attention. "Is that where you met Father Napier? He studied there, I'm told."

A faint line of tension touched d'Ailly's cheerful visage. "So he did." The Frenchman inclined his head toward Sorcha, as if conceding a point in a game. "My parents knew him. I was still a youth in those days."

Sorcha refused to avert her gaze, which seemed to hold d'Ailly's deep blue eyes captive. "And?" She fairly breathed the word, loading it with husky urgency.

But d'Ailly raised his palms upward in a typical French gesture. "And I grew up. Father Napier came and went, as was his calling." He shrugged. "Now, because he was a friend to my family, I assist him when I can." The white teeth flashed. "It's quite simple, is it not?"

There was a slight hesitation before Sorcha responded. "It would seem so. Your family is still at Amiens?"

In the shade of a beech tree, Rosmairi stirred as an insect buzzed close to her ear. D'Ailly watched with some concern and didn't speak again until the insect left Rosmairi in peace. "Alas, my mother and father have gone to their heavenly reward." He crossed himself briskly, the blue eyes abruptly cast down.

"You live at Ailly then?" Sorcha wondered briefly why she was bothering to wring these facts from the reluctant Frenchman, yet she felt obliged to press on. For such an extrovert, he aroused her perverse curiosity with his reticence.

D'Ailly sobered at the question. "Our chateau burned to the ground some years ago. That," he added with a sharp edge to his voice, "is how my parents died."

"Oh—I'm sorry." Sorcha sat back on her heels, feeling her cheeks flush. No wonder he hadn't wished to talk about his past. Certainly neither she nor Rosmairi would want to discuss their unhappy love affairs with a virtual stranger.

But d'Ailly had resumed his cheerful countenance. "We will be at Compiègne by supper time. It lies not quite an hour away along the river." He got to his feet, the short cape of his riding habit flowing gracefully from a high embroidered collar. As he raised his arms to stretch, a crackling sound from a nearby copse diverted his attention. D'Ailly turned, as did Sorcha, to see a young man in a white monk's robe emerge from the huckleberry bushes.

"Seigneur!" The young monk stopped in his tracks, leaves clinging to his garments, a brown smudge on one cheek. "I was told you would not be back." He spoke petulantly, his full lower lip thrust out, the colorless eyes accusing.

Under the birch tree, Rosmairi sat up with a start. She blinked at the monk, then at Sorcha and d'Ailly in turn, a bewildered expression on her pink face.

D'Ailly stood very still. "You were told an untruth, it would seem," he said mildly, and then smiled. "Brother Jacques, why have you strayed so far from Compiègne?"

In answer, the monk paced back and forth several times, shaking his head and clenching his hands. "I go to Paris. I promised God I would. Madame Serpent is dead."

Sorcha was standing up, moving slowly in Rosmairi's direction. Brother Jacques was the name Father Napier had mentioned in connection with Rob's summons. Doubtless there were a hundred Brother Jacques in the Île-de-France, but it seemed likely that this was the monk whose mission disturbed Rob. Sorcha recognized the reference to "Madame Serpent" as Catherine de Médicis, the Queen Mother of France. She had recently died, unmourned by a nation that had never taken the devious Italian to its heart.

The monk had stopped pacing, his hands now clasped in front of him. "She always lied, you know." Brother Jacques seemed to have eyes for no one but d'Ailly. "She was supposed to be a faithful daughter of Rome, but she was not. And she misled her son, Henri. She misled everyone. Except the Devil, who claimed her evil soul." He lowered his head slightly, the sun casting an unnatural glow on his tonsure. "So now I must go to Paris." The colorless eyes widened, like those of an innocent child who has just announced he is going to do a great mischief and expects to go unpunished.

D'Ailly chuckled good-naturedly. "Perhaps, perhaps. But not yet, Brother Jacques. For now, you must go with us to Compiègne. I have with me the charming sisters of Robert Fraser." He extended a hand toward Sorcha and Rosmairi, who stood close together in the shade. "You admire our *cher ami* Robert, do you not? Won't you honor his sisters with your company for a few days?"

As if he had noticed them for the first time, Brother Jacques all but jumped off the ground. "Ah! Sisters to Robert?" He leaned forward, peering at Sorcha and Rosmairi, who instinctively grasped each other by the hand. "They are very beautiful, are they not?" He turned quizzical eyes on d'Ailly. "Are they pure?"

Sorcha opened her mouth to snap back a reply, but d'Ailly moved swiftly between her and Brother Jacques. "Would you expect our Robert's kin to be anything but the most virtuous of demoiselles? Why," d'Ailly went on with a note of hurt in his voice, "they have been living in the Dominican convent at Le Petit Andely for the past year."

Brother Jacques considered this information carefully, then nodded his tonsured head. "Yes, I, too, am a Dominican. And Sainte Vierge is a holy house." He stepped aside to look beyond d'Ailly to the two young women. "Mayhap God has sent you to alter my course for reasons of His own. Could it be that I was going to Paris too soon?"

"It could," d'Ailly said with a sense of relief. "Come, let us go on to Compiègne. The sun is less intense, and there's a breeze off the river. Brother Jacques, do you have a horse nearby?"

He had a mule, tethered just beyond the copse by the road. A few minutes later the little party was following the Oise to Compiègne. Sorcha noted that d'Ailly rode close to Rosmairi, as if offering her protection. Brother Jacques plodded along behind them, occasionally humming snatches of Latin hymns. The monk seemed as pathetic as he was disturbing, and Sorcha's curiosity mounted. What task had Rob set for her in dealing with this peculiar young man? It would have suited her far better if d'Ailly had let Brother Jacques continue his journey to Paris. Surely he could not cause any more trouble there than he would for Sorcha at Compiègne.

She could have no idea how wrong Brother Jacques would prove her to be.

THE MOST OBVIOUS CHANGE THAT had overtaken Rob was a lush red-gold beard that grew almost to the cowl of his monk's robe. Both Sorcha and

Rosmairi marveled at how much older he looked, though he greeted his sisters with unbridled warmth. Rob offered d'Ailly a more formal welcome, but Sorcha observed a certain ease in their manner toward one another. As for Brother Jacques, he all but fawned over Rob, who expressed mild surprise— and perhaps relief—that the young man had returned to Compiègne.

"I feared you had not heeded my advice," Rob said in gentle rebuke as they seated themselves on stone benches in the priory garden. "You were very determined to go to Paris this morning."

Brother Jacques laughed without making a sound. " *'Justus ut palma florebit.'* " Is that not what is said in the offertory hymn from today's Mass celebrating the nativity of the great baptizer? 'The just man shall flourish like the palm tree.' And does not the palm withstand great winds and terrible storms by bending, yet never breaking?"

"That may be so," Rob replied, pushing at the unruly lock of hair that even cloistered walls couldn't tame. "But I've never seen a palm tree." He turned to d'Ailly. "Would you help Brother Jacques seek some refreshment? Despite the feast day, I fear he has fasted too long." Noting that the young monk was forming words of protest, Rob held up a hand. "Nay, Jacques, you grow thin. You would not bend like the palm—a great gust would blow you down. Go now with the Sieur d'Ailly."

Reluctantly, Brother Jacques traipsed from the garden, his sandals slapping on the flagstone walkway. The three Frasers waited without speaking, with the sound of bees buzzing in the night-scented stock and tall, rangy foxgloves. From where Sorcha sat, she could just make out the irregular roofline of Compiègne's uninhabited castle. To her right stood the priory chapel with its handsome row of cinquefoil windows. The campanile tolled the bells for Vespers, but Rob shook his head.

"I shall not go this evening. It's better that we talk while the others are in the chapel. Afterward, I will introduce you to our kinsman, Brother John Fraser—a most remarkable man, I might add." He gazed from Sorcha to Rosmairi as if to emphasize how much he respected his mentor.

"I had hopes we might meet him at supper," Sorcha said pointedly. "Rosmairi and I may not have been fasting, but neither have we feasted. At least not well."

Rob's serious demeanor fled as he grinned at his sisters. "Forgive me, I've been remiss in seeing to your creature comforts. But it's important that we speak privately while we have the chance." He paused as a half dozen monks walked in solemn silence from the priory through a side entrance to the chapel. When the heavy door closed behind them, Rob visibly relaxed and crossed his legs at the knee under his robes. "You have already met poor Brother Jacques. I assume he struck you as … odd."

"Simple, perhaps?" Rosmairi asked almost hopefully.

But Rob shook his head. "Only in that his mind works in a very direct manner. He is most devout, fanatically so. Make no mistake," Rob asserted, with a wave of his index finger, "there is need for militancy in the Church to oppose rampant heresy. That is one reason why I am determined to take Holy Orders. But fanaticism is another matter. It leads men not only into physical but spiritual danger. Fanaticism destroys humility. It is like a disease, gnawing away at one's very entrails."

For Sorcha, it was an unfortunate comparison, since what was gnawing at her own entrails was a great hunger. She fervently wished Rob would cease expounding and get to the point.

"You know, of course, that despite Catherine de Médicis' professed Catholicism, she played each side of the religious controversy off against the other when it suited her needs." Rob halted long enough to let the statement sink into his sisters' brains. Only a slight twist of his lips indicated that he noticed Rosmairi's glazed expression and Sorcha's impatient tapping of her foot. "Her son, Henri, has followed her example. It may be that he truly embraces certain precepts of the Huguenot religion. But to placate the Huguenot minority, last winter he had the Due de Guise and the Cardinal of Lorraine murdered." Rob bowed his head and crossed himself, rousing his sisters sufficiently to follow suit. Indeed, they had both attended at least three dozen masses at Sainte Vierge that Mother Honorine had offered up for the repose of the souls of her powerful kinsmen.

"The Guises and the Catholic League have turned on King Henri," Sorcha offered, hoping not only to appease Rob by her show of interest but hurry him along with his story. "But it's said that the League is only a tool for Spain to swallow France whole."

"Didn't the English show that Spain was weak?" asked Rosmairi, whose knowledge of politics had never been deep. "Or was that Portugal?"

"Spain, ninny," hissed Sorcha, and immediately conjured up images of plump, glorious oranges.

Rob ignored his sisters' conversational byplay. "Philip of Spain has a claim to the French throne through one of his daughters. But the point here is that the League holds Paris. And that Henri III and his Huguenot brother-in-law, Henri of Navarre, have joined forces against the League. The city lies under siege, barricaded, at war with itself. King Henri is weak, as were his brothers before him. And now the family's strength—Catherine de Médicis—is dead." Again, Rob crossed himself, though Sorcha thought he did so with less enthusiasm than he had shown for the murdered duke and cardinal.

"So," Sorcha surmised, in the hope that Rob had finally reached the climax of his account, "Brother Jacques wishes to go to Paris and join the Catholic League?"

But Rob smiled sadly and slowly shook his head. "Oh, no. Brother Jacques is going to Paris to assassinate the King."

During the next quarter of an hour, against the backdrop of the monks' clear voices chanting the holy office, Sorcha found herself utterly bewildered by Rob's request and the rationale behind it. She understood that Brother Jacques would consider King Henri a traitor to the Church of Rome, perhaps even a traitor to France. But since Henri de Navarre was an avowed Huguenot and next in line to the French throne, Sorcha couldn't see how eliminating the last of the Valois line would save France for Catholicism. Nor could she possibly envision how—or why—she might have any influence with Brother Jacques in deterring him from his lethal mission.

"You must realize how Brother Jacques has always been surrounded by women," Rob explained for the third time. "His father died before he was born; he was raised by his mother and four sisters. There were no other boys or men in the family. Never mind the years he has spent in the monastery. It is still women—our Holy Mother, the saints, the virgin martyrs—to whom he prays and asks for inspiration."

Sorcha was on her feet, pacing the flagstone walkway. "But he clearly admires you, Rob. If you can't dissuade him, how could I?"

"He may admire me, but he doesn't heed me." As Sorcha stamped her foot in front of him, he grasped her by the hand. "You dealt so well with King Jamie. In truth, he's not much different from poor Brother Jacques. Both were reared in unnatural situations. Both have disproportionate opinions of their own abilities. Both have never known how to act with lasses of their own age and station." He stopped as he heard Rosmairi sniff indignantly. "Forgive me, Ros, I meant before you became Jamie's boon companion." Rob looked at Sorcha from his place on the stone bench. "There is something else you should know about Brother Jacques. He visits someone across the river. It is a woman. She's a recluse—a hermit, really. He calls her Athene."

Sorcha withdrew her hand and abruptly sat back down next to Rob. "He has a mistress?" She gave herself a little shake. "God's teeth, I shouldn't wonder that Athene isn't a laddie. Or a sheep."

Rob stiffened, and Rosmairi giggled. "Sorcha," intoned Rob, wearing his adult, serious expression, "we are speaking of life and death, of heaven and hell. For once, could you not let your mind feast on less earthy matters?"

It was Sorcha's turn to look solemn. "It's not my mind that wants feasting, Rob, it's my stomach." She brightened as the monks began filing out of the chapel. "Please, dearest brother," she implored, hooking her arm through his and tugging at him in earnest, "isn't it time you combined Scottish hospitality with French cuisine?"

Despite a moral and spiritual obligation to impress upon Sorcha that the matter of Brother Jacques and King Henri of France superseded her hunger pangs, Rob succumbed to the importunate green-eyed gaze. "I'm not sure how," he remarked with irritation tempered by his usual good humor, "but you actually seem to have managed to make your cheeks look gaunt."

Sorcha clapped a hand over her midsection. "Not half so gaunt as here. I'm cavernous, Rob." She pulled again at his arm and plucked Rosmairi by the sleeve. "God's teeth, starving or not, it's good for the three of us to be together again."

"So it is," agreed Rob, putting an arm around each of his sisters. "I have tried not to think of home and family these past months. But," he added, with a little catch in his voice, "it's been hard to walk away from the past."

Neither Sorcha nor Rosmairi responded to Rob, but they took up a brisker step as they moved down the flagstone walk toward the monastery entrance.

THE SUPPER COMMEMORATING THE NATIVITY of Saint John the Baptist more than fulfilled Sorcha's expectations. "*La soupe à l'oignon, les escargots, la pâté de foie gras, le rôti de porc, les haricots verts, les pommes de terre, les pâtisseries, le fromage* and *les fruits.*" Sorcha recounted the courses in French, carefully stifling a gastronomic eruption. "Ah, food even sounds better in France!" With a deep sigh of satisfaction, Sorcha slumped sideways onto the little divan in the parlor where she and Rob had adjourned after their meal. Rosmairi, whose fatigue had not been feigned, went straight to bed. But while Sorcha was also extremely tired from the long journey to Compiègne, she hated to waste these precious moments she could spend with Rob. Given his usually strict regime at the monastery and whatever plans he might have for her regarding Brother Jacques, Sorcha felt their reunion might be brief.

"What did you think of Brother John Fraser?" Rob inquired, refilling their wine glasses with a sparkling Vouvray.

Sorcha couldn't suppress a yawn. "He's very learned. I must read some of his works. He is brother to Sir Alexander Fraser, is he not? I recall visiting him at Philorth once or twice. Our Lady Mother is fond of Sir Alexander but says he's given to bad judgment in money matters."

Rob shrugged. "Perhaps. But Brother John says Sir Alexander has done much to enlarge his estates. Our sire has had business dealings with him and has praised him for improving the harbor at Philorth."

"Hmm." Sorcha half closed her eyes, blurring the little room with its charming paintings of the Madonna and Child and its gilded triptych with angels surrounding the Infant Jesus and Saint John the Baptist. She found the history of Brother John and Sir Alexander Fraser extremely soporific. Indeed, she didn't quite catch most of Rob's next words until a single name made her eyes open wide and her body stiffen.

"… As I felt in following the example of Gavin Napier. It didn't matter that he wasn't a priest, I didn't know that then, but …."

"Rob!" Sorcha had twisted around to look more closely at her brother, who sat calmly ruminating in a tall, straight Spanish chair. "Have you heard news of him? Have you seen him?"

Rob avoided her eyes by taking a large swallow of wine. "Of course not. I have seen his brother—as you know, I had him send for you. But for all I know, Gavin may be in Cathay."

To Sorcha, it sounded as if Rob didn't much care, either. She sat up, pounding her fist into a small silken pillow edged in gold orphrey. "Damn your eyes, Rob Fraser, has Gavin Napier fallen off the edge of the earth as far as the rest of mankind is concerned? I may not bleat and moan like Rosmairi, but that doesn't mean I'm any less stricken!"

Rob put down his fluted wineglass and reluctantly met Sorcha's angry gaze. He was struck by how much she had changed since they had first set out from the Highlands four long years ago. The long, black hair was as tangled as ever, the wide green eyes still flashed their fire, the strong, full mouth was as prone to laughter as it was to rage. Even her attire was as simple and careless as it had been in their youth. Yet he sensed that beneath that familiar exterior, the faintly wild, untamed lassie of the glens and burns and peaty bogs had hardened her heart—or at least built a wall around it. If she had been a headstrong girl, she was now a willful woman.

"Maybe," Rob said slowly, "I didn't realize how much you … cared."

Sorcha waved her wineglass as if in defiance. A few colorless drops spilled onto her gray skirt, but she paid no heed. "I cared. I care. Would you have me set my grieving heart to the notes of a pibroch for the pipes to play over my grave?" She paused to watch her brother grimace at the fulsome words, then wagged a long, slim finger almost in his face. "What truly passes beyond my understanding is that Gavin loves me, too! So why did he leave me? Hasn't Father Napier—the real Father Napier—ever given any hint of what possesses his cruel brother?"

"No." Rob spoke with relief. Father Napier had rarely mentioned his brother, except to praise him for his efforts of impersonation on behalf of the Catholic faith. Had he revealed more, Rob felt he would have had to answer Sorcha honestly—and he also sensed that the truth might wound her more deeply than his ignorance. Calmly, Rob folded his hands inside his flowing sleeves. He'd had little experience offering spiritual guidance, but it appeared his sister needed counsel. "It's best to accept the will of God," be began, failing to note that Sorcha's eyes snapped at the words. "Give thanks to our Lord that you were spared being dishonored by Gavin Napier."

"Dishonored, my backside!" Sorcha leaned far forward on the divan's edge. "I gave myself to Gavin, and I did it freely, without the promise of holy matrimony to justify the act! God's teeth, Rob, do you think you're talking to a moonstruck milkmaid?"

Rob picked up his glass and drank with fervor. "I didn't know." He took another swallow, choked, and shook his head with vigor, as if he could erase the words his sister had just implanted upon his brain. "Have you confessed?"

Sorcha sat back on the divan, though her body was still tensed. "Of course. At Beauly Priory." She sighed and lowered her eyes to the hands which held the half-filled glass. "But I wasn't sorry. I'm still not." Lifting her head, she tossed the long hair back over her shoulders. "I know that's wrong. But I can't lie to myself. Or God."

"Jesu." Rob rubbed his bearded chin with agitated fingers. "Did you accept your penance?"

"Oh, aye, 'twas dozens of prayers and litanies and fasting and abstinence. I almost starved to death!" She made a strange little noise that was half cry, half laugh. "The true penance is losing Gavin. The other was easy."

For several moments, brother and sister sat in silence, neither looking at the other. Outside, a dog howled in the distance and from somewhere down the hallway, a door banged shut. Darkness had settled in, leaving the parlor in shadow as a half dozen candles burned on the marble mantel of the little fireplace.

Sorcha finally broke the silence, cradling the wineglass against her breast and offering Rob a wan, feeble smile. "Am I going to hell?"

It was Rob's turn to emit a truncated little laugh. "No one knows who will go to hell, except God Himself."

"Well," said Sorcha, standing up and stretching her neck muscles, "I've asked God to make me sorry. But nothing happens. I've asked Him to send Gavin back to me. But Gavin doesn't come. Mayhap God doesn't hear my prayers."

"He hears," Rob replied, still staring off into the far corner of the room. Slowly, he got to his feet, holding his wineglass before him as if it were a chalice. "I can't give you a second penance. But will you make yourself more pleasing in the sight of Almighty God by helping prevent the murder of the King of France?"

Sorcha gave her brother a wry smile. "It sounds like a bribe." She put a hand out to touch his chest just above where he held the wineglass. "I think it's all madness, especially your notion that there's anything I can do to dissuade Brother Jacques. But if it will please you, yes, I will help."

Rob's features relaxed slightly as he put one hand over Sorcha's. "You may be right—my idea's quite mad. But then, so is the rest of the world, Sorcha."

She felt the warmth of his fingers, the bond of flesh and blood their parents had forged from a union of love, and Sorcha knew that mad or not, she would play out her part with a fanatic monk, a heretic king, and a strange woman called Athene.

Chapter 19

THE MORNING DEW WAS STILL heavy on the grass when Sorcha emerged from the chapel to seek out Brother Jacques. He had not been at Mass, but Rob said that wasn't unusual. Brother Jacques, who was a Dominican and not in actual residence at the Recollect priory, often spent his mornings at prayer in his cell or in the company of Athene, the woman he called his patroness.

Since Rob had not found the young monk anywhere on the premises, Sorcha headed out across the meadow toward the river. It was much farther than she'd expected, and her feet, which had grown unaccustomed to rough tracks during her stay at Le Petit Andely, began to hurt by the time she reached the crossing. And even then, she had only traversed halfway to Athene's hut. Indeed, she became aware that Rob's seemingly precise directions were based on hearsay from Brother Jacques rather than firsthand knowledge. The path through the bracken was easy enough to follow, but Sorcha came to a standstill at a feeble stream flanked by tall evergreens. The trees inched up a hillside, the ground bare except for a few twigs and fallen branches. Relying on her Highland instincts, Sorcha followed the listless stream until she reached a plateau where burbling springs oozed out of a marsh.

There were fresh prints, but they belonged to deer and possibly squirrels. Sorcha felt her feet begin to sink into the mire and moved quickly to firmer ground. Gazing overhead at the filigree of branches against the bright blue sky, she wondered if there were any point in pursuing the trail farther.

Sorcha's worn shoes were not only damp, but one leather sole felt loose. Annoyed, she bent down to examine her footgear, and as she leaned storklike against a tree, she noticed a small cross carved in the bark. A blaze, perhaps, to mark the way to the hermit's dwelling. Sorcha decided that since she had no other signposts to indicate the way, she'd go farther into the woods, in the hope that other crosses might guide her.

The loose sole flapped on her left shoe, providing a constant irritant. But within another ten yards, she discovered a second cross. A third was cut into a young larch. The trees grew more densely, blocking out the sunlight. Fallen branches and moss-covered logs cluttered the forest floor as proof that the local peasants didn't come this way to gather firewood. From high up in a pine tree, a bird's screeching cry startled Sorcha, causing her to stumble over an exposed root. She righted herself quickly, but paused to frown at the dense berry vines barring her path. With a brisk swish of her skirts, Sorcha turned to her left, shoving aside a stand of tall, feathery ferns.

She was still searching for another cross when she heard a sound that wasn't identifiable as either bird or animal. It might have been the wind or a distant waterfall, yet as it sounded the second time, it had an unsettling human quality that was more like a heavy sigh or even a groan. Slowing her pace, Sorcha noted that up ahead the sunlight penetrated more easily through the tall, thick trees. She moved carefully, still listening for that strange, unnerving sound.

An immense, ancient evergreen all but blocked her way. Almost at eye level, Sorcha spotted a cross. It was larger and deeper than the others. As she drew closer, she saw that a real cross, delicately made of silver with the body of Christ etched upon it, had been placed into the carved wood of the tree trunk. The familiar sight was comforting, and Sorcha blessed herself before circumventing the tree's girth.

The scream that erupted from her throat scattered a family of quail and set at least a half dozen squirrels racing to safety. Sorcha rocked back on her heels and would have fallen had she not collided with the bulk of the great tree directly behind her. Even as she stared, wide-eyed and openmouthed, the weird, wrenching moan echoed in her ears once more.

There, virtually in front of Sorcha, stood a ten-foot stump still rooted in the ground. From the strong branch that had been affixed crosswise hung the body of a man, attired in the white robes of a Dominican monk, with a crown of brambles ringing his fair hair. He moaned again, writhing in apparent agony. Sorcha put a hand over her eyes, pressing at her temples. Her brain told her to flee, to escape, to go back to the priory and leave this grisly place, but her feet refused to move. Slowly, she slipped her hand from her eyes and forced herself to look at the crucified figure. It seemed like forever before she realized with a gasp of shock that the man was Brother Jacques.

"Jesu," Sorcha whispered, again crossing herself. Urging her feet to uproot themselves, she started toward the monk but stopped in her tracks when Brother Jacques spoke in a strangled, yet astonishingly untroubled voice.

"Do ... not be ... afraid. This is ... my ... test. My God ... will not ... forsake ... me." From under the brambles that bloodied his forehead, Brother Jacques fixed an ecstatic gaze on Sorcha's stunned face. "I will ... come down ... when it is ... time."

At last able to focus on more than the frightening apparition itself, Sorcha took in the ropes that held Brother Jacques's arms in place on the cross. His sandaled feet dangled a foot or so above the ground, though there were burls on the stump that would have permitted him adequate support if he had desired it.

Suddenly, Sorcha was no longer shocked or horrified, but angry. While she had not been exposed to many deeply religious persons in her life, she knew enough about piety from Mother Honorine, about zeal from Rob, and about dedication from Adam Napier to realize that Brother Jacques's self-crucifixion was not merely misguided but a mockery of faith.

"It's time to come down," Sorcha asserted through clenched teeth, "*now*." Lessons learned in the art of knot tying from her seafaring father served her well as she reached up to undo the ropes that bound Brother Jacques. He cried out in protest, raining down various curses in French so rapid that Sorcha lost their meaning, if not their intent. As the ropes came loose, he fell, face first, onto the ground, the crown of brambles rolling off into the dirt.

"Devil's whore!" screamed Brother Jacques, the attempt to pound his fists stymied by lack of circulation. "No one but Athene takes me down!" He again pumped his arms but succeeded only in a limp flail of flowing sleeves.

"Then Athene can put you back up, you silly wretch!" Sorcha's olive skin was flushed, the long hair more tangled than usual. "I refuse to be a party to such demented devotion!"

"Heretic!" Brother Jacques was scrambling about in the dirt, trying to get to his knees. "What of Saint Simeon Stylites and those other holy penitents?"

"If I may say so, I always thought they were a bit touched in the head, too." Sorcha pushed her hair out of her eyes and brushed some evergreen needles from her dress. Near her hem lay the sole of her shoe; angrily, she snatched it up and shoved it into her deep pocket. "Anyone who preached to people from a sixty-foot pillar in the desert under a scorching sun had to be deranged."

"You dare!" spat Brother Jacques, at last achieving a seated position. He was filthy, the white robes now torn in at least two places and the blood congealing above his beetled eyebrows. "What does a slut like you know of saintliness?"

"I prefer saints such as Helena, who went to search for the True Cross, or Monica, who managed to save her son Augustine from dissipation, or our own holy Margaret, who taught the Scots to eat with a fork. I can hardly imagine any of them hanging from a tree in the middle of a forest like some

great white bat." Sorcha stormed about the little clearing, skirts whipping at
her ankles, heedless of the rough ground.

Brother Jacques, however, had gotten to his feet and was attempting to
compose himself. "You don't understand," he said for the third time, aware
that Sorcha had paid no heed to his first two tries. "You must meet Athene—
then you'd realize why I'm so … fervent."

The word caught Sorcha in midstep. Flinging her hair out of her face
briskly, she turned to face Brother Jacques, who now looked almost rational
and vaguely repentant. "Fervent?" Sorcha shook her head. "Scarcely the word
I'd have chosen. As for Athene, if this," she emphasized, jabbing with her
thumb at the makeshift cross, "is her idea of religious fervor, I must send my
regrets. I hardly need to confront an addled old crone to further despoil my
day."

Brother Jacques looked shocked. "Oh, no, no, no!" He placed his hands
over his breast, inadvertently covering up one of the rents in his habit. "Athene
is neither old nor addled! She is astounding in her wisdom, and amazing in
her kindness." He swallowed, his face turned heavenward so that the sun
shown directly on his bland, yet exhilarated features. "And … belle. Très belle,
like the Virgin, like Aphrodite!"

The confusion of language and imagery puzzled Sorcha, though she knew
it shouldn't, considering Brother Jacques's peculiar mental state. It also piqued
her curiosity. Having gone this far, she decided that meeting one more maniac
could do little harm. And if Athene or Aphrodite, or whatever the weird
woman of the woods called herself, turned out to be as hopelessly mad as
Brother Jacques, Sorcha could honestly offer Rob her genuine defeat.

Brother Jacques was already traipsing along what had now become a fairly
well-traveled path. They moved across the crest of the hill, then through a
clearing where overhead the midday sun was beginning to intensify. Once
again, they plunged into a dense forest, where they crossed a tiny yet raucous
stream and followed it until the trees became so tall and close together that
the sun was almost blotted out. Only a few minutes earlier Sorcha had been
too warm; now, she actually shivered as a faint breeze riffled the evergreens.

Two fallen logs all but obscured the hermit's hut from view. To Sorcha's
surprise, up close the dwelling was neither as small nor as mean as it had
appeared at first glance. There was an open door, a window made of horn,
and a dormant little chimney rising from a fireplace at one end of the stone
building. In truth, Sorcha noted, it was far sturdier—and more commodious—
than many a crofter's home in the Highlands.

Sorcha disdained the hand that Brother Jacques offered to help her over
the logs. "I was raised in wilder country than this," she asserted, and scowled
at the monk, who motioned frantically for her to speak more softly. "Is this

a hut—or a shrine?" Sorcha demanded, though she consented to lower her voice.

Brother Jacques didn't answer. He was already approaching the open door with diffidence, reminding Sorcha of an errant serving boy being summoned into the irate presence of Lady Fraser.

Even before Brother Jacques's slight frame slipped inside, he gestured for Sorcha to stay back. Impatiently, she leaned against one of the logs, arms folded over her chest. Jacques Clement all but disappeared inside the darkened stone hut, though Sorcha could just make out his voice engaged in conversation with someone else.

The exchange between the monk and whoever dwelt beyond the entrance seemed to go on a very long time. Sorcha began to sigh rather loudly and tap her foot against a large, gnarled root. At last, in a flurry of earth-stained white garments, Brother Jacques turned to face Sorcha, his arms outstretched, a beatific smile on his seemingly innocuous face.

"Athene welcomes you! She is pleased to meet another female who has braved the wilderness to explore new dimensions of spirituality." He brought his thin hands together in a prayerful gesture, humbly stepping aside to let Sorcha enter the hut.

Despite the gloom of the surrounding forest, it took a few moments for Sorcha's eyes to grow accustomed to the virtual dark of the hut's interior. No fire burned on such a warm summer's day, nor did any candle dispel the inky void. Only the open door permitted any light at all, and at last Sorcha began to perceive the outlines of the fireplace, a few sparse furnishings, a huge kettle, and a cot covered with what appeared to be luxurious furs.

It was there that Sorcha's hostess reclined, a graceful figure enveloped in black draperies more suited to Araby than the Île-de-France. Indeed, as Sorcha peered into the opaque gloom, she saw that only the woman's eyes showed. They seemed to be a beautiful blue, but neither warm nor welcoming. Sorcha stiffened slightly and waited for the other woman to speak.

At last she did, in a honey-edged spate of French that Sorcha failed to understand. Nor were the words directed at her but at Brother Jacques, who leaped forward like a pony in leading strings and knelt before his patroness. Again, the white-clad monk and the black-draped woman spoke low and with some urgency. Standing just a few feet away and unable to catch more than her own name and Rob's, Sorcha began to feel not only annoyed but uneasy. Just as she was about to interrupt or beat a hasty retreat, Brother Jacques stood up and bowed himself out of the hut. Athene's fingertips emerged just enough from her draperies to beckon Sorcha nearer.

Espying a piece of wood that might have been a chopping block, Sorcha sat down without being asked. She sniffed once or twice, recognizing an exotic scent. Was there more of Araby about this strange woman than her flowing garb? Sorcha wondered.

"So," the woman remarked after a long, unsettling pause, "you are Sorcha Fraser, sister to the much-admired Rob."

To Sorcha's surprise, the woman's English was good. She spoke forthrightly, though her tone was too self-possessed for Sorcha's taste. "I am," Sorcha replied after more of a pause than she'd intended. "I've been living in France with my sister for about a year." She hadn't meant to divulge that much, but there was something compelling about those lovely, chill blue eyes.

The woman held a long index finger against the gauzy black veiling that concealed the lower part of her face. Fleetingly, Sorcha wondered who waited upon the hermit woman in her rude surroundings. Certainly her hands were better tended than Sorcha's.

"I've heard much of your history," Athene said at last, the honey tone sharpening, the sibilant sounds hissing with a trace of venom. Sorcha drew back in spite of herself and tried to hide her puzzlement. Except for the fact that she was Rob's sister, there was no reason for the inhabitants of Compiègne to be interested in her. Unless, of course, Athene, in her guise as Brother Jacques's mentor, paraded omniscience as part of her arsenal of influence.

Whatever Athene's reasons, the preliminaries had gone on long enough. "Let us get to the heart of the matter," Sorcha declared, making a move closer to Athene to prove her own staunchness. "I'm told that Brother Jacques has a mad plan to kill King Henri. If this is so," she ploughed on, despite a gesture on the other woman's part to interrupt, "then he must be discouraged. I frankly find him a troubled soul."

"You've barely found him at all," Athene replied with more verve than Sorcha guessed she usually cared to display. "You know nothing of Brother Jacques, nor the King of France, nor what goes on in our world here. I suggest you cease meddling and return to your peaceful convent in the Seine."

Athene folded her arms across her drapery-clad bosom, her hands disappearing up the flowing black sleeves. Sorcha was reminded of Mother Honorine, yet while the mother superior's movement suggested security and serenity, Athene's gesture was secretive, almost malevolent, as if a dagger might be hidden beneath the folds of her artful hangings.

Briefly, Sorcha reflected upon Athene's words, which seemed intended to dismiss further argument. One thing was clear—whatever Brother Jacques's mad plan, it was at the bidding of this mysterious recluse. Was she a nun, Sorcha wondered, a member of one of those strange contemplative orders that sought salvation through seclusion? But though her garb was black, it evoked eroticism, not mysticism. A darting glance confirmed that there was nothing—not even a cross—to indicate Christian zeal. It struck Sorcha that there was more evil in the hut than good, and she was suddenly not just uneasy, but afraid.

Taking a deep breath and summoning all her courage, Sorcha stood up. "The matter of men and murder is everybody's business," she asserted loudly enough so that if Brother Jacques were eavesdropping, he would hear. "I cannot think why a Catholic monk would kill a Catholic king, knowing that the heir to the throne is a Protestant from Navarre. I know little of French politics, but I do know madness." Sorcha swept at the air with her hand. "And herein, I see it; I smell it in my nostrils like any other foul stench."

In a breeze of draperies, Athene was on her feet, arms outstretched in warning. "Begone! Away with you, Scots whore!" She was close to six feet tall and towered over Sorcha like a vengeful raven. The long nails slashed just past Sorcha's face as the chill blue eyes glittered hard as diamonds. "You, who consorts with priests! Go, before I put a curse on you that will drag you into hell twice over!"

The shrieking babble that erupted from Athene's lips sounded like no language Sorcha had ever heard. Unwilling to concede defeat, yet aware of the need for retreat, Sorcha slowly began to move backward toward the entrance.

"A pox on your curses," Sorcha called out, again hoping Brother Jacques was listening. "You've no more power than a whipped egg! If you had the brains of a board, you wouldn't sit about in a pile of unwashed window curtains!"

Sorcha was back-pedaling through the door, hoping that the spate of invective would keep Athene off guard until the clearing could be reached. But the other woman was moving with long strides toward Sorcha, a hand wrenching at the flowing veils. "Bitch! *Chienne des chiennes*! Your wild, foreign face can't compare to mine, even now!" She yanked the veil away, revealing perfect features and golden curls. She was the most beautiful creature Sorcha had ever seen. With a little gasp, Sorcha stood stock-still, one hand braced on the rough doorway. Yet even as she took in Athene's stunning appearance, the hermit woman lifted a handful of shimmering hair to reveal a great puckered scar that ran from ear to shoulder. "Well?" demanded Athene, the blue eyes searing Sorcha with both malice and triumph. "Are you satisfied? Do you see that Athene is made of pleasure—and pain?" The golden hair fell back down over her shoulder to hide the brutal scar as Athene again marched on Sorcha. This time when the hand went inside the black draperies, it emerged with a sinister slender shaft. The ivory handle was carved into a death's-head; the steel blade shone like silver.

The time for courage was over: Sorcha whirled, half expecting to crash into Brother Jacques, but he was nowhere to be seen. Scrambling over the logs that barred the way to the hermit's hut, Sorcha regained her footing and raced off through the evergreens. The shrieking mockery of Athene's laughter followed her all the way to the bustling stream at the edge of the forest.

She began to slow down as the trees parted to let the early afternoon sun beat upon her perspiring body. Some time later, barefoot, dirt-stained and weary, Sorcha gratefully spied the walls of Compiègne. She was about to cross the river by the little footbridge when a lone rider raised enough dust to make Sorcha put a shielding hand up to her eyes. Stepping aside to let him go over the bridge first, she sensed, rather than saw the man in the saddle.

"Gavin!" she cried, half choking on dust and surprise.

At first man and horse didn't seem to pause, but just as he was about to guide his mount over the bridge, Gavin Napier reined up and stared in wonder at Sorcha's bedraggled form.

"Praise God!" Napier exclaimed, and leaped down from the horse. He moved as if to take Sorcha's hand, then rooted himself into the dusty road. Dressed in a white cambric shirt and black breeks, he wore the same high leather boots Sorcha remembered, and the long-handled dirk was at his hip. He was bareheaded and faintly sunburned, yet his skin seemed even darker, and the hunter's eyes were as deep and unrevealing as ever—save for that brief moment of relief when he had recognized Sorcha.

Despite his hesitation, Sorcha refused to let either time or distance keep them apart another moment. Without shame, she hurled herself at his chest, her arms wrapping tightly around him. "Thank the Virgin and all the saints! I've found you! I thought God had stopped answering prayers!"

Napier said nothing at first, though Sorcha could hear his deep breathing. Slowly, his own arms encircled her. "You should have forgotten me by now," he asserted, his tone too rough. "I prayed you had."

But nothing he said or did could spoil Sorcha's glorious happiness in finding him again. She looked up at him, the tangled black hair falling away from her elated face, the green eyes shining with joy, the wide mouth laughing with little gurgling sounds, like a brook gone berserk. "I told you at Fotheringhay I could never let you walk out of my life. But you did, and I kept waiting … and then"—she hurried on, trying to make sense and at the same time to drink in his presence—"I came to France, to be with Rosmairi, yet I knew I was searching for you." Sorcha pressed her face against the cambric shirt. "I found you, too, by all that's holy!"

Gavin Napier emitted a rumbling sound that was half rebuttal, half chuckle. "Or profane." He stood very still, the faint breeze rising from the river to ruffle their hair. Gazing over the top of Sorcha's head, Napier's features relaxed ever so slightly. "Rob tells me you came here at my brother's urging." He paused as two young boys drove a flock of geese over the little footbridge. "Have you seen Brother Jacques this morning?"

"Brother Jacques!" Sorcha all but spat out the name. She pulled away just enough to look up into Napier's face. "God's teeth, are you going to tell me it's Brother Jacques you were hastening to find just now instead of me?"

Napier had the grace to flush under his tan. "It *is* an urgent matter, after all." He let go of Sorcha to take his horse by the bridle. "Come, this isn't the place to chat. Let's return to the monastery." Deliberately, he led the big bay over the bridge.

Scowling, Sorcha followed him, forcing her tongue into silence until they reached the abbey's entrance, where a porter was eating strawberries out of a small wicker basket. "Back so soon, eh?" the man said to Napier and popped another fat red berry into his mouth.

"Aye," Napier replied pleasantly enough as the porter opened the gates.

"Hold on!" Sorcha tugged at Napier's sleeve. "Where are we going?"

The porter eyed her with curiosity as a young boy raced across the courtyard to tend Napier's mount. Napier flipped the boy a coin, then frowned at Sorcha. "To rejoin Rob, of course. He awaits news of Brother Jacques."

"A pox on Brother Jacques!" Sorcha folded her arms across her breast and rocked angrily on her bare heels. "Either you and I speak privately now, or I shall refuse to offer further assistance with this mad monk. Nor will I tell Rob—or you—what I learned this morning. Brother Jacques can eradicate the entire French court for all I care." Whirling around, Sorcha turned her back on Napier and ignored the now mystified porter, who had inadvertently allowed strawberry juice to besmirch his white cowl.

Gavin Napier stood on the dusty walkway, shifting his weight from one booted foot to the other and rubbing his bearded chin in vexation. With great effort, he stifled an urge to pick up Sorcha and haul her into the monastery. Instead, he took a deep breath and set his jaw. "There's an inn, Le Chien Rouge, just a few streets away, by the river." With forced gallantry, he offered his arm. "Shall we?"

"I have no shoes," she said, and saw his dark brows edge even closer together. "Though it *is* summer and many peasants are about," she added hastily. With far less enthusiasm than she had shown just a few moments earlier, Sorcha placed her hand on Napier's arm and let him lead her past the porter and back into the narrow street.

They walked the short distance in silence. Sorcha had not yet seen Le Chien Rouge since arriving in Compiègne, but noted that it seemed respectable, no doubt a haunt of the town's bourgeoisie.

Indeed, its very respectability was affronted by Sorcha's disheveled appearance. An owl-eyed young man wearing a white apron and carefully patched hose eyed the newcomers with a suspicion that bordered on panic. In a peculiar, high-pitched nasal voice, he inquired if Napier and his companion wished to eat. Before Napier could reply, Sorcha intervened. "Certainly, my good fellow. Pheasant and artichokes and onion soup and cheese and crusty bread. Wine, too, of course."

The young man, who called himself Bertrand Fils, seemed much relieved that his visitors desired food. He ushered them to a corner table, however, where they were somewhat shielded from the prying eyes of other patrons.

Sorcha watched his spindly-legged departure and snorted. "Monsieur Bertrand thought I was a strumpet, I'll wager! When will people cease mistaking me for what I'm not?" She glanced at Napier for commiseration, but noted his frown and flushed. "Oh, by heaven, you're thinking I'm a strumpet, too!" Distressed, she wriggled about on the bench, which was worn into grooves by at least three generations of diners.

The wolflike face softened. "You know that I think no such thing. It may be that I understand you better than anyone else." Forcing herself to grow calm, Sorcha contemplated his words. "Perhaps," she admitted at last, "though I can't say that I understand—or even know—you so well." She saw his dark eyebrows lift ever so slightly and resumed speaking: "So then—what brings you to Compiègne?"

Gavin Napier's impulse was to respond that it was fate. He could scarcely believe that after not having passed through Compiègne in over two years, he would arrive within twenty-four hours of Sorcha Fraser. He had learned from Adam that Rob was with his kinsman, Brother John, at the abbey. It had seemed prudent to visit his former protégé and offer an explanation— as well as an apology—for his deception. In the time that had passed since Fotheringhay, many things had troubled Gavin Napier; not the least of these was allowing the innocent, guileless Rob to believe in a vocation that didn't exist.

As Bertrand brought the platter of food and a bottle of wine, Napier sketchily answered Sorcha's question. Between mouthfuls of cheese and pheasant breast, she watched him closely, her disappointment mounting. Obviously, Gavin Napier hadn't ridden to Compiègne because he knew she was there. At best, it had been a fragile hope, but Sorcha had nurtured it all the same, not quite able to believe in the coincidence of their both arriving in the same place at the same time.

"Your brother was gracious when I offered my explanation," Napier said as he broke off a chunk of bread still warm from the oven. "Though he was preoccupied, of course. He seemed more concerned with Brother Jacques."

Sorcha peeled off an artichoke leaf and waved it at Napier. "Rob may be, but I am not! I am preoccupied with you—with us." Seeing Napier involuntarily draw back, Sorcha tore the artichoke leaf in two and threw it on the worn wooden table. "You're right—I should have forgotten you! I ought to hate you, despise you! You're a coward, Gavin Napier, a fiendish seducer and a damnable liar!" Her voice had steadily risen to a shrill shout. "To think I greeted you with open arms!"

Across the low-ceilinged common room, a half dozen nondescript travelers looked up from their meals to stare. In the doorway, three Franciscan friars paused, then discreetly turned away, and edged quietly toward a table as far removed as possible from Sorcha and Napier.

Gavin Napier's long mouth was clamped tightly shut in the dark beard. He gripped his wine cup with both big hands, lest he reach across the table and shake Sorcha into silence. From the arched doorway that led into the kitchen, Bertrand's owlish eyes gazed anxiously.

Napier caught Bertrand's apprehension and stood up. Slapping down a handful of coins, he nodded to the young man, snatched Sorcha by the wrist and led her out the back door of the inn.

"By God, you have the manners of a Highland poacher!" he fumed. "Couldn't you at least keep your voice down?"

Sorcha was struggling in vain to get free. A dozen baby chicks scattered near her hem as she tried to fight back a sudden surge of tears. "I don't care! I meant what I said! I've waited two years to speak those words!"

His profile was turned to her, the jaw set, the dark eyes brooding. Napier remained silent for several moments, then tugged at Sorcha's arm. "There, beyond the wooden gate—it's the stable. Or," he demanded, not without a glint of humor, "would you rather talk in the henhouse?"

It was Sorcha's turn not to answer. She let him lead her across the tiny flagstoned courtyard, past the fragrant herb garden, and through the gate, which creaked on rusty hinges.

The stable was small, though at least a half dozen horses and three cows were quartered there. From the rafters, a pair of pigeons cast indifferent glances from small, beady eyes. Napier spotted a bench by a wall that was covered with bridles and harnesses. Indicating that they sit down, he finally let go of Sorcha's wrist, but kept one hand over hers. His usually controlled features were in chaos—anger, doubt, remorse, and pain vied for supremacy. Sorcha forgot her own tears and waited apprehensively for Napier's next words.

"You're right," he said in that low, rumbling voice that bespoke the depth of his emotion. "I was unfair and dishonest." His gaze locked with hers, and despair seemed to dominate his face. "It was devious enough of me to let you believe I was a priest. But, in fact, I am as unsuitable for you as any man who's taken Holy Orders. I can't expect you to understand my heart—or that hard brown nut that has become my heart—but it is impossible for me to love you the way a man should love a woman."

He paused to worry his long upper lip with his teeth, and Sorcha couldn't help but interrupt. "But you did! I know you did! I could sense it!"

Gavin Napier gave a little shake of his head and a rueful smile. "I admit, I even fooled myself. For one fleeting, joyous hour, I thought I could love again." His fingers tightened on Sorcha's as one of the horses whinnied softly. "Yet I know that was an illusion." The hunter's eyes were black with sorrow. "I loved once, you see, and that love destroyed me forever."

Even in her anguish at his words, Sorcha's practical nature asserted itself. "That sounds like an excuse," she said, almost more to herself than to Napier. "Isn't at least one broken heart expected in a lifetime?"

He let out a long, painful sigh and passed his free hand through his hair. "Jesu, if only broken, it would be mended. I speak of destruction, Sorcha, of willful annihilation."

Despite herself, Sorcha made an incredulous face. "Whoever this woman was, she must have hated you. Why?"

Gavin Napier shrugged his broad shoulders, and somehow the gesture made him seem much younger and more vulnerable. "I never knew exactly, but you're right. She answered my love with hate. And feasted on my misery."

A brindle cat nosed its way from behind a wooden bucket, looked up yearningly at the pigeons, and slunk away. Sorcha paused before phrasing the next, obvious question. "Who was this wretched woman?"

His eyes seemed to sweep up over Sorcha like a great, towering wave of remembrance. "Her name was Marie-Louise. She was my wife."

"Ah!" Sorcha actually fell back, her shoulders striking a piece of harness. "Was? What happened to her?" For one frightening second, Sorcha was afraid to hear the answer.

"She died." Napier took a deep breath, his hand still wrapped around Sorcha's. "She was with one of her lovers at the time."

Despite Napier's tragic statement, Sorcha couldn't help but feel a sense of relief. "She was faithless, I gather. I'm sorry." The words sounded insipid and Sorcha cursed herself inwardly. "Was all this a long time ago?" she asked too rapidly, as if to cover the lameness of her previous remark.

"It was," Napier replied, staring straight ahead at a stall where a black-and-white-spotted cow regarded him with big, somber eyes. "I was twenty-two when I met Marie-Louise. Her mother was a Scottish exile, her father was French. Marie-Louise was sixteen, lovely as the lily, full of grace and charm. She already possessed wiles that would make a man go mad with desire. I sought her hand, and though there were others, I was the only Scot." He stopped for a moment, then turned slowly to Sorcha. "This must be unpleasant for you, to hear me speak thusly of another lass."

"She's dead." Sorcha shrugged. "I don't fear the dead." Seeing the vivid pain in Napier's eyes, Sorcha bit her lip. "Yet you do. Or her, at any rate."

"Aye," he sighed. "I hadn't thought of it that way. But it's so." Releasing her hand at last, he rubbed his temples. "It must sound daft to you, yet it's very real to me."

"So it seems," Sorcha said as matter-of-factly as possible. "But tell me the rest. If you wish to."

"It's strange—but I do." His gaze was almost diffident. "I've never told anyone else—except Adam."

Sorcha nodded in mute acceptance of his confidence. Napier took up his tale, relating how Marie-Louise's mother had favored his suit. "Her father had been dead for many years, and Marie-Louise had no dowry, though that would not have deterred most of the young men who wanted to take her to wife. Still, my ancestry stood me in good stead. We were married just after Eastertide that year, the ceremony performed by my brother, Adam. Within a fortnight she was unfaithful to me." His voice rose slightly on the last words, but before Sorcha could interject more than a gasp of astonishment, he continued: "The worst of it was, she made no excuses. She even told me I should take a mistress if it suited me. She had no shame, no guilt—nothing except her insatiable need for men. Some were old and ugly, some were poor and simple; it made no difference. She mocked my humiliation, flaunted her sins. Everyone knew—and sniggered and sniped behind my back. A few were even bold enough to hurl their insults in my face."

Sorcha could stand it no longer. She put her hands on Napier's arms and clutched him tightly. "The heartless whore! But why, Gavin?"

He shook his head with such fervor that his entire body quaked. "I swear, I don't know. It went on for almost a year. And then she told me she was with child. She insisted it was *my* child, though how she could be sure, I never could guess. Still, I wanted to believe her. I hoped that a babe might change her." He stiffened in Sorcha's grasp and took a deep, excruciating breath. "Two weeks later, she lay in my arms and looked at me with those lovely eyes and smiled with that beautiful mouth and announced that she had destroyed our child. I tried to kill her."

Sorcha's hand fell away from Napier's arms and went to cover her mouth. "Oh, sweet Virgin!" she murmured, laying her head against his shoulder.

"She fled. Marie-Louise was strong, a superb horsewoman, a fine archer, as accomplished in sports as any man. I was insane with rage and hurt. The dirk had missed its mark. It gave her time to get away. Or perhaps I wanted her to escape." Again, Sorcha felt his body tremble against hers. "She never came back, of course. And a year or so later, I heard she was dead."

Gavin Napier now sat very still, his head down, his shoulders slumped, like a runner who has just completed an arduous race. Sorcha felt his pain, absorbed his misery—and still could not reconcile it with her own experience.

"The fact remains, my love, Marie-Louise is dead. Why should you let such a vile woman ruin the rest of your life?"

He lifted his head just enough to look at Sorcha's face, which still nestled against his shoulder. "Can you imagine what marriage means to me? Can you think how I must feel about women? Do you believe I could ever trust another one?" Sorcha gave him a little shake. "God's teeth, Gavin, what proof of my fidelity do you need? I haven't even thought of another man since I met you! And I've spent a year in a convent doing nothing except wait for the day you'd return to me! Your wanton Marie-Louise was a foul mockery of womanhood. I'm no more like her than you're like … Brother Jacques!"

Napier turned on the bench, his arm tentatively going around Sorcha's waist. "I'd like to believe that," he said slowly, "but I've spent eight years thinking otherwise."

"Then think again," Sorcha persisted, the green eyes boring into his as if she could compel him to change. "Be honest. Do I strike you as faithless?"

The storm clouds seemed to lift from his face. "No." Napier leaned down to brush her temple with his lips. "Yet I would live in fear that someday you would leave me."

"Pah," retorted Sorcha, though the word was muffled by Napier's beard. "I could never belong to any other man, not even in my thoughts."

"I want to believe you." He was speaking low, into the masses of black hair that tumbled over her shoulder. "I want to make you mine, yet love exacts a terrible price."

Sorcha leaned closer, purposely letting her breasts touch his chest. She was jarred by the contact, unprepared for the surge of desire that enveloped her body. But, she reminded herself, there was far more to this moment than sensual gratification. Gavin Napier's heart and soul were in her hands; she must convince this haunted, tortured man that love could be kind, not cruel, and that despair could be dispelled by hope.

Though Sorcha didn't draw back, she willed her racing pulse to slow down. Carefully studying Napier's face, she asked herself why him, why this perverse, baffling, agonized man who had deceived her, abandoned her, avoided her? Who had no money, no rank, no visible prospects?

There was no explanation, save for that dark wolflike face, with the sharp, broken nose, the secretive peat-brown eyes, and the long mouth, with its infrequent but devastating smile. Perhaps it was the rigid self-control, which, when broken, could sweep them both away like a spring flood. Or the inner strength of conviction symbolized by the tall, broad-shouldered body of muscle and sinew. Then again, Sorcha realized, it was the very elusiveness of him, like a great, wily salmon—or the Master of Ness.

"Love is what it is," she said at last, watching his brow furrow slightly. "It's there. Or it isn't." Lightly, she touched her breast, just above where it met his shirt. "I can't will it away." Her hand brushed his chest. "Can you?"

Slowly, vehemently, he shook his head. "No. Though I thought I could, for I feared it." Napier's arms pulled Sorcha close, his mouth seeking the curve of her throat. She went limp as he lifted her off the bench and carried her to the soft mound of hay in the corner of the stable. "Hold," he whispered, going to the door to bolt it from the inside. "Let's hope that Monsieur Bertrand's patrons are enjoying a lengthy repast."

Sorcha knew she should protest, for this was not the place, yet it was the time, and past time. She was too exultant in her triumph over Gavin Napier's memories to exercise restraint. Sorcha had waited too long, with so little hope, while loving and wanting him so very much. This time there was no shadow of forbidden passion, nor, Sorcha fervently hoped, the specter of a faithless wife. There were only the two of them, lying breath to breath in the fresh summer hay.

Napier cradled her head under his arm and gazed into her expectant face. "You are changed," he said, and while his voice was serious, it had lightened considerably. "I left a lass at Fotheringhay. I find a woman in Compiègne."

Reaching up to tease the dark hair that curled just slightly where his neck met the cambric shirt, Sorcha smiled. "I hope it's a change you like. I sensed Rob merely found me more obdurate."

"No!" Napier grinned, and Sorcha realized how long it had been since she'd seen those white teeth flash in the dark beard. "It seems to me," he went on, letting his free hand caress her hip through the fabric of her rumpled kirtle, "that while you might grow more bonnie, it would be well-nigh impossible for you to become more stubborn."

"Never half so stubborn as you," Sorcha said on a little sigh as Napier nibbled at her ear and let his hand wander into the secret recesses of her skirts. She savored the male animal smell of him, the hard, lean body against hers. Until this moment, the memory of their first lovemaking had seemed hazy, almost dreamlike. Now she recalled every nuance of his touch, of how he felt and moved.

His hands trailed sensuously up and down her linen-covered thighs, and he delighted in the little shivers he provoked. "Wondrous strange, we mortals," murmured Napier, claiming her lips in a deep, possessive kiss that seemed to go on forever. Sorcha wrapped her arms around his neck, straining him closer, welcoming the throb of her body, which begged for fulfillment.

At last Napier released her lips and began unlacing her bodice. He paused before slipping the camisole from her shoulders to grin at her again, this time a mischievous, conspiratorial exchange that captured the joy they found in each other. With one swift, sure movement, he uncovered her, savoring the ripe flesh in silence with those hunter's eyes. Then his hands engulfed her breasts, molding them into aching mounds of desire. His tongue lavished fuel to the flame, stretching each peak full and taut. Sorcha writhed beneath him, moaning with unbridled pleasure. Still suckling at her breasts, Napier reached down to pull the garments away from her lower body. The fragrant hay tickled her skin and somewhere in the stable, a horse pawed anxiously at the ground, but Sorcha was conscious only of her need for Napier. Her hands tugged at his shirt until she could cover the dark hair of his chest with kisses and knead his hard-muscled back with her searching fingers. He had clasped the core of her in his palm, exploring the secret, tender flesh until she cried out with yearning. "Gavin! I've waited too long! Take me now, or I'll die of longing!"

Sorcha's head was thrown back, her body arched, her legs spread wide to welcome him. He entered her, slowly, deliberately, with a sensitivity that suddenly gave way to passionate abandon, elevating Sorcha to a place apart, a burnished realm of joy. At last, he unleashed the gift of his love, wrenching shuddering cries of exultation from them both. They trembled in each other's arms, then went still, and lay together in the exhausted peace of total fulfillment.

It was the loud banging on the stable door that finally roused them. Startled, Sorcha lifted her head just enough to peer over Napier's shoulder. "God's teeth! What shall we do?"

Napier made a face, then disentangled himself from Sorcha and hastily put his clothes back on. "*Un moment, monsieur,*" he called out as Sorcha frantically pulled on her own garments. Moments later, Napier was at the door, lifting the bolt. "Forgive us," he said with a self-deprecating smile for the group of travelers from the inn, "but my betrothed and I have not seen each other for some time."

The men responded with wry, knowing glances. One of them bowed to Napier and murmured something about "*l'amour*" while the others chuckled indulgently. Though she knew she was blushing, Sorcha marched briskly to Napier's side. He put a protective arm about her, thanked the men for their true Gallic spirit of understanding, and led Sorcha out of the stable.

Finding an exit directly onto the back street, Sorcha and Napier headed in the direction of the monastery. His arm still held her close, and Sorcha reveled in the sense of belonging. "I love you," she whispered, ignoring the stares of two young girls carrying big baskets of brown eggs.

Napier smiled down at her, though his expression was in sharp contrast to his solemn tone. "Dare I love you? Will you swear to be mine?"

Sorcha squeezed his arm. "Don't be absurd! I am yours always." They stepped aside as a stout woman wearing a mound of petticoats and pushing a cart laden with fresh-cut flowers barreled past them. Sorcha paused, forcing

Napier to stop, too. She turned to look up at him, the green eyes unwavering. "Did you mean what you said? Do you truly want to make me yours?"

Napier was no longer smiling. His hand still rested on Sorcha's waist, though lightly now, silent evidence of his uncertainty. "You speak of … marriage?" The word was almost inaudible.

Forgetting she wore no shoes, Sorcha stamped her foot and felt the rough cobblestones bruise her sole. "Aye, marriage! Damn your ancient nightmare. Think of today; think of all our tomorrows! Will you marry me or not, Gavin Napier?"

He was staring over her head, in the direction of a fishmonger's stall and a candlemaker's shop. Beyond, the bulk of Compiègne's great castle was outlined against the flawless blue sky. The long face might have seemed emotionless to a casual observer, but Sorcha recognized the haunted eyes and the tightening of his neck muscles. There had been a time when she had paid no heed to those storm signals, but no longer. Sorcha pointed a finger at his face and spoke in a low but compelling voice. "Would you go on using me like a strumpet, or salvage my honor in holy matrimony? I had considered you something more than a callous seducer."

Napier gritted his teeth and looked down at Sorcha. "I was never clear about who seduced whom," he asserted so somberly that Sorcha almost missed the glint of humor in his eyes. "But since you have a father to avenge your virtue and I do not, I shall have to take the blame." He leaned his head to one side, regarding her with irony. "As you will, mistress, I'll consent to marry you."

Sorcha was torn between elation and chagrin. Never in her wildest dreams had she envisioned her betrothal occurring in such an unorthodox fashion. "I'm overcome," she declared with some asperity. "Shall we name the day?"

At last, Napier grinned and cuffed her chin. "Any day you like. The sooner the better, lest I grow skittish. The Feast of the Transfiguration, mayhap, to celebrate the change which has overcome me."

"Most fitting," agreed Sorcha, taking his arm. "Let's tell Rob and Rosmairi."

They took up the pace again, more swiftly, and suddenly Sorcha burst out laughing. The high, joyous sound turned the heads of two goodwives who'd been gossiping across from the abbey, and set a spotted hound to howling. But Sorcha paid no attention; she went right on laughing while Napier eyed her with amused indulgence.

"God's teeth," she exclaimed, catching her breath and turning a radiant face on Napier, "I'm so happy! I've never felt like this before." They were at the abbey gate, where the same porter still sat, his white cowl now virtually pink from the strawberry juice. Napier was as oblivious of the rest of the world as Sorcha, as he caught her to him and kissed her soundly on the mouth.

"By the Mass," he murmured into her hair, "I'd forgotten what happiness was! I feel like Lazarus, as if I'd been raised from the dead!"

Sorcha's face was pressed against his chest. This is where I want to be forever, she thought fiercely, and jerked her head up. "Don't let this be taken away from us," she demanded in a voice that shook with intensity. "Swear it, by all you hold sacred!"

Startled by her vehemence, Napier soothed her with his hands. "I hold you sacred. And I hold you now. I do swear it," he averred with absolute conviction.

Sorcha grew quite still, her breathing slowed, her body relaxed. At last, she pulled gently away, and her smile was touched by a faint tremor. She nodded toward the abbey gate. "Does the porter think we're mad?"

Napier glanced over his shoulder. "Aye. No doubt he's right."

Chapter 20

IT HAD NOT RAINED IN the vicinity of Paris for over two weeks. The horses' hooves spewed dust in thick clouds along the road that passed the great forest of Compiègne, by Creil, Saint Leu d'Esserent and above Chantilly, where the Oise turned in its westerly course to join the Seine on its voyage to the sea. Sorcha closed her eyes for a moment, to ward off the late afternoon sun, which was settling down over the fields of golden grain beyond the hedgerows. Her teeth felt gritty, her already soiled clothing clung to her body, and the boots she'd borrowed at the abbey were too big.

It was distressing enough not to have had the opportunity of announcing her joyous news to Rob and Rosmairi, but it was even more upsetting to find herself galloping across the Île-de-France under a hot sun in a hopeless cause.

When Sorcha and Gavin Napier had joined Rob at the abbey, they found him in an uncharacteristically grim, even frantic mood. Word had reached Compiègne that the barricades were up in Paris, that Catholics and Huguenots were fighting to the death, and that while the situation was dire, it wasn't entirely hopeless. If King Henri could retain control of Paris, peace might still be preserved. But, as always, the city was as capricious as a courtesan, surrendering her allegiance not to her acknowledged master, but to whoever pleased her present whim.

For now, Paris chose the protection of Spanish troops. Overwhelmingly Catholic, the city's inhabitants were less interested in the bogus claims of Philip II's daughter, Isabella, or the befuddled Cardinal de Bourbon than the fifty thousand crowns a month the Spanish king paid to quarter his troops in the city.

While Sorcha had argued that none of this religious or political turmoil should disrupt their own lives as Scots subjects on French soil, Rob had vehemently disagreed. "As long as I have responsibility for Brother Jacques, I must remain involved. If," Rob had declared heatedly, "Brother Jacques has headed for Paris, my conscience dictates that I must at least try to avert tragedy."

To Sorcha's chagrin, Gavin Napier had concurred with Rob. At first, only the two men were riding off for Paris, but Sorcha, suffused with guilt for failing to deter Brother Jacques, insisted on joining them. Gavin Napier displayed as little confidence in Sorcha's ability to sway the mad monk as she herself did, but Rob persisted. And Rosmairi, loath to be left behind, asserted that she'd come, too. That decision prompted the gallant Armand d'Ailly to call for his mount.

"You are too delicate, too fair, to face danger without protection," d'Ailly had told a blushing Rosmairi. "If you go, I go, too."

So the five of them now approached the walls of the great city on the Seine. As far as the eye could see, troops ringed the outskirts with clusters of men manning the weapons that would be used to force the city's surrender. Tents had been erected, horses were quartered in every open space, and troops in a variety of multihued dress milled about. Even from such a distance, the shouts of men could be heard, accompanied by the clang of steel and the acrid smell of gunpowder.

Sorcha leaned over the pommel of her saddle to peer at the strange tableau. "Jesu," she murmured, holding a hand over her eyes to keep out the sun, "how will we ever find King Henri amid such disorder?"

"I should think there would be a royal insignia above his tent," Rob said, though his voice sounded unsure.

Gavin Napier rubbed his bearded chin. Sorcha watched him in bemusement, overcome with a sudden desire to reach out and clasp him in her arms. "I wonder if King Henri wants his whereabouts known," remarked Napier, more to himself than to the others. "It might be easier to find Henri of Navarre than Henri de Valois."

The Sieur d'Ailly, who had moved his mount next to Rosmairi, frowned at the dust on his finely cut blue doublet. "I have heard that the leaders of the siege are positioned on the other side of the city. It would make sense if King Henri has come to Paris from one of the chateaus in the Loire Valley," d'Ailly added in a self-effacing manner.

Napier nodded, silently cursing the heat of the late summer day. The first of August, he realized—how long had Paris been under siege? Only a few weeks, surely not enough to weaken the will of its inhabitants. No wonder the soldiers appeared to be in disarray. Between the hot, increasingly humid weather and no prospect of victory, it was a marvel they hadn't deserted in droves. Napier turned to the others. "We'll ride 'round," he announced, then noted how Rosmairi had begun to droop in the saddle. "D'Ailly, think you it might be wise to remain here with Mistress Fraser? Perhaps you can find some shelter out of the sun."

Rosmairi lifted a hand in feeble protest, but d'Ailly leaned from the saddle to clasp her fingers. "*Non, non, ma belle demoiselle,*" he admonished gently. With his free hand, he made a sweeping gesture. "These rude, stinking soldiers, the lack of even the most basic comforts, the sweltering sun—none of this benefits your delicacy." His gaze held Rosmairi captive. "Come with me; we shall refresh ourselves at Saint-Germain-des-Prés."

With a jaundiced eye, Sorcha watched the pair canter off. Apparently, it hadn't occurred to the Sieur d'Ailly—or her brother, or Gavin Napier—that she might also be squeamish about encountering the seamier side of military life. She wasn't, of course, though the thought of Rosmairi resting in a cool place, drinking chilled wine and nibbling on partridge made Sorcha feel a pang of envy. But Napier was leading the way westward, still keeping their distance from the actual concentration of troops. To their right, several small farms and sturdy windmills sat untended under the August sun. No doubt the soldiers had driven off the local tenants while plundering both harvest and horses to augment the royal supplies.

"That's the Porte Saint Victor," Napier called out, pointing straight ahead. "From what I know of Paris, that's the weakest point in the wall. It's also the closest portal to the Île de la Cité and Notre-Dame." He had reined up as Sorcha and Rob joined him on a little knoll that rose directly in front of an empty pigsty. "Strategically, that's where I'd judge King Henri and the Duke of Navarre would set up their camps."

Rob was looking dubious as he surveyed the scene in front of them. At least a hundred men were lolling about on what had once been a flourishing summer garden. Beyond them, another sort of garden grew, a maze of canopied tents, displaying pennons of various colors and design, none of which meant anything to Rob or Sorcha. Napier, however, pointed to a dark blue tent that bore no mark of any sort. "There—where the pious pair of ministers confer—I suspect we'll find one or the other of our Henris."

Gazing past the soldiers, whose dicing and drinking was in no way disturbed by the newcomers' arrival, Sorcha saw two somberly garbed men who would have been more at home in Uncle Donald's entry hall than on a battlefield outside Paris. "They look like Protestant divines to me," Sorcha declared as three young soldiers called out a bold, lascivious invitation. Napier glared at them, but Sorcha merely made an unmistakable gesture of disdain. "Boors," she muttered, then waited for Napier's reply.

"You forget, King Henri has acquired a great number of Huguenot advisers to placate those who criticized him for being under the Jesuits' thumbs. Come," he said, urging his horse to circumvent a cask-laden cart, "I'll wager fifty crowns those devout divines can tell us where the King is quartered."

"But will they?" queried Rob, still unconvinced that they would ever reach their destination.

Napier's answer, if any, was drowned out by the cacophony of men hauling a huge contraption up to the lowest part of the wall. A fire-throwing machine, Sorcha guessed, and wondered what it must be like to live under the constant threat of invasion.

Threading their way among the now-dense gathering of soldiers, the trio drew up in front of the blue tent. Napier addressed the two men in courteous French, aware that they regarded him with grave suspicion. Sorcha discerned from their terse, yet polite, response that neither was willing to offer much helpful information. She and Rob exchanged desolate glances, but Napier wasn't giving up so easily.

Indeed, the ministers' reluctance only fortified his own determination. At last, he got down from his mount and took three swift strides to where Sorcha and Rob waited. "I think King Henri is in that tent," Napier said, purposely making his Scots accent thicker than usual. "Otherwise, they would not be so evasive." He shielded his face with his hand. "Sorcha, could you faint?"

For just an instant, Sorcha stared at him in puzzlement. Between the searing sun and lack of food and drink, it occurred to Sorcha that she could almost accommodate Napier without chicanery. Napier had turned back to the ministers and was making a little bow. He was thanking them graciously when Sorcha caught Rob's eye and tumbled as carefully as possible from the saddle. Alertly, Rob reached out to stop her fall though he almost twisted an ankle in his stirrup. Napier cried out in alarm, then rushed to Sorcha's inert form which rested half against Rob and half on the dusty ground.

"My Lord!" Napier exclaimed, ignoring the tongue which Sorcha stuck out at him. "My sweet bride has fainted. For the sake of the babe in her womb, give us shelter!"

The divines seemed to freeze in place, but Napier had already scooped Sorcha up in his arms, while Rob brushed dirt from his laymen's riding garb. Only the bull-like surge of Napier making for the tent's entrance could have dislodged the clergymen. Even as they protested volubly, Napier parted them from each other and charged into the tent.

Though the canopy protected the tent's inhabitants from the direct rays of the sun, the atmosphere inside was fetid and oppressive. There was a mingling of other smells, too, of rose water and wine and roasted meat. Sorcha peered through the masses of heavy hair that concealed her face; her entire body gave a jerk in Napier's arms.

A small, thin man with a large nose and vacant eyes was seated in an elaborately carved red-cushioned armchair on a makeshift dais. His lack of substance made him seem young, though the lines in his pale face gave a more accurate count of his years. His startled reaction to the interlopers was reminiscent of King Jamie, yet more languorous and exaggerated. Fleetingly, Sorcha recalled an Italian conjurer she had once seen in the High Street of Edinburgh. If this was King Henri of France, he had inherited more Medici than Valois blood.

Sorcha's impression took only seconds; it was the two people flanking King Henri who startled her. To the king's left stood a nun, her entire body enveloped in the white and black habit of the Dominicans; even her face was hidden by the squarish black coif. Yet Sorcha knew at once who the woman was and had to suppress a startled exclamation.

But Rob's self-control wasn't as rigid as Sorcha's. An astonished oath escaped his lips as he recognized Brother Jacques standing to the right of the King. While the others in attendance gaped at Napier, Sorcha, and Rob with stunned curiosity, only the triumvirate of King, monk, and nun seemed real.

King Henri was looking vaguely at no one and yet at everyone. "Who intrudes?" he inquired in high, fluting tones. "By Saint Louis, are we to have no rest before our supper?"

As Rob moved toward Brother Jacques, the young monk wheeled around and cried out in a hoarse, terrifying voice, "You'll have eternal rest now, wicked King of Demons!" The long blade flashed from under Brother Jacques's robes. He fell across the king's seated form so swiftly that not one of the French attendants could intervene. It was Rob who hauled Brother Jacques away, the white robes splattered with blood, the knife still dripping in his hand.

Napier dropped Sorcha, somehow managing not to let her get bruised. She landed on her side, scrambling among the booted feet for a clear view of the mayhem that was unfolding not more than two yards away. Rob, now joined by Napier and two effete Frenchmen, was grappling with Brother Jacques. The other royal attendants, perhaps a half dozen in all, were clustered around the King, whose piercing moans seemed to make the sides of the tent inhale and exhale with a death gasp of their own.

To her rear, Sorcha sensed rather than felt other people pushing into the tent. The two divines and a clutch of soldiers joined in subduing Brother Jacques. The tent had become so crowded, so tumultuous, that Sorcha feared being trampled. She was making a mighty effort to get to her feet when she espied the black-and-white nun's habit flying past her. Sorcha reached out with one hand, lunging for the ankles. In a flurry of skirts and veils, the other woman crashed to the floor, her face almost level with Sorcha's. The coif was askew, and somehow a smear of blood had stained the white wimple under her chin. Fumbling at the heavy garments, Sorcha tried to get a firm grasp on her adversary. "Athene," Sorcha rasped, "you are as guilty as Brother Jacques! You will not escape!"

But Athene had already rolled away from Sorcha, pulling herself to her feet by gripping a silken cord that dangled from the top of the tent. Her feet kicked out, striking Sorcha in the temple. Momentarily stunned, she didn't see Gavin Napier looming over her, his fists clenched. "Gavin!" Sorcha cried, as she shook away the sudden daze, "it's Athene!"

Despite the uproar that still raged within the tent, Napier's breathing was quite audible to Sorcha. She was now on her knees, her gaze traveling swiftly from Napier to Athene, who still clutched the silken rope in her hands. Though Napier's voice was a low, harsh rumble, it seemed to ring out over the wounded King's cries and his courtiers' lamentations.

"Oh, no," intoned Napier, the words making Sorcha's head spin, "this is not Athene! This is Marie-Louise, my faithless bride!"

Napier all but stumbled over Sorcha's kneeling form to reach out to the woman whose azure eyes blazed contempt and fury. "Pig!" shrieked Marie-Louise, who, with the added height of the coif, stood almost as tall as Napier. "Touch me and your whore dies!"

Sorcha's gaze was drawn to a foreshortened hackbut that had been hidden in the folds of Marie-Louise's habit. Napier didn't back off, but Sorcha knew instinctively that he would go no further. Then there was a ripping sound and a rush of air as the tent collapsed upon them. Napier was pushed to the ground under the weight of at least two soldiers who fell on top of him, but he managed to shield Sorcha with his body. In less than a minute Sorcha, Napier, and Rob had extricated themselves from the copious hangings of the tent and stood staring into a sea of incredulous, grizzled faces. Waving aside the soldier's gruff questions, Napier pushed his way through, with Sorcha and Rob trailing behind. But even as they reached the outer edge of the circle, there was no sign of Marie-Louise. She had vanished, as if by magic.

THE STUDENTS WHO USUALLY MILLED about the walls of Saint-Germain-des-Prés had begun to scatter as soon as word of the attempt on the King's life filtered through the precincts of the University of Paris. Even as Sorcha, Napier, and Rob galloped within the shadow of the abbey's ancient walls, the usually bustling faubourg was all but deserted. The adjacent Merovingian abbey had already stood for two centuries before the founding of the university over three hundred years earlier. Generation after generation of young scholars had disported and disputed on the Prés aux Clercs outside the Porte de Bussy gate into the city.

The August sun had finally disappeared behind the steep towers of the abbey walls when the trio reined up in the abbey courtyard. It took almost a quarter of an hour to locate Rosmairi and Armand d'Ailly in the common room, drinking sparkling Vouvray and sitting side by side on a settee in front of an empty fireplace. It appeared that they were the only two people in the vicinity of Paris who had not heard about Brother Jacques and the King. It also appeared that they were too immersed in themselves to care much about either monk or monarch.

"A pity," Rosmairi murmured without much interest, the golden lashes dipping against her cheeks as she let d'Ailly take her hand. "Why must men hate when they could love instead?" She cast a demure sidelong glance at d'Ailly, who beamed his approbation.

"Because hate is sometimes easier than love," Napier snapped, and made both Rosmairi and d'Ailly jump. "Particularly when it's fueled by a wicked woman."

D'Ailly, however, wasn't put off by Napier's bitterness. He squared his shoulders and assumed an air of dignity. To Napier, he offered the merest inclination of his head; it was Rob whom he formally addressed. "Since I am unable to speak with Mistress Fraser's parents, I must ask you to favor me in their stead. I wish very much to marry your sister. She has," he continued, again smiling fondly down at Rosmairi, "done me the greatest of honors by consenting to be my wife."

Sorcha didn't know whether to burst into tears of frustration or shake both Rosmairi and d'Ailly until their teeth rattled. How dare fate be so monstrously cruel? This was to have been the day that she and Gavin Napier announced their love to all the world. Instead, it was her sister and d'Ailly whose eyes shone with the ecstasy of mutual adoration. As for Sorcha, her whole life had been ripped into shreds inside King Henri's encampment. Henri might die; no doubt so would Brother Jacques. But when Gavin Napier learned that the wife he thought to be dead still lived, something inside Sorcha had died, too.

It wasn't fair to let her own misfortune ruin her sister's happiness. Still, Sorcha was unable to greet Rosmairi's betrothal with enthusiasm. "You scarcely know each other," she blurted, interrupting Rob's studied response of qualified approval.

"Our hearts have known each other forever," d'Ailly replied with a little shrug. "Nothing else matters."

"You've reflected on your vocation, I assume," Rob said in sober tones.

Rosmairi's pink cheeks flushed more deeply. "I reflected upon it for a year, as you know well. I don't believe I'm intended for the cloistered life." She darted Rob a defiant look, then turned to d'Ailly. "Fear not, we will bide our time until we're home in Scotland and have the blessing of my parents."

Both Sorcha and Rob expelled audible sighs of relief. "That's wise,"

Sorcha asserted; then, noting the resentment in Rosmairi's eyes and the hurt on d'Ailly's face, she rushed to embrace her sister. "Oh, God's teeth, Ros, I didn't mean to offend either of you! It just seems so … so sudden!" Sorcha felt Rosmairi tremble slightly in her arms. "I like Armand," Sorcha whispered into her sister's ear. "At least what I know of him."

Rosmairi hugged Sorcha in return; then the two young women broke apart, though Sorcha's hands remained on Rosmairi's shoulders. "I certainly like him better than George Gordon," she said aloud and was joined in laughter by Rob. D'Ailly, however, looked mystified, and Sorcha realized that Napier wasn't looking at any of them. He had moved off to the end of the huge open fireplace, leaning against the intricately carved mantelpiece, glowering down at the worn hearthstone. It was Rob, rather than Sorcha, who went to him.

"This has been a momentous day in more ways than one," Rob began tentatively. "Shall we pour wine all around and drink a toast to the happy couple?"

If Sorcha had been devastated by the events of the past hour, Gavin Napier had been all but destroyed. The hunter's eyes shot past Rob to Rosmairi and d'Ailly, boring in on the Frenchman with an intensity that surprised Sorcha. "Who are you?" Napier demanded, leaning across Rob to speak directly to the young Sieur.

D'Ailly seemed affronted. He had regained Rosmairi's hand but let it go to take a step nearer to Napier. "You know who I am. My full name is Armand de Gréve, Sieur d'Ailly. I inherited the title through my late father, Gaston de Gréve."

Napier's dark brows drew together; the sudden silence was broken by a burly monk who did his best to ignore the obvious tension while he lighted a dozen wall sconces with a flaming torch. No one moved until he had departed, though Rob wished him a pleasant evening. The burly monk grunted a monosyllabic response.

"You had a brother," Napier said in calmer tones after the monk had left. "Raoul, I think."

D'Ailly's hands lifted palms upward. "Why, yes, that is so. He …" D'Ailly paused to take a deep breath, as if fortifying himself. "He died. As did my parents, in a terrible fire."

Napier's mouth was grim. "Set by his mistress, isn't that right?"

D'Ailly looked from Napier to Rosmairi's questioning face, then hung his head. "Alas, that is so. She perished also."

"Oh, no!" The words seemed ripped out of Napier's lungs. "She lives. I have seen her within the past hour." He took three long strides to stand directly in front of d'Ailly. "I, too, believed she had died. But like the phoenix, she has risen from the ashes." Napier's blazing dark gaze was still riveted on d'Ailly's face. "You have reason to hate her, I know. But my reason is even greater. She is my wife."

Rosmairi let out a little cry; Rob put one hand over his face; d'Ailly appeared stunned. Sorcha, her lips working nervously, made no sound, nor did she move. More than anything, she wanted to comfort Napier with her arms, but didn't dare. It was d'Ailly who broke the spell, suddenly galvanized into a fury almost as fierce as Napier's.

"*Mon Dieu*! It is impossible! You—and that vicious strumpet? But how heartless, how evil she was! I tried to warn my brother but he refused to heed me." D'Ailly began to storm about, hands snatching at his wavy blond hair, boots resounding loudly on the stone floor of the common room. "I vowed vengeance years ago. I never rebuilt at d'Ailly because I had not the heart. Yet there was no way to assuage my pain, no victim to hunt down." He whirled, turning to face Napier once more. "Where is she? I will show no mercy!"

Rob, who had busied himself by pouring wine for the others, passed around the cups and intervened. Carefully, he explained to d'Ailly and Rosmairi exactly what had happened under the walls of Paris that afternoon. This time the young lovers listened with rapt attention. When he had finished, Napier had regained control and d'Ailly had simmered down.

"I would hope," Rob said in a reasonable voice, his gaze moving from Napier to d'Ailly, "that neither of you would insist on revenge. 'Tis a sin, you know." The hazel eyes were very solemn.

"It would be a greater sin to let such a woman live," asserted d'Ailly. "Can you not see, even this very day, she has no doubt murdered a king?"

"She has also vanished," Sorcha pointed out as she drained her cup and picked up an apple from a wooden fruit bowl on the long trestle table. "Frankly, I don't see how she will ever be found. Hasn't she been able to disappear for the past eight years?"

"She has," d'Ailly responded slowly, "but she is not safe in France. She will go elsewhere, and I can guess that destination."

Napier lifted an eyebrow. "You can? How so?"

D'Ailly gave Napier his little self-effacing smile. "Perhaps I know more of her … history than you, since I felt obliged to search it out on my brother's behalf. Not," he added with a rueful shake of the head, "that it did any good. But among Marie-Louise's lovers were numbered two of her mother's people." He took another deep breath before uttering their names. "One called the Master of Gray. The other, Francis, Earl of Bothwell. I suspect she will flee to their protection."

Sorcha almost choked on a piece of apple. "Gray! And Bothwell! Aye," she declared with vigor, "isn't it said that Bothwell dabbles in the black arts, much as it would appear Athene—that is, Marie-Louise—does?"

"So say his detractors." Napier's brow was deeply furrowed. He set to pacing the length of the hearth, his hands clasped tightly behind his back. "But what is her game? Why this intrigue with Brother Jacques and the poor King?" He halted, lifting his wine cup from the place where he'd set it on the mantel. "Does she meddle in Huguenot politics? She was raised Catholic, of course …." He drank quickly from the cup, which caught the flame of the nearest sconce and shimmered brightly in his hand. "Christ," he muttered, pounding his other fist against his thigh, "or is it that she is set on destroying all manner of men, whether royal or commoner?"

"That she is a destructive force is without question," d'Ailly stated flatly. "And I would wager what is left of my inheritance that even now she seeks passage to Scotland."

"Scotland!" Sorcha all but wailed the word. "Why must the vile baggage pollute our homeland!"

Napier snorted and shook his head. "Why not? She has defiled all else in my world."

"And mine." D'Ailly put an arm around Rosmairi. "Except for you, *ma belle*. Shall we sail to Scotland on the morrow?"

Having behaved so impulsively with George Gordon, Rosmairi felt obligated to show at least some measure of caution. "Why … we don't know if it's possible, Armand. We should go back to Compiègne and make arrangements …." She appealed to Sorcha and Rob for support.

"*I* am going back to Compiègne," Rob said stoutly. "I belong there, you may recall." He forced a wan smile on his sisters. "What you others choose to do, is your own affair, of course. But I give thanks to God to be out of all this horrible mess and to seek the peace of the cloisters and the company of sane men such as Brother John Fraser."

Sorcha tossed the apple core into the empty grate and turned inquiring eyes to Napier. "I have nowhere else to go but home," she said in a surprisingly small voice. "I may as well join Rosmairi and Armand."

Napier glanced down at her, but the dark eyes were so suffused with pain that Sorcha had to look away. "Aye," he answered dully, "you may as well."

The awful finality of his words made Sorcha's heart turn over in her breast. With heavy steps, she made her way back to the trestle table and poured herself another cup of wine. It tasted bitter and harsh, like gall. Sorcha drank anyway, aware that it might as well be the dregs of her life that she was consuming as night came down over Saint-Germain-des-Prés—and all of France.

THE CELL THAT SORCHA AND Rosmairi shared was tiny and narrow, containing only two lumpy cots and a crucifix. But darkness brought cooler air through the ancient slit of a window some six feet from the faintly dank stone floor.

Rob had made the sleeping arrangements with the burly monk.

After a cold supper for which Sorcha had amazingly little appetite, the travelers had dispersed to their quarters. Rob and d'Ailly were a few doors down from Sorcha and Rosmairi; Gavin Napier seemed to have been swallowed up by the vast abbey, disappearing into its recesses like a hare gone to ground.

Despite the cooler temperature, Sorcha found it impossible to sleep. Rosmairi, however, had dropped off almost at once, and now murmured contentedly from her cot just a scant yard away from Sorcha.

The intervening hours since the horrifying moments in the King's tent had given Sorcha the opportunity to sort out the day's tumult. The shock of discovering that Gavin Napier's wickedly wayward wife still lived had given way to the quest for a solution on Sorcha's part. Surely a woman who had deserted her husband some eight years earlier could not be viewed, even in the eyes of the Church, as his lawful spouse. An annulment didn't seem out of the question. In fact, for Sorcha, it seemed the only reasonable answer. She had waited too long, wished too fervently, to be denied forever marriage with the man she loved.

But the darkness of the night and the lateness of the hour were no allies to Sorcha's peace of mind. She was restless, uncomfortable, and unable to relax on the unyielding pallet which served as a mattress. Her state of mind was further upset by the sudden eruption of church bells, distant in the beginning, then nearer and nearer, until the abbey shook with the ringing of its own great campanile. Rosmairi was jarred into wakefulness, sitting up with her hands over her ears.

"What's happening? Is it morning?" She squinted into the blackness of the cell, trying to make out Sorcha, who was already on her feet. "It's still the middle of the night," Sorcha replied with more impatience than she'd intended. "I'd guess from that doleful sound that King Henri has passed on to his royal reward." Absently, Sorcha crossed herself. "Damnation, I refuse to stay in this pokey place and twitch away the night." She felt for her boots, slipped her feet into them, and banged out of the narrow cell, ignoring Rosmairi's plea to wait.

It seemed that most of the abbey's residents had been awakened by the mournful tolling of the church bells. Sleepy-eyed monks, looking like so many aimless ghosts in the unlighted hallway, milled about, exchanging hushed comments. It only took a few seconds before someone in authority— the abbot or his subordinate—led them away, presumably to the chapel to pray for the King's soul. And for Brother Jacques as well, Sorcha thought, knowing that he surely could not have survived the fatal incident.

Even after the corridor emptied, Sorcha remained. Rob and d'Ailly would be awake, too, she was positive of that. But so would Gavin Napier. On silent feet, she moved down the hallway, peering on tiptoe through the small wrought iron apertures in the cell doors. The first five were empty; within the sixth, a tall, broad-shouldered form was outlined against the slit of a window, staring out at the sliver of moon that rose above the Seine. Softly, Sorcha called Napier's name. At first, he didn't seem to hear her. Then, slowly, almost reluctantly, he turned toward the door. "He's dead," Napier stated in that same flat voice he'd used earlier in the evening. "As ever, Marie-Louise has gotten her way with a man."

Napier was making no effort to move away from the window nor to open the cell door. Sorcha pushed at the handle, which gave with only a slight rusty protest. Boldly, she entered the cell and went to stand behind Napier but made no attempt to touch him.

"I feel sorry for the King. And for poor demented Brother Jacques. But," she went on with more fervor, "I feel even more sorry for us. They are both doubtless beyond pain. You and I are not. Will we stop living merely because that ghastly woman has come back into your life?"

Napier remained motionless, still staring at the moon. "You forget, 'that ghastly woman,' as you call her, is my wife. We are bound together forever in the sight of God and man."

"Rot!" Sorcha exclaimed, not caring if she roused anyone who had managed to sleep through the din of the church bells. They were subsiding at last, though the abbey campanile still reverberated throughout the ancient stone walls. "Eight years! She wanted you to think she was dead. Don't be a fool, Gavin. Go to your bishop, to the Pope if need be, and have the marriage annulled!"

The muscles under the cambric shirt flexed across the back of Napier's shoulders as he clenched and unclenched his hands at his sides. "Even if it were feasible, I could not do it." He paused, then heeled around to confront Sorcha. "Don't you see," he all but bellowed at her, his face suffused with pain, frustration, and rage, "the very day I resolve to fling off the past, Marie-Louise rises up to haunt me! It's like a judgment from God!"

"From the Devil, more likely," Sorcha declared with a vehemence as great as his own. She grabbed him by the upper arms, attempting to shake him, but achieving little more than wrinkling his already dirty, rumpled shirt. "She is like some dreadful, awful millstone. You don't deserve to live out your life in her ominous shadow!"

Napier's mouth twisted into a grim, mocking parody of a smile. "But I do, Sorcha. I swore before God that I would!" He lowered his voice, and his face softened ever so slightly. "It's a matter of conscience. Do you think I want it this way?"

Sorcha dropped her hands. "Mayhap you do." She spoke accusingly, the green eyes defying him to deny it. "After all, it spares you the effort of loving and being loved in return." Sorcha tossed her head, the long, tangled hair swinging over her shoulders. "It seems to me, Gavin Napier, that you prefer hate to love." Her gaze continued to hold his until, at last, she swept about and started to march from the little cell.

But Napier came after her and wrapped an arm around her waist to make her face him. "That's not so. Not at all." He suddenly looked very old, like a man who has fought the battle of life but knows that even though the struggle isn't over, he has already been defeated. "I beg you, don't judge me so severely."

"Jesu," Sorcha cried aware that her breasts were almost touching his chest, "I will not believe there is no remedy for this wretched predicament! Will you not at least return to Scotland with me to see what my sire can do? Or seek the advice of Brother John Fraser at Compiègne? He is most holy and very learned." She put her hands on his chest, kneading the fabric of his shirt in a pleading gesture.

Napier sighed deeply. "Oh, Sorcha you make it so very difficult! But all the holiness and all the learning of other men cannot alter my conscience!" He noted the desperation on her face and put a hand over his eyes. "By the Mass, I would change in an instant if I could, I swear it." Hesitantly, he put his hand under her chin. "I need time. This has been a most terrible shock." Sorcha couldn't be sure if he was appeasing her or was serious. But his words were the only hope she had. She blinked several times before responding in solemn tones. "As you will. But we've wasted years already."

His face seemed to shed its protective mask, like a warrior casting off his chin mail. "Saint Paul said it as well as anyone," Napier declared, his hand still under her chin. " 'By the grace of God, I am what I am.' For Paul, it meant certain things; for me, it means others. Yet the result is the same—I cannot change being the man I've become—solitary, inflexible, overzealous, even haunted. As a younger man, I was none of those things. I was open to life and to love, but experience taught me differently. To survive in this world, I will take no more chances where my heart and soul are concerned." The dark eyes bore down on Sorcha, willing her to understand. "If you love me, you will accept me as I am."

Sorcha's brain toiled deftly through the maze of words before she abruptly pulled away from him. "Don't quote Saint Paul's epistles to me! They're but an excuse, and furthermore, that great apostle spoke as a man who had undergone enormous change for the better. If he was flawed, as he admits, he was also satisfied with the man he had become. I can't think that you have reached that same place in your life, Gavin Napier. You ask me to accept you, when, in fact, you don't accept yourself!"

"That's not true—nor is it fair." Napier made an effort at calm reason, but his skin had darkened and his eyes gleamed with indignation. "I live comfortably enough in my own skin. There is no way you can guess how it feels or fits on me. Only I know that. Nor is there anything you can do to change it, even though I might wish it otherwise."

They had reached a point where Sorcha considered further words a waste of breath. Still, she could not give up so easily. "I should think so." Her gaze was reproachful. "Indeed, you just said you didn't want it this way."

Napier's broad shoulders slumped, and he started to turn away. Yet her seemingly helpless stance, the valiant effort she had expended for them both, reminded him of that night so long ago when Patrick Gray and the Earl of Caithness had dumped her on his doorstep in Edinburgh. He had been overcome then by desire, but through superhuman restraint, he had controlled his baser emotions. Now, he wanted to make love to her even more than he had then; having tasted the bounty of her passionate nature, having only the previous day pledged to make her his wife, he was uncertain how long he could withstand the power of her love.

Nor was Sorcha obliging him by offering rejection. She remained standing before him, the big green eyes all but begging him to take her. Napier crushed her lips with his, holding her in a grasp so intense that Sorcha thought her spine might snap. His tongue probed deep into her mouth, making her dizzy with desire. She tried to pull her hands free from where they were trapped against his chest, but the kiss went on and on until both had to gasp for breath.

"Never doubt my love for you," he muttered in a hoarse voice against her ear. "Never. Yet as you love me, don't try to kill my soul. Remember, Marie-Louise almost killed my heart."

Sorcha's response was to lift her head to nip at his ear and tantalize him with her own tongue. Her hands were now free, clinging to his back, tugging at the cambric until she tore a hole between his shoulder blades. "I will not give you up. If," she breathed into his neck, "I have to pursue you to the Indies, I will. Nothing, not even Satan himself, can keep me from you!"

Napier put his hands on each side of her face, marveling at the ferocity of her love. "I don't deserve you. Nor do you deserve the pain I can give you."

"Then give me pleasure now, my love." Sorcha's eyes glittered with wanting. "The pain can wait until later."

Napier knew he had gone beyond the point of self-control. Recklessly, he parted the thin material of her bodice and pulled down the camisole to bare her breasts. Sorcha offered them proudly to his eager fingers, feeling the tips turn to fire at his touch. Expertly maneuvering Sorcha to the narrow cot, he lowered her body down onto the single, worn covering. He all but fell on top of her, and Sorcha couldn't suppress her laughter. "By heaven, it's no wonder monks are celibate! There's no room to be otherwise!"

Napier grinned at her, suddenly restored to the youthful humor that Sorcha found as appealing as it was rare. "Let us hope the good brothers pray all night for King Henri's soul. I wouldn't want to scandalize them after they've offered us their hospitality."

Sorcha made a gurgling sound that was meant to be agreement. But Napier was inching up her skirts with one hand while the other stroked the flat of her stomach. He tickled her navel with his tongue as he deftly continued to disrobe her. At last they were both naked, entwined together with her legs wrapped around his. She felt the hard strength of his manhood pressing her thigh and arched her body to savor the length of his lean, sinewy form. Napier sought her buttocks, squeezing them with strong, possessive fingers until he felt her quiver like a bird that has flown too far too fast. His mouth captured hers once more, taking away her breath, blotting out everything but the frantic need to be one.

Sorcha clasped him to her with an almost violent urgency as he entered her body and seemed to plunge deep into her soul. They moved together in a frenzied rhythm, the small cot rocking precariously. The moon was already setting over the Seine, but their joyful union was like a sunburst, evoking great gasps of ecstasy that left them limp and replete. Sorcha was astonished to discover there were tears on her cheeks.

With great reluctance, Napier withdrew from her, and stood up by the cot, gazing down at Sorcha with a mixture of amazement and awe. "I had told myself this wouldn't happen." His grin was lopsided, faintly sheepish, as he ran a hand through his dark, rumpled hair. "Was it only yesterday that we made love in that stable?"

"Jesu," exclaimed Sorcha, "it seems like years ago!" She sat up, leaning on one elbow, surfeited by lovemaking, and suddenly sleepy. "My clothes," she murmured, peering at the floor. "I must go back to Rosmairi."

"Aye." Napier handed her the garments and started to put his own back on. He was dressed before Sorcha was and, to her surprise, had put on his boots. He saw the query in her eyes and sat down next to her on the cot, where she was lacing her bodice. "I am leaving this place tonight," he said, and recognizing that an argument was forthcoming, he put a finger to her lips and shook his head. "I could wait until Rob goes back to Compiègne in the morning, but I need to ride alone, to think alone. Do you understand?"

Sorcha wasn't sure that she did, but was too tired to argue. "Compiègne," she repeated tonelessly. "Why?"

"There are things I should find out about Marie-Louise. That's where I expect to garner some answers."

"And then you'll sail for Scotland?" Her eyes were very wide, very steady.

Napier's finger had trailed down her throat. "Aye. I will come to Scotland.

I promise." The hunter's gaze was as unflinching as her own. He gave Sorcha a little smile. "I make no other promise, though. I can't." The smile stayed in place, obviously costing him great effort.

Sorcha nodded once, then rubbed her chin against his hand. "I'll wait."

Lightly, he kissed her mouth and the tip of her nose. "Until Scotland," he said quietly, and got to his feet. Sorcha watched from the cot as he put on his dirk and picked up his gloves. She noticed the rent in his shirt and smiled ruefully to herself. At least he'd have a souvenir of their mutual passion until he arrived in Compiègne. Yet even as he saluted her from the doorway of the cell, Sorcha felt a cold fear creep over her and wondered if, once alone, Gavin Napier might follow his conscience instead of his heart.

PART FOUR
1589-93

Chapter 21

THE FIGURES ON THE MUSIC box were twirling and bobbing to a repetitious tune that was giving Sorcha a headache. But the Queen of Scotland clapped her hands and laughed with delight. "Enchanting! They are James and I, is right, *ja*, aye, you wager?"

"I believe so." Sorcha smiled without enthusiasm. During the first month of her attendance on Queen Anne, Sorcha had found James's bride kindly and good-natured, but decidedly lacking in wit or depth. The King of Denmark's daughter was tall, slender, fair haired, and white skinned, a typical Scandinavian lass. But at fifteen, she was too young to be wise, and by nature, too simple to be clever. Still, it was impossible not to like the new consort. Even Jamie, with his predilection for handsome young men, seemed quite taken with her. Sorcha had been amused by the change in him when he returned from his winter wedding in Oslo and a honeymoon in Denmark that lasted into spring. The stooped shoulders were straighter, the high voice seemed deeper, even the scant beard was thicker. Jamie was suddenly more than an unnatural boy—he'd become a husband, and perhaps a man.

To some, the change was not necessarily for the good. There were people at court, the Master of Gray among them, who preferred a less assertive, a more malleable James. There were others who preferred no James at all. It was rumored that someone, possibly Bothwell, or a certain woman known as the Wise Wife of Keith, had connived at sorcery to sink the King's ship on his homeward-bound voyage.

Sorcha had learned of these tales that previous month, after James and Anne had returned to court. It was the first inkling that Marie-Louise might actually be in Scotland, though far from conclusive proof. Yet it had been sufficient to lure Sorcha back to Edinburgh, where she had requested and received an appointment as lady-in-waiting to the new queen.

As Anne wound up the music box once again, Sorcha gritted her teeth and tried to think of other things. Her gaze fixed on a tall mirror across the room, its frame embellished with graceful nymphs. Noting her own image, Sorcha couldn't suppress a wry smile. Dallas had finally succeeded in transforming her older daughter into a noblewoman of fashion and style.

Yet Sorcha still hadn't grown accustomed to her new image. The upswept crown of black waves, with thick curls resting on her shoulders, the dark green satin trimmed in jet, with a flounce of black lace petticoats, the molded bodice cut to show just a tantalizing burst of bosom, and the stiff high-standing black collar that framed her face struck Sorcha as most peculiar apparel for daytime wear and, for her, downright ridiculous at any hour.

But it was expected at court, and Sorcha was forced to give in. Of course, she enjoyed the admiring glances men cast her way and the fulsome words of flattery proffered by gallants at court functions. They made no real impression, however, since the only admiration Sorcha sought was from Gavin Napier.

"I must learn the words to this song," Queen Anne exclaimed in her heavily accented Scots as the music box finally wound down. "Tell me, Sorcha, how does it go? 'My laddie and I to Birth we will bide ....'"

"That's Perth," cut in Sorcha, her chin in her hand as she regarded the Queen with forbearance. "It's a town in Scotland."

"Ah! That's good, a town!" Anne clapped her hands again while Jean Gordon Sinclair returned the music box to its honored place on the marble mantel. Jean was as blond as Anne and almost as tall. As George Gordon's only sister, she had been given to the Earl of Caithness in marriage to cement the Catholic bond between the two Highland families. She was a sweet-natured, indolent girl; Sorcha wondered how she put up with a lout like Caithness. She also wondered about Gordon and his Stewart bride, but in the busy weeks since her arrival at court, she had not yet had an opportunity to ask. She already knew that Gordon had been driven out of Edinburgh by an enraged citizenry when it was revealed that he had corresponded secretly with Spain prior to the armada's attempted invasion of England. While Jamie had shown remarkable leniency toward Gordon for conspiring with Catholic Spain, the capital's Presbyterian majority had not been so broad-minded. Consequently, Gordon was said to be pouting in his Highland stronghold, no doubt waiting for the King to invite him back to court.

It was not a notion without precedence; despite the convoluted, even treasonable, intrigues of Patrick Gray, Jamie had just announced his favorite's reinstatement as Master of the Wardrobe. Sorcha had seen Gray at court on several occasions, but fortunately, always from a distance. As for Bothwell, he had not been in attendance on the King since Sorcha returned to Edinburgh. Nor had she ferreted out even a trace of Marie-Louise. For all anyone knew, the dreadful woman had remained in France.

It seemed that Gavin Napier had stayed there, too. While the Queen twittered with Jean Sinclair over her toilette, Sorcha thought back to the last time she had seen Napier, in the monk's cell at Saint-Germain-des-Prés. He had promised, he had given his word, he would come to Scotland. But almost a year had passed, and only one letter had reached her. It had arrived at Gosford's End just before Christmas, and was brief and to the point. "Many obstacles have arisen to deter me from sailing to Scotland," Napier had written. "Not the least of these is the illness of my brother, Adam. I pray that he will survive the winter here at Amiens. I left your good brother and his kinsman in robust health at Compiègne, thanks be to God. May the Virgin watch over and keep you until I can be with you once again." To Sorcha's dismay, he had signed the missive, "Faithfully, Gavin." It seemed to her that Napier's pen had as much trouble expressing love as did the rest of him.

"Now we converse, *ja*?" Queen Anne was looking charmingly eager as Jean tucked the last curl into place with a turquoise-studded comb. "I ask today the questions." She beamed brightly at Sorcha. "It is charmed I am to meet you. Where from do you ail?"

"*Hail*. With an *h*," corrected Sorcha. "I hail," she replied, breathing heavily into the second word for emphasis, "from the Highlands. I love my homeland very much." The slow, stilted speech managed to carry conviction. Indeed, this time when she had returned home, it had been much harder to leave. Instead of loosening with the years, the ties of family seemed to grow tighter. Magnus and his wife had a new baby son and were building a home overlooking Beauly Firth, just an hour's ride from Gosford's End. Rosmairi and Armand had been married in the chapel at Beauly in late January. While the new groom was anxious to go to Edinburgh and seek out Marie-Louise, Rosmairi begged him to stay in the north at least until spring. By then, she was pregnant, and now Armand wouldn't leave her side until after the babe's birth in October. So Sorcha had gone instead, seeing herself as the envoy-designate in the search for a woman who could disappear for years at a time. Sorcha's reluctance, however, was tempered by the notion that if Gavin Napier ever came back to Scotland, he would first pass through Edinburgh.

The Queen had turned to Jean. "I admire your gown. It is yellow ..." She paused to point at Jean's sleeves. "And blue." Anne indicated the embroidered overskirt. "Your eyes are blue, too. Like mine."

"Excellent, Your Majesty!" Jean enthused. "Your gown is white and purple and ...."

A knock from the anteroom interrupted Jean's recital. Sorcha rose to answer it, but her hand froze on the crystal knob when she saw the Earl of Moray standing before her. "My Lord," she said in an uncertain voice. "I didn't know you were at court!"

"Only since yesterday." Moray smiled, the blue eyes taking in every detail of Sorcha's altered appearance. In the almost three years since Sorcha had last seen him, the Earl had matured; his handsome face was more finely etched, the auburn hair just a shade darker. He was as lean and fit as ever and, if anything, had grown even better looking. Sorcha marveled that she was not moved by his obvious attraction and wondered if her indifference showed.

There was no way of knowing, since Moray managed to tear himself away from studying Sorcha to hurry toward the Queen and kneel at her hem with an artful bow of homage. "Your Majesty," he exclaimed, introducing himself, "I have heard that our sovereign liege calls you his 'Juno of the North.' How apt!" He smiled winningly at Anne, who seemed quite overcome by his effusive, yet open manner. "I offer my humble self in your service, now and always."

Anne glanced questioningly from Sorcha to Jean, who both nodded imperceptibly. "But, *ja*, aye, for certain!" Anne replied heartily, bidding Moray rise. "You are cousin, *ja*? So many cousins, half of Scotland, I think!"

For once, Sorcha had to agree with the Queen's assessment. Moray was seating himself in a chair next to Anne's as she had insisted, and within moments, they were chattering away like old friends. Anne's conversational skills seemed to flourish in his company. Sorcha and Jean withdrew to the far end of the room, exchanging bemused glances.

The budding friendship was interrupted some twenty minutes later by King Jamie, who greeted Moray warmly and then announced that the court would move that very day to Falkland. "I must hunt," he announced, puffing up his thin chest in the direction of his bride. "I grow bored in Edinburgh, and you must see more of your new domain."

Anne was excited by the prospect. It had seemed to Sorcha that after less than two months in the capital, the Queen had also grown bored. But Anne's attention span wasn't long; Sorcha had the feeling that she would grow bored almost anywhere, unless she was dancing or playing cards, avocations frowned upon by the more stalwart presbyters.

Maids were summoned immediately, and a flurry of activity ensued. Sorcha was dismissed to tend to her own packing and, by chance, left the Queen's chambers at the same time Moray did. The anteroom was deserted, and Moray paused, blocking the outer door.

"It's been a very long time," he said lightly, his hands remaining motionless at his sides. "Time seems to have turned you from Circe into Aphrodite."

The comparison reminded Sorcha of Marie-Louise, and her alter ego, Athene. Unconsciously, Sorcha made a face, which Moray took for displeasure.

"Forgive me, I grow too familiar." His skin darkened, and he inclined his head to one side. "I know little of what has happened to you in recent times. Is it true you've been in France?"

Sorcha had been about to apologize for misleading Moray but changed her mind. "I stayed in a convent for a while with my sister, yes." She offered Moray a cool smile. "But these past months I've been at home in the Highlands."

Moray turned quite serious. "I see. Is it true that your younger brother is going to become a priest?"

Sorcha was at once on guard. For all his open-mindedness, the Earl of Moray was still a staunch Protestant. "Is that a concern of yours, My Lord?" she inquired archly. "I would have thought that Johnny Grant would be more interested, having been appointed by the Privy Council to search out Papists in the district of Moray."

The Earl's handsome face seemed to grow even darker. "Young Grant is more fanatical than I in such matters. But then," Moray said, with a forced shrug of indifference, "that is why he has been assigned the duty and I was not."

A sharp little laugh spurted from Sorcha's lips. "If I were Johnny, I'd not go searching for Papists at Gosford's End. He didn't dare venture near our property while I was there."

Moray started to speak, apparently reconsidered, and rubbed his forehead vigorously. "You are displeased to see me, that's clear. Why?" The blue eyes were genuinely perplexed.

Sorcha stared at Moray for a long moment without blinking. "Why, indeed," she echoed, on a weary sigh. She clamped her lips together as Jean Gordon Sinclair emerged from the Queen's chamber carrying three hatboxes, the top one threatening to topple over. "Here, let me help," Sorcha insisted, going to Jean and taking one of the boxes. Turning to Moray, Sorcha made an awkward little curtsy. "Pray excuse me, My Lord, but I must make ready for Falkland." Over her shoulder, she threw him a warmer smile than she'd offered earlier and was faintly touched to see the pleasure that clearly showed in his eyes. Another time, another place ... the words tripped unbidden through her mind, and Sorcha suddenly felt weighed down by more than Queen Anne's hatbox.

Chapter 22

Aɪʟɪs Fʀɪᴢᴇʟʟ ʜᴀᴅ ᴀɢᴀɪɴ ᴊᴏɪɴᴇᴅ Sorcha on the journey to Edinburgh. While the serving girl had rarely complained about staying in the Highlands during Sorcha's time in France, Dallas realized that once having been exposed to the stimulation of the city and the court, an alert, intelligent girl such as Ailis wouldn't be satisfied with the comparatively dull and unexacting routine at Gosford's End. At least not until she was married and had a family to tend, a prospect which was not yet imminent. So Ailis had gone south with Sorcha, and both young women were well pleased.

It was Ailis who now oversaw the loading of their baggage onto a cart already sagging with the other attendants' gear. Sorcha stood close by with the Countess of Moray and three of her children. Moray's wife had seemed genuinely pleased to see Sorcha again, and while rather pale, she displayed signs of having grown more self-confident and talkative since their last meeting. The countess spoke with pride of her four children, particularly the infant, May, who resided placidly in the arms of a chunky wet nurse.

"She's a good bairn," the countess remarked, motioning for the wet nurse to draw nearer so that Sorcha could get a better view. "Jamie and Francis and Meg cried a great deal. But," she rhapsodized, "my wee May is all smiles." To prove her point, the Countess tickled the baby's rosy cheek and was rewarded with a coo of pleasure followed by a hiccup.

Seeing that the courtiers were beginning to saddle up, Sorcha gave little May a pat on the head and turned to call for Ailis, who had momentarily disappeared in a sea of carts and wagons. But it was Doles McVurrich, not Ailis, who was hurrying up the drive of Holyrood, trying to wedge her way through the train of animals and vehicles that had begun to kick up dust and gravel as they moved away from the royal palace.

Doles was out of breath, and her cheeks were becomingly flushed when she finally spotted her cousin. Now maturing into adolescence, Doles had grown considerably taller, and while she was still rather plain, the promise of a handsome woman was unfolding in the regularity of her features and the soft new curves of her body.

"Coz!" Doles cried, waving at Sorcha. "Thank heaven I found you!" Hurrying with a coltish gait, Doles sketched the merest of curtsies to the Countess of Moray before taking Sorcha by the hand. "Please, come to our house! My father is very ill and my Lady Mother sent me to fetch you."

Sorcha hesitated only long enough to tell Ailis to ride out with the others to Falkland. After a minimum of protest, the serving girl shrugged her wide shoulders and turned away. Sorcha and Doles all but ran down the drive and past the Girth Cross into the Canongate. As ever, a number of local citizens had gathered to watch the King and his new bride ride out of the palace precincts. Doles led Sorcha around them by a shortcut through Lord Seton's garden, and moments later, they had emerged by the entrance to a goldsmith's shop, just above the old Canongate Tolbooth.

"What's wrong with your sire?" Sorcha asked as they slowed their pace upon sighting the house in Panmure Close just ahead. She had seen Uncle Donald and Aunt Tarrill twice since her return to Edinburgh, and except for looking somewhat tired the last time, he had appeared in good health.

Doles pushed open the wrought iron gate that separated the house from the street. "He complained of his stomach this morning and decided against going to his bank." From over her shoulder, Doles gave Sorcha a meaningful look. "You know how ghastly he must have felt if he wouldn't attend to his business." She paused to open the front door. "Then, just about half an hour ago, he collapsed. We sent for Dr. Hunter, who is with him now."

"Sorcha!" Tarrill's skirts gave a mighty rustle as she ran to embrace her niece. "I was afraid you'd already left! Dr. Hunter said he'd heard the court was going to Falkland." She stepped back, her long face drawn with anxiety. "Praise God, Donald seems better. The good doctor thinks your uncle works too hard."

"I wouldn't discount it," Sorcha said dryly, reminding Tarrill of Dallas. "Shall I go see him?"

Tarrill, momentarily lost in reverie, shook her head. "Dr. Hunter says he must sleep." She linked her arms with Sorcha and Doles, leading them into the parlor, where the sun shone in patches through the mullioned windows. "I have been a bit selfish," Tarrill admitted as she sat down in a big upholstered armchair while Sorcha and Doles seated themselves on a cut-velvet divan.

"For just a few minutes, when I feared the worst, I desperately wanted my own kin to comfort me."

Sorcha pulled off the suede gloves with their heavily embroidered cuffs and nodded in sympathy. "Of course. But where is Aunt Glennie?"

Tarrill rolled her dark eyes, shedding sentimentality like a second skin. She reached for the comfit dish by her side and passed it to Sorcha and Doles. "Your Aunt Glennie's comings and goings are quite unpredictable ever since she took up with that mapmaker from Leith. Morpeth, his name is, and widowed twice over like Glennie, but close to twenty years older, and colors his hair the most monstrous shade of red." Tarrill chewed aggressively on the sweet she had popped into her mouth.

Turning to Doles, she asked her to bring them some wine. "A chilled bottle," Tarrill called after her daughter. "I fear the day grows overwarm. Now," she said, rearranging her skirts and putting her feet up on the footstool that matched the one in front of Sorcha, "you must tell me of your adventures in England and France. We've had no opportunity to talk privately since you got back to Edinburgh."

Judging from her aunt's relaxed attitude, not only had her worries about Uncle Donald subsided but she also seemed to be in the mood for a long gossip. If Sorcha left right now, she could still catch up with the rear van of the royal entourage. Yet, she was loath to go, aware of how lonesome Aunt Tarrill must get for the companionship of her Cameron kin. If necessary, Sorcha could ride alone to Falkland. It wasn't that far, and the weather was certainly going to hold. Accepting a frosted goblet of white wine from Doles, Sorcha commenced her recital, careful to omit those parts that were too personal— or too distressing—for the ears of either her aunt or her young cousin. Yet, Sorcha knew, those intimate details, no matter how harrowing, were precisely what Tarrill would most enjoy. It seemed almost a pity not to confide in her kindhearted aunt.

It was midafternoon by the time Sorcha finally sallied forth from the McVurrich household. The doctor had long since departed. Uncle Donald still slept, and Aunt Tarrill was growing a bit drowsy after her fourth goblet. Sorcha was feeling faintly lightheaded herself as she paused by the Girth Cross to splash water on her face. Three young boys were trying to give a cat a bath in the trough that ran around the base of the cross but the youngsters were having little success. Sorcha noted that the boys seemed a great deal wetter than the cat.

Still smiling over their antics, Sorcha found the courtyard at Holyrood deserted, except for several riders who were just heading out through the Water Gate. She started to call after them to wait up until she could get a mount, but one of the men turned in the saddle, and Sorcha recognized him

as the Earl of Bothwell. Quickly, she drew back and waited until the company
had disappeared in the direction of the royal tennis courts.

So Bothwell was back, Sorcha thought to herself, gathering up her skirts
to avoid a large mound of horse droppings. Doubtless he was following the
King to Falkland, hoping for a royal pardon of his latest misdeeds. There were,
Sorcha knew, several: Bothwell was said to have dabbled in witchcraft; he had
publicly stated that Scotland would be better off joining the Spanish armada,
rather than fighting it for England's sake; and he had taken part in a street
brawl that had resulted in the death of Sir William Stewart, Arran's brother.

As always, Sorcha marveled at the blood feuds not just spawned but
nurtured by her countrymen. She was waiting for a load of timbers to cross
in the direction of Dalrymple's Yard when a figure in dark riding clothes
appeared, leading a horse out of Leith Wynd. Sorcha squinted against the sun
and felt her heart skip a beat. Surely, after all these months it couldn't be he!
Her mouth agape with surprise, she waited almost a full minute until he was
abreast of Saint John's Cross, then she rushed to meet him, her riding hat
clutched to her head.

"Gavin! Is it truly you?" Sorcha grasped his arm with both hands, her face
glowing with pleasure. "When did you arrive?"

"Within the hour," Napier replied, forcing his voice to keep level. "I had
Naxos here transported as well." He patted the stallion's nose. "Adam is staying
in Leith for the time being."

"Adam!" Sorcha exclaimed, embarrassed by not asking after Napier's
brother immediately. "Of course! How is he?"

Napier's taciturn expression didn't change. "Much improved, thanks be to
God." He paused to cross himself deliberately, devoutly. "Yet the sea voyage
cost him greatly, and I fear it will be a few days before we proceed north."

Sorcha's hands fell to her sides. Her sudden elation was fading fast. "You
aren't going to stay in Edinburgh, then?"

If the smallness of her voice dismayed Napier, he gave no sign. He was
walking his horse to the trough in the middle of the Canongate. The three
boys and the cat had vanished, permitting Naxos to drink in leisurely peace.
"I'm told there's fresh trouble afoot in the Highlands," Napier said over his
shoulder. "Have you been north recently?"

Gavin Napier's manner was so detached, so relentlessly formal that Sorcha's
disappointment gave way to rage. She snatched off her riding hat, flinging
it about in front of her like a warrior's shield. "God's teeth, Gavin, it's been
nigh on a year! Aren't you pleased to see me?" she demanded, disconcertingly
aware that she echoed Moray's recent words to her.

Napier stopped in the process of checking the stallion's bridle and looked
at Sorcha as if seeing her for the first time. The hunter's gaze was steady but

guarded, an expression Sorcha knew all too well. "Aye, why would I not be? Yet it would be unseemly to demonstrate my delight in the middle of the Canongate."

"Or the middle of paradise, if it came to that," Sorcha shot back. A passel of urchins had gathered round to watch the grown-ups argue. Two goodwives who had just emerged from the goldsmith's shop stopped to stare. "If you can't express your enthusiasm here, may I ask where you intend to do it? The Canongate Tolbooth, perhaps?" Sorcha gestured up the street with a wave of her hat. "Well?"

Napier abandoned the stallion to focus his full attention on Sorcha. He took a deep breath, seemed to grow ominously taller and broader in the process, and stepped a bit closer, lowering his voice so that neither urchins nor goodwives could hear. "You appear oblivious of one significant fact—I am married to another woman." He paused to let his statement sink in. "No, I didn't find her in France. But I did learn some things that may explain—if not excuse—her brutal behavior." Napier took another step nearer to Sorcha. "By chance, I happened to sail with a man who remembered a blond lad with a scar on his neck who'd taken the last ship out of Le Havre before the French ports were closed after King Henri's assassination. The lad's destination was Dunbar, and I'd stake my life on the fact that it was Marie-Louise in disguise. She would have to put her hair up to pose as a boy, which would have revealed the scar." Taking a third step, Napier was all but six inches from Sorcha's errant riding hat. "Making these inquiries, in addition to a great many more, as well as caring for Adam, have taken up the past eleven months." Napier stood where he was but leaned down so that his chin was almost touching the top of Sorcha's upswept coiffure. "And what have you and Armand accomplished in that time?"

Napier's looming, implacable presence forced Sorcha to rein in her temper. But she was still angry. "Armand has married my sister and got her with child," Sorcha asserted. "Manly deeds, I must say, which some would find more commendable than vengeance or rancor." To her left, the urchins crept closer; on her right, the goodwives pressed nearer. Sorcha glared at all of them, and Napier as well. "I refuse," she hissed at him, "to stand here another moment and argue as if we were part of a public spectacle. Will you come with me to Holyrood?"

Napier's thumb jerked in the direction of Panmure Close. "Why not to your kin's house?"

"Because Uncle Donald is very ill," Sorcha replied, perversely pleased that she had a good reason to foil Napier's suggestion.

Napier shrugged, then turned to take his horse by the reins. The urchins and the goodwives slipped away, obviously disappointed that what had promised to be a fine quarrel had fizzled out so quickly.

While the courtiers and their attendants had left Holyrood, a skeleton staff remained. Sorcha, who had consumed nothing but sweetmeats and wine since breakfast, led Napier into the small dining room just off the King's bedchamber and requested that a servant bring them food. Napier, who had never been inside the palace before, asked Sorcha if this was the infamous room where David Rizzio, Queen Mary's hapless secretary, had been stabbed to death by jealous nobles. Sorcha answered vaguely that she thought it was, but long-ago events weren't uppermost in her mind. She wanted to know precisely what Napier's plans were. And, though she didn't say so, most of all, she wanted to find out if they included her.

Napier didn't answer directly, but began instead by elaborating on the information he'd unearthed about Marie-Louise's background. It seemed that her father's family had turned Huguenot, but when the daughter of a Scots expatriate married him, their vows were witnessed by a Catholic priest. Marie-Louise was their only child, and her sire doted on her.

"But when she was about seven or so, Catherine de Médicis ordered the Saint Bartholomew's Day Massacre. Though Marie-Louise's father hadn't openly practiced his religion since taking a Catholic wife," Napier went on, "he was slaughtered by his neighbors—right before Marie-Louise's terrified eyes."

"Jesu," whispered Sorcha, surprising herself by feeling a pang of pity for the young Marie-Louise. "I must admit, that would leave a far deeper scar than the one on her neck."

"Aye," Napier agreed, as a servant, looking much put out, entered the room carrying a tray of cold quail, bread, wine, and fruit. He bristled when Sorcha asked if there was cheese, but she ignored his ill humor and set about decimating a quail breast.

"I knew none of this, only that her father had been dead for some years," Napier said, taking up his tale. "I can only guess that deep down, Marie-Louise harbored an abiding hatred of Catholics. Perhaps she hated everyone who professed to belong to a specific faith, since as a child, she must have equated religion with evil. It's even possible that she grew up hating men." Breaking off a crust of bread, Napier gazed at it with unseeing eyes. "I also suspect that somehow she decided to use poor Brother Jacques as her tool in destroying the King of France. She must have convinced him that she was as fervent a Catholic as he was. And then, as many believed, persuaded him that Henri was too sympathetic to the Protestant cause and had to die. If Brother Jacques questioned why she dabbled in black magic, she could explain that so did King Henri—and she was merely fighting fire with fire. So to speak." Napier shook his head, as if he were unsure that anything he had just said was credible. "I feel—and Adam thinks so, too—that Marie-Louise will try to stir up as much trouble here in Scotland as she did in France."

Sorcha was picking out a tiny piece of bone from her quail. "But Jamie isn't Catholic. What kind of havoc can Marie-Louise plan to make?"

Napier lifted his shoulders. "Anything to discredit or undermine the Church, I suppose. Perhaps she'll foment further dissension between the influential Catholic families."

Sorcha snorted. "As if they needed help! You mentioned trouble in the Highlands—did you refer to Johnny Grant?"

For the first time, Napier's face broke into a smile, albeit a wry one. "Aye, a name from out of your past, eh? But that's only part of it. Gordon and Errol are said to be riling up a rebellion."

"They plot against the Crown?" Sorcha saw Napier nod, and licked butter from her fingers.

"If the rumor is true, they will damage the fragile framework of a Catholic alliance. They must be stopped." He poured wine for them both into pewter cups and handed Sorcha hers. "You haven't yet told me what you've learned since coming back to Scotland," he reminded Sorcha, the smile gone.

The shadows were beginning to lengthen between the openings in the red velvet draperies, making dark, shifting patterns on the wine-colored damask table covering. Sorcha inspected a peach, then bit into it, skin and all. She cursed silently as a few specks of juice landed on the black suede slashings of her blue riding habit. "I have little to report. There are stories going round that Bothwell is using sorcery against the King and that he may have associates. Or are they called familiars?" Her face puckered over the distinction, but without waiting for clarification from Napier, Sorcha continued in a rueful voice, "Yet there is no mention of anyone like Marie-Louise, only some goodwives from North Berwick or some such place."

Napier washed down the last of his crust with the wine and pushed away from the table with one booted foot. The room was so narrow that as he leaned back in the armchair, his long legs almost reached the opposite wall. Sorcha was sorely tempted to leap from her chair and fall to her knees beside Napier—but she did not dare. "It sounds too coincidental not to be Marie-Louise," Napier said at last, thoughtfully rubbing his beard. "While I don't know everything she did during the eight years of her disappearance, I'm told she practiced the black arts in various places."

Sorcha put her elbows on the table and rested her chin on her folded hands. She regarded Napier levelly, and her voice was very serious. "Do you believe in such things, Gavin?"

He returned her unflinching gaze. "By the Mass, no! It's superstitious nonsense. The problem is, many—perhaps most—people do believe in witchcraft."

"I don't think I do." Sorcha reflected for a moment, realizing that she hadn't given the matter much thought one way or the other. "There have been burnings and hangings ever since I can remember," Sorcha said, trying to dredge up some of the crimes committed by alleged witches and sorcerers. "Not around Gosford's End, of course. My parents wouldn't permit such madness."

"Alas, they're not in the majority. King Jamie takes witches quite seriously, I hear."

"True." Having disposed of the subject of Marie-Louise, the Highland crisis, and black magic, Sorcha was more than anxious to discuss their own problems. But Gavin Napier was on his feet, brushing crumbs from his shirt and stretching his arms. "I must be off to the saddlemaker's. Naxos's girth is broken. And no doubt Adam is wondering what has become of me."

Uncertainly, Sorcha also got to her feet, brain whirling in an effort to think of some credible reason why Napier shouldn't leave—or why she ought to join him. Surely he wasn't going to simply walk away after all these months?

That, however, appeared to be exactly what Gavin Napier intended to do. He was at the arched door of the supper room, carefully ducking his head since it had originally been constructed for a much shorter race of people.

Sorcha flew to him, clutching at one arm. "Gavin! By all that's holy, don't you want to kiss me? Or at least hold me? How can you be so ... so cold?" Her voice quavered, and the green eyes glistened with tears.

Napier went rigid at her touch. He drew up very straight, just missing the outer edge of the doorway. "I can't kiss you. I can't even hold you." Deliberately, he pulled away from her grasp. "If I do, I will keep kissing and holding until I possess you. And that would be wrong." He had moved just far enough from her that his face was now in shadow. Napier spoke heavily, each word weighted to make Sorcha believe him. "I don't want you to be my whore. I want you for my wife. Since that's not possible, I won't demean you—or myself—by using your body, no matter how freely offered."

Sorcha listened to the leaden words with a sick, hollow feeling at the pit of her stomach. From somewhere, a small voice of memory pricked at her brain. She'd condemned Johnny Grant for his lack of fidelity and chided Moray for his duplicity. How ironic that the only man she really loved should possess the qualities the others had lacked—and that she should curse him for it. With a shaky hand, Sorcha brushed her eyes and swallowed hard.

"You'll take care in the Highlands?" She sounded very tentative, almost wispy.

"Aye." Napier nodded once. He had remained very still, and now the dark brows drew close together as he pulled his bearded chin. "Keep me in your prayers."

"Of course." Sorcha moved a pace backward, as if signaling to him that he was free to go. Still, Napier hesitated. Sorcha caught her breath and waited. But, with an abrupt swing of his body, he turned to the door and moved rapidly from the supper room.

Chapter 23

SORCHA DID NOT GO TO Falkland Palace after all. She sent a messenger to Ailis, telling her of the change in plans and to make up her own mind about staying on with the court or returning to Edinburgh. Sorcha went back to Panmure Close, and that night, over snifters of French brandy, she poured out her heart to Aunt Tarrill.

"I wondered," Tarrill remarked as the church bells tolled midnight. "It seemed you'd left certain gaps in your recital earlier today."

While Tarrill was understanding, she had no real advice to offer her niece, nor had Sorcha sought it. But separated from her mother and Rosmairi, temporarily deprived of Ailis's company, she'd desperately needed a sympathetic female's ear. And Tarrill Cameron McVurrich was a woman who not only listened but kept a confidence. For perhaps the first time in her life, Sorcha understood the abiding bond between her aunt and her mother.

During the next few weeks, Uncle Donald recovered from his frightening collapse and resumed his banking duties. Ailis had shown up on the McVurrich doorstep two days after Sorcha sent her message. She was not keen on staying at Falkland without Sorcha and reported that the arrival of the Earl of Bothwell had created an atmosphere of unease.

By coincidence, it was Bothwell who occupied Sorcha's thoughts late one sultry afternoon as she raced the rain clouds back to Panmure Close. She had been to the dressmaker's in the Lawnmarket trying on a new russet-and-gold riding habit. As she hurried away from Castle Hill toward the old Weigh House, she noted a handsome coach turning into Currier's Close. Sorcha's curiosity was piqued. She paused, feeling the first drops of summer rain on her face. Bothwell's house was in Currier's Close, and unless she was mistaken, that was where the coach was heading. Sorcha stepped back against an old brick wall and watched the coachman bring the horses to a halt. A moment later, the footman scrambled down from the back of the coach and raced round to open the door for a tall, black-clad figure wearing an enormous white hat that concealed her face. But the height and carriage of the woman were unmistakable. Marie-Louise was indeed in Edinburgh and staying at Bothwell's town house while the Earl waited upon the King. There was no reason why the wretched woman shouldn't show herself in Edinburgh. As far as the Scots were concerned, she was just another French émigrée at best and, at worst, Bothwell's mistress. Neither was a crime.

The rain was coming down much harder, and out over the Firth of Forth, lightning slashed the lowering gray skies. Sorcha picked up her pace, though her mind was going far faster than her feet. It had been more than a month since she'd seen Gavin Napier. Very likely he and Father Adam had left some time ago for the Highlands. She had no idea of their precise destination, though it occurred to her that they might pay a call on her parents.

Almost slipping on the wet cobblestones by Saint Giles, she skirted the Market Cross and the Butter Tron. She must write at once to Gosford's End and relay her information about Marie-Louise. Even if Gavin and Adam Napier didn't stop there, Armand d'Ailly would pounce on the news, though it seemed unlikely that he would leave Rosmairi before she had delivered their babe.

Turning into Panmure Close, Sorcha noted that her hair had come undone and drooped in damp tendrils around her face. She had not, in truth, been as careful about her toilette during her stay at the McVurrich house. Not, she thought ruefully, that it made much difference—Gavin Napier hadn't even noticed the dramatic change in her appearance. Suddenly, she was angry with him, infuriated at his indulgence in self-pity. Why, she wondered fiercely, as she yanked at the wrought iron gate, had he bothered to consider becoming a priest, when he'd already made a martyr of himself? Was he any less misguided than Brother Jacques?

Sorcha paused in midstep at the entrance to the McVurrich house, overcome by an odd sense of being watched. Fleetingly, she felt guilt assail her for being so hard on Gavin Napier. It was as if she were back in the nursery at Gosford's End, allegedly learning her prayers from one of the Beauly monks who had instinctively known that she was thinking of smoked salmon and steamed mussels instead of the Pater Noster and the Ave Maria.

Sorcha fumbled inside her cloak for her calfskin purse. She took out a little mirror, ostensibly rearranging her coiffure. In the glass, she could see a man whose sudden interest in the wares of a fruit seller was suspicious.

Sorcha couldn't be positive, of course, but she would have wagered that he was the footman she had seen in Currier's Close.

IT CAME AS NO SURPRISE the following morning when Sorcha received a note asking her to meet Marie-Louise at the Clockmill House on the edge of town. Studying the note, as well as the pigeon-toed lad who had delivered it, Sorcha crossed out Marie-Louise's suggested meeting place and substituted Croft-an-Righ. Sorcha's choice was just west of Clockmill House, but unlike Marie-Louise's choice, which stood surrounded by trees off the main byway, Croft-an-Righ was closer to the busy Water Gate entrance to the city, and thus, Sorcha decided, considerably safer. She would further ensure her well-being by having Ailis and Doles follow her at a discreet distance.

The summer rainstorm had worn itself out before dawn, leaving the city fresh and clean, with patches of steam rising from the cobbles where the morning sun struck. Sorcha set out at a brisk pace, from time to time glancing over her shoulder to make certain Ailis and Doles were still behind her. Both Clockmill House and Croft-an-Righ were part of the affluent neighborhood north of Holyrood Palace. Most of the courtiers who lived in the area were with the King and Queen at Falkland. Sorcha had no idea who resided in either of the houses, but vaguely recalled that one of the numerous Stewarts was connected with Croft-an-Righ, and either an Erskine or a Douglas owned Clockmill.

As she supposed, Croft-an-Righ seemed closed up. It was an elaborate house with corbeled turrets on the south gables and dormer windows that ran the length of the north front. It stood three stories high, with an attic as well. A wall surrounded the house, but Sorcha could make out a garden with handsome shade trees and carefully clipped shrubs. She was admiring a dovecote toward the back of the property when a tall, slender youth swaggered toward her from the direction of the royal bathhouse. There was something familiar about the lad, and Sorcha frowned in the effort of recollection. But from ten yards away, a glimpse of golden hair told Sorcha that this was no laddie, but the same disguise Marie-Louise must have used to gain undetected passage from France to Scotland.

"Forgive me if I don't doff my cap," Marie-Louise said by way of greeting. The honey-edged accent didn't seem as pronounced as it had in the forest at Compiègne. Indeed, attired in dun-colored breeks and a plain-cut brown doublet, Marie-Louise had assumed quite an ordinary air. The scar on her neck was camouflaged with a foppish cream-colored scarf, and the jaunty cap sported a jeweled brooch.

"I can't imagine what you have to say to me," Sorcha began, having no desire to engage in idle conversation with the loathsome woman who had all but destroyed Gavin Napier, "so let us dispense with pleasantries."

Marie-Louise's brilliant azure eyes widened, then narrowed. "Ah, but why not? We are both women of good sense, are we not?" She noted Sorcha's sour expression and ran a pink tongue over her full lips. "But then, you and I have much in common, *c'est vrai*? We have both thrilled to the embrace of the same man." She flicked the tip of her tongue with her little finger in a provocative gesture that made Sorcha's green eyes spark.

"Your prattle wastes time," Sorcha declared, aware that she sounded like a cantankerous old woman. "I have better things to do than listen to your maudlin memories."

"Oh, la, la," exclaimed Marie-Louise with a burst of tinkling laughter. "How stern you Scots all are! Not that Gavin was always so—why, in my arms he was as frolicksome as a child!" She erupted into laughter again, one hand stroking the curve of her bosom which was ill-concealed by the brown doublet. Suddenly, like a storm that gathers without warning, Marie-Louise's expression turned menacing. "I do not bring up these memories merely to titillate you, Mistress Fraser. They are a reminder that I am Gavin's wife and always shall be. If somehow your Scots mind, so typically legal, had led you to think of annulments and such, disabuse yourself. Oh," she continued, waving a long, languid hand at Sorcha, "don't deny it, I know how you Scots use the law to seek your own ends. As for that fool, d'Ailly, does he truly think to lay claim to his family property?" She smirked and patted her doublet. "Here, safely tucked away, is the deed to d'Ailly's land—made over to me, in gratitude, by his late brother."

A string of invective sprang to Sorcha's tongue, but for once, she held back. She could demand to see the deed, but no doubt it existed. If it was binding was another matter. Whether d'Ailly's brother could have handed over his family holdings while his parents still lived struck Sorcha as unlikely but not impossible.

"The law, which you so lightly dismiss, should disprove your claim," Sorcha said with forced calm. "French law, at that."

A faint breeze stirred the rowan trees behind the walls, and a dozen starlings took flight toward the turrets of Croft-an-Righ. Looking beyond Marie-Louise, Sorcha tried to spot Ailis and Doles. She had last seen them lurking in the vicinity of the tennis courts. While in the course of a normal day, the thoroughfare would be quite busy, the absence of its tenants lent a ghostly aura to the place, reminding Sorcha that she was in the company of a woman who didn't flinch at murder.

Still, Sorcha refused to bend to Marie-Louise's will. "You abandoned your husband years ago," she remarked in a tone meant to sound bored. "I find this conversation tiresome."

When Marie-Louise spoke again, it was as if she hadn't heard Sorcha. "You have noted that those who defy me earn an early grave," she said evenly, each word more honeyed than the last. "It matters not who they are or how highly placed." The beautiful azure eyes gleamed down on Sorcha. "The French learned that. So will the Scots."

Sorcha could barely believe the brazenness of her adversary. To admit openly her complicity in the assassination of a king and to boast about undoing other important personages clearly demonstrated Marie-Louise's confidence in her own powers. Sorcha stared up into those arrogant eyes and marveled at their clarity and steadiness. Somehow, she half expected them to roll about, like dice on a gaming table. But if Marie-Louise was crazed—and Sorcha was sure she must be—the evil that infected her was within and had no doubt long ago eaten away her heart and soul. "Why?" asked Sorcha, unable to control a little shake of her head, as if still doubting Marie-Louise's intentions. "Why such destruction?"

The lovely features hardened, though the voice remained sweet and husky. "If you Scots defy the law, we French worship fair value." Marie-Louise's fingers fluttered at the knot of her cream-colored scarf. "Wicked men took away someone I loved. Now I repay them. And all men are wicked." Her beautifully defined mouth curved upward in a smile that was almost confidential. "*All*" she repeated, her voice low and breathy.

In spite of herself, Sorcha looked away for a brief moment. Before she could respond, Marie-Louise had resumed speaking, this time on a more natural note. "You've heard how your king's ship was almost sunk by storms off Norway?" she asked in the same tone another woman might have remarked upon a loaf of bread that had failed to rise. "Some silly women who mumble nonsense over boiled cats are being held accountable." Her jaunty cap swayed atop the blond curls as she laughed derisively. "What folly! Yet they have served to frighten King Jamie and that suits my purpose very well."

The morning sun was growing warmer, and despite the faint breeze that rustled the nearby trees, Sorcha had begun to perspire. Her breakfast shifted unhappily in her stomach, and her legs felt vaguely unsteady. This tall, lovely creature who stood before her, whose femininity was poorly disguised by the masculine garb, whose mellifluous voice spoke Scots almost as well as French, might have brought her gifts of intelligence and grace and beauty to enhance a tawdry world. Marie-Louise could have been the chatelaine of an elegant home, the doting mother of happy children, the generous benefactress of the poor. And above all, a loving wife and companion to Gavin Napier. Instead, for whatever twisted reasons, she had chosen evil. It was a waste, a sham, a cheat—and yet, from somewhere deep inside, Sorcha was perversely grateful to Marie-Louise. Had she fulfilled the brighter side of her destiny, Sorcha would never have met Napier, never known the wonder of love, never have given her heart to the hunter. If she never saw Gavin Napier again, she still owed Marie-Louise a great debt.

Deliberately, Sorcha turned away and headed back toward the Water Gate without a further word. She sensed, even if she could not see, Marie-Louise's startled reaction. "Wait!" the Frenchwoman cried, the honey melted from her voice. "Where is Napier? Where did he go?"

Sorcha kept walking, urging her uncertain legs to maintain a brisk step. Just ahead, by the entrance to the royal tennis courts, Ailis and Doles wandered casually into the street, seemingly absorbed in their own conversation while keeping several yards ahead of Sorcha.

"I know he is in Scotland!" The voice was receding into the wind that had picked up off the Firth of Forth. "You'll regret not telling me! Where is …."

Grateful that Marie-Louise's words were swallowed up by the distance that separated them, Sorcha slowed her pace and took a deep breath. She had been certain that the other woman wouldn't follow her back into the bustling Canongate; even if she had, she could do no more than rant. As Ailis and Doles sauntered up to the McVurrich house, Sorcha paused by White Horse Close, oblivious of the pigs that rooted for food among the debris dumped by local residents.

Sorcha had not yet penned her message about Marie-Louise to send north. She had intended to write it as soon as she returned from meeting her nemesis. But as she stepped around two piglets who were trotting after a huge, lumbering sow, it occurred to Sorcha that a letter wouldn't do. Marie-Louise's threats weren't meant just for the King of Scotland, but for Gavin Napier as well.

Sorcha made up her mind to head for the Highlands that very day.

Chapter 24

WHILE GOSFORD'S END WAS ABUILDING some twenty years earlier, Dallas had set her heart on the inclusion of a solarium. She had mystified her husband and frustrated the architect by her persistence in putting the room at the north end of the manor house to capture the view of Inverness. Even with its perpendicular windows, which filled one wall almost from floor to ceiling, the sun penetrated only about three months of the year. Iain Fraser had called it "Dallas's Folly," a name that had clung over the years, much to his wife's chagrin.

But that August there were several rare, hot, brilliant days when Dallas could indulge herself by opening up the much-maligned solarium. She had supervised the cleaning and refurbishing of the room, ordering new upholstery for the divan, an armchair to match, and Delft tiles for the fireplace, which had never been quite finished to her satisfaction. Now, surveying the fruits of her creativity and the labors of a dozen workmen, Dallas went off in search of her husband, who had returned only the previous day from a voyage to Norway. To Dallas's consternation, she found him closeted with visitors.

"Who's in there with him?" Dallas demanded of Cummings as she jabbed her thumb in the direction of her husband's study.

Cummings's expression remained as imperturbable as ever. "I believe Lord Fraser is meeting with the priests from France. Unless," he added with an uncharacteristic lack of confidence, "one of them is not a priest."

Dallas bore down on Cummings, her ruby-studded choker catching fire from the sunlight that streamed through a recessed diamond-paned window at the end of the hall. "Priests? From France? Jesu!" she exclaimed, whirling around toward the study door, but thinking twice about barging in. "Not Gavin Napier and his brother?"

Cummings coughed delicately. "I believe so, yes."

Dallas tapped her cheek with her fingers. Had Napier managed to shed his odious wife and make an honest woman out of Sorcha after all? Dallas doubted it; such good fortune didn't seem destined for her elder daughter. Not that Dallas was convinced Gavin Napier would make Sorcha a suitable husband. As far as Dallas could see, he had no inheritance, no property, and no visible means of support. She could hardly wish an indigent husband on Sorcha. At least Armand d'Ailly owned land in France, and with any luck, Donald McVurrich would see that he profited handsomely from it.

"How long have they been in there?" Dallas asked at last, again gesturing in the direction of the study.

"Nigh on an hour," Cummings replied. He was about to add that Lord Fraser had requested supper in the study for all three of them, but was interrupted by a breathless serving lad who caromed around the corner of the hallway and almost collided with Lady Fraser.

"Have a care, Wee Willie," Dallas cried, gathering her pale green lawn skirts around her, "you all but toppled me!"

Wee Willie took no umbrage. "There's great excitement at the front door, My Lady!" The boy's red curls hopped up and down. "Some of the servants will offer hospitality and some will not. What shall be done?"

Dallas and Cummings exchanged bewildered glances. "That depends on the visitor's identity," said Dallas, turning back to the boy. "Who is this questionable character?"

The lad's blue eyes were as lively as his curls. " 'Tis the Laird of Freuchie, madam—he that used to be called Johnny Grant."

"Oh, a pox on Johnny Grant!" cried Dallas, shaking her head vehemently at Cummings. "Iain and I swore he'd never darken our door again! Come, let's throw the gap-toothed gargoyle out!"

Dallas was already around the corner of the hall before Cummings, favoring his painful bunion, could hobble after her.

Wee Willie trailed behind, determined not to miss out on what ought to prove a first-rate entertainment.

In the four years since Lord and Lady Fraser had seen Johnny Grant, his youthful affectations had grown into mature pomposity. His body had altered, too, broadening in the shoulders and even in the paunch. The beard he sported was thick but too long for fashion, though the gap between his teeth seemed less noticeable now that his face had filled out. His riding clothes were somber but well cut. While he assumed an air of dignity, the flickering of his eyes betrayed his inner apprehension. Indeed, as Dallas bore down on him, he unwittingly took a step backward, almost stepping on one of the Fraser collie pups that dozed in the sun on the doorstep.

"You are not welcome here, Johnny Grant," Dallas announced, fists on hips made formidably wide by a deep green farthingale. Over Grant's shoulder, she glimpsed at least two dozen men wearing the Grant plaid and seated on fleet-footed Highland ponies. Dallas wished she had not been so precipitous in ordering Wee Willie and the other servants to withdraw. "Fie," she breathed, frowning at the ominous company. "What manner of visit do you pay us?"

Grant pushed out his chest and pulled in his paunch. "On behalf of His Majesty's Privy Council, I am empowered to search these premises for seditious priests." He snapped his fingers rather clumsily, and one of the men strutted forward, carrying an impressive sealed piece of parchment. "This," Grant intoned self-importantly, "is the warrant of my office." He took the paper from his man, and with a flourish, handed it to Dallas.

Swiftly, she perused the seal to make sure it was genuine, then brandished it at Grant. "How neatly it's rolled! Pray tuck it back where it belongs, Johnny Grant!" Dallas shoved the parchment back into her astonished visitor's hands, forcing him to juggle it awkwardly against his puffed-up chest.

"Madam!" gasped Grant, turning quite pink, "do you realize what effrontery you commit? Effrontery!" he repeated, in his familiar quest for emphasis.

"It is you who commits effrontery by coming here in the first place." Dallas's eyes blazed with indignation. "My husband and I ordered you never to show your insipid face on our doorstep again." Dallas was wagging a finger under Grant's nose. "Now put yourself back on your horse before I summon Lord Fraser."

But Johnny Grant's office gave him the right, as well as the courage, to withstand Lady Fraser's onslaught. "This is not a matter of petty personal quarrels," he declared, summoning up the vestiges of his dignity. "This is the King's business. You will permit me—and my men—entry at once."

Inwardly, Dallas cursed herself for not first informing her husband about Johnny Grant's arrival before going to the door. Outwardly, she had to stall for time. Casting a swift glance over her shoulder, she was relieved to note that Cummings had slipped away.

"Well." Dallas remained in the doorway, effectively blocking Grant's passage. "Are you serious about all your men tramping through our house?" She made a sweeping gesture with one hand, indicating Grant's troops, who were growing restive under the hot sun.

"Uh …." Johnny Grant passed a quick glance backward toward his men, then looked upward, as if calculating how many would be needed to conduct a thorough search. "Some half dozen, I'd say." Grant nodded once, the overlong beard dusting his expanded chest. "Yes, some half dozen."

"And the others?" Dallas asked, now looking deceptively benign. "Perhaps they'd care for some refreshment. At least a cool drink." She worried her lower lip with her teeth, apparently taking mental inventory of the Fraser kitchen and cellar. "We have Dutch beer," she said brightly, "and something rather strange that Iain has just brought back from Norway in funny little wooden casks. There's wine, of course, but the day's so hot, I should think it might give your men spells or headaches …." Her voice trailed off as she underscored her indecision by twirling a strand of hair that had come loose from under her pert green cap. "Now, sack might please them …. Cummings could fetch that from the cellar." She turned slowly and caught her breath as Iain Fraser moved toward the front door, a pleasant, indolent expression on his face.

"What have we here, lassie?" he asked mildly. He stood next to Dallas, an arm around her shoulders. "Ah, 'tis Johnny Grant and a company of fine Freuchie fighting men." He gazed past Grant to the increasingly restless retainers. "They are armed, are they not? What's happened, Johnny? Are you fleeing From Highland reivers, or do you still have designs on my daughter's dowry?"

Grant's pink color deepened to puce. "My Lord, this is not a matter for … jocular behavior. My men and I are empowered by the King to search your house. We come to root out traitorous priests." He cleared his throat and again waved the sealed parchment. "Catholic priests," he added, in case there was any confusion.

"But first Cummings must bring beer. Or was it sack?" Dallas gave Grant a befuddled glance. Suddenly, she all but jigged with excitement. "And that sumptuous pickled herring in cream! Such a treat! Johnny," she said with a motherly smile, "aren't those laddies well-nigh famished? We'll have a picnic, to prove we Frasers can let bygones be bygones." With a firm but friendly shove, she marched past Grant to the others. "Good gentlemen of Freuchie, we've food and drink to put you at your ease. Come, under the larches, by the rose garden. It's cooler there, and your ponies may slake their thirst in the little pool. Just don't let them trample my pansies. I nursed them through that uncommonly late May frost."

The Grant supporters, who were uniformly wiping perspiration from their brows while their little mounts drooped under them, waited anxiously for a signal from their leader. Johnny Grant's face was set, however, and he turned to Iain Fraser, who was idly leaning against the doorway examining his fingernails. "My Lord," Grant said in a voice that he hoped conveyed mature authority, "while those men that I do not need just now refresh themselves, I must insist upon searching these premises at once. At once," he echoed, stamping his booted foot.

Fraser shrugged. "As you will, Johnny. But take care when you reach the solarium. One smudge of dirt, and my lassie will skewer you. She just had it prettified at a cost that made half the tradesmen in Inverness wealthy, while helping to impoverish me." He shook his head with mock self-pity. "It's as well you didn't marry Sorcha, Johnny; you could have ended up like me, a pathetic old man eking out a living by trading good Scots wool for Norwegian pickled herring."

To Johnny Grant, the tall, lean Iain Fraser, even at sixty, with his pantherlike grace and air of easy command, hardly seemed old or pathetic. Though his hair had more gray than black, and the lines in his face were etched deep by years at sea and a life lived well, Fraser's cool hazel eyes not only knew more, but still saw more than most men half his age.

"I shall search the, uh, solarium, myself," averred Grant, finally signaling for a half dozen of his men to follow. The others trotted eagerly after Dallas, while she shouted for Cummings to serve their guests.

It took two hours for Grant and his men to search the Fraser home. In the kitchen, Catriona stood by the ovens, wielding a basting brush and expressing displeasure at the invasion of her domain. After a cursory perusal of Dallas's bedroom, they were dispatched by an irate Flora, who was mending her mistress's best ballgown. In the servants' quarters, the ancient Marthe wheezed after them, making sure that they replaced every item that they touched. In Rob and Rosmairi's rooms, now converted into a suite for the d'Aillys, Armand gave them scant shrift. His wife was taking a nap, and in her delicate condition, they might risk sending her into premature labor, a crime for which they would pay dearly with specific members of their bodies. As for the nursery, which was in the process of being refurbished by some of the same workmen who had been hired for the solarium, Dallas herself intervened.

"I wouldn't hide the Pope himself in a place I was having redecorated," she declared, maneuvering Johnny Grant around a bucket of paste for the pastel wallpaper being hung by a finicky young craftsman. "If you can find a priest in yonder cradle," Dallas warned them, "I'll send him to the gallows myself."

At last, Grant and his followers reassembled in the entry hall, an overwarm, weary lot. "There's still some schnapps and kippers, I believe." Dallas informed them airily. "Feel free to partake. But," she admonished as the half dozen searchers gratefully headed outside, "mind my pansies!"

Johnny Grant did not follow his men outside, however. "There are stables and other outbuildings, My Lady. We are not yet finished." He cleared his throat importantly. "Not yet finished at all."

"You never are," Dallas retorted irritably. It had cost her greatly this past two hours to exert such good-natured amicability. "Go pry into every nook and cranny of Fraser property, then. Look until your funny little eyes pop out. But disturb one blade of grass, and there will be no sixth Laird of Freuchie!"

Grant had the grace to look vaguely embarrassed, but he also possessed a dogged tenacity that brooked even the most menacing of threats. "We respect your rights as Highlanders," he allowed, no longer making an effort in the heat of the late afternoon to restrain his paunch, "yet I must tell you, we have heard from unimpeachable sources that one, and perhaps two, priests visited you here within the last few days. Not to mention," he mumbled on, "the presence of that Frenchman."

"Oh, fie," exclaimed Dallas in exasperation, "that Frenchman is our son-in-law! Now beat your retreat, Johnny Grant. I've expended all the patience I possess on you today!" Dallas deliberately turned her back and stomped off toward the kitchens. But before she turned the corner of the hallway, she paused to make certain Johnny Grant had left the house. Then, picking up her pale green skirts, she raced off, all but hurtling into Cummings who was with Catriona, supervising preparations for the family supper. Ordinarily, Cummings would not have shared responsibilities with the Fraser head cook, but this afternoon, his presence was mandatory. On the hottest day of the year, it was one of those rare occasions when the ovens at Gosford's End had not been fired up. In their deep recesses reposed Gavin and Father Adam Napier, uncomfortable but safe from Johnny Grant's prying eyes.

Dallas was particularly concerned for the crippled priest; as for Gavin Napier, she wasn't entirely sure she wouldn't prefer roasting him anyway. But Adam insisted he'd rather enjoyed the dark solitude of the oven. "The sweet smell of bread lingers," he assured Dallas, as two kitchen boys assisted him into a chair. "I meditated on the bread and wine, on the Body and Blood of Christ. And," he added with a twinkle, "on fresh buttered rolls and biscuits."

Ovens or no ovens, Dallas declared that a sumptuous table must be set, to honor the deception of Johnny Grant. She was also pleased to meet Father Adam, though her emotions were far more mixed at seeing Gavin Napier again.

IAIN FRASER PULLED A FRESH shirt on over his shoulders and gave his wife a crooked grin. "Gavin Napier is in an awkward situation in more ways than one. Had I not opened my doors to him years ago, I might have run him through on the spot. But while Sorcha was once quite keen on having her honor avenged in the matter of Johnny Grant, I don't think she'd thank me for doing likewise with Napier."

Dallas tucked her hair up inside a heart-shaped cap edged with pearls. "Married to a so-called witch! Fie, I've known many a man who's claimed such was his plight, but Gavin Napier is the first who actually is. And Sorcha is fool enough to fall in love with him! Even if he could rid himself of that lunatic Frenchwoman, he has nothing to offer. Sorcha might as well marry a poacher."

Fraser came up behind Dallas at her dressing table and put a hand on her bare neck. "Oh, lassie, how you forget! You came to our marriage bed with naught but bluster and bravado. Yet I managed to overlook it, and we've done quite well, all things considered."

Dallas started to pull away, but caught her husband's half-serious, half-mocking reflection in the mirror and leaned back against him. "That was different," she grumbled, but her words lacked bite. "If Napier hasn't come with an honorable proposal, why did he—they—come at all?"

"The Napiers dream of Catholic unity to ensure the Church's viability. It's a fragile hope, yet not impossible if we could all put petty differences aside." Fraser stepped back, adjusting the cuff of one sleeve. "It would mean, of course, that we would have to reconcile with George Gordon."

Dallas made a face in the mirror. "That seems too great a sacrifice, no matter how noble the cause."

"Precisely." He waited for Dallas to rise and gave her his arm. "But if we cling to old grudges and ancient feuds, we risk destruction by the Protestant oppressors. As the Napiers point out, our only hope is to stand together."

"Protestant oppressors, indeed!" Dallas gave her damask skirts a swish. "Though what's to choose between George Gordon and Johnny Grant? Has that wretched little pest taken his mindless men from the vicinity yet? If I thought they were still prowling about, it would spoil my appetite."

"They may still be bothering our tenants," Fraser admitted as they headed out into the hallway. "If nothing else, Johnny Grant is efficient."

"I'd still like to know who passed on the information," Dallas persisted. "Have we a traitor in our midst?"

Fraser shook his head as they descended the carpeted staircase past the grouping of family portraits commissioned some ten years earlier. "Not necessarily. Anyone with Protestant leanings could have seen them headed this way. I imagine such informers are well rewarded."

Dallas was about to deliver her opinion of such grasping, weasel-like creatures when Armand d'Ailly rushed to meet them at the bottom of the staircase. "A most deplorable occurrence!" he cried, putting a hand on each of the Frasers' shoulders. His usually impeccable appearance was marred by the blond hair hanging down over one eye; his dove-gray doublet was askew at the collar, and the links in the silver chain he wore around his neck were badly tangled. "I have just come from seeking blackberries for my sweet Ros—you know how she craves such things—and there, beside the road that leads to the burn, I found young Grant and his men riding away."

"Good riddance," said Dallas, and gave a sharp nod of approval.

"Oh, but no, no!" D'Ailly's grip tightened on his in-laws. "With them was Mistress Sorcha! They have stolen her!"

Lord and Lady Fraser stared wordlessly at each other, then gaped at d'Ailly. "How did Sorcha come to be here?" Iain Fraser demanded.

D'Ailly lifted his palms upward in a helpless gesture. "I cannot guess. You will have to ask her serving girl and the young man who were left behind."

Iain Fraser's jaw hardened. He grabbed d'Ailly by the arm. "Where are those two?" he demanded, waving off Dallas's attempt to interrupt.

"In the kitchen," d'Ailly replied. "We came in that way. It was closer."

An unusually pale Rosmairi clung to the banister several steps above them. "What's happening? This entire day has been incredibly chaotic."

D'Ailly took the stairs two at a time to rash to his wife's side. She leaned against him, a hand on her bulging abdomen. "Even the bairn is distraught," she complained. "Besides, it's too hot."

With soothing words, d'Ailly led her back up the stairs. Fraser, with Dallas at his heels, was already headed toward the kitchen. To their astonishment, Catriona was serving Ailis a mug of ale and bread with cheese, while a young man not yet twenty chewed hungrily on half of a cold chicken.

" 'Tis Alexander—or is it Andrew?—McVurrich," Dallas whispered.

Fraser wheeled on Ailis and whichever nephew the ravenous lad happened to be. Tersely, he requested the details of Sorcha's alleged abduction by Johnny Grant. It was Ailis who responded, relating the incident with her usual economy of words. She and Sorcha, along with Andrew McVurrich, had ridden hard for three days from Edinburgh to warn Gavin Napier of possible danger from the Frenchwoman, Marie-Louise. As the weary trio finally drew within less than a mile of Gosford's End, a troop of men had blocked the road. Recognizing Sorcha, Johnny Grant had commanded his men to seize her.

"He said," Ailis recounted, choosing her words with precision, "that inasmuch as he believed that Lord and Lady Fraser were hiding seditious priests in some cunning place, he would hold Mistress Sorcha hostage until the priests were turned over to him as required by the King's command." Ailis stopped speaking and pursed her lips. "That is all he said, as best I can remember. Except," she added on a note of disapproval, "for an ill-mannered remark about 'coming to your senses.' "

"Fie," breathed Dallas angrily. "Such monstrous arrogance."

Fraser fingered the bridge of his hawklike nose and looked thoughtful. "How long ago did this happen, Ailis?"

Ailis tipped her head to one side. "Let me think—no more than half an hour." She peered at Andrew McVurrich for confirmation; the lad nodded over his tankard, then accepted a bowl of raspberries and cream from Catriona.

Fraser slammed a fist onto the table, rattling the dishes and causing

Andrew to look up from his berries. "I can guess where they've gone, but such a headstart hinders us considerably."

"Perhaps," suggested a mild voice from the corner by the butter churn, "you might wait for my brother to report back."

The others all turned to stare at the inconspicuous figure of Father Adam Napier, seated in a straight-backed chair, a light woolen blanket thrown over his crippled legs. He cradled a tankard of Dutch beer in his hands and assumed an apologetic air. "I'm at fault for what has happened, of course. Had you turned me over to young Grant, it would have saved a great deal of trouble. It's still not too late, you know."

Her maternal instinct rushing to the fore, Dallas started to agree with him, but Iain Fraser strode to Father Adam's side and placed a hand lightly on his shoulder. "We'll do no such thing. Johnny Grant won't harm Sorcha," Fraser asserted, though he wished his inner conviction were as strong as his words. "Now tell us, Father, what did your brother plan to do?"

Adam Napier gave a little shake of his head. "I'm never sure what Gavin plans in such circumstances. He … improvises." The priest uttered a self-deprecating chuckle. "He took Naxos, his own horse. He might overtake those ponies."

Fraser weighed the priest's words carefully. In the end, Magnus was summoned to confer with his father and his brother-in-law. However, young Andrew McVurrich was given the option of absenting himself from the family conclave. "You're not a Fraser," he was told by his uncle, "nor have you been brought up in the Catholic faith."

But Andrew surprised them by declaring that he would stand fast with his Fraser kin. "Sorcha is my cousin," he declared, setting his long jaw in affirmation. "While my sire may be a McVurrich and a presbyter, my Lady Mother is a Cameron, and Catholic to boot. She has always taught us that family keeps with family, and let the rest of the world go hang."

Iain Fraser clapped the youth on the back and silently thanked Tarrill for her sense of kinship. Magnus arrived just after sunset, and along with Dallas and Rosmairi, the family joined Father Adam in the solarium, where they could view the last streaks of pale purple light fade over the rooftops of Inverness and disappear into the sea. Their discussion was lively as well as urgent. Dallas never veered from her determination to seek Sorcha's swift and safe return, while Father Adam repeated his offer to surrender himself to the Grants. Iain Fraser and Magnus concentrated on rescuing Sorcha by force, while Armand d'Ailly extolled the virtues of negotiation. When Andrew grew excited at the prospect of possible armed confrontation, Rosmairi disagreed vehemently, asserting that the one factor everyone was overlooking was Sorcha herself.

"I'm confident that Sorcha is sufficiently resourceful to find a way out of this silly situation. Hasn't it dawned on anyone else that Johnny Grant may be more embarrassed over being humiliated in front of Gavin Napier years ago than he is motivated by religious zeal?"

Rosmairi's comments were duly considered, but Dallas's determination remained fixed. "I care not for whys and wherefores," she asserted, as a cool breeze stirred the new Flemish draperies. "I want my daughter back home. At once."

No one in the room contradicted her; it was, despite the divergence of opinions on how to achieve such a goal, exactly what they all wanted most.

The candle wax collected in thick clumps on the twin candelabra that stood at each end of the refurbished mantel. Rosmairi dozed on Armand d'Ailly's shoulder, and Father Adam's face took on a pinched, careworn look. Andrew McVurrich turned silent, occasionally biting his fingernails. Only Lord and Lady Fraser and their eldest son talked on, while the gilt hands of the Austrian clock across the room edged close to midnight.

And still, Gavin Napier did not return.

THE SWEET, WILD CRY OF the lav'rock called from the pinewood, and somewhere farther off, a dog howled at the risen moon. Sorcha yawned and grimaced at herself in the wavy mirror that hung above a solid but ugly oak dressing table. The room in which she was held prisoner was large enough and furnished adequately, but despite her weariness, she wasn't in the mood for sleep. Only in the past hour, after supping on overdone beef and wrinkled peas, had her temper come under control. That Johnny Grant, of all people, should kidnap her in the name of religion was more aggravating than it was frightening. She had not wasted her breath on him during the arduous ride to the bank of the Spey, but once they had reached Johnny's modest outpost, Sorcha had berated him and his followers with a stream of bitter reproach. Johnny's response had been to have her hauled off bodily by two of his men and locked into the bedroom where she now paced in frustration. In truth, she had not been mishandled, and while she had first threatened to hurl the supper they'd brought in their faces, she'd finally decided that food was a better ally than malice.

The night had grown quite still; both bird and dog were silent. Sorcha had opened the window, with its square-shaped panes, many of which were cracked. From what she recalled of Johnny's holdings, this was where the high country moor met the great green glens of Strath Spey. The building itself was a hunting lodge, situated close to Gordon property. This room was located on the second floor, facing the river. Leaning over the sill, she noted that heavy vines of ivy covered most of the stone facade, but even if she dared try climbing down to the ground, a guard was posted almost directly below her. Sorcha left the window open, for the room was musty, and the heat of the day still lingered.

Resignedly, she marched to the bed and tested the mattress. The straw was bunched up into clumps, and she began to pound the surface to distribute the stuffing more evenly. A knock at the door evoked an irritated grumble, but she moved briskly to inquire who her visitor might be. At least whoever it was hadn't barged in. From the other side of the door, she heard Johnny Grant, sounding officious. The key scraped in the lock, but he waited for Sorcha to turn the knob.

Johnny had changed his clothes since their arrival at the hunting lodge, and in his tan shirt and scuffed house slippers, he looked too young, too nondescript to be a clan chieftain. "You've supped?" he inquired, folding his hands at belt level.

"Aye," replied Sorcha in a cool tone, "if poorly."

Johnny inclined his head this way and that, as if making up his mind whether to be offended. "I'm afraid my people here at Ballindalloch were unprepared. We all had to make do with the meager offerings of an ill-provisioned kitchen."

Reluctantly, Sorcha chose to accept Johnny's words as an apology. "These forests must have sufficient game," she added in a conversational tone. "I trust your men will hunt tomorrow."

"Mayhap," he hedged, "though we have more serious matters on our minds." He shuffled his feet, glanced about the room, and gazed yearningly at the only chair, but remained standing. "Very serious," he amplified, "inasmuch as we must discover why a clan such as the Frasers, who've not meddled much in politics, would suddenly conspire with priests." Johnny did his best to look severe but managed only petulance.

Sorcha gave a little snort. "How should I know, not having been in my family's house for three months? Hasn't it occurred to you that since my brother is studying for the priesthood with one of our kinsmen, it would be quite natural for our parents to offer hospitality to other priests? Why must you think only of politics?"

"Napier was at Gosford's End several years ago," Johnny said doggedly. "I saw him there. He was in league with the Gordons."

"He was, for a time. They had a falling-out." Sorcha didn't choose to enlighten Johnny Grant about Gavin Napier's real identity.

"He went to England with your brother. You went, too." Johnny's voice was accusing.

"That I did," Sorcha admitted readily. "Oh, my, I did indeed." She frowned at the stale rushes, a flood of memories washing over her.

Johnny sensed her shift of mood and moved about the room uneasily, straightening a candle by the bed, twitching at the faded hangings by the window, inspecting a loose brick in the little fireplace. At last, he spoke again, forcing Sorcha to turn and face him. "The Frasers must not become involved in Catholic intrigues." He wagged a finger at her. "They absolutely must not. Your sire has maintained virtual neutrality all these years. And so it must remain."

Sorcha lifted one shoulder. "I can't speak for my father. No one ever could."

Johnny tried to ignore Sorcha's withering glance. "On a map of the Highlands, you see the Sinclairs to the northwest, the Frasers around Inverness, your mother's Clan Chattan, with those warring MacKintoshes and Camerons. Then, my own Grants, and farther east, the Gordons with all their allies, almost to the sea. We Protestants are wedged between those Catholic clans. Until now, we have considered the Frasers, though Catholic, a buffer. If your family changes its political stance ...."

Johnny droned on in a soporific voice that made Sorcha aware of how tired she was. Stifling a yawn, she suddenly opened her eyes at the sight behind Johnny's back. There, at the open window, was Gavin Napier, gesturing for her to keep silent. Sorcha pressed her hand against her lips, let her eyelids droop to hide her surprise, and nodded several times to indicate her interest in Johnny's diatribe.

With one strong, swift movement, Napier leaped from the casement to wrap an arm about Johnny's neck and clap a hand over his open mouth. Eyes popping like a beached salmon, Johnny struggled in his captor's grasp. Napier let go of him at the neck just long enough to unsheathe his dirk, which he pressed against Johnny's cheek. "One word and I'll shave more than that scraggly beard, Johnny Grant! Now do as you're told, or prepare to die a dubious hero."

For the first time, Sorcha took in Napier's apparel. He was dressed much as usual, but wore the red-and-green plaid of the Grants and the clan's dark green bonnet with its crest badge. Apparently he'd overcome the inattentive guard under her window and borrowed some of his gear. Sorcha couldn't help but bestow a wide, grateful smile on Napier, not just for coming to her aid, but for coming at all.

Napier was asking Johnny if there was a guard outside the door. A jerky nod affirmed that there was. "I'm going to let you call to him," Napier said evenly. "The dirk stays on your flesh. Tell him to come in." He looked at Sorcha. "Quickly, find rope or rags or some such item with which to secure the guard. I'll have to hold onto Laird Johnny. Can you tie a strong knot?"

Sorcha tossed her hair back over her shoulders. "You ask that of a sea captain's daughter? I could tie up half the Highlands."

Grinning, Napier steered Johnny closer to the door. "One wrong word," he warned, pressing the cold steel even further into Johnny's cheek, "and you'll meet your Maker!" The hand dropped abruptly from Johnny's mouth; Napier's knee nudged him to speak. To his credit, Johnny sounded almost natural. A moment later, a rawboned young man, blue eyes turning almost black in consternation, stared at his captive laird. Napier ordered him to let Sorcha tie him up with a long piece of tattered, yellowing lace she'd found in a drawer. Quickly, Sorcha tested the piece to make sure that age and mildew hadn't rotted the fine threads.

The young man gaped at Sorcha in disbelief. "On the floor," she commanded. "Are you daft enough to risk your laird's life?"

The young lad might be slow, but he wasn't daft; giving his chieftain an apologetic look, he lay down as Sorcha ordered and submitted to her expertise with knots at his ankles and wrists. Her supper napkin was used as a gag, his keys were removed from the ring at his belt, and his dagger, sheath and all, was secured at Sorcha's waist.

"Good work, lass," Napier said in approbation. He propelled Johnny Grant toward the hall, pausing to make sure no one else was in the vicinity. From around his shoulder, Sorcha peered into the gloom, aware of stale smells of a neglected house and cooking odors that had drifted up from the kitchen below.

Napier prodded Johnny with the dirk. "You'll take us out of this place by whichever route is safest. Waste no time," he admonished, "and head for the stables."

Moving noiselessly, but without hesitation, Johnny led them down the passage to a narrow, winding back stairway where the footing was uneven and treacherous. Sorcha felt her way along the rough stone wall and twice collided with Napier's back as he held on firmly to his captive. At the bottom of the stairs, they could hear voices to their right. A half-opened door made a wedge of light near their feet—the kitchen, judging from the food smells which had grown much stronger. Sensing that Johnny was weighing the risk of bolting to sound an alarm, Napier brought the side of his hand crashing down onto his captive's neck. Johnny crumpled, but Napier caught him before he could hit the floor, then stood stock-still, waiting for repercussions from the kitchen. From within, a man laughed carelessly, and another voice responded in casual tones. Sorcha and Napier took deep breaths in unison, then turned into the passageway.

Luckily, the outside door was just around the corner. "No guards were here earlier," he whispered, "but we'll take no chances."

Hauling the inert Johnny Grant to the door, Napier dumped him unceremoniously against the wall, then peered outside before boldly steeping into the moonlight. "It's quiet," he whispered, taking Sorcha's arm. "The stables are just beyond the smokehouse."

Napier had left Naxos tethered to a fencepost near the well. Except for the Highland ponies and Thisbe, there were no other signs of life. Speaking in gentle, reassuring tones, Sorcha led Thisbe outside where Napier was already mounted, anxious to be off. Johnny Grant wouldn't stay unconscious forever; there was a good chance he was already awake, raising the cry to rally his men.

In high summer, the Spey was placid between Ballindalloch and Aberlour. They were riding north, rather than west toward Fraser country. The moon was sliding down over the gaunt, stark moors, and far away, a wolf howled as if bidding goodnight to his silver companion in the sky.

Napier had explained to Sorcha that Grant's men would assume they'd ride for Gosford's End. "They won't figure us to stay in Grant's territory. In the morning, we'll get our bearings and head west."

An hour or more from Ballindalloch, where the Spey meandered through a glen dotted with birch and yew on one side of the river, and a rocky outcropping on the other side sported a carpet of heather in full bloom, Napier suggested they halt for awhile. "Now that the moon's down, we risk a fall with the horses. They've both ridden hard today, especially Thisbe. I suggest we sleep," he said, testing the ground beneath his feet. "We've no blankets, but it's dry enough."

Bemused, Sorcha stood quite still, noting Napier's sudden preoccupation with their surroundings. He had taken off the Grant plaid and was spreading it on the grass, pulling and tugging it this way and that. "This might offer you some comfort, at least," he said rather woodenly.

"It could offer us both comfort if we slept in each other's arms," Sorcha declared in a voice that was tinged with annoyance. "Or perhaps you'd prefer sleeping on the other side of the Spey."

Napier stood up straight, and Sorcha could have sworn that even in the dark, she could see his skin deepen in hue. "Don't taunt me," he said sharply. "I can't live with your wrath and my misery."

Sorcha wanted to tell him that if he'd set aside that misery, she'd willingly dispense with wrath. Instead, she spoke in a cool, almost detached voice. "Marie-Louise is living in Bothwell's house in Edinburgh. I met with her. I've reason to think she not only intends to foil your plans for Catholic unity, but to cause the King harm as well."

Napier took an inadvertent step closer to Sorcha, the brown eyes amazed. "Christ," he breathed. "Is that why you came north?"

"Aye. I had to warn you. And someone must warn King Jamie." Sorcha smoothed the skirts of her burgundy riding habit with fingers not entirely under control. "Marie-Louise spews evil the way an evergreen oozes sap.

She must be stopped." The glittering green eyes bore into Napier's face as she moved deliberately to stand in front of him. "Can you stop her, Gavin? Can anyone?"

His features twisted painfully, then went slack. "I don't know. No one in France could. And that success has doubtless made her overconfident." He fingered his bearded chin between thumb and forefinger. "It's madness, of course. She is like a great boulder, rolling downhill, scattering all that's in her path. But even a boulder eventually crashes at the bottom of the hill."

Sorcha said nothing. Napier's analogy was quite apt, his frustration understandable. But now that Sorcha had delivered her message, she was determined to break down that terrible barricade Gavin Napier had erected between them. It was fruitless to argue. Sorcha knew from previous experience that in a verbal exchange, she was doomed to failure. Nor would some vague remnant of pride allow her to hurl herself at Gavin Napier. Indeed, Sorcha had nothing left to offer in their battle of wills—except herself. She stood quietly before him, her green eyes turned to jade with longing, the full, wide mouth slightly parted, the streaming black hair framing her face like a veil of osprey feathers.

A muscle along Napier's jaw tightened; the hunter's gaze turned as hard as the hills outlined against the night sky. Then, a tremendous shudder overtook his big body, and he swallowed up Sorcha in his arms, burying his face in her hair. "Sweet love!" he cried on a strangled note, sounding not unlike the lonesome wolf that had mounted the passing of the moon. He cradled her face in his hands, and his eyes were suspiciously overbright. "Could it be that you've been sent not to damn me but redeem me?"

Awed not only by the sudden change but by her power over him as well, Sorcha found it difficult to speak. "God knows I'd never want to bring you harm." She placed her palms against his chest, trying to dredge up the right words. "You must trust my love for you. You must also trust your own instincts, no matter how deeply you've buried them. You talk of being bound to Marie-Louise, but her hold is one of hate. Can you honestly tell me such ties nurture your soul and make it more pleasing before Almighty God?"

A hint of a smile touched Napier's long mouth. "As ever, your touch drives moral argument from my mind." He bent to sear her lips with his kisses, slowly, inexorably bringing her down onto the red-and-green patch of plaid. His passion at last unleashed, Napier fell upon her, crushing the breath from her body. Sorcha paid no heed; he could snuff out her very life and she would know only the ecstasy of surrender. Her hands caressed the hard muscles of his shoulders, her cheek felt the delicious savagery of his heavy beard, her teeth and tongue taunted his ear. Napier's hands worked at the fastenings of her riding jacket, with its padded shoulders and black velvet trim. It had cost a goodly sum, but Sorcha submitted the garment—and herself—to Napier's reckless plundering. The thin shift she had worn under the habit slipped away from her breasts, baring them to Napier's hungry mouth. Sorcha felt for his buttocks, kneading the sleek masculine flesh through his leather breeks. Under his demanding tongue, her nipples preened, her body ached for consummation, her soul cried out to be filled with him.

For a brief instant, he looked up into her face and smiled that wry, half-guilty, half-ecstatic grin that rent Sorcha's heart from top to bottom. "Denying you is like denying life itself. You are the earth—like wind and fire and sun and rain. I thought I lived in spite of you. But no—I live because of you."

"Living is loving. There should be naught else," Sorcha declared with breathless fervor. She wriggled under him as he pulled off the rest of her clothing and then his own. Though the night air was kind, she trembled as she felt the source of his manhood, her long, slim fingers stroking him into groans of pleasure. Greedily, yet lovingly, her mouth captured his and he clasped her by the hips, guiding her into a sitting position.

The black hair streamed down her face, and she shoved it out of her eyes with an uncertain hand, delighting in the faintly dazed, glorious happiness of his face. She was straddling his thighs as he lay on his back, his off-center grin no longer touched by guilt. "You're a wanton wench, Sorcha Fraser. Thank God." His laughter echoed out over the rambling waters of the Spey. "I confess to being seduced. Take me, then. I'm yours!"

Momentarily puzzled, Sorcha ran a finger over her lower lip. She stared uncomprehendingly down at Napier; he made an encouraging, if impatient gesture with his hand and suddenly she understood. Her own laughter chimed on the night air, and even as it seemed to roll out over the moors, she moved forward a few inches on her knees and then lowered herself over the pinnacle of possession.

The shock of feeling him invade her being in this unanticipated manner rendered her breathless. Sorcha closed her eyes, and began to rock back and forth as Napier moved forcefully within her, numbing her brain and stunning her senses. Just as she was certain she could no longer endure the agony of desire, the outpouring of his passion overwhelmed her. With a cry of delirious fulfillment, Sorcha went rigid, her head thrown back, the long masses of hair brushing Napier's thighs, her breasts thrust upward, her body outlined against the darkness like a mythical Valkyrie riding her steed into the fiery twilight of the gods.

And in that moment of exultant triumph, Sorcha knew that the power of her love had brought Gavin Napier out of the shadows and into the light of life.

Chapter 25

THE FIRST HEAVY SNOW FELL early that autumn, covering the Highlands from Strathnaver in the far north to Glen Clovo in the southeast. The roads were impassable, the last of the harvest had been hastily brought into the barns, and farmers struggled through four-foot drifts to round up their livestock. Even after the storm let up, the wind continued to blow from the north, piling snow up against the very walls of Gosford's End.

From her bedroom window, Sorcha grudgingly admired the pristine white landscape that stretched almost unblemished to the roofs and spires of Inverness. But the heavy fall had also delayed the return of Gavin Napier and Magnus Fraser, who had ridden out the last of September to confer with the Earl of Moray at Donibristle.

"Keeping watch won't make them come any sooner," Rosmairi said in a faintly waspish voice. "No more than will wishing make my bairn get itself born." She put a hand over her bulging abdomen and tilted her head to one side. "I feel a foot—or is it an elbow?"

Sorcha gave her sister a fond smile. "Frankly, it looks like a group. Ros," she queried, leaving the window and going to warm herself by the crackling fire, "are you happy?"

The smooth brow furrowed as Rosmairi gazed at Sorcha. "Aye," she replied with conviction, "I am indeed. Yet bearing babes is a tiring task. And it takes so long!"

Pushing a half-burned log back farther into the flames, Sorcha set the poker down and came to sit on a footstool next to Rosmairi. "Yet it's the fruit of your love. I wonder if I shall ever bear Gavin's child."

Rosmairi noted the wistful look on Sorcha's face and smiled encouragement.

"If he has the support of his brother and John Fraser, surely the Pope will grant an annulment. Does Gavin still plan to go to Rome in the spring?"

"Oh, yes." Sorcha nodded vigorously. "But even after eight years of desertion and Marie-Louise's refusal to live as his wife, I still fear that the grounds may be insufficient. Annulments are difficult at best, and despite Brother John and Father Adam's influence, they have neither wealth nor political power." Anxiously, she raked the long hair that had fallen over her forehead. "I have visions of waiting so long that I'll be too old to care."

"Now, now," Rosmairi said in kindly reproach, "that's not like you to lose heart. You're conjuring up obstacles where there may not be any."

Sorcha was about to respond that sometimes she felt their only real hope was having Rob elected to the Papacy—yet, knowing Rob and his deep-seated sense of justice, even he might say no. But arguing the matter did as little good as worrying about it. Sorcha had to be comforted by the fact that Gavin Napier had finally agreed to seek the annulment at all. Indeed, he was eager to head for Rome and would have already left had not a new crisis erupted in the Highlands.

When Sorcha and Gavin Napier had returned to Gosford's End, the family's elation over their safety had been considerably dampened by news of George Gordon's incursion into Grant territory and adjacent MacKintosh lands as well. For Lord and Lady Fraser, Gordon's brazen move was a dangerous insult to Dallas's clan.

Despite Father Adam's reminder that the Church was best served by Catholic families who put aside petty clan feuds for the sake of religion, Dallas asserted that lawlessness was lawlessness, no matter what the nominal faith of the perpetrator. Iain Fraser eventually, if reluctantly, had to agree with his wife, pointing out that a Highland chieftain, such as Gordon, who flouted the King's command, served neither his country nor his Catholic faith.

King Jamie had obviously agreed, sending a force north to quell the burgeoning war. To everyone's relief, Gordon retired from the field, though no one believed he had given up completely. It was said that the great earl was too ambitious to live forever in the King's shadow. If George Gordon couldn't rule all of Scotland, he intended to reign over the Highlands. Consequently, Iain Fraser had decided to seek an alliance, not with his Catholic brethren who were in complete disarray, but with the one man whose judgment he trusted: that other James Stewart, the Bonnie Earl of Moray. Fraser had sent his eldest son and Gavin Napier to Donibristle to discuss the combustible political situation and to consider what might be done to prevent further military confrontations. Resignedly, Sorcha had watched Napier and Magnus ride out one crisp fall morning and knew that her hopes for a wedding in the near future were dashed.

At least, with Napier gone from Gosford's End, the awkward situation of living under the same roof with her parents and Father Adam was not a problem. During the month after their return to the Fraser manor house, Sorcha and Napier had agreed not to make love. At first, with the promise of an annulment and the prospect of marriage shimmering on the horizon, their mutual restraint had not been too difficult. But as the heat of summer fell victim to the chill of fall, Sorcha's yearning for her lover's embrace grew stronger. Nor was there much comfort from Napier, whose hunter's eyes burned with the intensity of his own desire. It was almost as if they'd come full circle, from those days of agonized uncertainty at Fotheringhay to the acknowledged, still-unsanctified passion they were forced to deny at Gosford's End.

While Sorcha hated being separated, she had waved Napier off to Donibristle with a sense of relief. But that had been more than a month ago. Now, a week after the unseasonable snowfall, there was still no sign of a thaw. The next day would be All Hallows Eve, and Sorcha suddenly thought of Marie-Louise and shuddered.

"Are you that cold?" Rosmairi asked with concern. "Here, take my shawl," she offered, starting to pluck the fleecy blue wool from her shoulders.

"No, no," protested Sorcha. "I just thought of something unpleasant. Ros," she said, her tone turning brisk, "I should go back to court as soon as possible."

Readjusting the fleecy shawl, Rosmairi regarded Sorcha quizzically. "Why? To avoid Gavin?"

Surprised by her sister's acuity, Sorcha stared, then laughed. "That's part of it—but we're out of touch here; we have no one at the King's side who can give us an unbiased report of what's happening."

"I thought you were going to wait until Armand and the bairn and I could go with you in the spring, so that we could discuss disposition of the French properties with Uncle Donald." Rosmairi was verging on petulance. "After all, you told us that dreadful woman claimed ownership of Armand's land. We've got to get the matter settled so that we can arrange to build a home in Scotland."

"That's my point," Sorcha asserted. "Who knows what Marie-Louise is doing in our absence? Her lover Bothwell's plots grow more daring by the day." Always a thorn in his royal cousin's side, the Border earl's reputed involvement with witches had caused Secretary Maitland to urge imprisonment. At the same time Bothwell's harassment of King Jamie seemed to have increased dramatically since Marie-Louise's arrival in Scotland.

"My original intention was to watch Marie-Louise like a hawk, should she show her evil face at court," Sorcha explained. "Yet when she finally came to Edinburgh, I fled north, to warn Gavin. Now, perhaps I can serve him—and

Jamie—better by returning to my place with Queen Anne." Concluding her explication, Sorcha waited for Rosmairi to comment.

But Rosmairi had turned rigid, her normally pink cheeks gone gray as the snow clouds that hung low over Beauly Firth. "Sweet Mother of God," she breathed, her eyes startlingly bright, "my water broke!"

Marie-Louise's witchcraft, Bothwell's treachery, even Gavin Napier and the Fraser-Grant mesalliance were all swept aside by that most natural, yet most incredible of occasions—the birth of a baby. As Rosmairi groaned in her labor, Sorcha held her hand and whispered encouragement. The midwife, a hefty, capable cousin of Catriona's, stood in for Dr. Macimmey who was stranded by the weather in Inverness. Margery Syme had helped birth dozens of babies born to Fraser tenants and clansmen, but Dallas would have preferred to have the taciturn, pedantic Macimmey in attendance.

If Margery Syme was aware of Her Ladyship's preference, it made no difference. The broad-beamed midwife gave orders like a commander in the heat of battle. Even Dallas was pressed into service, assembling the linen with which to wrap the newborn babe. As for Armand, Margery dispatched him early on, to be cosseted by his father-in-law with large amounts of strong spirits.

"Breath in, now out, there's a good lassie," she ordered, red, work-roughened hands helping Sorcha hold Rosmairi on the bed. "Ochs, you're fighting it, push the bairn; the wee mite wants out!"

Dallas winced as Rosmairi erupted with another soul-searing cry. "Does Margery Syme think my sweet daughter is a cow birthing a calf?" she whispered in annoyance to Flora. But Dallas acknowledged Margery's skill and said no more.

A short time later, as Rosmairi's agony seemed to brook no respite, Margery Syme called for whiskey to dull the pain. When Rosmairi waved away the brimming cup, Margery downed it herself. Aghast, Dallas was about to remonstrate when the baby finally emerged. Margery triumphantly held the infant aloft, a husky boy, bellowing his greeting to the Fraser clan.

A short time later, Sorcha was overcome with a sense of awe—and a tinge of envy—as she handed the baby to Armand. "*Mon Dieu*," murmured the much-relieved, slightly tipsy father, "he looks like *un petit Chinois!*"

"Nonsense," snapped Dallas, "his eyes aren't open yet. And with that mop of black hair, he looks just like Iain."

His own eyes not quite in focus, Armand d'Ailly gazed in bewilderment at his son. "He shall be Adam, in honor of the good priest who has shared our roof in Scotland and France."

Rosmairi smiled wanly, her face looking very small and pale against the mound of pillows. "He is lusty, is he not?" she asked as tiny Adam let out another thin, piercing wail.

Armand grinned and gently bobbed the baby in his arms. "He is quite perfect. Though," he added rather wistfully, "I should have thought he'd be fair, not so … dark."

"Imagine my surprise when Rob was born with red hair," Dallas remarked, leaning over d'Ailly's shoulder to touch the infant's rosy cheek. "Ah, dear bairn, we'll build a fine home for you yet, and never mind Gordons, Grants, or muddleheaded strumpets who stand in our way! Your grandmother promises, and she so hates to be wrong!"

"That being the case, he'll no doubt end up owning Ireland." Iain Fraser was standing a little apart from the others, but Sorcha noted that he looked every inch the patriarch of his growing brood.

The squalls of the baby and the happy chatter of the household members had a sudden, unexpected fatiguing effect on Sorcha. She wandered to the window, where she was astonished to see the first frail light of dawn filtering over the snow-covered eastern moors. "It's morning," she said to no one in particular. "It's All Hallows Eve Day."

Her words went unremarked. Sorcha gazed at Rosmairi and d'Ailly, who were totally absorbed in their new creation. Some day, God willing, she and Gavin would wrap themselves in the wonder of a tiny child. Yet if the sight of her sister and husband and their babe evoked a pang of envy, the day itself called to mind the formidable image of Marie-Louise. While many would swear that they saw witches ride the lowering storm clouds in the night to come, Sorcha had no fear of such fantasies. What filled her with foreboding was the evil reality of Marie-Louise. The black arts she practiced were surely bogus, but the plots she contrived were all too genuine.

Sorcha felt a draft blow through the casement, and shivered. She turned to observe the others: a drowsy Rosmairi surrendering her babe to Margery Syme, Armand d'Ailly gently kissing his wife's brow, Iain Fraser with his arm slung around Dallas's neck, Ailis helping Flora put the soiled bed linen into a hamper—the scene was so ordinary, so comfortable, so rich in familial affection. Sorcha squared her shoulders and went to take one last peek at little Adam before he was placed in the elaborate cradle fit for a prince. Marie-Louise might command all the powers of darkness, but Sorcha was fortified by the realization that in the end, love was always stronger than hate.

A DOZEN DEER CARCASSES WERE STRETCHED out on the frosty ground by the stable. Gavin Napier pulled off his kidskin gloves and passed a hand over his brow. "It's not true sport when the animals are forced by the weather to come so close in. I'll wager we could bring back twelve more tomorrow."

Iain Fraser nodded absently, the hazel eyes resting on a set of magnificent antlers. "Any other day, I'd claim those as a trophy," he remarked, "but not this time."

"Then I will," declared Magnus, signaling to one of the stable boys to sever the head. "Jeannie and I have none so fine to decorate our walls at the Muir of Ord."

Fraser shrugged. "As you will." He turned to Sorcha. "Was that one yours?"

Sorcha twisted her mouth in concentration. "I don't recall—I think it was Gavin's." She averted her eyes as the stable boy fetched a broadax. "At least the poor things won't starve," she said, stamping her feet, which had grown quite numb despite the fur-lined boots. The snow had finally melted over the course of a week, but after intermittent rainfalls, the weather had turned bitterly cold again. Gavin Napier and Magnus had ridden into Gosford's End at the end of the first week in November, bringing optimistic news from Donibristle. King James had ordered George Gordon's imprisonment in Borthwick Castle. The earl's incarceration would stave off further trouble in the Highlands, at least for some time. Gavin Napier and Father Adam had been of two minds about the matter. Gordon's ploy for power had rallied both Catholic and Protestant lords around him. Bothwell, Caithness, and the Master of Gray were numbered among his coconspirators. At best, Gordon's aggression could not be considered solely a Papist plot. On the other hand, as the nominal leader of Scotland's Catholic Church, George Gordon was in disgrace. It was yet another frustrating, if typical, obstacle in the way of religious unity.

The dull thud of the ax made Sorcha wince. A hand at her elbow guided her away from the hunting party, toward the rear entrance of the manor house. "I've made up my mind," Gavin Napier said, the long mouth set, though from somewhere in the depth of his eyes a touch of warmth began to wash over Sorcha. "I leave for Rome tomorrow."

A surge of contradictory emotions surfaced in Sorcha's breast. She was overjoyed that Gavin Napier was committed to pursuing an annulment; she was also afraid that his quest might end in failure. Now, after less than a week of being reunited, he would be gone again, this time for several months, perhaps a year or more.

"Does Father Adam go with you?" The question covered the disarray of her feelings. Somehow, standing there under the lackluster November sun, Sorcha felt suddenly shy. Indeed, she had grown increasingly awkward in Napier's presence ever since their return to Gosford's End. It was as if the constraints they had put on their lovemaking had also robbed them of any other sort of intimacy.

Napier, seeming to sense her unease, took one gloved hand in his bare, yet warm fingers, "Nay. I can travel faster without him, and in truth it's best for his own health that he remain here. That is," he added with a little smile, "if your family will be gracious enough to have him."

"You know they will." Sorcha's mouth curved upward though the green eyes failed to conceal her distress. "Yet without Father Adam, who will gain you an entree to see the Holy Father?"

Napier let out a grant of laughter and squeezed her hand. "Which Holy Father? This past year, we have gone from Sixtus to Urban to Gregory, at last count. The Holy See is in chaos."

Sorcha covered his hand with both of hers, feeling the strength of him flow through her suede gloves. "I've worried about that," she admitted, looking at him through her lashes. "A stable Papacy would greatly aid our cause, don't you think?"

Napier's smile turned grim. "*All* of our causes," he emphasized, glancing beyond Sorcha to Iain Fraser, Magnus, and Armand d'Ailly, who were supervising the butchery of the stags. "The Church has been moribund ever since Sixtus died. He took a strong line against Protestant propaganda. I sometimes think it was his influence that forced Henri de Navarre to become Catholic when he assumed the French crown."

"That seems so long ago, yet it's been only a little over a year since we were all in France." Sorcha's memory traveled back to the languid, pristine days at Le Petit Andely, to the great forest of Compiègne, to the turmoil of Paris under siege. She thought of Rob, as she often did, and brightened. "Gavin, why not take Rob to Rome?"

The heavy brows drew close together, then lifted. "Why not? With Brother John Fraser's blessing, Rob might aid our cause." Napier leaned down to brash Sorcha's temple with his lips. "We spoke before of their possible intercession. Even now, Adam is writing up the background of the … matter." His face clouded at the allusion to his tragic marriage. "If nothing else, it will do Rob good to see the glories of Rome."

"It would do me good to see Rob," Sorcha remarked, her gaze fixed on her elder brother, who was holding up the dripping stag's head with it four-foot span of antlers. The faintly swaggering stance, the black hair, the strong, yet blunted features, the sense of substance, made Magnus seem as unlike Rob as two brothers could be. Yet their open, honest smiles and the candor of their gaze marked them as not just kinsmen, but as kindred spirits.

"Magnus reminds me of you," Napier said unexpectedly as he followed Sorcha's eyes. "He is dauntless, irrepressible, genuine." His arm slipped around Sorcha's shoulder. "Not nearly as bonnie, though."

Sorcha's eyes slid round to look up into Napier's wolfish face. "Am I truly bonnie?"

"Sufficiently bonnie to send me to Rome. Having pledged my heart, it seems I'd go halfway to hell for you, Sorcha Fraser." He nudged his chin against her russet hat and grimaced.

Her voice was a muffled, desperate cry against his leather jacket: "Come to me tonight, Gavin. Please!"

His reply was a quick, fierce hug. Briefly, she went limp against him, then straightened, pulled away, and offered Magnus an extravagant wave as he and Armand carried off the great stag's head with its spikelike crown and cold, dead eyes.

THERE IS A STARK, GAUNT quality to the Highlands in November that is at once forlorn and comforting. The bare trees, the wan gray light, the permeating damp chill, the sharp wind from the north descends upon even the hardiest inhabitants of glen and moor. Yet the season also brings with it a sense of peace, of silence, of fulfillment, with the harvest brought home and the approach of the Yuletide season. From the old Caledonian forest in Cameron country to the relentless waves of Moray Firth, nature tucks itself underground, to wait with tireless patience through the long, dark nights of the Highland winter.

Sorcha Fraser, having learned those lessons of time and place and seasons, instinctively put aside her fears and anxieties to offer Gavin Napier the unleashed passion that sprang not just from the depths of her femininity but from the very earth itself. Another woman might have wept and clung on their last night together before a long, uncertain parting. But Sorcha had looked out over the hills of Cawdor and Nairn to the east and the mysterious, shrouded sea to the north to find hope. In a few months, those hills would erupt into a bounty of color and life; the sea would grow calm, and sunlight would dazzle the waters. All things would change—except the love that she and Gavin Napier shared.

It was well after midnight when Napier rapped softly on Sorcha's door. She had been sitting by the fire, watching the orange-and-gold flames dance among the dry logs. On eager, noiseless feet, she flew to greet her lover, clasping him in her arms and savoring the virile intensity of his embrace.

"I thought you'd never come," she breathed, her face pressed against his chest.

His grip tightened; he rocked slightly on his heels as she swayed gently, yet securely, in his arms. "Adam and I had much to discuss. And, as it turned out, so did your sire."

Sorcha pulled away enough to stare up into Napier's wry face. "God's teeth! You mean to tell me my father talked about your intentions?"

Napier lifted his shoulders. "It's his duty, after all. I've marveled that he hasn't put me on the rack before this. Surely you've spoken of the matter with your Lady Mother?"

Sorcha had. And to Dallas's credit, she had displayed remarkable restraint. "You seem to know what you want," she'd told Sorcha. "I only hope that having got it, you'll not be disappointed." At first, the words had stung Sorcha. Until she recalled that there was a time she'd wanted to marry Johnny Grant, that she'd wanted a titled, wealthy husband above all things. But those were whims, not wants. And never need, which was the fuel that fired her tenacity to become Gavin Napier's wife.

Sorcha offered Napier a fulgent smile, her head tipped back against his arm. "Parents, Popes, plots, a pox on them all!" She watched those dark eyes turn black with desire, saw the long mouth curve upward in anticipation, admired the strong, white, even teeth that were revealed as the grin widened at the wonder of her own yearning.

Though the bed was turned down and a single rushlight flickered on the nightstand, Napier slowly went to his knees, his hands sliding down over the curves of her body, which the clinging moire of her night robe enhanced more than concealed. She moved enticingly at his touch, her hands wrapping themselves in his hair, the long, slim fingers transmitting messages of urgent longing. Adroitly, he parted the robe, chuckling appreciatively to find her naked. "You wanted to waste no time, I see," he said, wrenching his eyes from the magic black triangle to look up into her resplendent face.

"We only have this night. For now," she added hopefully. "Would you rather I'd layered myself in petticoats and chemises?" She had meant to sound lighthearted, but he found her inflection far more provocative than amusing.

"We've wasted too much time—too many months and years—already." Napier's expression had sobered, the hunter's gaze mesmerizing Sorcha. "Every part of you is vibrant," he said in low, rambling tones. "Your body doesn't just live—it offers life."

"It's freely offered only to you," Sorcha averred, feeling him draw her down onto the carpet by the hearth. The moire robe fell apart of its own accord, allowing the firelight to cast a fulvous glow across her ripe, proud breasts. Napier filled his hands with them, covering the flat of her belly with kisses. Dazed and aching with desire, she wrapped both her legs around his, hugging him with her thighs in urgent appeal for completion.

Moments later, after experiencing the delectable agony of his hands and lips seeking out every inch of her body, Sorcha gasped as he thrust himself into that moist, secret, throbbing chamber where infinite joy awaited them both. Their cries broke the silence, lighted the darkness, dispelled the loneliness of separate souls.

A half-moon was fretfully fending off the rain clouds that had rolled in from the North Sea after sunset. The wind had risen up off Beauly Firth, moaning with a weary sound among the chimneys of Gosford's End. In the grate, particles of fir crumbled into glowing crimson embers. The shadows grew long across the room; the rushlight had long since guttered out.

Their bodies spent, their spirits healed, Sorcha and Napier lay in each other's arms for a quiet, blissful time. The days and nights ahead would bring separation and anxiety and pain. But for now, Sorcha and Napier were together, inextricably united, bound by love, their union forged in passion, their future as uncertain as a November morning.

Sorcha could see Napier's dark hair curling slightly along the nape of his neck, and the hard, sure muscles of his shoulder. Nothing else matters but now, she told herself fiercely. Nothing will ever matter but him. Not even, she promised, the thought of defeat.

Chapter 26

IN JUST SIX SHORT MONTHS, fashions at court had changed drastically. Queen Anne's youthful love of elaborate finery had influenced her ladies'—and to some extent, even the gentlemen's—apparel. There was more color, a greater variety of fabric, and a lavish use of jewels, lace, ribbons, and exaggerated ruffs for embellishment.

Sorcha, however, found the often cumbersome and always gaudy toilettes not only unsuitable, but uncomfortable as well; the great four-foot flare of farthingale across the hips made most women look like galleons sailing into port. A dressmaker recommended by the Countess of Moray had accommodated Sorcha's more moderate tastes by refining the cartwheellike adornment into a trimmer, more graceful drape. While the décolleté necklines emphasized her full bosom, the heavy ornamental detail that usually descended from the shoulders to well below the waist was much too rigid. Instead of weighing herself down with rows of gold braid or bugle beads, she chose seed pearls and satin ribbon. Nor would she endure wiglets and falls, heated tongs and primping irons. With her own thick mane, she could pile her hair atop her head, and weave in several strands to create a simple, yet striking coiffure.

On this mild June night at Holyrood, Sorcha fanned herself with a clutch of ostrich feathers and watched the other courtiers join in a dance she hadn't yet learned. Not that there hadn't been time in her two months at court, but Queen Anne was so enamored of dancing that hardly a night passed by without the introduction of new steps. But the Queen was enamored in another, more sinister way: To Sorcha's great chagrin, she had found Marie-Louise in attendance on Jamie's consort.

It was only natural, of course, that the blond, statuesque foreign-born Anne had felt instant empathy with the Frenchwoman who was so similar in coloring and stature. Bothwell had dared introduce Marie-Louise at court that spring while his wife remained at their Border home of Crichton. Even after he had been warded in Edinburgh Castle for his involvement with witches, Marie-Louise had been kept on as one of the ladies of the bedchamber. Since Sorcha's appointment was as a lady-of-the-wardrobe, their paths seldom crossed. It was just as well, Sorcha realized, since upon those occasions when the two women did meet, Marie-Louise was invariably and insinuatingly snide.

She was also seemingly innocuous within the household, at least as far as Sorcha could discern. Perhaps, with Bothwell imprisoned, Marie-Louise was biding her time until sentence should be pronounced. At the moment, Marie-Louise was cutting a graceful figure on the ballroom floor, despite a damask farthingale that stretched out almost as far as her arms could reach. She was dancing with the King, who seemed to be eyeing her with a quizzical, yet amused expression. The tune ended on a rapid series of tinkling notes, and the partners bowed low to each other before parting company. Somewhat to Sorcha's surprise, the King shambled from the dance floor, to join her by the long banquet table at the far end of the room.

"Oh, Coz," Jamie said with a sigh, sorting through a pile of oysters before he found one small enough to his liking, "I've seen too little of you since your return to court. We have yet to find you a husband. I feel quite guilt-laden over my neglect."

Sorcha smiled wryly at her sovereign. His beard had grown out and his features had sharpened, but he still cut an insignificant figure. He had, however, taken a firmer grip on the reins of Scotland in recent times, and the acquisition of a wife had increased his esteem among his subjects, if not his nobles. And while it was whispered that he continued to prefer the company of handsome men, he didn't shrink from his marital duties. Sorcha found him changed, but not sufficiently to either lessen her affection or increase her respect.

"I can find a husband on my own," Sorcha assured Jamie, though her voice held more conviction than did her heart. Gavin Napier had now been gone for almost eight months; his most recent letter, received in late May and written in mid-April, recounted further disarray in the Holy See. Neither he nor Rob had yet talked to anyone more influential than the secretaries of a handful of relatively unimportant cardinals. Napier's letter reeked of frustration. Sorcha responded with encouragement, but to herself she admitted disappointment.

"Bonnie Rosmairi married a Frenchman, did she not?" Jamie glanced inquiringly at Sorcha, then gazed down at the empty oyster shell with distaste. "I think these are off-season. Perhaps I shall try the scallops instead."

"Rosmairi and her husband are due in Edinburgh any day now," Sorcha said, deciding to test the oysters for herself. "I'm sure they're looking forward to seeing you." Out of the corner of her eye, she saw Marie-Louise dancing with the Earl of Moray. Sorcha wondered how Armand d'Ailly would react when he encountered the woman who had destroyed his family. More to the point, she wondered how Marie-Louise might behave toward a man whose property she claimed to have in her possession. She swallowed the raw oyster whole without tasting it, and shuddered.

"Ah!" exclaimed King James, "I told you—they're tainted! Eat no more, Coz, or you'll be sick."

Sorcha didn't bother to tell her royal cousin that the oysters had nothing to do with the creeping fear that had overtaken her. Nor could she have done so had she wanted to. The Master of Gray had sidled up to the King, managing to rake Sorcha with a malevolent eye before he put an all-too-familiar hand on his monarch's arm. "I must speak alone with you, sire," he murmured in his most intimate, mellifluous voice. "It's a matter most urgent."

"Oh, Patrick, dear Master, it is always urgent with you." Jamie sighed with an exasperated air defused by affection. The King bowed to Sorcha. "Forgive me, Coz, the Master must beleaguer me with weighty matters of state."

Sorcha ignored Gray's smirk as he led the King away. A new dance tune was beginning, a galliard which Sorcha knew from her previous service at court. She was just reaching for an almond tart when the Earl of Moray bowed low before her. "Will you honor me with this dance, mistress? I feel as if we are strangers since you've come back to serve Her Grace."

"Never that," Sorcha said rather absently, dropping the tart back onto the silver tray. She let him take her arm to steer her out onto the floor, her pine-green gown fashionably short enough to reveal silver slippers with pearl-gray buckles. "I've not seen your wife tonight," Sorcha remarked as they moved in unison to the lively music. "Is she here?"

If Sorcha's inquiry had been intended as a reminder of the earl's marital status, he gave no indication of embarrassment. "Nay, she has been unwell the past few days. I've no doubt," he went on cheerfully, "that with the warmer weather, her health will improve."

"Pray convey my heartiest wishes for her recovery," Sorcha said. While she and Elizabeth of Moray were not close friends, the two women had developed a certain camaraderie.

"I will tell her," Moray replied, his hand resting lightly on Sorcha's waist as they made a difficult turn and leap. The blue eyes regarded her with a mixture of amusement and admiration. Sorcha was vexed by his attitude, though she would have been hard put to say why. Moray, however, maintained impeccable decorum even as they moved and touched and all but embraced in the course of the fast-paced dance. "You have heard, I presume, that George Gordon was recently released from Borthwick Castle?"

"Aye," Sorcha answered, pausing as they made their final exacting twirl to end the dance. "His freedom disturbs me."

Moray bowed as Sorcha curtsied. "It does that to me as well." His smile remained in place, but his face clouded over as he led Sorcha back to the buffet table. "He has wished me ill for some time. I think he still resents the fact that years and years ago, Queen Mary wrested the Moray earldom from his grandfather and bestowed it upon my wife's sire. The Gordons don't give up their grudges easily."

"Few Scots do," Sorcha pointed out, popping a sliver of smoked salmon into her mouth. "We nurture old hurts and humiliations like exotic flowers in a cold climate."

Several other hungry courtiers were milling about the buffet, chattering and laughing, a brilliant mélange of color and gloss, of musky perfumes and fresh rose water, of precious stones and gleaming metal. Sorcha edged away, with Moray in her shadow.

"The irony is," she said, when they'd gained a refuge not far from the empty royal dais, "these nobles seem so congenial at court. Yet I know that underneath all that hearty good fellowship, they plot and connive." At that moment, she glimpsed Marie-Louise on the Earl of Argyll's arm, her blond head thrown back in exuberant mirth. "How many here, I wonder," Sorcha murmured, "wish us ill?"

If Moray had an answer, he never had the chance to give it voice. King Jamie, the Master of Gray, and Secretary Maitland emerged from a side door, their faces a mixed study in anger, contempt, and outrage. Queen Anne, who had been allowing the Earl of Morton to feed her chocolate-covered strawberries, paused with her mouth open to stare at her lord, who was stamping past Sorcha onto the dais. James raised his hands for silence, though most of the assemblage had already gone quite mute.

"Good friends," Jamie began, his high-pitched voice deeper and more resonant than usual, "we have received calamitous news!" He halted for a moment, sufficiently in control of his emotions to judge the dramatic effect of his words. "The Earl of Bothwell has decamped from Edinburgh Castle!"

A gasp rose from the crowd, followed by a burst of murmured babble. No one had ever escaped from the castle, with its stout stone walls set atop the sheer cliffs that dropped straight down to a bed of jagged rocks. Sorcha locked glances with Moray, whose look of surprise was tempered by a sudden spark of humor. Knave that Bothwell was, Sorcha recalled that the kinship he shared with Moray forged a seemingly unbreakable bond.

King Jamie's voice rang out again, immediately stilling his courtiers' tongues. "Bothwell will be apprehended, of course. We hold everyone here responsible for his recapture and will tolerate no assistance on his behalf." Jamie glared at his nobles, then made a lax, almost whimsical gesture with one hand. "So be it. Let us continue our entertainment."

At Argyll's side, Marie-Louise had assumed a bland countenance. Sorcha watched her keenly, wondering if Bothwell would risk coming to her at Holyrood. But such audacity would be too much even for him. On the other hand, his daring escape had put an end to the myth of Edinburgh Castle's invincibility. Even if Bothwell were captured within the hour, he had already enhanced his reputation for wizardlike powers.

"You're fond of Bothwell, aren't you?" Sorcha asked as Moray nodded politely to dour Secretary Maitland.

"I am." He offered Sorcha his boyish smile. "Bothwell is an impossible rogue, but boon company. I'd rather he didn't persist in his efforts to plague poor Jamie, but it's almost as if he's driven by demons." Moray fingered his chin thoughtfully as he watched Sorcha's eyes return to Marie-Louise, who was now dancing with the Earl of Atholl. "His mistress is very beautiful, is she not? I hear he met her some years ago in France."

The green eyes slid up to meet Moray's. "So he did." Fanning herself with the ostrich feathers, she suddenly felt quite impotent, and afraid—for herself, for Gavin Napier, for the King, and even for Moray.

AILIS HAD JUST RETURNED FROM airing out Sorcha's summer gowns prior to packing them away for the colder weather. The court had spent the past month at Falkland, hunting almost every day under clear, calm skies. As if on cue, the morning that the royal caravan headed out for Edinburgh the weather turned cool and damp, with fog rolling in from the Firth of Forth to shroud the travelers' route in a wraithlike mist.

Now, on the day back in the capital, the sun had finally dispersed the thick hoar, though the late September day held a sharp chill. "I suppose," Sorcha remarked to Ailis as she set the lid down on the bulging clothes chest, "Ros and Armand will be going home soon. I do hate to see them leave." While her kinfolk had not stayed with the court, but in Panmure Close, there had been the opportunity for many visits during the past two months. Much to Sorcha's surprise, there had been no interference from Marie-Louise concerning the d'Ailly property in France. Uncle Donald had dutifully sent off the requisite letters of inquiry and had learned that there were indeed conflicting claims to Armand's inheritance. However, despite the loss of the house itself, the land was worth a substantial sum. Negotiations were now being conducted through the good offices of a Huguenot banker in La Rochelle who was a longtime business associate of Uncle Donald's.

Sorcha's prediction concerning Rosmairi and Armand turned out to be all too accurate. Within the quarter hour, a messenger arrived, saying that the d'Ailly entourage was about to depart for the Highlands. Sorcha and Ailis hurriedly got on their cloaks and raced from the palace precincts to cover the short distance to Panmure Close.

All was abustle inside the McVurrich house, as the wet nurse, two Fraser retainers, and the McVurrich's servants busied themselves with the sudden preparations for leave-taking.

"The weather has been so fine," Rosmairi said to Sorcha as the wet nurse stuffed a frolicsome baby Adam into a cashmere bunting, "that I think we were lulled into thinking that summer would last forever. But now that it's grown colder and more damp, we must head home. If we weren't traveling with the bairn, it might be different." Her voice trailed off when Tarrill entered the room, carrying a wicker basket bulging with foodstuffs.

"To enjoy along the way," she said, tucking a linen napkin more securely over the top of the basket. "But do save the blackberry jam for your mother, Ros. It's a great favorite of hers. I made it myself, from Marthe's old recipe."

"Lovely." Rosmairi smiled, while Armand d'Ailly vigorously pumped Uncle Donald's hand. For Sorcha, there was reassurance in the gesture; at least under the McVurrich roof, Catholic and Protestant could dwell in harmony.

Andrew McVurrich, with Doles at his side, was regarding his Highland kinfolk with envy. "Is it true, sir, you'll be fighting Gordon troops soon?" he asked Armand.

The Frenchman's brow furrowed. "Let us hope not, my fine Andrew. We hear unfortunate rumors, that is true. But we also trust that George Gordon will not commit a folly similar to the Grant of Freuchie incident." He put a firm hand on Andrew's shoulder, seemingly grown broader in the past year. "I take it that if we should need reinforcements, you'd march north?"

Andrew's long face grew very solemn. "Oh, aye, I would! Gordon of Huntly flirts with treason. I have pledged myself to defend King, Kirk and country."

Uncle Donald, moving his substantial form with stiff dignity like a Calvinist icon, came to stand behind his second-born son. The long, graying beard dipped in approval. "A worthy promise," he intoned, "as long as it doesn't prove expensive as well."

Tarrill assumed an expression of mock exasperation. "I swear, Donald McVurrich, if St. Peter asks you for the price of heaven, you'll count his change!" She rolled her dark eyes, and neither Sorcha nor Rosmairi could help but laugh at their aunt.

The merry mood was broken with the announcement by one of the servants that all was in readiness for the journey. Sorcha waited quietly until Rosmairi turned in her direction, the gray eyes glistening with unshed tears. "So many partings," Rosmairi sighed, embracing her sister. "Why couldn't we all have stayed at home in the Highlands?"

Sorcha brushed Rosmairi's cheek with a kiss. "Some day, perhaps," she said, and then gasped. "God's teeth, what is this?"

Rosmairi and the others turned to where Sorcha was staring. Marie-Louise, attired in a voluminous black cape trimmed in white fox and a tall black hat with a white bouquet of plumes and flowing veil, stood in elegant arrogance on the McVurrich threshold.

"May I?" Marie-Louise murmured, the beautiful azure eyes fixed on Uncle Donald. It was a shrewd choice, since Donald McVurrich's mastery of European finances had not dulled his awe of a dazzling woman.

At his acquiescence, Marie-Louise floated into the parlor, scattering startled younger McVurriches and servants in her wake. Her gaze seemed to take in every member of the household, even little Adam, who had begun to fuss in the wet nurse's arms. Sorcha refused to avoid those azure eyes and stared back boldly, arms folded resolutely across her breast.

Marie-Louise adjusted the flowing veil that hid her scar and reached inside the fur-trimmed cape to withdraw a folded piece of parchment. "This," she said pleasantly, as she turned to a white-lipped Armand, "is the deed to the d'Ailly lands. I thought it best to show it to you in front of various witnesses. It will save you and your good uncle-by-marriage further exertion in trying to sell something that is not yours." Slowly, she unfolded the paper, smoothed it out with one gloved hand as if caressing a pet, and held it out for Armand and Donald McVurrich to read.

McVurrich looked up to meet Marie-Louise's cool gaze head-on. "This appears to be in good order," he admitted with a frown. "You have three witnesses, including the mayor of Amiens, the pastor of St. Genevieve's Church at d'Ailly, and a certain Monsieur André Ferraud of Chaulnes. You also," he added with a touch of chagrin, "have the signature of Raoul de Greve." Uncle Donald turned to Armand. "Would that be your brother or your father, sir?"

Armand's crimson cheeks seemed to implode in his face. "My brother," he said in a voice that was little more than a whisper. "My late brother."

With a graceful gloved hand, Marie-Louise waved the parchment like a battle pennant, then refolded the deed carefully and tucked it inside her black cape. "Then there is nothing else to be said." She offered the entire company a brilliant, self-satisfied smile before turning toward the door. "That being the case, I shall depart. *Bonne chance.*"

In a flash, Sorcha was on her adversary's heels. Just as Marie-Louise stepped over the threshold, Sorcha dove, knocking the larger woman off balance. With frenzied hands, she clawed at Marie-Louise's cape, seeking out the folded parchment. Armand and Uncle Donald were the first to follow, while the others pressed into the entry hall.

"Meddling strumpet!" screamed Marie-Louise, righting her hat and steadying herself on the stone steps. "You don't care about d'Ailly and his silly land! All you want is my husband in your bed!" Whirling away from Sorcha, Marie-Louise all but fell into the waiting grasp of Gavin Napier. The Earl of Moray was at his side, looking as bewildered as Napier was thunderous.

Marie-Louise exercised sufficient good sense not to struggle with Napier. She tamed her fury and regarded him with contempt. "Your conjugal caress is as swinish as ever," she jeered.

Napier's grip on her arms tightened so hard that it seemed Marie-Louise's bones might snap. But she never flinched. He tore his dark visage from her sneering face and looked to Sorcha. "What did you search for? What is she hiding?"

Sorcha moved down a step, aware that Moray's eyes were on her, rather than on Napier and Marie-Louise. "She has a deed—to Armand's French property. She insists it's legal, but I don't believe the lying baggage for a minute!" Leaning on the rail, Sorcha was momentarily taller than her rival. She stared Marie-Louise down, then flicked at her nose in that defiant gesture of dismissal. "It's a fraud! I don't care what anyone says!"

Marie-Louise glared at Sorcha, then spat on the ground. "That for your pitiful allegations!" She gazed past Sorcha, Armand, and Uncle Donald, searching for Rosmairi. "Madame d'Ailly! Hear me! Tell this brutish lout to let me go in peace or"—she shot Napier a scathing look before turning to Rosmairi who was now clinging to her husband's arm—"I shall call down a curse on that babe of yours! Do you understand?"

Napier didn't loosen his grip, but his taut features went slack. Moray uttered an oath, and Tarrill crossed herself rapidly. But it was Sorcha, not Rosmairi, who replied: "We don't believe in that puerile pap," she declared. "You have no demon powers. You're no more than an overblown, oversized bag of wind!"

But Rosmairi's maternal instincts were malleable clay in Marie-Louise's conniving hands. "You're right, Sorcha, but …." Rosmairi looked helplessly at her husband. "Sir," she called to Napier, "let that wretched woman go. We'd rather lose all of France than our sweet child!"

Very slowly, Napier let go of one of Marie-Louise's arms, but not the other. She eyed him with disdain as cold as hoarfrost. Deliberately, he picked up the loose end of her veil and wound it around her throat, over the puckered scar, across her neck, and back again. Then he began to pull, easily at first, and then tighter and tighter. Sorcha stood stock-still, a hand against her mouth.

Marie-Louise's white skin was beginning to turn pink, but she made no sound, offered no resistance. Napier began winding the veil around a second time, drawing it so taut that Sorcha was sure either the fabric would rip or Marie-Louise would collapse.

Without warning, Gavin Napier dropped his hands to his sides and walked away. He stood by Tarrill's herb garden, his back turned to them all, his broad shoulders slumped. Sorcha started toward him, but paused, her legs unsteady. Marie-Louise sucked in several deep breaths, then unwound the veil with a steady motion that must have cost her mightily, and rearranged her fox-trimmed cape. Head held high, she took a single step toward the street, then gave Moray a sidelong glance. "Who do you side with, My Lord? Do you know? Your life depends on it." She ignored his handsome, baffled stare and swept out of Panmure Close, leaving a wake of terrified silence behind her.

THE SEPTEMBER SUN CAST AMBER light across the chamber, gilding the paneled walls and the big oak bed. The filmy curtains that hung from the canopy stirred as the two figures under the single silken sheet moved in languorous contentment. On the carved mahogany mantelpiece, an Italian marble clock chimed six times. Sorcha rolled over onto her back and stretched, the sheet sliding unheeded to her waist. The green eyes grew soft as she contemplated the quiet form of Gavin Napier, now lying on his side, facing her but apparently asleep. The dark hair was rumpled, falling boyishly over his forehead; the long mouth was slightly parted, his breathing deep and even; one arm was bent at the elbow, the big hand slack against Sorcha's breast. He looked so serene, so peaceable, that even Sorcha could scarcely believe he'd all but engaged in a murderous act earlier that same day.

It had been an eventful day for them both, with the turmoil unleashed by Marie-Louise, but at last, after seeing Rosmairi and Armand off, Sorcha and Gavin Napier had gone on to Holyrood Palace. Initially, Napier had been distant and abrupt. He had said little about Marie-Louise, but Sorcha sensed that he was at once regretful and relieved: Had he actually strangled his wife on the spot, it would have been only righteous revenge for the murders she had committed or instigated. On the other hand, his act of mercy had spared him the burden of having her death on his conscience.

It was not words but gestures that had ultimately released Napier from his own private cell. With gentle determination, Sorcha had kissed and caressed him into emerging from that dark, secret place. Once unshackled, his emotions were intense, fierce, almost savage. He claimed Sorcha in a violent, shuddering embrace that seemed to rock the palace's stone walls. Had not the pleasure overwhelmed the pain, she would have cried out in protest rather than exultation. Later, after they had drank from the same goblet of red

Bordeaux wine and talked about the frustrating delays he had experienced in Rome, Napier's touch turned tender, almost languid, playing Sorcha's body like the strings of a Highland clarsach. She responded in kind, with as much sensuousness as sensuality, exploring every inch of him, leaving the imprint of possession on every muscle, sinew, and bone. They came together in a voluptuous crescendo of rising passion, oblivious of everything except the union of their fervid flesh.

No matter, Sorcha thought dreamily, that the new Pope had not yet studied the request for an annulment. Neither Napier nor Rob could have remained in Rome forever. And the papal secretary had all but promised to send word when the decision was finally handed down. Four Popes in two years had created a chaotic situation in the Holy See; the plight of one obscure couple in Scotland must be put aside until more important matters were considered.

Sorcha jerked her body suddenly, aware that she, too, was almost asleep. In just a little over half an hour, she was due to help select the Queen's finery for the evening's entertainment. "Gavin," Sorcha whispered, sitting up in bed, with the long hair brushing his upper arm, "wake up, my love! The sun is setting."

Napier's eyes opened slowly, his hand reaching vaguely for Sorcha. "What? Is aught wrong?" With effort, he focused on her, his fingers touching her bare stomach.

"Nay." She laughed, clasping his hand with both of hers. "I must dress to tend the Queen."

Napier shifted his weight, leaning on his elbows. "Send word you're ill. I've a mind never to leave this bed." He grinned, an unwonted flash of mischief in the dark eyes.

"I can't do that," Sorcha declared with resolution. "I want to, but I can't. Besides," she added seriously, trying to ignore the fingers that crept up her thigh, "I thought you wanted to see Moray."

"I do." The fingers pranced upward, to sink between her legs. "I will—in good time."

Setting her mouth, Sorcha started to swing her legs away but only managed to part them enough for Gavin Napier to capture the mound of her womanhood in his hand. Effortlessly, his other arm pinned her shoulders down against the pillows. His beard tickled her abdomen as Sorcha felt a single probing finger move within her, stretching, seeking, inciting. The other hand brushed back and forth across her breasts, then made lazy, maddening circles around the pink plateau of one nipple. With a groan of delight, Sorcha surrendered to his delicious, relentless torment. The Queen could wait; the world could wait. She was in the arms of the man she loved, and nothing else mattered.

Chapter 27

Hours later in the same chamber, with the fire turned to ashes and the only candle burned down almost to the nub, Gavin Napier bade Sorcha good-bye. After Sorcha had thrown on her clothes and raced off to the Queen, Napier had met with Moray at the Earl's town house. Fresh news had arrived from the north, relating George Gordon's further encroachment of MacKintosh property around Badenoch. The MacKintosh chieftain had formally asked for the help of Moray and the Earl of Atholl. Neither noble was anxious to engage in a Highland war, but realized that Gordon must be stopped before he gobbled up huge chunks of the northern kingdom. Moray, in turn, had asked Gavin Napier to join them; they would leave immediately.

Sorcha had been distressed not only at her lover's precipitous leave-taking but because the situation in the Highlands had deteriorated. Ironically, Napier was being forced to side with the Protestants he nominally opposed, against the Catholics he had promised to protect.

"It would seem," a grim-faced Napier had told Sorcha, readying his gear to head out into the dense fog, "that the Church's only real hope of surviving in Scotland lies with the achievement of peace. Perhaps," he added, donning light chain mail over his leather jerkin, "the ultimate hope is union with England."

For Sorcha, such conjecture seemed irrelevant compared to the imminent danger Gavin Napier would face in the north. The mere sight of him wearing chain mail and carrying a steel helmet had made her shudder. "I know it's not like me," she'd admitted, clinging to him, yet hating the jagged feel of the chain mail against her cheek. "Ordinarily, I'm quite a sensible person. But this time you're actually going into battle."

"To parley, more likely," Napier had replied.

Sorcha remained unconvinced. She'd argued that he must take her with him, but Napier was adamant. If ever there was a time when Sorcha was needed to watch the devious plotting of Marie-Louise and Bothwell, it was now. "She threatened Moray, you know," Napier reminded her. "It makes no sense, since he and Bothwell have always been friendly. Yet Moray was alarmed—not that he'd admit it, but I know he was."

That the Earl of Moray would take anything Marie-Louise said seriously only added to Sorcha's mounting fears. Yet Moray must know that Marie-Louise was not to be dismissed lightly. She had already dared to connive at the murder of a king.

"I wish now you'd stayed in Rome," Sorcha had exclaimed. "You might have been bored, but you would have been safe."

Napier had gazed down at her tousled dark head and sighed. "Except for loving you, I feel as if I've lived a useless life. What have I accomplished here in Scotland?"

Sorcha had known better than to try to dissuade him further. In some vague, instinctive way, she understood that he was a thwarted man who felt he'd failed his mission, his faith, even his own brother. The fact that he had successfully concluded Father Adam's initial task with Mary, Queen of Scots was no consolation. Gavin Napier would count himself a failure until he had unified the Catholic clans and forged a policy of toleration.

At last, with the heavy fog swirling around the walls of Holyrood Palace and the owls hooting mournfully from the eaves of the Chapel Royal, Gavin Napier kissed Sorcha an ardent farewell and rode out toward the Water Gate to meet the Earl of Moray.

"LA!" CRIED THE QUEEN, BRACING herself against the gaming table with the palms of her hands, "I have now the seven!" Her broad smile beamed at the other players. "Who can defeat me?" Her blue eyes danced from Jean Sinclair to the Earl of Morton to Marie-Louise, and finally to Sorcha, who was sitting between Lord John Hamilton and his wife, Margaret. Despite Queen Anne's high good humor, the company was attired in black, mourning the Countess of Moray, who had died of a wasting sickness the previous month. As she was cousin to the King, the court had observed her untimely death with a subdued Yuletide season. Now, two days after Christmas, the Queen had rebelled at the ban and had insisted on an evening of gaming.

After more than two hours, Jamie had long since tired of the game. Sorcha, who had been forced from the table by a pair of luckless ivory dice, crossed the room to join her royal cousin, who was whipping off the covers from various dishes and sampling most of them.

"I hunted all day," the King declared, stuffing smoked mussels and capon legs and jellied lamb into his mouth. "The winter weather gives me a hearty appetite." Still chewing lustily, he waved a crisp cabbage leaf in her direction. "Alas, I forget my manners—you must be starving, too; you always are. Try the lamb first."

To Jamie's amazement, Sorcha shook her head. "Nay, sire, I'm not hungry." Indeed, her digestion had been unruly for some time. "I'm overanxious these days—for many reasons."

Even if Jamie had evinced interest, there was no opportunity for Sorcha to relate her concerns. Secretary John Maitland stood in the doorway, his dour face a peculiar shade of sickly gray. He headed straight for the King and spoke without preamble. "Your Majesty, I have the most astounding news!" Maitland's usually smooth voice was lowered to a gruff whisper. "The Earl of Bothwell has invaded the palace!"

Jamie's brows drew together. "Maitland, dear Maitland, you have a tendency to bring me the most exasperating news about Bothwell. What do you really mean? That he has inserted spies among our royal presence?" Jamie giggled. "I don't fear spies; I make friends of them!"

Maitland's nostrils were flaring like those of a racehorse at the finish line. "I'm quite serious, sire. Bothwell is inside this very palace!" Maitland's whisper grew more frenzied, attracting the attention of the players at the gaming table. "He came to my chambers to kidnap me! A pot-boy heard him and warned me."

In a flutter of black brocade and lace, Queen Anne rose from her chair. "Good Maitland, you speak of Bothwell, *ja*, aye, for certain?"

The answer came from outside the door to the gaming room. "Damn!" breathed Jamie, making a fist and waving it ineffectually. "I hear Bothwell, I truly do!" He whirled around, looking both helpless and desperate. "Where is the Master when I need him? Where are my servants?" His outrage mounting, he charged at Maitland, his face as petulant as a child whose parent hasn't kept faith. "Where is my army? You said I didn't need an army, Maitland! Well, I sorely need one now!"

John Hamilton quietly intervened. "What Your Majesty needs now is a barricade." Signaling to the Earl of Morton, Hamilton moved briskly to a tall armoire at the end of the room. "We'll put this in front of the door. It should hold them off until help arrives."

"What help?" wailed King James, oblivious of the clutching hands of his frightened consort. "Listen! They are battering down the very walls!"

Sorcha winced as she heard wood splinter outside but kept her gaze on Marie-Louise, who had insinuated herself between the King and Queen. It was clear that somehow she had helped her lover gain entrance to the palace.

The armoire shuddered but remained in place against the door. Crouched over the gaming table, King Jamie was beating the green baize cover with his fists. "He's gone too far this time! I won't have it!"

Sorcha sidled up to Lord Hamilton, who was bracing his not inconsiderable weight against the armoire, while Morton huffed next to him. "What does Bothwell really plan on doing, sir?" she asked in a low voice.

Hamilton's grave countenance took on a wry expression. "I couldn't guess. If I had to, I'd say he wishes to embarrass his royal cousin. I'm afraid," he added with an avuncular air, "I've never quite understood how that laddie's mind works."

It seemed a fair assessment, though Sorcha wondered if John Hamilton was taking Bothwell too lightly. While the hammering noises had all but stopped, she could make out other ominous sounds in the hallway. Indeed, she thought she heard voices and footsteps coming from another part of the palace. She took a deep breath and suddenly stiffened. The air was tainted with smoke; gray wisps curled ominously from under the door.

"Your Majesty," she called out in alarm, "I fear Lord Bothwell has set a fire in the hallway." Sorcha moved toward the King, who regarded her as if she had lost her wits.

Lord Hamilton, however, was nodding in reluctant agreement. "Mistress Fraser is right, sire. It would appear that Bothwell intends to smoke us out."

The smoke was growing quite thick, obscuring the far end of the room from Sorcha's view. The Queen and the Earl of Morton were coughing. Sorcha, feeling queasy as well as choked up, put a handkerchief over her mouth. Outside, a crackling sound could be heard; the King slumped against the gaming table, his thin shoulders shaking. "May God curse the man!" he wailed into the green baize cover.

The King of Scotland's lack of composure distressed Sorcha, who forced herself to move toward one of the open windows. Marie-Louise had already steered the Queen to the nearest casement, where Anne was taking in deep gulps of air. Sorcha leaned against the embrasure, one hand clutching the damask draperies. It was ridiculous to feel so puny, she reproached herself. The situation was precarious; the smoke was thick as a lowland fog, but it was hardly likely that any of their lives were threatened. Bothwell's antics smacked more of a prank than of danger.

Loud voices and scuffling sounds erupted on the other side of the door. Sorcha strained her ears to catch a sound or a voice that might reveal what was happening in the hallway. Shouts and running feet, the ring of steel, the sound of blows—the melee ascended to deafening proportions. And then, astonishingly, it spiraled down into silence.

Jamie Stewart had gotten to his feet, standing unsteadily and wiping saliva from his chin. The Queen was half fainting, leaning on Marie-Louise, who was not only looking supremely smug but curiously unaffected. It suddenly occurred to Sorcha that the Frenchwoman had been through a far more frightening trial by fire than this, at Armand d'Ailly's family home. Despite the weakness that still nagged at Sorcha, she cast a withering, scornful look at Marie-Louise, who deigned not to notice.

Someone was calling from outside the door, a frantic voice begging for entry. Recognizing one of his lieutenants, Jamie heaved a sigh of relief and commanded that the armoire be removed. Moments later, a dozen members of the household guard and twice as many staunch burghers crowded into the still-hazy gaming room. Jamie had by now assumed an air of nonchalance, thanking his loyal subjects who had rallied to their sovereign's aid. A sheepish Maitland, who, Sorcha realized, had disappeared during the crisis, clumsily crawled out from under the gaming table.

"I must insist upon justice, sire," Maitland said to Jamie as the troop of armed men trailed out of the room. "Clearly, Bothwell has committed high treason."

"Oh, indeed." James sighed, wiping his reddened eyes with a fist. "Yet," he went on, finally remembering his husbandly duties and going to stand by the chair into which his wife had collapsed, "I should like to know who helped him gain admittance to the palace in the first place."

"Bribery," stated the Earl of Morton. "Palms crossed with gold. It's as simple as that."

"I wonder," mused Hamilton, pouring whiskey for his monarch and the others.

Surprised by Hamilton's perspicacity, Sorcha gratefully sat down on a petit point covered bench. Servants had already removed the battered, burned door from its hinges and were busily cleaning up the debris in the hallway.

One of the guardsmen had returned, bowing his way over the threshold and looking crestfallen. "My Lord, Bothwell has escaped, apparently the same way he entered, through the Duke of Lennox's stables." The man hung his head, as if he were solely responsible for Bothwell's brazen behavior.

King Jamie's eyes grew very round. "By the Holy Cross, the man must be found! He *will* be found!" Jamie whirled on Maitland. "I swear it, I've done with that sorcerer! He means me great harm! I'll have everyone in the palace interrogated, tortured, if need be. See to it, Maitland!"

"We could start in this very room," Sorcha announced with a calm she didn't feel. Her green eyes traveled deliberately to Marie-Louise, who stood next to the King, behind the Queen's chair. "It is no secret," Sorcha declared in a reasonable tone, "that the Frenchwoman in our midst has been Bothwell's paramour for some time. Who would be more likely to conspire with him?"

Marie-Louise lifted her shoulders in a little shrug. "*Ma foi.*" She laughed in her throaty voice. "How the Scots love to accuse the foreigners! Do they ever make us feel welcome instead of suspect?" The question seemed to be posed to everyone, yet Sorcha knew it was directed at Queen Anne.

Indeed, Her Majesty was sitting bolt upright, squinting at Sorcha with bleary eyes. "That is so," she remarked in careful tones. "It is difficult to be a stranger here, I think."

Sensing a major confrontation, John Hamilton chose the role of peacemaker. "It's been a nerve-racking night," he intervened tactfully. "I suggest we all withdraw to rest, so that on the morrow our minds will be fresh to contemplate these problems with more clarity."

Morton was about to voice his eager agreement, but Sorcha was on her feet. "I crave your pardon, My Lord, but I didn't speak lightly. I must stress that if Bothwell was aided in entering Holyrood Palace, it was through the offices of his mistress." She stood erect, her chin jutting, the green eyes level. "I trust that upon reflection, you will all see the common sense of what I say."

Jamie, digging at one nostril with thumb and forefinger, pondered Sorcha's words. "Women—whether French or not—do strange things for love," he admitted, though Sorcha noticed he would look neither at his wife nor her favorite lady-in-waiting. "I should hate to think that anyone would betray our consort's trust," he added, not without bite.

A great guffaw of contempt erupted from Marie-Louise's red lips. "That women do strange things for love is so true, Your Majesty!" She took two gliding steps around the Queen's chair and pointed a long finger at Sorcha. "This trollop, for example, is my own husband's mistress, and even now seeks to shame me to hide her harlotry!" In two more swift steps, Marie-Louise was glowering down at Sorcha. "I see through your childish game! You wish to dishonor me because you carry my lord's bastard!" The long fingernail wagged dangerously close to Sorcha's eyes. "Deny it, Highland whore! You, who eats like a pig, can't bear the sight of food! You, brown as a berry, now pale as ash!" Her menacing finger dove downward toward Sorcha's belly. "You, with your quaintly unfashionable waist, bulging like a birthing bitch! Dare you accuse me of betraying our sweet Queen?"

Only the terrible truth of Marie-Louise's damning onslaught could force Sorcha's surrender. She reeled—the room was far more hazy than it had been earlier—and would have toppled over had not John Hamilton caught her in his arms. She knew nothing else until she awoke in her own bed, with a worried Ailis sitting by her side.

Chapter 28

THE KING OF SCOTLAND AND a garishly feathered parrot were scrutinizing a small round dish that contained coarse yellow powder. Jamie grunted as the parrot squawked. Both looked up with startled expressions when Sorcha was announced.

Jamie jabbed at the bowl of yellow powder with his index finger. "See this? It's a witch's concoction, seized from that last batch of hags we roasted in North Berwick." He gazed up at Sorcha with eyes that were as righteous as they were frightened. "Our justice consumed their earthly bodies. Those evil crones can't harm me now, can they, Coz?"

For all his bravado, uncertainty tainted his voice. Sorcha sought to reassure him, but wished he'd first bade her sit. She had spent a sleepless night, overcome by her own terrors. Ailis had bathed her forehead with rose water, plied her with brandy, massaged the tension out of her neck and shoulders. But still Sorcha had not slept. The episode in the gaming room had undone her usually staunch nerves.

"I suspect," said Sorcha carefully, leaning one hand on the table to support her flagging body, "those so-called witches never did Your Majesty harm when they lived. I shouldn't worry about them now if I were you."

Instead of relief, James evinced a scowl. "Coz, are you saying that we acted unjustly? Surely you can't mean that after last night. First, Bothwell escaped from Edinburgh Castle; then he harasses us in our very chambers. Who else but a wizard could manage such feats?"

Risking reproach, Sorcha sat down unceremoniously in an armchair anointed by dried white streaks that looked suspiciously like parrot droppings. "Bothwell is an inventive, athletic, daring sort. He's also calculating, despite his daredevil manner. Getting out of Edinburgh Castle was probably not nearly as dangerous for him as it would be for most men. Besides," she went on pointedly, "I still say he had accomplices in both circumstances. Queen Anne may disagree, but I believe that Marie-Louise has been in league with Bothwell all along." She gazed boldly at the King, though the parrot had assumed a far more defiant posture than its master.

"Yes, yes," Jamie agreed irritably, "I—we, that is—have always given considerable weight to what you tell us. Yet Marie-Louise is so devoted to the Queen, and I—we—are so indebted to her, since often we aren't able to be with Her Majesty due to … uh, affairs of state." While Jamie didn't have the grace to blush at his own subterfuge, he at least allowed Sorcha the hint of a wink. "Even now, Anne is quite inconsolable, between Bothwell's outrageous escapade and your accusations concerning her favorite lady-in-waiting." He rapped his knuckles on the table, making the small bowl bounce, its contents shivering like pollen in the wind. "I wish Moray were here—he's the only other person who can soothe our Queen."

At Moray's name, Sorcha looked away, her thoughts diverted to Donibristle, where even now she supposed Gavin Napier was meeting with the Bonnie Earl. The Highlands remained on the verge of a blood-letting, with George Gordon's troops still poised at the edge of MacKintosh and Grant territory. She had received two letters from Napier since he went north, the first from Gosford's End, the other from Badenoch. In neither had his news been good.

King Jamie had risen, taking the parrot off its perch and onto his shoulder. Heedless of whether Sorcha sat or stood, he began to pace the audience chamber in his bandy-legged, graceless gait. "I have had to assure Anne that Marie-Louise will not be punished," Jamie said, dispensing altogether with ceremony and reverting to the first person pronoun. "For her own part, Marie-Louise has forsworn Bothwell." He heard Sorcha's snort of disdain and whirled about; the parrot nervously flapped its wings and flew noisily over to the mantelpiece. "She gave guarantees. Don't think me foolish, Coz—I insisted she prove her allegiance. This very day she rides north to George Gordon, with a letter of Fire and Sword to use against Bothwell."

Sorcha gripped the edge of the table with rigid fingers. Her brain whipped into a frenzy of thought, torn between basic mistrust of Marie-Louise, her fear of George Gordon's vaulting ambition, and most of all, what this unexpected development might mean for Gavin Napier. "Do you think George Gordon will desist in his Highland aggression to come south and pursue Bothwell? They used to be allies, you know."

"Of course I know! I'm the King!" Disgruntled, Jamie prowled next to the mantel, pausing to pat the parrot, which flexed a claw in the King's direction. "But George is basically loyal. More to the point, he must see Bothwell—who, after all, possesses royal blood—as a serious rival. I should guess that would mean more to him than acquiring a forest full of stags and rabbits."

"Canny," murmured Sorcha, offering the King a little smile. "You could be right," she allowed, though fear still tugged at her heart. "I pray you've defused the situation in the north."

"Aye, and why not? As I said, I'm the King." He puffed out his narrow chest and smiled in that lopsided manner Sorcha found quite endearing. "Now," he said, marching in his ungainly way toward the chair where Sorcha perched not unlike the anxious parrot on the mantel, "I must inquire, being not just your sovereign lord, but as your kin, is it true that you are with child?"

The question, posed with that unexpected candor James increasingly exhibited, caught Sorcha off guard. Her fingers slid from the table into her lap, as if protecting the babe in her womb. "Aye," she replied softly, glancing up through her lashes at Jamie, "I am."

"Ah." James's response was equally soft-spoken. "Good Christ," he muttered, "is it all true? Is Marie-Louise's husband truly your lover?" Before Sorcha could reply, Jamie frowned deeply and wagged a finger at her. "Wait— his name is Napier; I remember that now. But long ago, there was another, an ancient drone you sought to insert in my mother's household. I recall hearing later, after she … she died, that this Napier was neither ancient nor a drone." Jamie was leaning over Sorcha, his small eyes like slate. "Did you deceive me, Coz? Have you deceived us all?"

"Certainly," Sorcha replied, her own frown a match for Jamie's. "I had no choice."

Sorcha's frankness diverted Jamie's wrath. "Good Christ," he said again, tugging at the surcoat that hung awkwardly from his shoulders. "How could you? You've dishonored our name, our royal house!"

"Oh, God's teeth," expostulated Sorcha, "had it not been for your grandfather dishonoring my grandmother, we wouldn't be related in the first place! Please, Sire, this is no time for homilies on virtue! Gavin Napier doesn't know about the child yet; no one does, except my maid, Ailis. At least I didn't think anyone else knew until that vile Marie-Louise sniffed out the truth last night." To her horror, Sorcha had begun to cry. "I just … want to … go home," she sobbed, covering her face with trembling hands.

Disturbed by Sorcha's outburst, the parrot flapped from the mantel to a curved wall sconce across the room. Equally discomfited, Jamie shifted from one foot to the other, then clumsily patted Sorcha's heaving back. "Now, now …. If you'd like to go home, why not?" Certainly Sorcha's departure would save the embarrassment of having one of the Queen's ladies—and a cousin to the King at that—bear a bastard child at court. "Let me think." Jamie ruminated, chewing on a fingernail. "You can't marry this Napier because he's already married to Marie-Louise. Now, I know I promised you a husband years ago; mayhap all this is my fault—I didn't keep my word." He fretted his beard, worried his nether lip, and fussed with the sable trim of his black surcoat. "There was never anyone quite suitable, at least not someone you'd want to marry. Truly, Coz, I'd hoped to find you a noble, wealthy, braw bridegroom, a man worthy of your ...." He halted, snapping his fingers. "By our Sweet Savior! Why didn't I think of it sooner!" Jamie beamed down at Sorcha, who was regarding him dismally through her tears. "Moray! He's perfect! I'll speak to Maitland at once!"

Staggering slightly, Sorcha got to her feet. "Oh, nay, Sire, he's but widowed a month! It would be unseemly, such haste! Nor would he wed someone who carried another's child! Think again, I pray you!"

But the hard, chilly slate had returned to Jamie's eyes. He wore a cunning expression, though he gazed not at Sorcha but across the room, in the direction of the parrot, which appeared to be going to sleep on the wall sconce. "Our consort grows overfond of him," the King mused, as if to himself, or possibly the parrot. "I would see the Bonnie Earl otherwise occupied." Abruptly, he swung back to Sorcha. "It's a marvelous match, dear Coz, fashioned by fate. Besides, he already has children by another woman. They need a mother, just as your bairn needs a father. Think on it; you'll see I'm right. So will your good parents."

What her parents would think of Sorcha's pregnant state was something she had shut out from her mind. Yet, for the moment, it would do no good to consider their explosive reactions. Sorcha knew that only one thing mattered—now that she was past the early, nauseated state of her condition, she must brave the winter weather and head for the Highlands. Never mind that Lord and Lady Fraser waited there—in the north she would find Gavin Napier and the haven of his arms.

Hastily, she wiped her eyes with one lace-trimmed cuff and straightened her shoulders. "A litter, perhaps, if you'd be so kind."

Momentarily puzzled, Jamie pulled his right ear. "Ah? Oh, in which to seek out Moray? Well enough, though wait until I've conferred with Maitland." He made a face at his chancellor's name. "I wonder, sometimes, how well he serves me. What if Bothwell intended to kidnap him because Maitland wishes me ill?"

Drained and weary, Sorcha had no desire to discuss John Maitland's skittish politics. She was saved from responding when the parrot suddenly opened its eyes and swooped onto the table. Before King James could stop the bird, it pecked freely from the little bowl, devouring beakfuls of yellow powder.

"Holy God!" Jamie shrieked, batting at the parrot, which squawked raucously before flying high above their heads, circling twice, and landing on one of the heavy rods that held the dark green brocade drapes over the room's west window.

Jamie was waving his arms at his pet, cursing and cajoling. "He ate witch's brew! He'll die! Or turn into a demon!"

Her composure regained, Sorcha inspected the bowl's contents closely. She sniffed, touched the coarse powder with her finger, then put it to her tongue. James cried out, aghast. But Sorcha tasted a few grains and gave a little shrug. "Don't fash yourself so, Sire. 'Tis nothing more than maize, or corn that the Indians eat by the bushel in the New World."

The King of Scotland goggled at his cousin, looking as if he expected her to turn into a gargoyle before his very eyes. "Maize? Nay, nay! It was taken from those witches! At least three savants have attested to its Satanic properties!" He paused, realizing that Sorcha stood calmly before him, idly rearranging her disheveled coiffure, but otherwise quite unaltered. "I don't believe it," he asserted, looking very much like the petulant boy Sorcha remembered from their first meeting at Stirling Castle. "How do you know of this maize?"

Sorcha screwed up her face in the effort to recall. "Some years ago a sea captain my father knew brought some to our home. Our cook, Catriona, baked it into a sort of bread. It was very tasty."

Jamie's shoulders slumped, though his expression grew speculative. "Then," he asked, eyeing the yellow meal in the bowl warily, "it might be … harmless?"

Sorcha shrugged again. "It is harmless."

In silence, he considered the implication of her words. "Are you saying those hags might have been harmless as well?" His tone begged her denial.

"I did not sit in judgment." Sorcha sounded more severe than she'd intended. Seeing Jamie's stricken look, she took pity on him and his ill-founded fears. "Perhaps they wished you ill. Thoughts can sometimes be powerful weapons. If I were you, I'd consider witches less and wickedness more."

The King gazed at Sorcha in puzzlement. "Well put, I think." He brightened as the parrot shrieked and sailed back down to the mantelpiece. "Now put your mind at ease, dearest Coz; we shall set about our task at once to arrange your marriage with our Bonnie Earl."

Trying not to look askance, Sorcha offered James a feeble smile. Over his shoulder, she saw the parrot stare with a seemingly critical eye, then wink. The bird would ordinarily have amused Sorcha, but now, in her pregnant, distraught state, it only seemed to mock her misery.

FRANCIS HAY, NINTH EARL OF Errol, was a squarely built young man with square facial features, and square, blunt hands. His only remarkable physical attribute was a cluster of chestnut curls, which dipped gracefully over the short white ruff of his collar. To Gavin Napier, Errol looked more like a fledgling Flemish merchant than chieftain of the second most powerful Catholic family in Scotland.

Sitting across a trestle table from Errol and George Gordon, Napier braced his booted feet against a stout rung and stroked his dark beard. "My Lord," he said, addressing Errol and ignoring Gordon's angry countenance, "my brother, Adam, has found you a most reasonable sort. How can you involve yourself in a feud opposed to your interests and those of your Catholic faith?"

Errol shifted uneasily on the hard bench next to Gordon. The three men had agreed to meet on neutral ground, at an inn in Glenlivet. Magnus Fraser, three family retainers, and a handful of MacKintosh supporters were posted in a nearby copse, lest George Gordon not keep his word to parley rather than fight. Napier was justified in his suspicions; a scouting expedition had discovered some two hundred Gordon troops quartered across an ice-choked burn.

"My future is entwined with the fate of My Lord of Huntly," Errol finally replied, giving Gordon a sidelong glance that indicated his ally had rehearsed him. "Our houses have a history of standing together."

Over his tankard of ale, Gordon gave Napier a sly little smile. "Even against Queen Mary, the Hays bolted and stood with the Gordons."

"And lost." Napier knew the Battle of Corrichie Moor as well as any Highlander. He looked archly at Gordon. "Even now, you have surrounded Darnaway Castle, laying siege to MacKintosh and Grant leaders. Lord Fraser is there, too."

Idly, Gordon dragged a chunk of rye bread through his platter of congealing beef gravy. "Over time, the Frasers have proved to be more trouble than they're worth." The small blue eyes fixed themselves on Napier, little pinpricks of censure.

Under the table, Napier clenched and unclenched his fist, but his face remained impassive. "I'm here to ask that you withdraw your men from Darnaway. If not, the Fraser clan will officially join forces with the Grants and MacKintoshes."

Gordon rolled the chunk of bread around in his mouth and fingered a signet ring on his right hand. "They won't," he said in that light, deceptively good-natured voice. "They'd betray the Catholic cause."

Napier pushed an empty jug out of his way as he leaned forward on the table. "Your cause is not Catholic, it's cupidity. You take the Holy Mother Church's name in vain as a sop to your greed and ambition. The Frasers want peace in the Highlands. War profits no one; it only divides men of good faith—and no faith at all." The hunter's gaze was piercing, like arrows loosed from a bow. "You have three days to withdraw. If not, Moray and Atholl will join the Frasers as well."

Gordon's mouth worked soundlessly; Errol seemed absorbed in wiping up a daub of butter sauce with his sleeve. "Don't threaten me," George Gordon muttered. He summoned up the pride of his clan and the vanity of his name to sit up straight and fix Napier with angry, warning eyes. "Go back to Moray or Atholl, or whoever sent you, and say that the Earl of Huntly is no weak-willed woman, to be frightened by a handful of renegade lords!" With a mighty heave, he got to his feet, almost upsetting Errol's ale tankard in the process. "Better yet, I'll make sure you deliver that message exactly as I give it." He turned to scan the common room, which was all but empty on such a chill, wintry afternoon. "*A Gordon, A Gordon,*" he called, and before the words had echoed off the walls, Patrick, Master of Gray, and a half dozen men charged through the door.

Gavin Napier's hand had flown to his dirk, the blade cutting through the inn's peaty air. Gray didn't hesitate. He flew at Napier, his own weapon unsheathed. Napier had already assessed his chances for escape. Except for the door through which Gray and the other men had entered, the inn's only exit was through the kitchen. But instead of maneuvering himself in that direction, Napier broke right, toward the trestle table, forcing Gray to move off balance. Napier's dirk lunged at the Master, but missed. Gordon and Errol were now armed as well, but with a powerful shove of his booted leg, Napier sent the trestle table across the floor, pinning both men to the wall. He dove under Gray's thrusting blade, and even as the other men rushed forward, Magnus Fraser and a dozen red-and-green-clad MacKintoshes followed on their heels.

The diversion cost Gray the edge. Napier's dirk crashed against the longer, slimmer French sword brandished by Gray. The weapon clattered to the stone floor, where Napier kicked it out of reach. Gray's saturnine gaze raked his opponent as the dirk came within a half inch of his chest.

"My Lord of Huntly wants his message delivered accurately," said Napier, his tone sardonic. "Will you do us such an honor?"

Gray's handsome face was distorted with wrath. Magnus and his men had subdued the Gordon followers, holding them at bay in the far corner. A stringy-haired serving wench and the innkeeper gaped with mingled fear and excitement, while the only other occupants, two portly Aberdeen merchants, scrambled for safety under a table.

"Whoreson." Gray spat the word between clenched teeth. "I remember you—from Stirling, long ago, with that troublesome Fraser chit."

Even before Napier could say a word in defense of Sorcha, Magnus's voice cut across the common room like a whip. "Lock your lips, dung-arse, lest I cut them off!" Leaping over a chair, his sword gleaming with menace, Magnus flew at Patrick Gray.

Napier planted himself between the two men, cautioning his irate comrade with a purposeful gaze. "The Master is of more value alive than dead. For the moment." He looked beyond Magnus to Gordon and Errol, who had managed to push the table away but were both standing uncertainly, their weapons useless at their sides. Napier planted a firm hand on Gray's arm, but kept his eyes on George Gordon. "When you have removed your men from Darnaway, send word to Gosford's End with Iain Fraser. We will send Gray back to you then—more or less as you see him now." Gray glared, Gordon was an apoplectic shade of scarlet, and Errol failed to conceal his sense of shame.

The MacKintosh soldiers started backing toward the door, their hackbuts trained on Gordon's followers. But Napier waved them in his direction. "Remember, there are many more troops across the burn." He gave Gray a shove. "We'll take our leave, out the back way." He paused on the threshold, ducking his head under a low beam. "Don't try to come after us, My Lord," he said in a quiet mellow voice that was nonetheless laced with formidable compulsion. "In our encounters, you have always been one step too slow—or one thought too late." Flashing the dirk in mock salute, Napier led Magnus and their men out of the common room.

Chapter 29

DALLAS FRASER COULD NOT RECALL being so agitated since the early days of her marriage. A quarter of a century ago, during their years at court, Lord and Lady Fraser had been swept up in political intrigue, hounded by adversaries, beset by plots both grand and petty. Ultimately, Iain Fraser had chosen not to live at the center of Scotland's turmoil, but to retire to the isolation of the Highlands, where they could raise their family in peace. While Dallas had often longed for the city she loved so well, she had understood and accepted the wisdom of her husband's decision.

But now, caught up in the maelstrom of a Highland feud, with an unwed daughter carrying a married man's child, with her eldest son joining forces with her daughter's lover, and most of all, with her husband held a prisoner by Gordon of Huntly, Dallas felt like a piece of flotsam being battered by an ocean storm. Only sheer force of will prevented her from a nervous collapse. And without Iain Fraser or Magnus or George Gordon or Gavin Napier on the premises to act as targets, Dallas directed her frustrated outrage at the one source of aggravation who was present—Sorcha.

"For the fiftieth time, I tell you that addlepated Jamie has finally generated a plausible idea," Dallas asserted, kicking at a faded, discarded holly wreath left over from the Yuletide season. "His plan to have you wed Moray is brilliant. Hasn't the Bonnie Earl been panting after you for years?" She paused to stare down at the wreath, mute evidence of a holiday season passed with little cheer. "Even Christmas was spoiled with your father gone." Tears welled up in the dark eyes, but she struggled mightily against shedding them.

For a fleeting moment, Sorcha pitied her mother—but not as much as she pitied herself. "It would be indecent for Moray to take a bride so soon after

Elizabeth's death," Sorcha insisted, also for the fiftieth time. "Nor will I marry anyone but Gavin. The annulment will come; I'd stake my life on it."

"Don't." Dallas bit off the word. She had regained her composure, now stomping about her bedchamber in a swirl of tawny silk. "That latest holy relic—Innocent or whoever, I've lost track now—is rumored to be in ill health. By the time the College of Cardinals elects a Bishop of Rome who can breathe in and out for more than six months, your poor bairn will be more marriageable than you!"

Ordinarily, Sorcha would have found her mother amusing. But after almost a week of vituperation, Sorcha was more inclined to hostility. "I absolutely refuse to become Moray's wife. Neither the King—nor you—can command it." She had risen from the padded footstool by the bed to face her mother, well aware of the advantage her height gave her. The green eyes glittered dangerously, defying crown and kinfolk, determined to defend the right to forge her own future.

The recent days of argument had taken their toll on Dallas, too. She gazed steadily at Sorcha, noting, yet somehow resenting, the same fierce pride, the same hardheaded obstinacy she herself possessed. Most of all, she perceived the enormity of her daughter's love for Gavin Napier. It was a bulwark no mother could assault, and Dallas knew it.

"Fie," she breathed, looking away and rubbing her palms jerkily against the tawny silk of her overskirts. "You should not have let him use your body," she murmured. "We have been dishonored."

Her head high, Sorcha put a hand over the curve of her abdomen. "I am honored to carry Gavin's child, honored to have his love. Will Father Adam condemn me?"

Moving to a panel in the wall, Dallas turned a gilt-edged latch and gave Sorcha a baleful backward glance. Adam Napier had gone to spend the Yuletide season with the monks at Beauly Abbey. He was due to return by now, but the latest heavy snowfall of the season had detained him. "I can't speak for Father Adam," said Dallas, taking out a decanter of wine and two crystal glasses with the slimmest of stems, "nor do I condemn you, if it comes to that." She poured dark red wine into the glasses and handed one to Sorcha. "I'm sick at heart, afraid for you, worried half to death about your father." She sank into an armchair, the silk billowing, then collapsing into long, limp folds. "These past few weeks …." Her voice seemed to swallow itself. Dallas drank deeply and cleared her throat. "I feel so … helpless. Where can Magnus and Napier be? They've been gone over a fortnight."

Sorcha had been asking herself the same question ever since her exhausted arrival at Gosford's End. Yet the complexity of the task set by her lover and brother, compounded by the winter weather, no doubt explained their prolonged absence. Taking advantage of her mother's softened mood, Sorcha attempted to divert the conversation. "Is it true that Johnny Grant is also under siege at Darnaway?"

Dallas's nose wrinkled at the Laird of Freuchie's name. "Aye. So I hear. They can hang the wretch by his heels, for all I care. If it weren't for him, we wouldn't be in this debacle."

Her mother's logic eluded Sorcha. She sipped her wine and wished she felt more like taking Thisbe out for a canter on the deep, hard-packed snow. But except for rare intervals, her usual vigor had deserted her since conceiving a child. Listlessly, she brushed at a stray lock of hair. "If only I could have caught up with Marie-Louise." She sighed. "But the strumpet rode like the demon she is, and I was too enervated to keep up the pace."

"Marie-Louise!" Dallas intoned the name on a scathing note. "I can scarcely believe anyone that wicked exists! I wonder, did Bothwell flee to his damnable Borders?"

"He must have. Where else would he go?" Sorcha and Dallas both swerved toward the door as Cummings called to them. Dallas bade him enter, but frowned at the disturbed expression on his usually imperturbable face.

"Father Adam is back," said Cummings, looking very ill at ease. "He would like to see you." Cummings covered his mouth as he coughed slightly. "He says he has bad news."

Sorcha and Dallas both swung to their feet, firing questions at Cummings, demanding to know if the priest had word of the men they loved. But Cummings held up a hand, shaking his head in apology. Father Adam had related no details. He was downstairs, warming himself by the fire in Iain Fraser's study.

Adam Napier was more gaunt and strained than when Sorcha had last seen him. He sat in her father's big armchair, a thick woolen blanket thrown over his useless legs. At the sight of his hostess and her daughter, he bowed from the waist, a kindly smile on his thin lips. "May God be with you," he said in greeting, waiting for the women to sit down. But when neither moved toward the room's other two chairs, he began to speak again.

"Even a short journey takes me a long time, I fear," he began by way of apology. "I have spent the better part of the day traveling from Beauly Priory."

Patience not being a virtue either Dallas or her daughter possessed in great measure, both Fraser females briskly waved aside the priest's explanations. "Bad news keeps ill, Father," Dallas urged. "Please speak your piece."

Father Adam nodded in understanding, then withdrew a thickly rolled document from his robes, which he proffered not to Dallas, but to Sorcha. "Alas, the Holy Father has ruled against an annulment. Despite his failing health, Pope Innocent was gracious enough to hear Rob plead your case. You might not agree with his conclusions, but I believe you will find them fair and judicious."

With trembling hands, Sorcha unrolled the long sheet of parchment. It was written in Latin, a language she had learned in childhood and knew quite well, but the blow she had just received rendered her wits useless. The elegantly formed letters blurred before her eyes, the papal seal at the bottom of the page looked like nothing more than an amorphous blob. "Here," she said to her mother in a hoarse voice, "take it. I don't even want to touch the wretched thing!"

As Dallas grabbed the parchment before it glided to the floor, Sorcha flung herself into a chair. She covered her face with her hands, though the tears refused to fall. Dallas, her mouth set in a tight, angry line, scanned the papal verdict. "Pope Innocent indeed!" she snapped. "Pope 'Imbecile' would be more like it! This sounds like it's concerned with two completely different people! It reads as if Gavin and Marie-Louise have merely had a nasty little lovers' tiff!" She waved the document at Father Adam, whose mild dark eyes blinked at his hostess's fervor. "Tell me, Father—is it the Pope's body or his mind that fails him?"

"My dear Lady Fraser," murmured Father Adam placatingly, "I was not in Rome. I'm certain your good son will write you with details. He sent this in haste, from Paris, on his way back to Compiègne."

Oblivious of the exchange between her mother and Father Adam, Sorcha rose on shaky legs from the chair and slipped quietly from the room. She heard her mother call after her, but paid no heed. Stumbling up the stairs, she retreated to her bedchamber and collapsed onto the bed. For several minutes, she forced her mind to go blank in an attempt to erase all the disturbing, conflicting emotions that beset her. At last, she sat up, the green eyes drawn to the crucifix that hung over her bed. "Sweet Savior," she prayed, "let good triumph over evil. Surely it cannot be Your will to allow the wickedness and snares of the Devil to overcome what is right and true. Let me be the vessel to do Your work on earth. Amen."

Crossing herself, Sorcha frowned. What had she asked God to do for her? How could she expect Him to hear her prayers if she had sinned by surrendering herself to Gavin Napier? Worse yet, she had all but coerced Gavin into sin as well. He had struggled against temptation, while she had yielded to it. And now they were paying the price of disobeying God.

Except that God was merciful and forgiving, Sorcha reminded herself, edging off the bed and going to the window. Surely her sin had grown out of love, not—as with Marie-Louise—out of hate. Marie-Louise was a harbinger of death and destruction, killing a king, Armand's family, even the babe she and Gavin had conceived. How could God let such a vicious creature prosper?

Why hadn't He struck her down long ago, before she could blaze such a trail of mayhem and murder?

The white landscape was dotted with prints made by men and horses: Father Adam and his companions; the Fraser servants; and even now, Rosmairi, Armand, and little Adam, romping in the snow. Through the leaded glass, Sorcha could just make out their voices, raised in happy banter. Wee Adam, who had learned to walk in the past two months, was tumbling about, sprawling and sliding until his heavy clothing was almost as white as the ground itself.

A bittersweet smile touched Sorcha's lips as she watched the merry scene. Was it possible that she and Gavin would never be together to see their own child frisk about under the loving gaze of both his parents? She turned away from the window, trying to tell herself there must be another solution to her problems. Perhaps that was where the answer lay, not with God, but with herself. She recalled once having flippantly told Gavin Napier that justice shouldn't be left to the Lord, since He had enough to do already. If that were true, if Sorcha actually believed her own words, then it was a waste of time waiting for divine intervention.

At least, she told herself, going back to lie down on the bed, Father Adam hadn't brought the news she'd dreaded most—that Gavin was dead. As for the papal decree, she should have paid more attention to its wording. Vaguely, she recalled that her mother had indicated it didn't seem to make sense. Maybe it could be appealed; if Pope Innocent were indeed a dying man, they might seek another ruling after a new Pope was elected. Yet time was running out. The baby would be born in June. Sorcha drummed her fingers on the counterpane and wondered if Rob would be able to return to Rome in the spring.

Moments later, the sound of voices and the jingle of harness could be heard outside. Sorcha hurried back to the window, where she saw Rosmairi and Armand, the baby high on his shoulder, greeting a troop of men. The tallest of the company was Gavin Napier; her father and the Earl of Moray flanked his weary black gelding, with Magnus and Johnny Grant at the rear of the little van.

Ever mindful of the precious burden she carried, Sorcha again made cautious haste down the central stairway. Dallas was already in the entrance hall, with Cummings trailing in her wake, like a longboat being towed by a galleon. Iain Fraser was the first through the door, bracing his feet for his wife's welcoming onslaught. Before Sorcha could set foot on the bottom stair, the hall was filled with at least fifty men, a dozen Fraser servants, and several barking dogs. From his unrivaled vantage point, little Adam burbled with excitement, while the snow dropped from the men's boots and clothing to melt in small puddles on the flagstone floor.

Still clinging to the balustrade, Sorcha took a deep breath. As relieved as she was to see her father and her brother safely home, she saw only one person in that cluster of humanity. Gavin Napier, still clad in chain mail and helmet, with the snow clinging to his beard and the heavy gloves frozen almost stiff, was making his way through the crush of people.

"My love!" Napier breathed with a big grin as he lifted Sorcha into his arms almost as effortlessly as Armand had picked up little Adam. He held her so that their faces almost touched. "You look wan," he said, the grin fading. "Surely you knew we'd prevail?"

"Oh, aye, I had great confidence in all of you." She forced a smile and lowered her lashes. Through the soft wool of her winter gown, she could feel the caked snow on his gloves, and it made her shiver. He brushed her cheek with his cold lips, then set her on her feet.

"I'm not suitable for a loving reunion," he said with a rueful little laugh. "Nor is this the place." He turned swiftly to look at the others, but most of the gathering had focused on Iain Fraser and Moray, who seemed to be taking turns telling how George Gordon had suddenly decided to withdraw his troops from Darnaway.

"It seems," said Fraser dryly, "that he preferred the company of Patrick Gray to ours. I can't imagine why—Magnus and I are much more amusing."

He offered his listeners that familiar crooked grin and squeezed his wife's shoulders. "To be candid," he continued, as Dallas reached out to bring Magnus into the family group, "Darnaway is too difficult to assault in winter weather. Mayhap we should have kept Gray as a hostage against attack when spring comes."

"We gave our word otherwise," Moray remarked, while Johnny Grant scowled at his side. "Two Frasers … and the Laird of Freuchie," he added hastily noting Grant's unhappy expression at being relegated to the background, "are thirty times the value of one Master of Gray."

Moray's words evoked a hearty cheer from the little crowd. Young Adam squealed deliriously, bouncing in his father's firm grasp. The gathering was breaking up into smaller groups, with some of the men already being led away by Cummings to the great hall, where food and drink would be served as soon as Catriona could marshal the kitchen forces. Magnus was inquiring after the welfare of his wife, Jeannie, who was eight months gone with their second child and had been unable to travel to Gosford's End to wait out the vigil with her husband's kin.

Napier slipped an arm around Sorcha as they discreetly climbed the stairs to her bedchamber, where he washed up and changed clothes. Now, away from the noisy rejoicing of the Fraser household, Gavin Napier pulled Sorcha into his arms and kissed her hungrily on the lips. She responded with affection, yet Napier sensed she was holding back—her body was stiff, her fingers lax around his neck. The assertive passion Napier had come to expect and delight in was missing, supplanted by a detachment that mystified him.

At last, he released her mouth and held her at arm's length. "Is my memory playing tricks on me?" he asked with a wry little smile. "I seem to recall leaving behind a much more hot-blooded lass."

The unintended irony of his words made Sorcha's mouth twist upward with humor that had nothing to do with mirth. Gavin Napier had ridden north from Edinburgh with no idea that his seed had borne fruit in Sorcha, or that Pope Innocent would rule against him in Rome. Now, in the wake of his triumphant return to Gosford's End, Sorcha, so normally glib, couldn't find the words to tell him the shattering news.

With his hands still resting lightly on her shoulders, she met his gaze. "Your brother's here," she said in a flat voice. "He arrived from Beauly Priory no more than an hour ago."

Napier's big hands slid down from Sorcha's shoulders to hang awkwardly at his sides. "Is he ill? Has he worsened?" The peat-brown eyes clouded over with anxiety.

Sorcha shook her head. "Nay, he's the same." She swallowed hard, lilting her chin as if to give herself the inner courage she had suddenly found so uncharacteristically lacking. "He received word from Rob that Pope Innocent has refused to grant the annulment."

Napier's big body seemed to shrivel under the weight of her words. He was silent for some time; the only sound in the room was the ticking of the little clock on the mantelpiece. When he finally spoke, his voice was sharp and jerky. "It's impossible. We ... Adam, Rob and I ... we prepared such a reasonable, logical case." Napier lapsed into silence again, his hands now clenched into fists. Then, like an unexpected crash of thunder during a winter snow storm, he whirled about, battering the oak paneled walls until the very room seemed to quake under his assault. "Sweet Christ!" he cried, "does the Church itself—the Church I've risked all to defend—oppose my life, my love, my very salvation?" Seemingly spent, he leaned against the wall, breathing hard.

Hesitantly, Sorcha edged toward him. Her throat felt constricted, her hands like lead. How could she tell him about the child when he was already so distressed? Later, perhaps, after he'd had time to absorb this dreadful blow.

She had come within a foot of where he stood, now rubbing his beard with agitated fingers and striving to collect his thoughts. Instinctively, Sorcha put a hand over her abdomen. Under the artful draping of her gown, the curve of her belly could not be detected yet, and Sorcha was thankful.

"Why can't we plead the case again?" she asked, still not daring to touch him. "It's said that Innocent is very ill."

Napier regarded her with concentrated effort. His self-control was all but regained, though the hunter's gaze held that haunted look Sorcha had not seen in some time. "It's possible." He moved away from the wall, reaching out to hike a lock of Sorcha's dark hair in his fingers and tuck it under her pearl-edged bandeau. "It would be the greatest folly to give up now." From the depths of his inner strength, he resurrected a smile that held more confidence than he could justify. "We've waited this long to become man and wife. What does it matter if we must bide a few more months?"

"None." The single syllable dropped between them like a rock in an empty bucket. Sorcha licked her dry lips and tried to form them into a cheerful expression. "Shouldn't we go down to the banquet hall? They must be serving by now, and I know you're ravenous."

"I am at that." The white teeth showed in the dark beard; the brown eyes glinted with yearning. Napier hooked his thumbs in the strips of brown braid that marched down Sorcha's bodice, molding the outline of her breasts. "Food can wait, though," he asserted, pulling her close and kissing her forehead. " 'Tis you I've hungered for all these months." He searched her face, noting the unwonted pallor and fatigue that showed up around her eyes. "You've been worrying too much, my love. Surely you knew we'd manage to outwit George Gordon."

"Oh, aye, I never really doubted that." Sorcha nodded with less enthusiasm than she would have wished for. She felt his hands slip down to cup her breasts, now grown even more full and ripe with pregnancy. Yet she flinched at his touch and saw the sudden surprised mixture of pain and puzzlement on his face.

"Sorcha—what is it?" He leaned backward, though his hands remained on her breasts. "Do you find me … repugnant?" The idea struck him as so unlikely, so incredible, that he laughed outright. "Good Christ, sweetheart, what troubles you?" Noting the strained, grave expression, he sobered immediately. "Is it Marie-Louise? Has she done something to turn your heart against me?"

Sorcha vehemently shook her head and put both her hands over his. "Never that. Never. I love you as much as before." But his question had summoned up the vital information she had forgotten to relay. Her own troubles had seemed so overwhelming that they had all but erased everything else from her mind. "The King gave a letter of Fire and Sword to Marie-Louise to convey to George Gordon. I tried to follow her from Edinburgh, but I … I lost her."

Napier was frowning, not just in dismay over this most recent development, but in perplexity at his beloved's failure to keep up with Marie-Louise. Sorcha was as expert a horsewoman as Marie-Louise. Not for the first time in his life did Napier wonder if his estranged wife's self-proclaimed magical prowess was all too real.

"Did Marie-Louise somehow obscure her path?" Napier asked, finally taking his hands away from her breasts to clasp her fingers in his.

Put off by the question. Sorcha groped for words. "It was … snowing," she explained, truthfully enough. "I suspect she reached Strathbogie or whichever Gordon stronghold she was heading for a week or more ago."

Since Gordon had obviously not known about the letter of Fire and Sword during the encounter at Glenlivet, it was apparent to Napier that Marie-Louise had sought the Earl of Huntly at one of his more distant residences. Yet even this foreboding news didn't explain Sorcha's lack of ardor. "I suspect you have much more to tell me," Napier said, the words etched with meaning. "Shall we talk now, or should I see how my brother fares?"

"Father Adam is no doubt eager to see you," Sorcha replied too quickly. Seeing the rejection well up again in the peat-brown eyes, Sorcha squeezed his fingers. "Gavin, my dearest love, don't think I'm being coy or changeable. But right now, with the news from the Pope being so fresh, I can't … I just can't give myself to you." The green eyes pleaded for understanding. "Surely you—of all people—can comprehend that?"

Taking in the pale, unhappy face and fervid speech, Gavin Napier knew he should be able to accept her feelings in good faith. She was, after all, quite correct about his own earlier ambivalence. Yet now, coming from Sorcha, he found her reluctance almost impossible to take in. It was out of character; it was wrong; it struck a jangling, harsh chord, like a trumpet blaring over the soft, mellifluous strings of a harp.

Yet he had no choice but to accede to her wishes. Even if they had not been under her parents' roof, Gavin Napier was not the sort of man to force his embrace on any woman—not even the one who had sworn to love him through eternity. Nor was he the type to conceal the pain. There had been a time—long years, in fact—when he had kept all his emotions, even his identity, hidden behind a curtain of cynicism, arrogance, indifference, even deceit. But Sorcha had managed to break through that aloof, dispassionate barrier. Though Gavin Napier might mask his feelings from the rest of the world, Sorcha's love had stripped him of pretense.

Or so he had thought—until now. For Sorcha herself was concealing something, and for the first time he sensed an erosion of the mutual trust they had shared. He could beg and badger her to confide in him. He could threaten and bellow. He could even shake the truth out of her by sheer brute strength. But that would defeat his own code of honor. Instead, he disengaged his fingers from hers and shrugged.

"I'll try to understand," he said in a dull, heavy voice. Then he turned his back and was gone.

IT COST SORCHA DEARLY TO attend the celebration in the great hall that evening. By the time she arrived, another fifty or more Frasers had made their way through the drifting snow to applaud the return of Iain Fraser. At least half the company was well-nigh raucous with drink, and even Johnny Grant wore a silly grin above his long, whiskey-stained beard. At the far end of the table, Gavin Napier sat next to his brother. With the exception of Iain Fraser himself, they seemed to be the only two whose wits were not befuddled by strong spirits. Even Magnus and Armand were engaged in a seemingly hilarious arm-wrestling match, which Dallas and Rosmairi eyed with wary good humor.

Sorcha squeezed into a place at the long table between a Fraser she didn't recognize and a Grant she had seen several times in Johnny's company. She was exchanging pleasantries with them both when she realized that the Earl of Moray was sitting almost directly opposite, his handsome face neither drunk nor sober. Tentatively, she lifted a hand to wave at him. He smiled back broadly, making lazy arcs with his whiskey cup. His mouth formed several words that Sorcha was unable to make out over the din. The great hall smelled of roasted fowl, meat fat, overheated bodies, drying wool, wood smoke, wine, and whiskey. Though Sorcha's nausea had passed now that she was in the fourth month of her pregnancy, she took one look at a pig's head wearing a garland of cranberries and fervently wished she'd had the sense to stay in her room.

After toying with a bit of Flemish cheese and a glass of Rhine wine, Sorcha excused herself, aware that Moray's eyes followed her from the table and that Gavin Napier's did not. Napier had moved from his brother's side to sit with Iain Fraser. The two men were speaking earnestly, no doubt of the King's letter of Fire and Sword. As Sorcha escaped through a side door, she wondered if her father would announce this latest piece of news to the assemblage. Probably not, since—assuming any of them were still capable of reasoning—it would dull the festive tone considerably. Most would spend the night within the walls of Gosford's End, bedding down on the floor of the great hall, sleeping like bricks until well past dawn. That would be soon enough to inform the men of Fraser and Grant that George Gordon was not only still in the King's good graces but that he had been empowered to exact Jamie's justice. The recent triumph over George Gordon would turn to ash, like the giant logs that even now burned down in the great hall's vast fireplace.

Back in her room Sorcha poured out her heart to Ailis, who listened with stoic patience, evincing surprise only at the news of Pope Innocent's refusal to grant an annulment. "You'll find a solution," Ailis said when Sorcha had finally worn herself out with talking. "Justice is sometimes slow," the maid went on in her brusque, yet sympathetic manner, "but eventually, it runs its course."

Burrowing down between the sheets to find the places touched by the warming pan, Sorcha took comfort in Ailis's words. As she closed her eyes in search of sleep, she remembered back to her childhood, to a sunny April morning when she and Magnus had disobeyed their mother and gone too far into the forest. After an hour of fearing that they were utterly lost and would be eaten by wolves, they had discovered a gurgling spring. Excitedly, they began to follow the trickle of water until it joined forces with other springs and became a tumbling burn, hurtling down the hillside. Yet once it reached level ground, in the shadow of the tall firs and pine trees, the stream seemed to backtrack, to flow in circles, to wind among the evergreens like a tangled skein of thread. The children had plodded through marshland, across a meadow where the dew still clung to the long grass, fighting their way among the blackthorn bushes, the leafless branches catching at their clothes. At last, when they were weary and exhausted and the sun was riding high in the flawless April sky, they found that the burn flowed heedlessly into Beauly Firth, not more than half a league from the manor house. So it seemed that this was how her love for Gavin wound its way in search of a happy ending— through darkness and sunlight, through fear and hope. Yet someday, like those long-ago children following the burn that led them home, Sorcha and Gavin must finally come to rest.

ALL BUT A FEW STRAGGLERS had cleared out of Gosford's End by noon of the following day. As Sorcha had guessed, Iain Fraser had waited until morning to pass on the word about George Gordon and the letter of Fire and Sword. Even then, he had confided only in Moray and Johnny Grant. There was no use in weighing down the others with such alarming news until after they had completed the cold, icy journey to their various far-flung destinations.

Sorcha had spent the morning visiting with Magnus before his departure for his home at Ord, and then playing with Rosmairi and little Adam in the nursery. The old nurse, Marthe, her joints now so stiff and painful that she had to be conveyed in a chair, joined them for the better part of an hour, elated, as always, that she had lived to see yet another generation of Fraser and Camron offspring. Adam had just upset his bowl of porridge on Rosmairi's pink lawn skirts when Cummings summoned Sorcha to join her parents in the study. With a sense of apprehension, Sorcha made her way downstairs, while Rosmairi scolded wee Adam, and Marthe soothed them both in her ancient cracked, wheezing voice.

Opening the door to the study, Sorcha took a deep breath before stepping over the threshold. Drifted snow piled up outside the windows, and in the grate, a trio of logs glowed but refused to burn. While her mother's perfume lingered and her father's newly acquired clay pipe sat on the desk, neither parent was in the room. Instead, the Earl of Moray sat in one of the armchairs, his booted legs crossed in an attempt to appear at ease.

"Please, Sorcha, don't look so upset," he urged, the blue eyes warm and candid. "Close the door and sit, I pray you. Your parents thought it best if we spoke privately."

"God's teeth," Sorcha murmured, then saw the wounded look on Moray's face and was repentant. She shut the door, careful not to let it slam lest Moray mistake such a gesture for anger. "Well?" she asked, vainly trying to keep her voice light. She sat down opposite Moray in the matching armchair and deliberately turned away from her father's vacant place, as if somehow he could still observe her.

Moray leaned forward, his hands draped across his knees. "I wish I lived up to my own legend as the 'braw gallant,' " he declared, the blue eyes quite still. "Rather, I feel like a clumsy country lout, possessed of few words and no wit at all." He made a wry face, moved one hand as if to reach for hers, apparently thought better of it, and ran his fingers through his wavy auburn hair. "I'm here to ask formally for you in marriage. I greatly fear you're going to refuse me, but be forewarned, I intend to persist."

Sorcha went rigid in the chair, her green eyes wide. She should have guessed, of course. Somehow, she had assumed that Moray had ridden out earlier with the others. Yet here he was, not two feet away, looking abject yet vaguely hopeful. Sorcha used both hands to brush back the stray hair that had escaped from her heart-shaped linen cap. "It's impossible. You must know I love another," she asserted, her green eyes fixed on his face. "There is no way I can become your bride. My parents must have misled you."

This time Moray took the risk of touching her knee. Gentle, undemanding, comforting—no doubt, thought Sorcha, the same gesture he'd use with an ailing mare. "I assure you, they have neither misled nor deceived me. This morning, they explained your plight, that you carry the child of a man who cannot marry you. I've waited five years, Sorcha. I don't intend to wait any longer."

From any other man, the words would have sounded not merely precipitate but callous. The Countess of Moray had been dead for less than three months. She had borne him five children, graced his name with her quiet goodness, dignified his title with her gentle beauty. Yet here he was, admitting to his long-standing desire for another woman. Yet it was Moray's frankness of heart, his lack of hypocrisy, that prevented Sorcha from being shocked by his proposal.

Behind her hand, Sorcha murmured a foul oath and hoped Moray hadn't heard. If he had, he gave no indication, the handsome face still serious and searching. If he were impatient for some sign of favor, he gave no sign of that, either; his features were as controlled as his emotions.

"I don't know what to say," Sorcha admitted at last, settling her chin in the palm of her hand. "Sweet Virgin, has any woman ever suffered from such a dilemma? Why couldn't Gavin and I—or even you and I—have met, fallen in love, and gotten married? Like Rosmairi and Armand, like Magnus and Jeannie, like a thousand other people in this sad, sorry world? See here, My Lord," she went on, the words coming rapidly, "if I married you, I'd forever long for Gavin. You'd be forced to bring up a bastard who has no claim to either your name or your property. People would laugh at you behind their hands; they'd call you cuckold. Besides," Sorcha added with her usual practicality, "while you might have once wanted me as your mistress, what makes you believe you'd be equally delighted to take me to wife? They are two quite different things."

Moray had listened to this lengthy, impassioned speech with rapt attention, his eyes never leaving Sorcha's face. "I'm told the King wishes us to wed. You must take on the raising of five bairns you've scarcely even seen. As for my possessions, I trust we'll have children of our own, and while my earldom may be a grand one, in truth, I'm not a man of great means." He spread his hands in an appealing, self-deprecating manner. "More to the point, I can offer you only myself—and as your husband, not your leman. I love you, Sorcha. I have always loved you, from that first night at Doune."

Sorcha sighed deeply, contemplating the sincerity of Moray's words. It would be cruel to dismiss his love out of hand. Love was too rare, too fragile, to throw away. Reality told her that if one Pope had refused an annulment, another might do the same. Her child would be born in June, just five short months away. If she married Moray, her babe would have a name and she would have her honor, albeit tarnished. She knew what kind of pressure her parents—at least her mother—would bring to bear upon her to accept Moray's suit. What she didn't know was how Gavin Napier would react. With his commitment to virtue, might he not be as determined as Dallas that their child be born in holy wedlock? Would it not be in character for him to persuade her to save her name and her honor by sacrificing him so that she could marry Moray?

Sorcha sighed again and briefly closed her eyes. "Give me a day or two. My Lord. I must think—and pray—upon this momentous matter." The green eyes were wide open as she gazed at Moray. He lifted her hand and put it to his lips; then he started to speak, apparently considered that further words might do more harm than good, and got to his feet to bow his way out of the study.

To SORCHA'S IMMENSE SURPRISE, GAVIN Napier received the news of her pregnancy with a minimal expression of shock. Over the twenty-four hour period following his return to Gosford's End and his unsettling reunion with Sorcha, he'd taken time to reflect in solitude, as well as to confide in Father Adam. While neither brother had guessed that Sorcha was with child, both had concluded that she was deeply disturbed over something of such magnitude that it even impinged upon her limitless love for Gavin Napier.

So, when Sorcha revealed the truth to Napier that evening in the small parlor, her brief, forthright explanation brought enlightenment rather than astonishment. Sorcha was seated on the settle in front of the hearth, while Napier stood with his back to one of the two bookcases that flanked the stone fireplace. He was silent at first, his face darkening as he clenched and unclenched one hand. While Sorcha sat with her fingers clasped together in her lap and her head held high, Napier went to one knee in front of her.

"I am filled with joy that you will bear my babe," he declared, his features softening. He placed his hands on her thighs, though it was the touch of affection rather than desire. "I have never loved you more than I do now." He paused, the white teeth capturing his lower lip as he pondered his next words. "I am about to lose you, am I not?" He spoke barely above a whisper, and there was a catch on the final syllable.

Sorcha could scarcely look at him. Her heart felt heavy and dull in her breast, and her own voice quavered when she answered him. "I don't know yet." With a trembling hand, she touched his hair. "My lord of Moray has asked me to be his wife." The green eyes were questioning, helpless. "What shall I tell him?"

Napier's face twisted as if it were following the convoluted pattern of his thoughts. For several moments, he gazed beyond Sorcha, seeking an answer in the far shadows of the little room. Then, with an agonized smile, his eyes fixed on her pale face. "Does he … know?" Napier watched Sorcha as she nodded once. "Then," he said, in that same low voice, "you must consent."

It was what Sorcha had expected him to say, but now, after the words had been given life, she cried out in protest, "Nay! I will not!" Sorcha took Napier's head in her hands, all but shaking it back and forth. "The annulment! You said we could submit the case again! I'll go away, I'll bear the babe somewhere else, I'll wait forever, if need be! Please, Gavin—you don't really want me to marry Moray!"

Grasping her firmly by the wrist, he took her hands away from his temples. "Of course I don't want you to marry him. But you must marry, and while I'd do anything—anything at all—to make it so that I could marry you, I fear our chances are virtually nonexistent." Sadly, he shook his head. "I once told you that Marie-Louise might as well have cast a spell on me. For a time, I thought you'd broken it. But," he went on, his voice rising, yet hollow, "I've come to believe that I shall live out the rest of my life in thrall to her."

"Don't believe it," Sorcha enjoined him. She was leaning so far forward in the chair that their foreheads almost touched. "The reckless life she leads, the trail of death and destruction she leaves behind her—no one can go on forever living on the precipice as she does."

Outside, the wind howled, heralding a new storm. Though the drapes were drawn, Sorcha could feel a draft blowing across the room. It had started to snow again just before supper, and no doubt by now the drifts were piling up outside the manor house. Winter, like her suffering, seemed to go on forever.

Napier kissed the palms of her hands and uttered a sharp little laugh. "What you say may be true, my love. But what you mean is that we should wait for Marie-Louise's death." The hunter's gaze fixed her squarely. "That is the reality, is it not? I can't live like that, waiting for someone else to die. I don't think you can, either."

The intensity of his stare forced Sorcha to look away. "You're right," she murmured, "I cannot."

They were quiet for a few minutes while the fire hissed in the grate and the wild cry of the wind swept over the moors and through the glen. I should weep, Sorcha thought, yet I have no tears. I feel drained, empty, aimless.

Still on his knees, Gavin Napier had shifted his weight. Tenderly, he put his hands on her curving abdomen. "My bairn," he said, and gave Sorcha a smile that held the warmth of summer and the pride of mankind. Desperately, she tried to summon an answering smile, but before her lips could do more than tremble, Gavin Napier laid his head in her lap, and the broad shoulders shuddered with emotion. At last, Sorcha felt the tears fill her eyes and roll down her cheeks, like snow melting in a sudden thaw. She wrapped her fingers in Napier's dark hair, and when he finally lifted his face to look at her, his own eyes brimmed with tears. Startled by his unabashed feelings, Sorcha wiped one cheek with the back of her hand, then pressed Napier's face, mingling her love as well as her grief with his.

"I will not say good-bye," Napier said in that low, rumbling voice Sorcha knew so well, though now it was touched by a faint tremor. "I will only ask that God hold you—and the bairn—in His hands."

"Where are you going?" Sorcha's question was a choked, rasping jumble of words.

Napier had gotten to his feet, looming tall and broad, blocking out the persistent draft, though the wind still shrilled outside the windows. "I don't know yet. But I'll be gone by morning." He was under control again, speaking tersely, his long face arranging itself into the mask he would show the world beyond the little parlor's door.

For more long moments, they gazed at each other, as if trying to commit every detail to memory. For one searing second, Sorcha considered flinging herself into Napier's arms for a last embrace. But she willed herself to remain seated; she knew that once in each other's arms, they might never again be pried apart. And, for the sake of their babe, that could not happen.

Finally, he tore his eyes from her, though he made no move to leave. Motionless, he stood staring at a small Italian marble statue of the Madonna and Child that rested on a slender teak pedestal across the room. Sorcha didn't have to turn her head to discover the object of Napier's unblinking attention. Silently, she offered her own prayers to the Virgin and her Divine Son.

Gavin Napier didn't speak again, nor did he look at Sorcha. He wheeled about with a swift, sure movement and crossed the little room in four long strides. Sorcha continued to sit very still, her hands folded against the curve where their child grew. Even after Napier had closed the door behind him, she remained as she was, while the fire in the grate flickered out and the wind howled its mournful song far into the night.

Chapter 30

IRONICALLY, THE MID-JANUARY BLIZZARD HAD presaged an early spring in the Highlands. In less than a week, a mild, if relentless rain had washed away all but the most secret, hidden patches of snow. Eager yellow primroses appeared in the forests around Loch Ness, the black grouse fanned its tail in anticipation of the mating ritual, and the wildcat crept back up into the hills.

While most Highlanders rejoiced at cruel winter's end, for Sorcha it meant that her wedding day would come much sooner than she'd expected. The last week of January was spent in a frenzy of preparation, with seamstresses brought in from Inverness, arrangements worked out by Iain Fraser for Sorcha's dowry, trunks being packed, and a rapid, if chaotic exchange of letters between Gosford's End and Moray's house at Donibristle. The latter caused the most consternation within the Fraser household. While Moray made no demands concerning the dowry, he was insistent upon being married in a Protestant ceremony. Father Adam, who had once more retreated to Beauly Priory, this time in Gavin Napier's company, was consulted. The only comfort he could give was to suggest that perhaps once the ceremony had taken place, Moray might be persuaded to convert to Catholicism so that he and Sorcha could be remarried in the Church of Rome. After much soul-searching, Lord and Lady Fraser agreed that such was their best—and only—hope. Sorcha was frank to admit that she didn't much care. If she could not be married to Gavin Napier, then the rites under which she wed with another were of no importance.

The family was scheduled to leave Gosford's End on the third day of February, but late in the afternoon of the preceding day, a messenger arrived saying that Magnus's Jeannie had gone into premature labor. Magnus begged his mother to come to the Muir of Ord. Torn between her children's needs, Dallas raced about the manor house in a flurry of indecision and fell down the main staircase, spraining her ankle. Gritting her teeth against the pain, she insisted on traveling to Magnus and Jeannie's home by litter, but Iain Fraser refused to let her go unless he went with her. Her parents were visibly distressed at abandoning Sorcha and parted from her with unusual tenderness. But Sorcha sensed a hint of relief in them both, as if neither parent truly wanted to be a witness to an occasion of which, deep down, they didn't approve.

Yet Sorcha wasn't terribly upset by Lord and Lady Fraser's defection. Indeed, the days that had followed Gavin Napier's departure from Gosford's End were a blur. Nothing seemed quite real. It was as if Sorcha were watching some other young woman prepare for her wedding while she observed from a distance, indifferent, detached, with only a perfunctory acknowledgement of the events that surged around her.

Rosmairi and Armand, however, would accompany her, along with the indispensable Ailis and a half dozen Fraser retainers. Little Adam would remain in the care of his nurse and Marthe at Gosford's End. So it was that on a cool but sunny February morning, Sorcha set out for Donibristle House in the ancient kingdom of Fife, where she would become the Countess of Moray and try to put her past behind her.

Yet, even as they rode out of Fraser country toward the shimmering lochs and high, rugged peaks of her mother's Cameron clan, Sorcha knew that she carried the past within her. At that moment, she felt a fluttering in her abdomen and let out a little gasp of astonished awe, then gently touched the place where the babe had moved. No, thought Sorcha, the past lives and will be with me always, and I rejoice in the gift of life Gavin Napier has given me.

Sorcha crossed herself devoutly and let the swaying of the litter lull her to sleep.

IT TOOK ALMOST FIVE DAYS to reach Donibristle House, high above the Firth of Forth, where the waters narrowed before sweeping inland toward Edinburgh. This close to the sea, winter still had its grip on the countryside, with ice floating on the little pond in the courtyard and a brisk wind blowing down from the east.

Sorcha and her companions had been greeted by an oddly distracted Earl of Moray. While he seemed delighted to welcome his bride to Donibristle, there was an unwonted tenseness in his manner, an unexplained air of expectancy. At supper in the manor house's handsome dining hall, Sorcha attempted to draw out her future husband, but he turned aside each question with a merry jest. Finally, she gave up, concentrating instead on the roasted boar and haunch of beef that constituted the main courses.

Though avoiding Sorcha's inquiries, Moray was otherwise talkative. Now that she had arrived safely under his roof, he planned to hold their wedding the following afternoon. "The preparations have been completed," he told Sorcha as servants removed their plates from the table. "Now that you're here, I see no reason to delay." His warm fingers stroked her palm, and the blue eyes twinkled.

"I suppose that's so," Sorcha responded, trying to work up an enthusiasm she didn't feel. Gazing at the high, timbered ceiling, she changed the subject by remarking upon the excellent proportions of the house. "Doune is barnlike, by comparison," she said, catching Rosmairi's sympathetic eye across the table. "I should think it more pleasant to reside here."

Moray nodded, his hand still on hers. "Elizabeth thought so, too," he replied, referring to his first wife without the least bit of self-consciousness. "The children also prefer it." He paused as a moon-faced youth with pale blond hair refilled their wine glasses. "Tomorrow I shall formally introduce you to the wee ones. They miss their mother very much, but I know they'll come to love you, Sorcha, as I do." The smile broadened but receded when Moray saw one of his household guards hurrying toward him. The man leaned over the earl's chair, while Sorcha discreetly turned in the opposite direction. She caught only two words: "sheriff" and "Huntly." A flicker of fear crept along her spine, though Moray was still smiling when he let go of her hand and stood up from his chair.

"There's some sort of minor fracas going on outside," he said, carefully placing his napkin down on the table. "I must speak with the sheriff."

Sorcha watched him leave the room, each step increasing with urgency. After he'd disappeared through the timbered doorway, she allowed herself to be drawn into conversation with the elderly gentleman on her left, a distant Stewart cousin. Indeed, most of the other guests were somehow related, either to Moray or the late Countess. Among them was the earl's elderly, ramrod-backed mother, Lady Margaret, a Campbell by birth. Upon meeting Sorcha, she had presented a polite, yet appraising façade. There were no more than ten others in all, but Moray had promised that by the same time the next evening, the dining hall would be jammed with celebrants from the town of Aberdour and its environs.

With such a full day ahead of her, Sorcha wished Moray would return soon so that she might excuse herself and retire for the night. The journey from Gosford's End had wearied her, and she wished that her groom had allowed for a few days' respite before the wedding ceremony. On the other hand, Sorcha would be relieved to have it over and done with. Postponement might give her false hope that the marriage would never take place. Not only was that highly unlikely, it wasn't in her—or the unborn child's—best interests.

After almost a quarter of an hour, Moray returned. The guard had been supplanted by a bluff-looking bald man of middle age, and Moray introduced him to Sorcha as William Dunbar, the sheriff.

Moray, aware that his other guests were regarding him with curiosity, stood behind Sorcha's chair and raised a hand. "Honored friends and kinfolk," he began, smiling pleasantly, though his casual tone was forced, "it appears that there is some trouble brewing outside. George Gordon, the Earl of Huntly, has accused me of sheltering the Earl of Bothwell." He stopped speaking for a moment as some of the guests chuckled richly. "While I've been known to offer my lord of Bothwell hospitality in the past, he has not visited here recently. Indeed, I would think it more likely that he would call on George instead of me."

Again, Moray's words evoked laughter among his guests, except for Sorcha, whose anxiety had mounted to disturbing proportions. She was certain that Moray wasn't being completely frank; she was also certain that if George Gordon was stirring up fresh trouble, Marie-Louise lurked in his shadow. For the first time since she'd conceived, Sorcha dipped deep into her reserve of common sense and energy to emerge from the cocoon of pregnancy.

"My Lord," she said quietly but firmly, a hand on Moray's arm, "I think there is more cause for alarm than you've admitted. Is George Gordon actually here at Donibristle?"

Moray avoided her direct gaze and looked to the sheriff instead. "He is rumored to be in the vicinity, yes." Sorcha sensed rather than saw something pass between the two men. "Under those circumstances," Moray went on, taking Sorcha's hand to assist her in rising from her chair, "it would probably be a wise precaution to withdraw to a safer part of the house." Gracing his guests with a reassuring smile, Moray led Sorcha out of the dining hall, the others straggling behind, voicing opinions ranging from amusement to outrage. Lady Margaret was the most indignant of the lot, declaring that her sire, the late Earl of Argyll, had always said the Gordons were a muddled-brained, irresponsible passel of fools. The indictment sounded so much like Dallas that Sorcha decided that her mother and mother-in-law would get on very well.

The best-fortified part of the house was a small sitting room on the second floor built inside thick turret walls. It was there that Moray herded his guests, stopping along the way to collect his five children and their nurses. Once crammed into the dark, unheated room, Sorcha and the others began to realize that their plight was far more dire than Moray had indicated.

"Are we under attack?" asked Rosmairi in a whisper.

Sorcha didn't dare respond, but Armand, wedged between the two women, was craning his neck in the direction of one of the turret's two narrow window slits. "I hear voices outside," he said keeping his own words low so as not to frighten the others. "It is, I think, someone calling to Moray."

Moray had also heard someone shout from below. He pressed his way through the others, ignoring the wails of his two youngest children and the warning offered by his mother. Tall as the earl was, he had to step up onto a chair to get a clear view. Sheriff Dunbar had squeezed in behind him, burly shoulders tensed as he waited for Moray to tell him what was happening. The nurses shushed the children, the adults turned silent, and even Lady Margaret kept still.

"It is George Gordon and his followers," Moray finally announced, speaking over his shoulder from his perch on the chair. "He is demanding that I surrender in the name of the King."

Lady Margaret snorted with contempt. "*Paugh*! By what right does that puffed-up pig issue such an order? He ought to be outlawed, along with that silly Bothwell."

Moray descended from the chair, his face grave but his manner respectful. "I'm afraid, my Lady Mother," he said with a note of bitterness in his voice, "that George has a letter of Fire and Sword from King Jamie. It appears he intends to use it against me rather than Bothwell."

"That's nonsense!" snapped Lady Margaret while several others echoed her opinion.

"Perhaps," Moray conceded, picking up his steel helmet with its silken plume, "but George is carrying out his threat by setting fire to some sheaves his men have piled against the house."

Sorcha heard Rosmairi gasp and Armand utter an indecipherable French oath. For her own part, she was reminded all too vividly of the recent night at Holyrood when Bothwell had tried to burn the King out of the palace's gaming room. There was much irony in both earls attempting to flush out their prey by fire, but there was also too much coincidence. Sorcha's eyes darted to Armand, who was tight-lipped with fury. Perhaps he, too, guessed that this latest conflagration bore the mark of Marie-Louise's dastardly handiwork.

Indeed, the flames could now be heard crackling below, and the cluster of faces inside the turret were illuminated by the dancing light that filtered through the narrow window slits. The young ones were crying again, and immediately Moray ordered the sheriff to lead them and the women to safety. As Sorcha grabbed Rosmairi, who was trying to cling to Armand, Moray leaned down to brush his betrothed's cheek with his lips. "I hadn't expected such a rude prenuptial celebration," he whispered with a self-deprecating little laugh. "Will you forgive the interruption?"

Sorcha didn't feel like laughing, but she managed a sound that passed for mirth. "George always did have a terrible sense of timing," she said and started to lead Rosmairi away. Abruptly, she stopped, her sister almost falling over her. Staring up into Moray's candid, kind blue eyes, Sorcha bestowed a genuine smile upon him, born not of love or desire, but of respect and affection. "You *are* a braw gallant, My Lord," she declared with fervor. "I intend to make you a well-contented husband." Impulsively, she kissed him on the lips, then smiled again as he stared back with pleasurable surprise. A moment later, she and Rosmairi were following Lady Margaret's ramrod-straight back down the winding staircase.

The sheriff took them through the kitchen, where the smoke from outside mingled with the cooking odors that lingered from earlier in the evening. "They've ringed the house with fire," Dunbar called out as he gestured for the servants to test the kitchen door, "but since the wind has died down, we should have a better chance of escaping back here where the house faces the sea."

Rosmairi appeared dubious, but there wasn't much choice. From somewhere at the front of the house, they could hear the crackling of timbers. Feeling the babe kick in her womb, Sorcha pressed forward with the others. Just ahead of them, Lady Margaret and another elderly woman who appeared to be her maid were exchanging irate commentaries about George Gordon's reckless audacity. Sheriff Dunbar was standing by the open door, urging his charges to hurry. The children and their nurses went first, their frightened cries carrying back into the kitchen. Sorcha could see the flames licking at the doorway, the brilliant glow turning night into day. At the threshold, she held Rosmairi by the arm as they both put handkerchiefs over their faces.

"Now," murmured Sorcha, as the two women plunged straight ahead. Tongues of fire leapt out at them, but except for some sparks that showered on their skirts, neither was burned, though both were flushed with the heat, and coughing from the smoke. They joined the others close to the edge of the sea cliff, just as several men wearing the green Gordon plaid approached with swords drawn. Sorcha turned to Rosmairi who was sobbing softly, begging the Virgin to preserve Armand.

Her prayers were answered almost immediately as Armand and several other men hurtled out of the house. Despite his command for Rosmairi to keep back, she rushed toward him, hurling herself into his arms. The dagger that he had worn with his supper finery was more ornamental than lethal; he now held a club in one hand. Steering Rosmairi back toward the other women and children, Armand hurried to aid the sheriff, who was making a futile effort to throw up a barricade between Gordon's men and the cliff.

Sorcha, Rosmairi and the rest were now encircled by Gordon followers, their backs to the sea. The wind had suddenly picked up again, and Sorcha shivered in her yellow taffeta gown, with its deep, lace-edged neckline. Yet while the enemy soldiers stood within a few yards of the frightened, chilled little band, the men made no move to come closer. To their left, a horseman leading another dozen riders cantered toward the house, then halted as the heat became too intense. It took Sorcha several moments to recognize their leader as George Gordon.

"Swine!" called Lady Margaret, though Gordon couldn't hear her over the crackling of the flames or the sound of timbers breaking in the house. "Bloated son of a pig," she railed, "fight with men, not bairns and women!" She raised a thin arm and swung her fist in Gordon's direction.

But George Gordon paid no heed. He, too, was shouting, calling for Moray to show himself. At last, the Bonnie Earl appeared at a window toward the far end of the house. For several seconds, he teetered on the sill, then broke the glass with his sword and jumped through the lapping flames to land on his feet several yards from Gordon's horse. With a bold salute of his hand, he raced for the sea cliff's edge, untouched by the fire, except for the silken plume of his helmet where sparks danced like fireflies. Gordon spotted his adversary and cried out to his men. Sheriff Dunbar, a handful of Moray followers at his heels, charged straight for Gordon, who wheeled his horse about and swung his sword with deadly intent. Dunbar dived for Huntly's reins, just managing to catch them in his burly grasp. George Gordon swung again with the sword, striking the sheriff in the chest. He staggered, dropped the reins, and crashed onto the ground, rolling over twice before landing on his back and staring wide-eyed up at the smoke-filled sky. Sorcha gasped and would have run to aid the wounded man, but Rosmairi grabbed her by the arm.

"It's hopeless," she whispered in a choked voice. "He's dead."

Noting the awkward angle of Dunbar's motionless body, Sorcha knew that Rosmairi was right. Yet she shook free of her sister's grasp, and though Rosmairi cried out after her, she ran not toward the inert sheriff, but down the path that Moray had taken to the sea. Now afoot, Gordon and several other men plunged over the cliff in tenacious pursuit. Gathering the taffeta skirts in her hand, Sorcha picked her way over the rocks, heedless of anyone who might be following her.

While Sorcha might know the forests and the glens by heart from her youth in the Highlands, she was ill acquainted with the vagaries of the seashore. However, during the course of the supper conversation, she had heard one of Moray's cousins remark upon the caves that had been carved out of the cliffs just below Aberdour. It seemed a likely hiding place for the Earl of Moray, who seemed to have disappeared.

Stumbling over a large rock, Sorcha righted herself and said a little prayer, asking the Virgin to guard her bairn. Regardless of what happened to Moray, Sorcha would not risk the life of the child she carried. Nor, she realized, making her way around a shallow tide pool, did she have the remotest notion of how she intended to aid her future husband against a swordwielding company commanded by George Gordon.

Gripped with fear and uncertainty, Sorcha peered up ahead, where she could barely make out George and his men, scrambling along the base of the cliff. Away from the burning house, there was no firelight to guide her, just the slender slip of a moon, hanging on its side over the dark, lapping waters of the Firth. A noise nearby made Sorcha gasp. She whirled and saw more men running in her direction, brandishing a variety of weapons, including a pitchfork and a meat cleaver. With a sob of relief, she recognized Armand, his dagger in one hand, the club in the other.

Breathing hard, Armand raced up to Sorcha. "Where is Moray?" he demanded as the others drew up behind him.

"I don't know." Sorcha turned to look over her shoulder. Gordon and his men had also vanished. "I think he must have hidden in one of the caves," Sorcha said. "Perhaps he'll be safe. He must know this terrain far better than George does."

Armand leaned on the club and considered Sorcha's words. "That's so," he replied thoughtfully. "Yet we must try to find him—and the others." Gesturing with the little dagger, Armand indicated that they should follow him to the caves. Somehow, in the wake of Moray's absence and Dunbar's demise, the Frenchman had been designated as their leader. "Which of you are familiar with the beach?" One of the older men, no doubt a Stewart cousin, replied that he'd been down in the caves that very day, playing hide-and-seek with the earl's older children. Slinging the club over his shoulder, Armand turned to Sorcha. "You must go back with Ros. It's too dangerous here."

"It's dangerous up by the house, too," Sorcha retorted. "I refuse to abandon my lord at such a time."

Noting her jutting chin and glittering eyes, Armand shrugged. There was no time to argue, nor could he guarantee anyone's safety within a mile of Donibristle. He walked swiftly to catch up with the other men, while Sorcha doggedly followed in his footsteps. They had covered no more than a hundred yards when they spotted the first of the caves, an angular opening in the rocks, too small for anyone of George Gordon's ample proportions. The second cave seemed much larger, and when the group paused to investigate, they could hear voices echoing inside. Sorcha and Armand exchanged anxious stares, then led the way between two big boulders that sat on opposite sides of the entrance like a pair of primitive doorstops.

Within a few feet, they could see nothing but black, oppressive darkness. Water dripped nearby, and the cave smelled dank and stale. Someone with a stammer—or a severe chill—suggested lighting a torch. Armand dismissed the suggestion; they didn't dare risk giving themselves away when they weren't exactly sure of the enemy's whereabouts. Sheathing his dagger, Armand felt for Sorcha's hand, leading her over a bed of small rocks toward the sound of the Gordon men's voices. It was obvious from their questioning tone that they had not yet found the Earl of Moray.

A split second later, a loud, excited cry erupted close by. Rounding a bend, Sorcha blinked against the sudden glow of light. One of the Gordons held a flare aloft, his other hand pointing toward a tendril of flame that dodged and darted straight ahead of them. Sorcha stifled a cry as she realized it must be the Earl of Moray. The sparks that had smoldered in his headgear's silken plume must have finally caught flame, betraying his presence to his pursuers.

Pausing to pull off the steel helmet, Moray cast it onto the floor of the cave, stamping out the fire with his booted feet. Exerting all of his athletic prowess, he veered toward an opening on his right, easily outdistancing his opponents. Yet as he ducked to squeeze through the slender, jagged aperture, a shower of dirt and rocks came tumbling down over his unprotected head. Momentarily stunned, Moray reeled, then fell against the sheer wall of the cave.

Gordon's men pounced, their chieftain bringing up the rear. Sorcha screamed and Armand shouted, but none of the green-clad men paid any heed. Even as a half dozen armed soldiers assaulted him, Moray tried to drive them back with his fists. Barking a command for Sorcha to stay where she was, Armand rushed forward with the others, though their every step was impeded by fresh falls of earth and rock. Four Gordon henchmen held Moray fast as George struck to the heart with his lethal dirk, then withdrew the blade and savagely stabbed the Bonnie Earl in the face. With his life's blood spilling out on the floor of the rock-strewn cave, Moray turned bemused eyes on his enemy and spoke his last words, "Oh, Georgie, I fear you've spoiled a better face than your own!"

As Moray slumped in the grasp of his assailants, Sorcha's screams pierced the dank air of the cave and echoed in her ears even after Armand had rushed to her side and put a hand over her mouth. "We can do nothing for him," he said in a thick, shaken voice. "Come, let us leave this grisly place before we are also made victims."

But the blood lust bred into generation after generation of Highlander had been sated. It was the hour of exultation for the Gordon clan, the making of a legend, which would be handed down to kinsmen yet unborn. Stumbling through the darkness, Sorcha thought she could hear laughter rumbling behind her, penetrating the haze of shock and terror that seized every inch of her body. She leaned on Armand, who swore at intervals, not having stopped to strike a light to guide them. After what seemed like an unendurably long time, they reached the entrance of the cave. Fresh salt air swept over their faces as they paused to revive themselves and adjust their eyes to the frail moonlight.

"Sweet Jesu," whispered Sorcha, still clinging to Armand, "I hope Jamie hangs George Gordon high as Haman!"

Armand was about to utter his total agreement, when a tall, hooded figure emerged from the other side of the large boulders that guarded the cave's entrance. With an effort, Sorcha disengaged herself from Armand and tried to focus on the shrouded apparition. With the swift movement of one hand, the hood was flipped back, revealing Marie-Louise, the moonlight tipping her long blond hair with silver.

"Has your bonnie bridegroom gone to meet his Maker?" she asked insolently.

Armand started forward, a low growl in his throat. But Marie-Louise held a long Italian dagger, and several Gordon retainers had materialized from behind the rocks. One of them had Rosmairi firmly in his grasp. Armand cursed volubly, then stepped back next to Sorcha. "What evil game do you play now, whore of Satan?" he hissed with such intensity that Sorcha jumped.

Marie-Louise didn't flinch. She uttered a throaty little laugh and waved the dagger at Sorcha. "A bride should be with her groom, think you not? Was I not with mine the night he died in the fire at d'Ailly?"

Armand went rigid at Sorcha's side, then frowned in puzzlement, before exploding once more at Marie-Louise. "Speak not of d'Ailly to me, Mistress of Death! What do you mean, you were with your groom? You'd left him long years before you came to d'Ailly!"

Marie-Louise's broad shoulders lifted in an indifferent shrug. "Ah, yes, *that* groom—the father of your child, eh?" She was regarding Sorcha with amusement, not unlike a snake playing with the mouse it planned to consume for supper. Her malignant gaze shifted back to Armand. "I speak of another groom—your brother." She smirked as Rosmairi called out for Armand to hold his tongue, lest Marie-Louise and the Gordons murder them all.

Armand, however, was not so easily intimidated. "You couldn't have married my brother! You already had a husband!"

The laughter that rolled out of Marie-Louise's throat held a genuine sound of amusement. "I've had many husbands, *mon cher* Armand—one way or the other. Your poor, deluded brother didn't know that, of course."

Enlightenment suddenly dawned upon Armand, but it was Sorcha who spoke. "You tricked Armand's brother into deeding the property to you! Then you set fire to the house and killed them all! Vile trollop, why did you commit such a terrible deed?"

Marie-Louise casually waved the dagger from side to side. "I was impatient for my inheritance. And bored with my so-called husband. I always grew bored with them." She spoke matter-of-factly, as if admitting to no worse a flaw than biting her nails.

A commotion from inside the cave momentarily distracted Marie-Louise as well as the others. George Gordon and his men were filing out, dragging Moray's bloody corpse behind them. George walked within a foot of Sorcha but didn't give her a glance. Instead, he hailed Marie-Louise, a broad smile on his ruddy, dirt-stained face. "This night we have triumphed over villainous Moray! The King will thank us for ridding Scotland of such a viper!" He paused, huffing noticeably, and scanned the shingle for his followers. Several more were descending down the sea cliff path, while the glow from the fire was beginning to fade. Gordon leaned toward Marie-Louise, making certain his bulk didn't obtrude between the dagger and her quarry. "We ride on to Aberdeen now. What do you claim as your reward?"

Marie-Louise gestured at Sorcha and Armand with the dagger. "I've claimed it." Without ever taking her eyes off her intended victims, she threw a wide, triumphant smile at George Gordon. "Leave me an escort, and I will join you shortly."

Gordon saluted Marie-Louise, then joined his men, who dragged Moray's battered corpse behind them over the wet, rocky sand. Sorcha watched with renewed horror and felt as if she were going to be violently ill. She was only vaguely aware that Armand was pulling her along with him as he edged an inch at a time closer to where Rosmairi stood with her captors.

After Gordon and the others scrambled back up the sea cliff path, Marie-Louise tossed her flowing blond hair and laughed, a rich, ribald, jarring sound. "I've waited such a long time for this," she said in that pleasant, throaty voice. "Who will not believe that Moray's bride and her relatives were murdered by George Gordon?" The blue eyes darted in the direction of the remaining Gordon retainers. "Not you, my good fellows, since if you disclaim the crime on your master's behalf, I shall take credit for the Bonnie Earl's death. Or blame you for what becomes of these three pathetic creatures."

Already suitably cowed by the formidable Frenchwoman, at least two of the men mumbled their acquiescence. Marie-Louise turned smug, then commanded the soldiers to move d'Ailly out of her way. "I'll deal with you later, cher Sieur. I've yet to decide whether it would be more amusing to let you live, a poor—and possibly blind—wanderer, or to dispatch you with your simpering wife and her obstinate sister."

Strong arms were hauling Armand away from Sorcha. Rosmairi let out an ear-splitting wail before a hand was clamped over her mouth. Struggling against his captors, Armand kicked one in the groin, sending the man sprawling onto the strand. "Enough!" Marie-Louise cried out, springing at Sorcha. The dagger flashed in the moonlight, but Sorcha leapt to her left.

The soft sand had grown mushy where Sorcha and Armand's feet had dug in to edge toward Rosmairi. While they might not have ever reached her side, the damage had been done. Marie-Louise slipped in the muddy sand, her cloak flying about her like the wings of a great malevolent bat. Her hand still held the dagger tight, and it was those clutching fingers that Sorcha went for, dropping beside the other woman, wrenching at the dagger with a frenzied, clawing grasp. Marie-Louise rolled over, refusing to surrender the weapon. Sorcha sunk her teeth into her adversary's wrist and at last Marie-Louise let out a howl of pain. Tasting blood, Sorcha ground the clasped hand against a rock as Marie-Louise's other fist pounded her back. The babe fluttered in Sorcha's womb, and she froze, her fingers still clutching at the dagger.

One of the men who was not engaged in restraining Armand and Rosmairi rushed to aid Marie-Louise. Grabbing a handful of Sorcha's hair in one hand, and her right arm in the other, he pulled mightily, at last forcing her to let go. Sorcha kicked her feet and swung her arms wildly, but the man held her just off the ground in a virtually helpless position. Cursing under her breath, Marie-Louise, her blond tresses caked with muddy sand, struggled to her feet. The beautiful azure eyes blazed hatred as she once more raised the dagger and with an exultant cry of "Bitch!" sent the steel slashing down toward Sorcha's heaving breast.

The night seemed to come apart in a volley of thunder as the dagger dropped onto the sand only inches from where Sorcha's feet swung ineffectually. Marie-Louise screamed and staggered, her momentum carrying her several yards down the strand. Yet she didn't fall; with a superhuman effort, she kept on her feet and straightened her body. Head flung back, she stared beyond the others to the running group of men whose booted feet reverberated in Sorcha's ears like church bells on a festival mom.

The hackbut's muzzle gleamed in Gavin Napier's hand as he drew closer. Shouting at Gordon's men to release their prisoners at once, Napier raced toward Sorcha, whose captor was unceremoniously dumping her on the sand. Dazedly, she shook her head, which throbbed in tandem with the pounding surf and the tramp of the other men following Napier. As her eyes came into focus, she saw the Italian dagger almost touching the bruised fingers of her left hand; to her right, she could make out Napier's calfskin boots. Then she felt his sure hands lifting her carefully to her feet, his arms wrapping around her trembling body. "The babe," she whimpered, "the babe! Did I harm our child?"

Napier smoothed her tangled hair with one hand. "Don't fash yourself. Nothing matters except that you're safe."

Craning her neck, Sorcha saw Armand give Rosmairi a reassuring hug before he left her to see what was happening to the men who held Marie-

Louise. To Sorcha's surprise, she recognized several Fraser kinsmen, including Magnus, rounding up George Gordon's outnumbered soldiers.

"Your shot only grazed the witch's arm. Do we carry out justice or not?" Armand had taken over custody of Marie-Louise, with a firm grip on one wrist and his dagger at her throat.

Over Sorcha's head, Napier frowned. "With the sheriff dead, there is no one to act in the King's name. I suggest we take her into Edinburgh."

As far as Marie-Louise was concerned, Armand was done with mercy. "She's not to be trusted! You of all men know that!" Aghast at Napier's apparent lack of fortitude, Armand yanked Marie-Louise by the wrist. "She calls herself a witch! Let us prove we believe her! Up there where the fires of Donibristle still burn, let us roast this sorceress and forever destroy her evil-doings!"

Fleetingly Napier gazed at Marie-Louise, who wore an expression of mingled contempt and rage. Her muddied hair fell over her smudged cheeks, her billowing cloak was torn in several places, and blood ran down her right arm.

"We have no right," Napier asserted, his expression suddenly haggard. "At least," he added in a hushed, shaken voice, "I do not."

Sorcha felt his arm tighten around her. She knew she ought to say something, either to encourage his sense of equity or at least to support his magnanimity. Yet she could do neither. Marie-Louise was his wife, and her fate was held solely in his hands.

Bristling with self-righteousness, Armand propelled Marie-Louise toward Sorcha and Napier. Magnus, with Rosmairi at his side, had joined the little group. "In Scotland, every person has the right to a fair trial," he told his brother-in-law. "Judgment may be a foregone conclusion. But the process is still maintained under our laws."

Armand waved his little dagger at Magnus. "Was that justice that sent the honorable Moray to his death? Did this villainess deal fairly with my family or the King of France? Was she, right here on Scottish ground, going to give your sisters and me a fair trial? Come, come, my good Magnus, such altruistic talk of the law is a farce!"

Magnus pulled at his long chin and regarded Armand ruefully. Yet before he could speak again, Marie-Louise, taking advantage of Armand's diverted attention, broke free and raced toward the sea, her cloak flying behind her. With a stunned cry, Armand started after her, Magnus on his heels. Napier would have joined them, but Sorcha held him back. "They'll never catch her," she whispered hoarsely.

Napier swallowed hard and nodded once. At the water's edge, he saw Armand and Magnus waving their arms and calling out to Marie-Louise. She had plunged into the waves, and the moonlight shone on her golden hair.

"What are they doing?" demanded a shaken Rosmairi, whose face was blotchy with anxiety.

Neither Sorcha nor Napier answered her. Marie-Louise's cloak spread out behind her on the water as she moved purposely out to sea, then let the outgoing tide carry her away. Armand had waded in up to his knees, but Magnus, always the family's strongest swimmer, had dived into the water. They could make out his rapid, sure strokes as he swam after his elusive prey. He was within a few yards of Marie-Louise when her head disappeared in the wake of the undertow. Magnus's shouts could be heard over the waves; he swam out further, then dove and dove again. Mesmerized, the others watched in silence. At last, they saw Magnus heading back toward shore, much more slowly, his strokes laboring in acknowledgment of defeat. Armand waded out farther to meet him; then the two men walked back close together over the damp sands of Aberdour.

Leaning against Napier, Sorcha shuddered violently. She tried to speak but found no words. Napier was still staring straight ahead, out to the undulating waves where he had last glimpsed Marie-Louise. "Fire was a tremendous force in her life," he said at last through lips that barely moved. "Mayhap she should have died at the stake as witches do. Yet, somehow, it seems fitting for the sea to claim her. After all, water quenches fire."

Rosmairi was running toward Armand, her arms outstretched. Sorcha watched husband and wife reunite with great joy, and suddenly the enormity of what had just transpired struck Sorcha with the force of a hurricane. For all the horror of the past few hours, despite the tragedies she had witnessed, one fact suddenly overwhelmed her: Gavin Napier was freed from his awful burden, liberated at last from the evil spell cast by Marie-Louise.

Yet, noting his grim expression, Sorcha realized this was not the moment to speak of his freedom. As her sister and brother-in-law walked wearily over the strand, with Magnus expressing his regret over not having been able to rescue Marie-Louise from her act of self-destruction, Sorcha jumped as the bairn kicked vigorously. Excitedly, she grabbed Napier's hand and pressed it against her abdomen. "Feel," she whispered, "new life. *Our* life." Sorcha turned a radiant smile on his anxious face. "Marie-Louise would have taken that life—and mine."

Napier looked down at Sorcha, the corners of his long mouth slowly turning upward, though the smile that emerged in the dark beard was bittersweet. "I need no reminding, my love. I know all the things you'd wish me to know." He paused, signaling for the others to join them. "But there is still pain," he said, dropping his voice so that their companions couldn't hear. "Only time—and you and our child—will ease that for me."

Sorcha's smile didn't falter. As Magnus put a brotherly hand on her shoulder, she reminded herself that at last she and Gavin Napier had all the time in the world.

Chapter 31

A FORTNIGHT LATER, A YOUNG LAD searching for mussels near Dunfermline found the body of a beautiful woman washed ashore a few miles east of Aberdour. His initial shock was overcome by how perfectly preserved and unmarked she was. Except for a graze on one arm and what looked like teeth marks on the other wrist, she might have been asleep under the old dock's pilings. Being a responsible sort, he reported his discovery to the local magistrate. Since no one in the vicinity had any knowledge of the dead woman, the magistrate ordered that she be buried in a nearby potter's field. Two grave diggers set about their work, but the first broke his pick, the second, his shovel. New tools were acquired, but the ground refused to yield, and the day, which had begun in sunlight, turned dark and threatening. The grave diggers retired to a tavern in the town, where they mulled over their difficulties and quaffed several tankards of ale. At last, just as the sun set over the Firth of Forth, they reeled back to the potter's field. The hastily built coffin had disappeared; the earth beneath it was freshly turned and smoothed over. What appeared to be a tiny silver cross had been stuck into the dirt at one end of the plot, but upon closer inspection, the men were astonished to see that it looked more like a dagger. Utterly bewildered by such a turn of events, they raced back to the tavern to down more ale before collecting their wages, and pledged to each other that they would never discuss the unnatural doings at the grave site. Later that night, shortly before the storm broke, a newly married couple strolled past the potter's field hand in hand, their pet terrier frisking up ahead of them. As the pair lingered to exchange a kiss, the dog ran off toward the new grave, stopped abruptly just where the freshly turned earth met the old, and let out a mournful howl. Puzzled, the newlyweds went after the animal, which seemed rooted to the spot. They coaxed and petted and finally became exasperated, but still the terrier refused to budge. At last, a black cat prowled out of the darkness, and the dog barked sharply, then gave chase. The cat seemed to vanish almost at once, and very soon the terrier came panting back to his master and mistress. From that time on, the potter's field was said to be haunted, and no one ever walked that way again by night.

THE LINGERING JUNE LIGHT GUIDED Gavin Napier all the way to Falkland. For that he was grateful, since he had ridden south only with the greatest reluctance. The bairn was already overdue, and if it hadn't been for Sorcha's insistence that he race to warn the King of Bothwell's mad new intrigue, Napier would still be at Gosford's End. But with that huge bulge of new life thrust out before her like the bow of a mighty galleon, Sorcha had been virtually impossible to refuse. Indeed, in the four months since Father Adam had married them in the chapel at Beauly Priory, Gavin Napier had found it difficult to deny his wife much of anything. The peace she brought to him, the surcease of pain, the sense of joy that might be marred but never supplanted, all made up the myriad gifts Sorcha readily offered in the name of love.

To gainsay her, even as the hour of her labor approached, would have been unthinkable. Certainly her request was not only reasonable but of great consequence. Word had reached Gosford's End that Bothwell, having once more been chased from his Borders by the King's men, had sought sanctuary with the turbulent Earl of Caithness. In the most northern reaches of Scotland, at Castle Sinclair, Protestant Bothwell connived with Catholic Caithness to make yet another attempt to capture the King's person. Yet Caithness's wife, Jean Gordon Sinclair, had dissuaded him from active participation in the plot. While her brother, George, remained at large following Moray's despicable murder, Gordon lands and holdings had been ravaged by the combined forces of Grants, MacKintoshes, and Frasers. The circumspect Jean, Countess of Caithness, saw any further violation of the King's law or person as inviting calamity for both her husband and her brother. For once, Caithness heeded her words.

But, according to the Flemish trader who had called at Inverness after a stop at Sinclair's Bay, Bothwell remained undeterred. Accompanied by a clutch of his faithful Border rowdies, he had planned to ride south the same day the Fleming had lifted anchor off Noss Head. Fortunately, his vessel had had the benefit of a favorable wind, and with any luck, Gavin Napier should be at least a half-day's ride ahead of Bothwell.

Slowing Naxos to a trot as they entered the town through the West Port, Napier could make out the palace's sturdy twin gatehouse towers outlined against the rose-tipped sky. Falkland's High Street was all but deserted so late in the evening, no doubt in deference to the local curfew. While the palace guards at first eyed him with suspicion, when Napier identified himself as son-in-law to Lord Iain Fraser, Baron of Beauly, he was escorted promptly into the King's presence.

A long, if profitable, day of hunting had left King Jamie faintly irascible. When Gavin Napier arrived, Jamie was in the company of Patrick Gray, who still clung tenaciously to his post as Master of the Wardrobe. Gray eyed Napier with hauteur; the King studied the newcomer with curiosity.

"After all these years," James said somewhat querulously, "we finally meet face-to-face. Did you know that for some time we believed you to be an ancient pedant, bowed down with learning and dried up with virtue? We were duped, so that you might dash off to England and insert yourself in my mother's household as a Papist spy!" Jamie had worked himself up into a fairly impressive royal rage. When Napier merely inclined his head to one side and offered no apology, the King turned to Patrick Gray. "I hate it when my subjects deceive me! Don't look so smug, Patrick, my Apollo-like confrere, you're no better than the rest!"

To Napier's surprise, Patrick Gray wore a sheepish expression, though the smile he bestowed upon his monarch was engaging. "Mayhap some of us hide the truth to spare you, sire. Your responsibilities weigh so heavily."

Jamie snorted and took a deep drink from his sapphire-studded wine goblet. "Paugh. I've been King since I was a bairn. If any sovereign could recognize responsibility in the dark, it's me. *Us*," he amended pettishly and drank again. "We grow weary of having others try to carry it for us." Still peevish, he turned back to Napier, whose studied patience was fraying around the edges. "So? What gives you call to burst into our chambers this late in the day?"

Napier gazed blandly at the King, then at Gray, and back again. "I'd prefer speaking with you privately, sire."

Patrick Gray lifted an elegant hand. "Speak freely, Master Napier. His Majesty and I have no secrets."

Napier's dark brows drew close together, but before he could utter a rejoinder, Jamie broke in. "A pox on your impertinence, Patrick! I'll share with you whatever I choose to share! Now, begone. Go sort through my small-clothes or whatever needs to be done in your exalted capacity." The King glared at Gray, who did his best to conceal his humiliation. With an offhand remark about always being ready to serve his sovereign, he made an exquisite bow and left the room.

With time running out, Gavin Napier came right to the point. He explained Bothwell's latest brazen plot and was met with a mixture of fear and exasperation. "What was I just saying?" Jamie ranted, getting up from his chair, and crossing the room to pull the bell cord. "Protestant, Catholic, friend, foe, minister, priest—I can count on none of them to be loyal! Self-seeking, that's the whole lot of them. Rapacious, greedy, grasping knaves on every side." Giving the bell cord an angry tug, he stared at Napier. "What's your game? What is it you want from this?"

"To please Sorcha," Napier blurted. Noting the King's look of surprise, he laughed. "She insisted I come. She's fond of Your Majesty, as I'm sure you know."

Jamie's lords of the bedchamber and several servants were at the door in response to his signal. Still regarding Napier with speculative amusement, the King finally nodded. "I almost believe you. Aye," he said, more to himself than to Napier, "in fact, I think I do."

The King and Queen, along with Napier, Maitland, Gray, and several other important personages in the royal household, sought safety in the palace's main tower. Some time after midnight, Bothwell and his men were sighted in the town. The alarm was spread by the watch, and though the earl and his followers surrounded the palace, no attempt was made to storm the gates. Shortly after sunrise, when the townspeople learned what was happening, they armed themselves and put Bothwell to flight. The King made a brief, yet surprisingly eloquent speech of thanks, which the good burghers cheered before heading back home to take up their daily routine. Having done his duty, Gavin Napier asked the King's permission to return at once to the Highlands. Jamie, however, was reluctant to have him leave.

"You have shown your loyalty to us," King James told Napier over a belated breakfast. "Strange, isn't it, that being a Papist, you'd ride at breakneck speed to save your sovereign from Bothwell. We could use such a man at court, Master Napier." Jamie waited anxiously for Napier's reaction.

It came only after careful consideration. "I'm not cut out for life at court, sire, though your words honor me. I'm a plain-spoken man, who has had little success in attempts to negotiate between Scotland's Catholic families. I intend to raise Highland ponies on some property that makes up part of my wife's dowry," Napier said, with a wry smile. "Talking to horses doesn't require artful diplomacy."

"True," Jamie agreed, dumping the contents of a jam pot on his bread, "but it requires something even more rare—horse sense. See here," Jamie went on earnestly, as strawberry jam oozed out of the corners of his mouth, "it's impolitic to discuss our claim on the English throne. But it would be simpleminded to ignore the possibility. If we—I—am to some day wear the crowns of both Scotland and England, I must persuade English Catholics I don't intend to persecute them. If I don't demonstrate a tolerant attitude, they'll press for a Spanish succession, since my mother"—he paused to make a rueful face—"willed her right to the English crown to King Philip of Spain. Not to mention the fact that it's in my best interests here at home to play off Protestant against Catholic." He shrugged, wiping at a daub of jam on his pale blue satin shirt. "I must play one faction off against the other, because it's best for Scotland. If you won't join the court, will you serve as special envoy to England?"

Gavin Napier was nonplussed. His efforts as envoy of the Catholic Church had failed. How could King Jamie consider involving him in what would be an even more delicate political and religious mission? Napier said as much, but Jamie merely shrugged. "You didn't fail at bringing unity to Scotland. My, no," reiterated the King, wiping out the rest of the jam pot's contents with his index finger, "you brought the Highland families together—Grants, Frasers, MacKintoshes, Camerons—all those old enemies united not only in self-interest but against George Gordon's treachery and injustice. Never mind religion; it often masks far baser motives. You unerringly fought on the side of what was right. I—we—should like to have you do the same for us in England."

Weighing the King's words carefully, Napier had to admit that they held an element of truth. Catholic leaders such as Gordon and Errol, Caithness, and even the will-o'-the-wisp Gray, had used their faith, rather than lived by it. They were far less interested in religion than in self-aggrandizement. Yet despite the turmoil of the past few years, George Gordon's hold on the Highlands had been broken. If he had succeeded in ridding himself of his hereditary rival, Moray, he had also weakened his own position as a threat to the Crown. It would serve no purpose for Napier to discount his own contribution.

"Let me think about your generous offer," Napier said at last, shifting his body in the armchair and tugging at the cuff of one leather boot. "Right now," he went on with a grin, "I have other matters uppermost in my mind."

Jamie turned a puzzled face on Napier and then let out his jarring laugh. "Aye, the bairn! By all means, point your steed northward and ride to my dear Coz's side! We'll send a splendid gift, I promise! Indeed, if all goes well, mayhap I'll bring it in person!"

The King's piercing cackle followed Napier out of the room and halfway down the corridor. Somehow, the sound seemed almost musical to Gavin Napier.

THE MONTH OF FEBRUARY HAD rolled round again at Gosford's End, bringing two important visitors. While some might judge the arrival of the King of Scotland as the more impressive, for the Frasers it was Rob who had sparked the most exuberant celebration. He had come to visit his family before heading for Rome, where he would study to become a Jesuit. The cloistered life of a Recollect friar did not suit him as well as the more active vocation he could exercise as a disciple of Ignatius Loyola.

"Missionary work appeals to me," he explained one rainy evening to the King he had not seen in six years. "You and I may not agree on religion, but I trust you will permit me to submit that there are many heathens who have no knowledge of the Gospel."

"Oh, many," conceded King James blithely. "A great many, indeed. And if any of them ever learn to read, they ought to have a Bible that makes sense. I like the Bible very much, don't you, Cousin Robert?"

Sorcha stifled a giggle behind her hand. She wasn't sure if Jamie was teasing Rob or merely being polite. Certainly the King had dispensed with formality since arriving at the head of a large troop of men the previous day. After a year of halfhearted endeavor to bring George Gordon to justice for the murder of Moray, King James had finally ridden north with a formidable army. George, like Bothwell before him, had fled across the Highlands to seek shelter from their old accomplice, Caithness. Upon reaching Gosford's End, Jamie seemed content to give up the chase. It appeared that Moray's tragic murder would go down as one of the great unprovoked and unpunished crimes in history.

Gavin Napier stood up and stretched in front of the sitting room's crackling fireplace while his father-in-law poured more whiskey for everyone except Jeannie Simpson, who was already practically asleep on Magnus's shoulder. "Drink up," Iain Fraser urged, lifting his cup, "tomorrow is Saint Valentine's Day and Sorcha and Gavin's first wedding anniversary." He offered his eldest daughter and her husband that familiar crooked grin and drank deeply. The others followed suit, toasting the happy couple with fulsome praise. Father Adam smiled as broadly as the rest, though he discreetly asked Rosmairi to water down his whiskey before he took another sip.

The King of Scotland appeared to be the merriest of them all. He had burst into that faintly jarring cackle, slapping his thigh, with his head thrown back and a trace of whiskey trickling into his beard. "Such irony!" he exclaimed, controlling his mirth and gazing around the family circle to which he was tied by blood as well as affection. "Here I—we, that is—are pursuing the leading Catholic lord of the realm for murdering the most eminent Protestant lord, and sharing hospitality with a passel of Papists and priests!" Lurching in his chair, he turned to Napier. "Well? You've had eight months to mull over our offer. What say you, Master Napier?"

A sudden uneasy silence filled the sitting room. Napier fingered his dark beard and glanced at Sorcha. "My wife and I would like to see more of England," he said evenly. "Especially without watchdogs like Sir Amyas Paulet looking over our shoulders."

Jamie all but jumped from his chair. "Excellent! You will serve us well at Queen Bess's court! You know, of course," he said offhandedly, "that our first order of business these days is to reorganize the Presbyterian Kirk." He paused to make sure his statement had hit home. "However," he went on in an airy manner, "we shouldn't wish to see power concentrated in the ministers' hands as has so often been the case in the past. Power," Jamie emphasized, one gangling hand touching his breast, "lies here." His gaze was level with Napier's; the two men understood each other perfectly. Henceforth, Scotland would not be ruled by the Kirk, but by the King, and in so ordaining, Jamie would coincidentally grant qualified protection to his Catholic subjects. Napier could not suppress an exultant smile.

"I can only speak for myself," he said to Jamie with a deferential nod, "but I think you are demonstrating a great deal of wisdom, sire."

"Wisdom?" Jamie giggled. "Aye, some call me 'the wisest fool in Christendom.' I like that title. What think you, Coz?" He turned to Sorcha and gave the silver lace on her sleeve a little tug.

"I like it fine, Your Majesty," she replied with a bright smile. "You always were canny when it came to deceiving your elders."

"Not all of them," interjected Dallas with a wince, as Jamie sloshed whiskey onto a petit point cushion. "I'm told you made a promise to present our new grandchild with a gift. It occurred to me that Scotland is much indebted to our Gavin—and will be again, it seems. Might a humble, doting grandmother make a request?"

Jamie was trying to keep a straight face. "For what? Denmark?" Seeing Lord Fraser roll his eyes toward the ceiling, while Magnus choked on his drink and Rob stared at the Persian carpet, Jamie slapped his thigh again and howled with laughter. "Well, Madam?" he gasped between cackles, "is Denmark too large even for your acquisitive nature?"

Dallas was the only undismayed—and unamused—person in the room. "Too large? What about Jutland, then?"

Jamie was wiping his eyes with his sleeve and shaking his head. Dallas, wearing a blandly innocent expression, which was belied only by the quick wink she gave Sorcha, primly folded her hands in her lap to present a fetching portrait of maternal concern. "Of course," she said in a deceptively demure voice, "if Your Majesty intended a more modest gesture …."

King James had finally regained control of himself. He blew his nose loudly and scooted to the edge of the petit point cushion. "Somewhat more modest, aye. Where's my sword?" he asked, turning to Armand, who was standing behind the settee where Rosmairi and Rob were seated.

"I believe, Your Majesty, you are wearing it," replied Armand, the blue eyes twinkling.

"Ah! So I am!" Jamie reached around to pull the weapon from its bejeweled scabbard. Peering at the hilt, he frowned. "I fear I've lost a ruby. By heaven, war exacts a terrible price!" He shrugged, then motioned to Gavin Napier. "Step forward, good Master Napier. Your perspicacious mother-in-law is right. We do owe you a debt. And we can't send you to Queen Elizabeth's court in our service as plain Master Napier." James had grown quite serious. "To that end, and in gratitude, we now endow you with lands and privileges east of Inversnaid, between Loch Lomond and Loch Katrine. Kneel, sir, I pray you."

Startled by the King's unexpected words, it took Gavin Napier a moment to react. Then, with a glance at his wide-eyed wife, he knelt before Jamie, who touched the broad shoulders with his sword and pronounced the rite of ennoblement: "We hereby proclaim you, Gavin Napier, as First Laird of Lomond, your lands and titles to be passed down in perpetuity to your lawful heirs. So be it, in the name of the King and God Almighty."

Jamie raised his sword and bestowed a smug smile on the rest of the company, then looked sideways at Armand. "Are you not about to spend your inheritance on the building of a fine place near Loch Ness?"

Armand, whose inheritance had finally been secured by a diligent Donald McVurrich, happily replied that such was indeed the case. Jamie lifted his palms face up. "Then the future is bright for all of my Fraser cousins! How pleased we are with this evening's piece of work!"

"As are we," murmured Sorcha, who came to slip between her husband and the King. "While I'm overwhelmed by your generosity, my own request would have been of a different nature." She juggled a handful of almonds she'd scooped from a silver bowl and regarded James conspiratorially. "I should have asked if you've considered sending that worrisome rascal Bothwell and the Master of Gray into exile."

Jamie's munificent expression went blank. "Ah …." The sovereign dug in his ear with great zeal. "Actually, that's a brilliant suggestion, one I've—we've— toyed with for some time, of course. At least," he amended quickly, "regarding Bothwell." Jamie lowered his voice so that only Sorcha and Napier could hear. "But Patrick Gray is another matter. He may be bad—but he's so beautiful." Emitting a little sigh of rapture, James offered Sorcha his most winning smile. "But fear not, the Master has been mastered. He knows that if he wants to keep our favor, he must behave. That," Jamie added solemnly, "I promise you."

Sorcha accepted the King's words in good faith; she stepped forward to hug her royal cousin tight. Jamie giggled with pleasure and demanded more whiskey. As Iain Fraser again made the rounds with the decanter, a now wide-awake Jeannie proffered her cup, while the King proposed yet another toast. "This time we drink to Scotland! Good family, I give you our kingdom—and the kingdom to come!"

Everyone cheered lustily at his somewhat cryptic words, even Father Adam, who made no request to water his whiskey this time. The conversation grew less formal and more raucous as the whiskey decanter was emptied, refilled, and emptied again. Outside, the rain dissipated into a fine mist, and the heavy gray clouds began drifting out to sea. In the nursery, Magnus's son and daughter slept in their cradles next to little Adam's brand-new trundle bed. And in her wet nurse's arms, wee Dallas Napier suckled greedily, her tiny fists swinging as if she were impatient not just for the flow of milk, but for the future.

SEATTLE NATIVE **MARY RICHARDSON DAHEIM** lives three miles from the house where she was raised. From her dining nook she can see the maple tree in front of her childhood home. Mary isn't one for change when it comes to geography. Upon getting her journalism degree from the University of Washington (she can see the campus from the dining nook, too), she went to work for a newspaper in Anacortes, Washington. Then, after her marriage to David Daheim, his first college teaching post was in Port Angeles where she became a reporter for the local daily. Both tours of small-town duty gave her the background for the Alpine/Emma Lord series.

Mary spent much of her non-fiction career in public relations (some would say PR is fiction, too). But ever since she learned how to read and write, Mary wanted to tell stories that could be put between book covers (e-readers were far into the future and if she hadn't seen her daughter's iPad, she might not know they exist). Thus, she began her publishing career with the first of seven historical romances before switching to mysteries in 1991. If Mary could do the math, she'd know how many books she's published. Since she can't, she estimates the total is at least 55. Or something. See below—count 'em if you can.

At the time of her husband and mentor's death in February 2010, David and Mary had been married for more than 43 years. They have three daughters, Barbara, Katherine and Magdalen, and two granddaughters, Maisy and Clara. They all live in Seattle, too. Those apples don't move far from the tree ... literally.

For more information, go to: www.marydaheimauthor.com.

Other Camel Press Titles by Mary Daheim

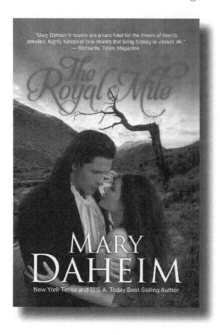

The Royal Mile

You've read the sequel, now read the story of Sorcha's parents, Dallas and Iain.
In the time of Mary, Queen of Scots, a young girl left destitute by her father's death meets a pirate in the service of the Queen. They make a bargain: he will marry her, giving her security, and she will not reveal his profession or curtail his freedom. By the time love begins to blossom, it may be too late. First they must survive the turmoil plaguing the court of their Queen. Originally published in 1984 under the title, *Love's Pirate*.

Reunion

Serena Farrar dreams of being a journalist in Massachusetts. First she must obey her family and marry sea captain Brant Parnell. Her coldness drives him back to sea, so when an ugly scandal erupts, Serena has no choice but to flee to her sister in New Bern, NC. Brant arrives as conflict engulfs the city. Serena is not only a Yankee in enemy territory, but also a woman at war with her heart. Originally published in 1986 under the title, *Pride's Captive*.